BECAUSE I NEED YOU

A ROMANTIC SUSPENSE NOVEL

CLAIRE

NEW YORK TIMES BESTSELLING AUTHOR

CONTRERAS

Edited by: Kay Springsteen
Proofread by: Liza Tice
Formatted by: Champagne Book Design
Cover Design: Hang Le

To my day 1 Crew,
who one-click anything I write with no hesitation,

to BookTok, for renewing my love of writing after
three extremely difficult years,

and to anyone who has ever felt like they didn't belong

PREFACE

Dear reader,

I don't normally write trigger warnings, not because I don't believe they're important, but because very few things trigger me and I'm always unsure of what to write. However, I feel inclined to let you know that there is talk of rape in this book. It is not on the page, but it is discussed.

I hope you enjoy this book as much as I enjoyed writing it!

Xo,

Claire

BECAUSE I NEED YOU

A ROMANTIC SUSPENSE NOVEL

CHAPTER ONE

Isabel

THE PAST TEN DAYS WERE A BLUR. I FELT LIKE I'D BEEN STRUCK BY A force that was too great for me to bear. It wasn't just the loss of my father. It was the terrifying way in which it happened. To have him, a force of nature, just collapse in the kitchen right in front of me right after telling a joke. The ride to the hospital was shocking, and leaving without him after being told he was "gone," even more so. That was how the doctor said it, too, before he gave me a moment alone with my father. *"I'm so sorry. He's gone."* GONE WHERE? I'd demanded. *GONE WHERE?* I knew it was an impossible question to answer, nearly an impossible thing to consider without delving deep into existentialism and religion, and yet, I'd rather deep dive into both of those than let him go. I wasn't ready to do that, and I needed an answer. The days that followed had been much muddier than that. Thankfully, Dad had his funeral arrangements all planned out, from the service to the casket to the burial plot. I was grateful for his foresight, because I'd never had to plan one before, and I wouldn't even have known where to start.

The actual funeral brought more questions, more blurred memories. I'd expected his employees to show up. I hadn't expected more than fifty men in dark suits to be there. Men who were hard and rough around the edges. I'd only recognized a handful of guys my father employed in his painting company. The rest were just bodies. Each of them squeezed my shoulder as they walked through and said a sentiment. I'd clung onto William the entire time, kept my face mostly buried in the sleeve of his suit jacket, grateful I hadn't been *completely* alone. My boy-friend had enough things on his plate, but he set them all aside to be there for me that day.

Later, he asked who all those men were, and I didn't know how to answer him. I shrugged. I'd never seen them. William said nothing to that, but insisted I go back home to New York with him. I told him I couldn't, since I had to figure out what to do with my father's things. I was his only family, after all. If I didn't do it, who would? Shortly after Will had gone back to New York, I received a call from my father's attorney—I didn't even know my father had one—telling me to go to their offices so they could read me his will. Considering my father had a small painting company, and lived in a modest three-bedroom, I couldn't imagine what he'd left behind. The house, sure. His old red Ford truck, maybe. Both things I did not want. I just wanted my dad to come home. I wanted him to make up for all of the years we'd lost while he was working in Chicago, and I was living with my grandmother in Miami and later New York. So many years compounded into occasional weekend visits in-stead of the day-to-day presence that I needed. He'd just started making up for it, too. He'd just started visiting me more and ask-ing me to visit him more. I'd been in Chicago for five days when it happened. I'd planned to stay the entire summer while I was on break from teaching. And now he was gone. Just like that. I willed the unshed tears that burned my eyes away.

"Isabel Bonetti."

I snapped back to the present at the sound of my name and swallowed as I stood up and followed the woman to a conference room. I stood by the door for a moment, assessing the room. There was one man in a suit and one woman, also in a suit. Both were standing on the other end of the room, an odd sympathetic smile on their faces. A fake one, really. Besides teaching middle school, I was dating the current—and youngest—mayor. I was used to being in a room full of assholes. This room, however, felt different. There was a certain uneasy charge to it, as though both of them knew that I was in the dark about whatever they were about to tell me.

"Thank you for coming in, Ms. Bonetti," the man said, "I'm terribly sorry for your loss."

I nodded in appreciation. I couldn't thank one more person verbally for that statement and I shouldn't have to. I shouldn't have been here at all. I pushed that feeling back.

"I'm sure this is a lot for you," the woman said.

"I'm not sure what I'm dealing with, so I can't say whether or not it's a lot yet." I walked over.

"I'm Dave Hunt," he said. "This is Parker Evans."

I shook both their hands.

"We're only here to help and facilitate, answer any questions you may have, and make this as easy and painless as possible," Dave said, while Parker smiled.

"Help and facilitate what exactly?" I asked, taking a seat in one of the chairs they signaled at.

"Your father's trust, reading his will, signing a lot of papers. Things like that," Parker said.

"I can't imagine what he would have left. My father painted houses for a living."

"Let's begin." Dave cleared his throat, shifting in his seat uncomfortably.

Within the first three minutes, I was told the large sum my father left me. Within ten, I was told about his properties. In the thirty minutes that followed, I was given more papers to look through. I took my time with each one of them, knowing I'd have to either have William do me the favor of looking through them, or hire my own lawyer. It wasn't that I didn't trust my father's lawyers, but I'd seen the way Will conducted business and he always had his own at his beck and call, which made me think I should do the same, just in case. It was just too much for me to wrap my head around, let alone understand. He had property everywhere, it seemed. Not just homes, but warehouses, as well. Chicago, New Jersey, Rhode Island, Brooklyn, Miami. I took a deep breath and kept looking at the rest of the papers, pausing when I got to the marriage license. *He'd been married?* That was news to me. I looked up at Dave, who was chewing on the edge of his pen. Parker stood and excused herself.

"My dad was married?" I asked, confused.

"And divorced. We have those papers as well."

"Oh." The marriage license stated he'd been married to a woman whose name I didn't recognize before I was born. I looked at the divorce date. I would've been twelve years old, then. He'd been married to someone I'd never even heard of for twenty-years? My frown deepened. I glanced up again. "This doesn't make any sense. Was this like, an agreement for a green card or something?"

"No." Dave shook his head. "This was his actual wife. He was with your mother...you know. I'm sorry."

My jaw dropped. I looked back at the marriage license and divorce. My mother had been his mistress? That made me, what, his love child? I whispered those words aloud, feeling fresh tears prick my eyes. I swallowed them back. My childhood had been a mess, to say the least, with the back and forth between my parents' on and off relationship and the moving, but my mother and grandmother made it work for a while. We got to New York when I was fourteen, and I'd been instantly thrust into a fancy state-of-the-art school, rubbing elbows with celebrity kids and politician's kids. It was where I met Will during our senior year. We weren't high school sweethearts, though. We weren't anything until we reconnected a year ago at a teacher luncheon he'd hosted. I'd continuously asked my mother once how we could afford that school, and she'd yelled to stop asking questions and be grateful I could attend—period. So, I didn't ask any more questions. If I was a love child, surely, my grandmother, who I was with most of the time, would've slipped up and told me, especially during one of her rants about how I should've never been born. You'd think she would've thrown it into those jabs, at least.

I racked my brain for any clues, but there was nothing. My parents were cordial when they saw each other. My mother never had anything bad to say about my father and vice versa. Mom was always busy working and dating, anyway. That didn't leave much room for conversation about their relationship. I knew they'd never married, but never in a million years would I have thought I was the product of an affair. Knowing that made me feel dirty. I kept staring at the dates, kept wishing my math was all wrong, but it was clear as day. He'd lied to me. My entire life, he'd lied to me. The only person I trusted, the only person who loved me unconditionally, and he'd been lying to me my entire life.

"Did he have any other kids?" I asked, voice shaky.

"One," Dave said. My eyes snapped to his. "A son. He passed away a few years ago."

"Passed away?" I whispered. I had a brother I'd never met and would never meet.

"He was involved in questionable things," Dave explained.

My brows hiked up. Questionable things? That could mean anything. I glanced at the papers on the table. This could literally mean anything.

"What was his name?" I licked my lips. "My brother, I mean. Half-brother. Whatever."

"Vincent Bonetti."

"Vincent."

"Look, Isabel," Dave started as I continued to stare at the stack of papers that knew more about my father's life than I ever did, ever would. "I know this is difficult, but we haven't even hit the tip of the iceberg, so if you want to take a break to process this part and come back tomorrow, please, by all means."

"What do you mean?" I felt my lip wobble. "There's more? More secrets?"

Dave nods gravely. I shut my eyes, breathing through tears. I'd never been much of a crier. I had my parents to thank for that. All of the broken promises my mother had made. All of those weekends I'd waited by the window for my father to pick me up and he never showed. Had he been with Vincent? Had he been with his real family? A sob raked through me as I buried my face in my hands. Dave set a hand on my shoulder. He didn't soothe me, didn't move it, just set it there, letting me know I wasn't alone. Except, I *was* alone.

My mother was long gone, living in Spain with her new husband. I couldn't even remember the last time we spoke. My grandmother was in a nursing home now, dealing with onset dementia and a body that may not hold her up much longer. I had Luke and Noah, who were the closest thing I had to family, but they had their own lives, and I didn't want to depend on them for everything. I had Eloise, but she was like a little hummingbird, showing up and disappearing whenever she wanted. I had Will, but he was just a boyfriend. Of less than a year, at that, and he was always busy. All my life I'd told myself I didn't need anyone. I'd *acted* like I didn't need anyone. And now that the world had presented me with this, I wasn't sure I could handle it alone. I took another deep breath, wiped my face, and told myself to put my game face on and get this over with.

"Let's continue," I said. Dave took his hand off my shoulder. I didn't even look at him to confirm the wariness on his face. When I did, I shot him an expectant look. "We can continue."

"Okay," he said slowly, bringing out another marriage license.

"Jesus Christ, how many times did my dad get married?"

"This one is not your father's," he said quietly.

My eyes snapped to his, then to the marriage license, which had my name on it. It took me a moment to process that. MY NAME on a marriage license I'd never seen in my life. I was twenty-eight and had never even come close to getting married. *What the fuck?* I looked at the date. My birthday. My eighteenth birthday, to be exact.

"What the fuck is this?" I held up the paper in question.

"Do you not remember signing it?" he asked.

"Obviously not. I think I'd remember signing a marriage license." I looked at it again, then raised my voice to say, "I couldn't even legally drink, for God's sake." I waved the paper. "It can't be real."

"It's real." He looked down at the table, then met my eyes again. "Look. I had many conversations with your father and pleaded with him to tell you about this double-life he'd been living. None of this is fair to you. None of it."

"And what did he say when you suggested he tell me?" I asked, my voice suddenly quiet, what was left of my heart cracking wide open while I waited.

"He didn't want to hurt you."

"He didn't want to hurt me," I scoffed, shaking my head, hating the tears that filled my eyes again. "No. He just didn't want to see my face when he hurt me. He didn't want to see my face as he wedged the knife between my ribs." I flicked the tears from my cheeks. "I never knew my father to be a coward."

"He wasn't," Dave said. "But I guess it's different when your own children are involved."

"Why would he do this?" I whispered.

"He wanted to protect you. That much I do know."

"Protect me by forging my signature on a marriage license?" I held it up and shook it again. "Protect me by keeping me his dirty secret and never telling me about his son?"

"I don't think the paper is forged," Dave said, "Your father was a smart man. You must have signed it at some point and maybe you didn't know what you were signing off on."

I was shaking, so I lowered the paper again. I wanted to rip it, but I knew it wouldn't make a difference. How could it? This was real in the eyes of the law. He'd met Will. He had lunch with his family for Thanksgiving, for God's sake! He'd smiled and brought pumpkin pie and sat across from Will's dad—a fucking judge—all the while he was, what, a conman? A drug dealer? What the hell was he? What did this mean?

"After we discuss his investments, we will come back to this," he said, his blue eyes holding mine. "I promise."

I swallowed and kept my left hand on the paper. I'd listen to the rest of this, but I was not letting this go. Over my dead body was I going to stay married to a stranger. I didn't even know why he'd do that. Why would he marry me off? Like this was the 1800's and I was payment for cattle or something. What the fuck? Was it an arranged marriage? Was it some kind of ploy to hide other things? Dave continued talking about investments and stocks and I nodded along but couldn't hear the words coming out of his mouth. My mind was stuck on this paper. Finally, I sighed heavily and interrupted him.

"I'm sorry. I'm not listening. I can't wrap my head around this." I tapped the paper twice with my pointer.

"I understand."

"Who the fuck is Giovanni Masseria?"

Dave's brows hiked up to his hair line. "You don't know who he is?"

"I wouldn't be asking if I did."

"He's…a businessman," he said carefully in a way that made me think he was a freaking drug dealer or something.

"Oh, my God. Is he a drug dealer? A loan shark? Did my dad owe money to a loan shark? Is that what this is?" I asked, clearly having read enough fictional books that led to this.

"A loan shark? No." Dave laughed but grew serious when he saw that this was not a joke to me.

"So, who is he?" I asked. "I need to find him and ask him for a divorce. He doesn't know me. I don't know him. How hard can that be?"

He stared at me for a long moment, as if trying to read

something on my face that wasn't there. Then he said, "You really don't know who he is."

"I already told you I don't know who he is." I slapped my hands on the table and stared at him.

"I see you get your temper from your father."

"It's not a temper," I said, through my teeth. "I just don't like to waste time, and this feels like a waste of time if you're not going to outright tell me what my dad was involved with or who the hell I'm secretly married to. Does this guy know I even exist?"

"I'm just as much in the dark here as you are. I only know just enough."

"Look, Dave." I shut my eyes for a moment and drew in a breath then opened them again. "I'm a middle school teacher. My father owned a painting company. My mother worked at restaurants most of her life, and now you're telling me that my dad left me millions of dollars and investment properties, when he drove the same beat-up truck for ten years?" I stared at him. "Do you understand why I'm having a very difficult time wrapping my head around all of this?"

"I know it's a lot to take in," he said calmly. "I think the second marriage license is probably the worst of it."

"The worst of it?" I barked out a laugh. "Living a lie my entire life isn't the worst of it? Being the product of an affair? Finding out my father had a whole other family?"

"I'm sorry." He cleared his throat.

"Was his name even Charles Bonetti?"

"Yes."

"There were a lot of people at his funeral," I said, "Why'd he leave it all to me?"

"It was under you and your brother's name, but considering Vinny is dead…"

"Right." I swallowed.

"Did you ever meet any of your father's friends, employees, or acquaintances while you were visiting him?"

I thought about it. I'd met a few of his employees, of course. I'd met Sal and Andy, who were super nice to me and always gave me a Cadbury Crème Egg on Easter. Every year, they'd give me one if I was with my dad. If I wasn't, he'd give it to me next time he saw me. I couldn't even remember what they looked like. All my memories from that time were a haze. I remembered names, not faces. It was the opposite for me now. I remembered faces of all my students, but not all of their names. I'd met a man named Joe. I remembered him the most, because he was so tall and built and reminded me of one of those badass guys in the action movies Dad and I watched together.

"I remember some guys named Sal and Andy and a guy named Joe," I said. "I remember Joe had a construction company and Dad worked with him a lot. I went out to dinner with him and his wife." I smiled, remembering. "It was my birthday, so his wife brought a special cake to the restaurant, just for me. It was a My Little Pony cake."

"Joe. Do you know his last name?"

I shook my head. "I was too young. Why? Would he know anything about this marriage thing?"

"He might." Dave cocked his head in a way that told me he felt uneasy talking about this Joe guy.

We continued. I signed off on everything I needed to sign off on. When we finished, Dave said he'd walk me downstairs. We made small talk about Cubs games and the weather as we took the elevator down, but my head was still spinning from everything that had just occurred upstairs. When we reached the lobby, I turned to thank him, and noticed his face was serious again.

"Isabel," he started, "I couldn't tell you this before, and I probably shouldn't be telling you now, but I couldn't live with myself if I didn't. That Joe person you met? It was probably Joseph Masseria."

"Masseria?" I whispered. "Like Giovanni Masseria?"

"Yes."

"How do you know this?" I asked.

"I'm his lawyer. It's my job to know as much as possible."

I scoffed. "And I'm his daughter, and he didn't tell me shit about shit."

"Your signature was on a lot of those papers upstairs," he said. "That's probably how you ended up unknowingly signing the marriage license."

Fuck. I remembered signing a lot of papers growing up. *This is for my company. I want to make sure your name is on my things just in case.* I'd just sign. Blindly. Because that was the kind of trust I had in my father. I swallowed and met Dave's blue eyes again.

"I take it he was involved in illegal activity," I whispered, looking down at the toe box of my red bottom heels. A gift from my father.

Jesus. *Had I been blind?* No. I refused to believe any of this had been written on the walls and I just didn't catch on. He'd taken me to work with him when I was little. He'd driven me around in his truck. He hadn't hidden me from anyone. At least, it didn't seem that way.

"Nothing your name is on was illegal," Dave said, which should have made me feel better.

"My boyfriend is the mayor of New York, Dave." I met his eyes. "I can't have anything on me that'll tarnish his name."

"The mayor?" His brows shot up. "You're kidding."

"I wish I was." I let out a laugh that held no amusement as I looked away. "I seriously wish I was."

"I only know one address for The Masseria Family. It might be where you can find Giovanni," he said. "If you tell him you didn't know about the marriage license and explain your situation maybe he'll agree to a divorce." He shrugged. "It can't hurt."

"Right." I nodded absently. "Just, yeah, give me his information."

He did and we said our goodbyes as I walked out of the building. I didn't know Chicago. Not really. I hadn't even stepped foot here since I was eighteen, just before my high school graduation. Dad always visited me when he wanted to see me. I'd stopped visiting frequently when I was fourteen, because he was never home. He was always getting late night phone calls and taking off. Sometimes he'd be back by morning. Other times, he'd be gone an entire day. I never told my mother out of fear that she'd pick that to pretend she cared and somehow stop letting me see him all together. Instead, I told him I was busy with school and activities and friends, and he'd understood. He started visiting me instead on random weekends.

Sometimes he'd get us both rooms at fancy hotels and let me order room service and bring a friend. I loved those visits. That stopped me dead in my tracks, just feet away from my rental car. Holy shit. He'd never missed a child support payment. He'd paid all of my college tuition, books, and expenses. He'd bought me my first car—a brand-new white Volvo. The safest car at the time—and I'd never, ever thought to question where he got the money. He was always busy, always working, growing his business. Once I was inside my rental car, I gave myself a moment to let it all out. I cried harder than I'd cried all week, screamed louder than ever, and hit the steering wheel a few times, accidentally hitting the horn once. Then, I took a deep breath, wiped my tears, and collected myself, the way I always did, and I set out to find out who the fuck Giovanni Masseria was.

CHAPTER TWO

Gio

I HADN'T EVEN FINISHED SHAKING THE SAND OUT OF MY SHOES FROM my week-long vacation in Turks & Caicos and I already had my brother-in-law and my right-hand-woman, Nadia, staring me down from across the desk. When Nadia called me, demanding I come into the office, I knew it was important. When she said Lorenzo was flying in for the meeting, I knew it was very important and involved money. There was always a problem, always an obstacle, and always a solution, but I wanted to deal with none of the above right now.

"Let's hear it." I waved a hand, impatient. "How much money am I losing?"

Lorenzo cracked a smile at that, but grew serious when he said, "Charles Bonetti is dead," Lorenzo said.

"Shit. Really?" My brows rose. "Was it a hit?"

Lorenzo shrugged a shoulder.

"That's important," I said, "Because if it was a hit, someone may be trying to take the remaining four members out."

"Dean said it was natural causes," Nadia said.

I sat back in my chair, letting it rock a little. It wasn't that I didn't like Charles. He'd grown up with my father and was still very close friends with him. Growing up, I called him Uncle Charles, but I called a lot of people who weren't my uncles "uncle." My father was the reason Charles Bonetti had a seat at the table with The Family. There were five occupied seats. Well, four now, with Charles gone. I wondered if Dad had caught wind of this yet. Probably. No, definitely. There wasn't much he didn't know about. I looked at Lorenzo again.

"Why'd you call this little meeting? Because of the empty seat?" I asked him, then looked over at Nadia. "You shouldn't be in here for this."

"I don't think I'm going to be dragged into jail for this conversation." She shrugged. "And what I have to discuss is related to this."

Interesting. My eyes cut to Loren again. "You think Vinny will claim it?"

"Fuck, no." His answer was definite.

"He came after Cat last time."

"Under a completely different circumstance. He's not a threat, G."

"He got Frankie killed."

Nadia flinched. I felt bad, of course, he was her brother after all. He'd been my brother, too, but in a different way.

"Vinny won't come back. His family is too precious to him," Loren said. "Your dad already killed his mother, you think he's going to risk losing his wife? His kids? I know I wouldn't. He wants out of this life. He changed his name, forfeited everything."

"He forfeited everything when he faked his death, but that didn't stop him from coming back and kidnapping my sister." I pointed out. "He should already be dead."

Loren's jaw worked. It was the only indication I got that he was still pissed at the situation. He took a second to stop grinding his teeth and address me. "You think I didn't want to kill him? Cousin or not?"

"But you didn't."

"Your father didn't either."

"My sister begged him not to," I said, knowing I struck a nerve when his jaw twitched again, his eyes growing cold.

This was the Loren people worried about. He was a lawyer and was a boss when it came to racketeering. He didn't exactly get his hands dirty, he didn't have to, but if he wanted to, he would. I'd heard enough stories to know that to be true. With the look he's giving me, I knew this was the guy you didn't want to fuck with, but I did it anyway, because I liked pushing buttons and I knew my sister would kill him if he killed me.

"Enough about Vincent," he snapped after a moment. "He's out of the picture. Period. He won't be back."

"You're sure about that," I said.

"Gio, I swear to fucking God…" He let out a rough laugh, shaking his head, and I knew this was my final sign to stop fucking with him. I did, mostly because I was tired and didn't want blood on my new Prada suit.

"Let's move on," Nadia said. "If Vinny was going to come back, he would've showed up at the lawyer's office and claimed at least the money Charles left behind."

I rolled my eyes. Fucking Nadia always taking Lorenzo and my sister's side. It was because of her brother that she had this job, overseeing my nightclubs and any other business ventures I decided to get into. I didn't want to hire her at first. I kept hearing my father's voice in my head. *Women don't belong there, you fucking imbecile.* Every couple of days, when he called me and I chose to answer the phone, he said those words to me. Every time, he'd tell me to fire the women I'd hired. Every time, I'd stayed quiet, which was enough of an answer. I didn't really give a fuck about patriarchal bullshit. For the most part, at least. It wasn't like I wanted my sisters or Nadia involved in anything illegal. I couldn't say the same for Petra, my other right hand. She knew what she signed up for and she enjoyed getting her hands dirty.

"Do you want the seat?" I asked Loren. "Vinny's your cousin. You'd be next in line. You should probably just take it."

"Me?" He barked out a laugh. "Have you met your sister?"

My lip twitched. My point exactly. "They say you can't let women make your decisions."

"Who said that? A single man?" Loren asked.

Nadia snickered. "Definitely a single man."

"I'm good with acting as an advisor and putting my two cents in when necessary." Loren shrugged. "I don't want or need it a seat in that table."

Obviously, Midas over here didn't *need* it. The stingy motherfucker had more money than he knew what to do with *and* he was the consigliere's son, which put him higher than me in this hierarchy, and he was full Italian, which I wasn't. It didn't matter how much time passed and how much the world changed, me being half-Italian, half-Colombian, meant I had to prove myself at every turn. And I had. It didn't change the fact that the only reason I had a seat at the table right now was that my father was a fugitive on the run. Lorenzo, though? He could do whatever the fuck he wanted and still be guaranteed everything. If he didn't want the seat vacated by Charles, that meant it was for the taking and none of us knew what that really meant. Our fathers, grandfathers, and so on, had wars. Real ones that ended with a lot of people dead. It was a funny thing. People often talked shit about the Mexicans and Colombians and any organization from any other country, when in reality we were all the same.

We were all monsters. Some of us wore fancy suits. Others wore plain clothes. It didn't matter what we wore, though, it didn't change the fact that we were bad human beings. The Italians treated organized crime the way the Catholic Church treated their organization. The irony shouldn't be lost on you there, for obvious reasons. Staying organized sometimes meant doing messy shit, and that was exactly what the men who came before us did. They did what they had to do to ensure we all had a shot at this. Times change though, and they were changing rapidly. It was something my father didn't want to accept. Something Silvio Costello didn't want to accept. Something Charles Bonetti sure as shit didn't want to accept. Something Angelo Costello, Lorenzo's dad back in Italy, didn't want to accept. They were all the same, cut-outs of their fathers before them. Our generation was different. We followed rules, but they were rules we made. We were constantly looking for a way to bend the old rules just a little, to forge change that would hopefully reflect the time we lived in. They may not want to understand that, but we did, and we knew if there was any way in hell to keep all of this afloat, we'd all have to adjust. So, while they had their meetings that we were privy to sometimes, we had our own meetings. Our meetings didn't matter, though. We all needed *those* seats.

"Besides, that's now how it works," Loren added. "We can't just pick who takes the seat. There's a process, and we're not part of it. That's for Silvio, Angelo, and Dean to handle. And you at the moment, since you're acting as your father."

"Right. A process." I reclined back in my chair.

The only reason I even had a seat was because my father was a fugitive and was currently hiding out in another country. Otherwise, I'd still be beneath him. Waaaay beneath him actually, but he announced that I'd be a sit-in. That was exactly what he'd called it. He thought having me take his place showed strength, showed that he was still calling the shots. But now, there was an empty seat up for grabs and I needed to find out who I was running against if I decided to snatch it. Me taking it meant my father was automatically tossed aside. We couldn't have two members of the same family in these seats.

"Who wants the seat? Dominic?"

"Maybe." Lorenzo shrugged a shoulder. "You'd have to ask him."

"As if you don't already know the answer."

"I don't speak for Dom."

"Dean should choose on behalf of you guys," Nadia said. "He's the boss of your little squad anyway. All of you answer to him."

Lorenzo scowled. I felt myself scowl as well. Nadia laughed, shaking her head because she knew she wasn't wrong. Dean was practically all of our older brother. He was the oldest, definitely the wisest, and the one who had truly, one-hundred-percent grown up getting his hands dirty in this life. He'd also killed his stepfather, who'd once been the boss of bosses, and that earned him everyone's fear. And respect. And a damn seat. It didn't help that he knew every single detail of everyone's life. Dean could probably tell you at what time each of us took a shit every day. It was annoying, terrifying, and awe-inspiring.

Nadia sighed heavily. "Fine."

"Fine what?" I asked, shooting a bewildered look in her direction. If she was about to say she'd take the seat, I would laugh in her face. Yes, women were allowed at the table and mostly everywhere else, but not at *that* table. Not yet anyway. It was already a hell of a process, as Lorenzo pointed out.

"Charles left something for you in his will," she said. "So, I have to ask about it."

"For me?" *What the fuck?* I looked at her, then at Loren who shrugged, and back at her. This was the reason she was in my office to begin with. "You're making me nervous."

"So, do you...are you...don't even know how to ask this question," she said, laughing. She started trying again and as I watched her struggle with words, my heart started to pound hard. Nadia was never unsure or uneasy. Finally, she squinted at me and asked, "Are you married by any chance?"

"What?" I blinked, then let out a laugh. "Now is not the time for this kind of joke. You know I'm not married."

"It's kind of not a joke," she said quietly.

"What the fuck are you talking about?"

"You, Giovanni Masseria, are married to Charles Bonetti's daughter," she said. "According to the document he left for you, which, of course, would mean, you're entitled to that seat if you want it since his daughter can't take it."

I blinked. Looked at Loren again, who appeared confused as fuck. I blinked again. Looked at Nadia, as I tried to process this. Married to Charles' daughter? I didn't even know Charles had a fucking daughter. God. This had my father's name written all over it. I wasn't even going to try to understand his reasoning behind pulling this shit. I'd stopped trying to understand anything he did long ago. When I turned fourteen, he started whoring me out. Only to women, and according to him, I should've been grateful I was getting laid by beautiful, experienced women in the first place. I couldn't lie. I may have seen it that way once or twice, but using your body as your weapon, against your will gets exhausting and starts to make you feel dirty, even if you're a horny teenager. It was all he ever did with me, use me as a pawn in his sick game of human Twister. At the time, I thought, better me than my sisters. I still felt that way. I would've had to kill him if he ever did that to them.

And he considered it once or twice.

The final straw, for me, was when he tried to get me to seduce Loren's twenty-year-old cousin, Violeta. I took her out to dinner, of course, but I couldn't bring myself to give her false hopes. I couldn't even bring myself to kiss her. It had very little to do with me being a nice guy and everything to do with the fact that I had two younger sisters. Besides, it wasn't like Violeta had any information or anything valuable that I could use. My father just wanted me next to her to keep her father in check. Once it was clear that no one was safe from the Masserias, I broke things off. And still, without kissing or touching her, I broke the poor girl's heart when I told her we couldn't continue to see each other. None of that mattered now. I may have grown up a pawn, but I was a king now, or getting close to it. Still, this information threw me for a loop. Out of all the things my father has used me for this may have been the worst. He married me off? Anger hit me in the chest. I felt like hopping on a flight to Barranquilla and killing him myself. I could call one of my cousins to do it. Good relationship or not, they'd do it willingly. I knew that much.

"I didn't even know Charles had a daughter," I said, finally. "Do you have a copy of this certificate?"

She unfolded a sheet of paper and slid it over to me. I didn't even want to touch the thing. Instead, I stared at it. It was a New York marriage license. Not even Chicago. I looked at the names and the date. I had been twenty-two at the time, but the signature was undoubtedly mine.

I let out a laugh. "That motherfucker."

"I don't even know what to say about this," Loren said.

"As my lawyer, what would you have me do? This has to be illegal." I tapped the paper. "I never signed this."

Loren picked it up on an exhale and looked at it. "It's signed by a judge."

"Do you know this judge?"

"Yeah, he's a real prick." He set the paper back down and looked at me. "Probably great friends with your dad."

"Sounds about right." I looked at the paper again. "This happened eleven years ago according to the certificate, and I'm just now finding out, so it probably won't matter. We just have to get it erased somehow. Make it like it never happened." I shook my head again, looking at Loren. "Did you know Charles had a daughter?

"Nope."

"She's your cousin," I said unnecessarily.

"Not really. Vinny was, is, my cousin through his mom's side of the family. I'm a Costello, not a Bonetti."

"I should've stayed on that god damn island." I ran both hands down my face. "What the fuck?"

"Are you sure you didn't sign this yourself?" Loren asked. "Maybe you were drunk? Or high?"

"I don't get drunk or high, asshole." I glared at him.

"At twenty-two?" he asked.

Fuck. "I never would have gotten married. Not drunk, high,

or whatever else. Married?" I scoffed. "Fuck no. This had to be my father's doing. Some agreement with Charles."

"Can't argue there," he said.

"What do you have to do with this anyway?" I asked. "Why are you here?"

"He was one of my movers. I need access to his warehouses."

"Seriously?" I massaged my temples and closed my eyes. "Who the fuck is *not* your mover, Loren?"

"People who don't like making money."

I opened my eyes just to roll them. He smirked. Nadia bit back a laugh. I sighed, dropping my arms.

"Okay, so what do you want from me? Who the fuck is this Isabel person?" I asked. "Do we have any information on her?"

"She's pretty low key. She went to Rutgers. She's currently dating the Mayor of New York." Nadia paused to grin after saying that.

"You're fucking joking," was the only thing I could manage. "William Hamilton?"

"Yep." Nadia was still smiling. My stomach turned. I couldn't stand the guy and the feeling was mutual.

"Who cares?" Loren said. "What does he have to do with you staying married to her secretly until we figure out the warehouse situation?"

"Married to her secretly?" My voice rose. "How the fuck am I going to explain this to Natasha?"

"Really?" Nadia raised an eyebrow. "You're worried about Natasha's feelings all of a sudden?"

I frowned at that. Natasha was the woman I'd been seeing for six months now. Six months was a big deal for me. She'd met my sisters. On purpose. Not some run-in at a dark club or restaurant. That was a bigger deal. So, yes, I was worried about Natasha's feelings.

"Was Natasha in Turks & Caicos all week?" Nadia asked.

I glared at her. "You know she wasn't."

"My point exactly. The minute Natasha had to fly to Paris, you had a replacement waiting for you in the lobby."

"It's not my fault women want me," I said, eyes narrowed. "You act like I had someone flown in or something. How'd you find out about that anyway?"

"I have eyes and ears everywhere."

I let out a laugh. Of course, one of my men went and gossiped about this. My money was on Joey Z. Across from me, Loren chuckled, shaking his head.

"You better not do that to my sister." I pointed at him. "I'm not married to Natasha."

"I would never do that to your sister." He said seriously, then grinned. "And I know you're not married to Natasha. You're married to Isabel Bonetti."

"Oh, fuck off."

"And you need her for the warehouse locations, and potentially the seat, if you choose to go that route," Nadia added.

I sighed. "What I'm hearing is that I can't get a divorce from a woman I've never even met?"

"Only until I get I access to the warehouses," Loren said.

"Jesus Christ, Lorenzo, again with the fucking warehouses?" I threw my hands up.

"Those warehouses are currently costing me two-hundred-thousand a week, so yes, again with the fucking warehouses," he said, and I knew that again, he was just seconds from losing his cool. Midas loved making money, that was for damn sure. It was good for me, too, so I couldn't complain.

"Why not break into the warehouses?" I asked. It seemed like the logical thing to do.

"Break in?" he repeated back to me, as if I asked the dumbest question.

"Yes. Have one of your guys break in. Hell, have one of mine break in."

"Charles has warehouses everywhere, and he never told me where the exact locations were, you know, for plausible deniability."

"Some of them are on Russian territory," Nadia said, "According to Tony."

"There you go. We know Russians. Call one of them."

Nadia laughed. "We know a *few* Russians, and they all work against *the* Russians. They have no pull."

"I'm going to kill my father for this." I sat back in my chair. "Maybe Loren's right. Maybe she won't find out about this marriage, and we can just keep it a secret until we figure out a way to gain access."

"Uh, if Charles left this for you, he definitely left the same thing for her. She knows," Nadia said.

"Or here's an idea," Lorenzo began, and I already knew I wasn't going to like where this was going. "Maybe you should meet your wife and tell her straight up you need to see the documents."

"Or," Nadia started; I shot her a look, but she continued, "maybe you stay married until the big meeting. The one with the other four families. If Angelo Costello finds out about this, and he will find out about this—"

"If he doesn't already know," Loren interrupted.

"He's your father. Why don't you find out if he knows?" I asked.

"Eh. Not a good idea."

"Maybe Vinny gets the seat, as next of kin?"

"Hell no. Fuck Vinny," I said. "He gets that seat over my dead body."

"What if Silvio Costello finds out and wants Vinny back in?" She looked between the two of us. "Frankie used to say Silvio always had a soft spot for him."

I looked at Loren. "Is that possible?"

Loren shrugged, sighing.

"Would you allow it?" I asked, because that was more important.

"You think I can go over my father and uncle, two of the

top bosses?" Lorenzo's brows rose. "I'm crazy, but not *that* crazy. I actually have something to lose now. Nadia's right. We need that seat."

"I already told you that you can have the damn seat," I said, even though, I really fucking wanted it. I wanted all of the damn seats so I could plant the exact people I wanted in the exact places I wanted them. I was dying to get rid of these geezers, but Loren having a seat was a good alternative. He was my brother-in-law, and it would mean we were almost halfway there.

"I already speak on behalf of my father. I practically have a seat. I don't want it. Besides, Catalina—"

"Will kill you. I know." I sighed. "I guess I'm going to New York. And here I was hoping for a boring workday."

"Boring?" Loren stood with me. "You launder money through a bunch of nightclubs."

"Exactly." I stood and looked for my jacket while they stood and started walking out of my office.

Truth was, I actually enjoyed my nightclubs, and sure, the laundering. I'd tried to go one-hundred-percent legit with the nightclubs in the beginning, but in this life, that can only last so long. I tried to go to each one, frequently, but the one I went to the most was Devil's Lair, since it was the newest one. Natasha hated the nightclubs with a passion. If it were up to her, I'd sell them all. Leave it to me to find the one runway model who hated the night life. It was just one more thing I liked about her, though. She wasn't needy or clingy and she was always traveling abroad for a job, which meant I was the perfect boyfriend when she was in town (barely ever). The only downside was that my sisters didn't care for her, and unfortunately, that was a big downside. Neither of them could tell me what it was they had against her. They just said, *"it's just a feeling"* or *"her vibes are off"* as if that meant anything. The only thing I knew was, in my bed, her vibes were definitely on.

CHAPTER THREE

Isabel

As it turned out, my alleged husband, had a house in Lincoln Park. A beautiful one, too. Unfortunately, according to the housekeeper, he wasn't home. She'd been kind enough to direct me to his office, though, and now I was back in downtown Chicago, staring at a building. I walked around, found a little park tucked in between two buildings, and decided to sit there for a moment. I hadn't even called Will to tell him about any of this. I wouldn't even know where to start or what to say. *"Hey, I just found out my father, whom you shared multiple meals with, was maybe in the mob or something"*? or should I have started with, *"Apparently, I'm rich"*? God, this was bad. *Bad*, bad. I just…I couldn't wrap my head around any of it. I kept going back to drugs. Maybe he was a drug dealer, right? But my father was Italian, through and through. His parents were immigrants from Sicily, and that made me think of organized crime, because I wasn't an idiot. Also, I'd Googled, not that it'd helped *much*.

I did find a photograph of a time my father had been arrested when he was a teenager, though. Arrested. My father! The man who preached about staying on the right side of the law. He'd been arrested for stealing and let go quickly, but still. That wasn't the right side of the law. It had to be mafia related, right? How did that even work? Wasn't there a hierarchy or something? Were they going to kill me now that I knew who he was? It wasn't like I knew what he did. What did the mob do these days anyway? It wasn't the 1940's and we weren't in *The Godfather*. I lived in New York. I'd know if Italians were still running around killing each other. People were killing each other, all right, but it didn't seem very organized from where I stood.

I took a deep breath and marched over to the building, taking the elevator up to the twelfth floor before I lost my nerves. I channeled all of the strength I'd channeled when I walked into school, because I didn't care what anyone said, a room full of middle schoolers was worse than the mob. I knocked on the door, three times, just in case. Then, I walked inside and felt stupid for knocking at all. I hadn't expected to find an actual... business. There was a secretary sitting in front of a fancy glass that read *Valley of Kings*. I walked up to the man at the desk, who was smiling brightly.

"I need to speak to Giovanni Masseria, please."

"Was he expecting you?" he asked, frowning.

"No."

"Mr. Masseria left for New York an hour ago."

"You're joking."

"I'm not." He offered a sympathetic smile.

"Do you know where in New York I can find him?"

"Try one of his nightclubs. Maybe Devil's Lair? Or his restaurant, Masseria's." He shrugged a shoulder. "I don't keep tabs on him. Nobody really can." His eyes laughed as he said that last part and I didn't really like it.

I swallowed, thanked him, and left. I guess I was going back home after all.

"There she is." Will smiled wide as I strode into his office. He was so handsome, with blond hair, blue eyes, and a boyish smile. He was like that in high school, too, but he'd been too popular back then for me to stand a chance. He'd always been kind, though. Always. He stood and rounded his desk to give me a tight hug and kiss. "How'd it go?" he asked.

"It went." I sighed. I still hadn't told him about my father's secrets. I didn't know if I wanted to. I pulled away slightly. "How'd it go at the fundraiser?"

"It got postponed."

"No way. Why?"

"My father thought it was best if we moved it to Saturday afternoon. More people."

"Oh." I nodded. His father had a good read on the pulse of the city when it came to politicians and donors. And criminals. As a judge, he dealt with all of them.

"But the good news is, you get to come with me." He tapped my chin. I smiled for his benefit. I hated these events more than I hated grading papers on a Saturday night.

"Well, I'll leave you to it." I reached up and kissed him softly.

"Wait, you didn't tell me, how'd the thing with the lawyer go? Did your father leave you a grand estate in Europe?"

"More like a beat-up truck and a three bed-room in Chicago." I laughed softly. I didn't know why I didn't just tell him the truth. I should have. Will would've understood it, I knew that, but I just couldn't.

"I'll call you when I leave." He winked as I walked out of his office.

I was exhausted. Beyond exhausted. Yet, my body wouldn't let me rest and my mind was running a mile a minute. It was the only reason I'd talked Luke and Noah and their girlfriends to accompany me to the club, which, of course, earned me a lot of looks and questions that I didn't want to answer. I'd used grief as my excuse, and they'd readily agreed. The five of us were on our way to Devil's Lair, and only one of us knew the true purpose of the outing. Getting in was a lot easier than I thought it'd be. Once inside, though, I didn't know what to do. I'd been to nice nightclubs. This wasn't just nice, though. This was extravagant. It was mostly black, but everything that accented it was gold and looked expensive, which was saying something when you were dating someone like William Hamilton, who lived the lifestyle of the rich and famous. Will wasn't flashy, though. This was one step past flashy. After a few songs, I told my friends I'd be right back. I'd sort of filled Luke and Noah in on my meeting with the owner of the club, but I'd left out any details beyond that I needed to give him something from my father. They didn't question me, probably because I usually told them everything, and they had no reason to think I'd be lying about this. I felt a little bad about that, but until I knew what and who I was dealing with, I didn't want to involve anyone else.

I took the elevator upstairs, where I figured the office had to be. It stopped on the second floor, where there was another large bar, and some kind of VIP area. Instead of going left, I went right and walked the hallway until I reached double doors. I opened them and stepped inside, turning around to close them gently, grateful that the music was no longer blaring in my ears.

"May I help you?" A woman behind me asked, making me jump out of my skin. I turned around and faced her. She was Black, with platinum blonde hair cropped all the way to her scalp and dressed in an all-black tight leather outfit that fit her like a glove. She looked like a fucking badass, with dainty features and an air of femininity, though her features were the only soft thing about her.

"Um. Hi," I managed.

"Hi." She eyed me curiously.

"I'm looking for Giovanni Masseria."

"For what exactly?" She gave me a full, slow, once over now.

"I need to speak to him. It's urgent."

"It's always urgent." She set a hand on her narrow hip.

She was trying to make me nervous, and maybe I should have been, but a part of me thrived in situations like these. It was a weird thing, what traumatic events did to you. I'd seen some people succumb to them and become a shell of themselves, and others break past it and become total badasses. I was somewhere in the middle, if I was being honest, and I really couldn't afford to be scared right now.

"Please. Tell him Isabel Bonetti is here to see him."

"Bonetti." She raised an eyebrow, eyeing me closely again. "Interesting."

"Will you please relay the message?"

"Wait here." I watched her walk over to the next set of double doors, which she pulled open slightly, not even putting her entire face in as she spoke. I heard a man bark out words but couldn't catch quite what he was saying. She shut the door and turned to me with a polite smile that threw me off slightly.

"He's not taking visitors at the moment."

"Did you tell him my name?"

"Didn't get to that part." She pursed her lips. "Would you like to wait? I can fetch you a drink, but I can't promise he'll see you."

"Why are you being cordial all of a sudden?" I narrowed my eyes slightly.

"Because you're a Bonetti," she said, as if it were obvious.

"And that means?"

She just stared at me, kind of smiling, kind of curious, as she walked to the door. "What do you like to drink?"

"Tequila on the rocks, with a lime," I said, looking at the double doors in front of me.

As soon as I heard her walk out, I looked over my shoulder to make sure she was no longer there, and stepped forward, pounding on the door.

"What the fuck, Petra?" a man barked from the other side so angrily that even I stiffened, but it only fueled the anger I'd already been bottling up, because *how dare he?*

He'd signed a freaking marriage license without my consent.

He was probably just waiting for me to let my guard down before barging into my life and demanding whatever it is he wanted. I'd looked him up, too, this Giovanni guy. Total womanizing playboy. He was hot, yes, but everything else I'd read about him made him a little less hot in my eyes. He owned a ton of nightclubs and a couple of restaurants. *Definitely* involved in organized crime. There were dozens of message boards dedicated to discussing his underground businesses. That angered me further, because it meant that my father, my sweet, funny, caring father was also somehow involved in organized crime. With that in mind, I turned the doorknob and walked inside uninvited. The office was massive, the lighting dim. It reminded me of a restaurant or a spa. The chair was turned around, so he hadn't seen me yet. If this was any more ridiculous and Godfather like, I would have laughed, but I wasn't in the mood to laugh.

"What is it now?" he asked, sounding tired or bored. I wasn't sure which pissed me off more. "Did you find the bitch or not?"

"If the bitch you're referring to is your wife, the answer is yes."

The chair swiveled around quickly, his dark eyes landing on mine and narrowing instantly. I stopped breathing for a moment. For the sake of my own sanity, I tried very hard not to find him attractive. I tried, and failed, because the man sitting in front of me, claiming to be my husband, was by far the most attractive man I'd ever seen in person. The internet pictures definitely hadn't done him justice. It didn't matter, though. I wanted my name out of whatever equation he and my father had come up with. Besides, he was looking at me like he wanted to rip my head off, and that was all I needed to find him less attractive at the moment. I squared my shoulders.

"So, you're my husband?"

"I'm sure you're pleasantly surprised," he said as he looked over my shoulder. "Where's Petra?"

"The dominatrix?" I shrugged a shoulder. "I had to take her out."

At that, his brows lifted slightly, his eyes lighting in amusement as he continued to stare at me. I allowed it because I would not cower. These last six months, I'd been in many rooms filled with many men who thought they were too good for everyone else and each and every one of them had at some point proven otherwise. I took a step forward. He stood up, and I watched as he straightened to his full height. Shit. I hadn't expected him to be so tall or have those wide shoulders and that athletic frame to go with that too-handsome-face of his. I swallowed and reminded myself that I was there to get a divorce and move on, so I walked until I reached his desk, setting the tips of my fingers on it, mimicking his stance on the other side of it, and held eye contact. He gave away nothing as he watched me.

"I'm sure you know why I'm here."

"I don't assume anything about anyone, so maybe you should just tell me why you're here," he said.

"I want a divorce."

He stared at me. I tried not to blink. If this was a staring contest, I'd win. I'd won them against the best of them back in Queens and at the state of the arts high school I'd attended. I won against middle schoolers who thought they were hot shit. I wasn't going to let this man step all over me.

"A divorce," he repeated.

"That's what I said."

He took his eyes away from mine and for the first time, gave me a once over, that unlike Petra's, set my skin ablaze. He tapped the tips of his fingers on the desk, before sinking back down into the seat. I continued to stand, crossing my arms now. To his credit, he didn't drop his eyes to ogle my breasts, the way every other man seeing me in this tight hot pink corset dress would have. I was so glad I'd worn it. More importantly, I was so grateful for what I was wearing underneath it. Not that he'd ever know or see it, but when I had my good lingerie on, I felt like I could conquer the world. Tonight, was one of those nights.

"Here's the thing, Isabel," he said, nodding for me to take a seat across from him.

"What's the thing?" I uncrossed my arms and sat down but leaned forward in the seat so he knew I meant business. The movement pushed my breasts higher in the corset, and this time, he did look, but only for a brief moment. "The way I see it, there is no *thing*. What you and my father did was illegal."

"What I…" He laughed lightly, shaking his head. "You think I did this?"

"Obviously. Apparently, my dad was important in your world."

"My world," he repeated. "What do you know about my world?"

"That it's illegal."

"Illegal?" His mouth twitched. "What exactly do I do that's illegal?"

"I don't know. Things." I threw my hands up. "What does it matter? I don't care about organized crime, or your illegal or non-illegal activities. I just want out." I glanced away, hating that my emotions chose this moment to come out. Once I'd steadied myself and when I made sure I wasn't going to cry hot angry tears, I looked at him again. "I don't want to hurt you or get you in trouble or whatever. I just want out."

"Out of the marriage or out of this world?" He looked entirely too pleased with my display, and I had the sudden urge to grab the envelope opener on his desk and stab him with it. Maybe I did have a temper, after all.

"Both," I said, taking my eyes off the envelope opener and looking at him again.

"But you don't even know anything about this world. Maybe you'd love it."

"I wouldn't."

"How do you know?" He waited. When I didn't say anything, he continued, "How do you know someone won't knock
on your door tomorrow and tell you that you're next in line to
rule an empire, and then you'll feel like you walked away from
something big."

"I don't…" I shook my head. "I don't think you understand,
I don't care if it's big or makes millions or whatever the fuck. I
want out."

He raised his eyebrows, rocking back in the seat as he continued to look at me. "Where do you live?"

"Here."

"Where?"

"Queens." I swallowed, then rolled my eyes. "Chelsea."

"Big difference there." He cocked his head. "Which is it, you
a Queens girl or a Midtown girl?"

"Both. Not that it should matter since it has nothing to do
with the conversation at hand."

"What do you do for a living?"

"Again, nothing to do with my wanting out of this marriage
and this world."

"I can find out, you know," he said. "One phone call and I'll
know every dirty little secret you've ever tried to hide."

"Go ahead. Make that call." I smiled at that; it was the first
thing he'd said that gave me real courage. Men like him were so
used to getting their way at all costs, because men like him didn't
deal with women like me very often. "I have nothing to hide."

"Everyone has something to hide."

I let out a laugh. I almost felt like I was sitting across from
Will.

"What's so funny?"

"You reminded me of someone just now."

"A boyfriend," he said, and there was no question in the
statement, he was sure of it. So sure, of it, that I didn't bother
to deny it.

"Yes, a boyfriend, which makes this situation a little more urgent."

"Why? Has he proposed?"

"No." I bit my tongue, then let it go, because fuck this guy. "None of this is your business. I am not your business."

"You're my wife." He crossed his arms, rocking back again, a sexy grin on his stupid beautiful face. "So, that kind of makes you my business."

"This is so stupid." I threw my head back and groaned. I felt like one of my middle schoolers, but I didn't even care. This was a waste of time. He thought this was a joke.

"Just answer some questions for me and I'll think about it. Would that be so difficult if you have nothing to hide?"

"Fine. Ask." My eyes snapped back to his.

"Queens or Chelsea?"

"I currently live in Chelsea," I said. "Spent a chunk of my life in Queens."

"What do you do for a living?"

"I teach English and History."

"Really? A teacher?" His brows rose. He assessed me again, this time a little closer, his gaze heating as if I'd just said I was a Playboy model or something. My heart skipped a beat, even though I tried to contain it, because that was completely inappropriate considering I had a boyfriend. I glanced away.

"Yes, really," I said to the wall.

"What grades?"

"Seventh and eighth."

"God." He laughed, a real laugh, though it was so short I missed seeing it on his face when I finally looked at him again. "That must be a nightmare."

"Can't argue there," I said.

His eyes crinkled, but he didn't smile this time. "Why a teacher?"

"Why an astronaut? Why a firefighter? Why a...whatever it is you do?"

"You have a very short temper for a middle school teacher."

I ran my tongue along my teeth and drummed my fingers on his desk. "Is that all?"

"Is your boyfriend a teacher?"

"No." I almost laughed at the thought of Will as a teacher. He didn't even like kids.

"You're in love."

"So, you do make assumptions, after all."

This time, he did smile, and holy shit I wished he hadn't. It was slow forming, his eyes sparkling as he grinned. If he looked hot before, it was nothing compared to this. I brushed my hair behind both ears, knee bouncing. I didn't want to answer his question. I loved Will, but I wasn't in love with him. Not yet anyway, but sometimes love takes time, and I was giving myself that.

"I make you nervous," he said.

"You make me annoyed and angry and disgusted."

"Wow. All within, what, fifteen-minutes of meeting me?" He kept smiling. "That's a new record."

"Yep. Now, can you please for the love of God grant me the divorce?"

"No."

"No?" My jaw dropped. "What do you mean no?"

He tilted his face, running his tongue along his bottom lip. "I need things, some assets that your father has that don't belong to him."

"Like what?"

"I'm not at the liberty to say without my lawyer present."

"Oh, okay." I laughed. "You're one of those."

"One of whom?"

"One of those people who need their lawyers present for every conversation and sues everyone for everything," I said.

Will was also one of those. He'd just sued a freaking newspaper, for God's sake.

"And this annoys you."

"Kind of. It means you're going to stall, and I don't have time to stall."

"Because the boyfriend is going to propose soon?"

"Will you stop it with the proposal stuff?" I placed both hands on the sides of my face and looked up at the ceiling again, asking for patience and serenity and anything else that would help me. Will was nowhere near close to proposing, but I wasn't about to admit that to the man in front of me.

"I have a right to know when my wife is going to be proposed to by another man."

"Your wife?" I squeaked, looking at him again. He looked so smug, too. "Will you stop saying that? I am not your wife."

"The law says you are."

"Fuck the law. I'm not your wife!"

"Fuck the law, huh?" He raised an eyebrow. "Sure, you're not 'part of this world'?"

"Yes, Arielle, I'm positive."

He barked out a laugh and looked as surprised by it as I felt. It was a genuine laugh and I felt myself smile, proud that SOMEONE FINALLY UNDERSTOOD THE REFERENCE. I'd quoted Disney movies to Will for five months and my students longer, but they were too young, and Will had been too preoccupied with boarding schools and the violin and never saw those movies growing up. Citizen Kane, he'd seen multiple times, though. Go figure.

"Look, Isabel. I can't grant this divorce until I get what I need from this arrangement, and that's going to take a little while. Are you staying here? Going back to Chicago to tie things up? Where will you be?"

"Where will I be when?"

"This summer," he said. "School is out for the summer.

Where will you be? Do you have to be in school all summer doing paperwork and shit?"

"I hate to be the one to break this to you, but teachers usually leave the premises after school and actually have lives outside of teaching."

"I always wondered about that."

"Now you know." I shrugged a shoulder. Fuck. Was I still smiling? I got serious again. "How long do you think it'll take to sort all of this out?"

"If you give me full access to everything your father left? Sooner rather than later."

"Full access? Are you insane?" I blinked. I didn't know what that even meant, but if my father wanted anyone to have full access he'd have granted it himself. "Just tell me what you want, and I'll figure out how to get it to you."

"That might actually be a possibility," he said slowly. "If you leave me your contact information, I'll let you know what I need."

Contact information. As if I was merely leaving my email on a resume. I stared at him for a beat. "How 'bout I give you my number like a regular person in the twenty-twenties?"

"That works," he said, in a completely serious tone. "I'm getting tired of sending pigeons with my messages."

I bit back a laugh and looked away. If I wasn't dying to go back to my regular life, I might just be charmed by this interaction. I gave him my number. He gave me his in case I needed him for anything. I assured him I wouldn't. And I left. It seemed painless enough.

CHAPTER FOUR

Gio

DEAN HADN'T GIVEN ME ALL OF THE INFORMATION ON ISABEL, AND if I thought I wanted it before, I felt like I *needed* it now. She'd stumped me. I wasn't expecting her to be drop dead fucking gorgeous, with golden skin, light brown hair that hit her at the elbows, and eyes that nearly matched the shade. I definitely wasn't expecting her to be funny or sarcastic or a teacher. *A fucking teacher.* How could Nadia have left that part out of her one sentence pitch? That was my fucking fantasy growing up and my teachers looked nothing like Isabel Bonetti. This took my fantasy to a whole new level. I spent the rest of the night Googling her and wondering why she was dating William Hamilton. I just couldn't picture it. She was all fiery and funny and he was...well, him. Out of all the douchebags in the world, why pick that one? I scrolled through pictures after picture of her idiot boyfriend just to get a glimpse of her in a few of them. She was never front and center, always a few steps behind him, smiling a polite fake as fuck smile. She looked the part in all of them, though. She looked beautiful in all of them.

Beyond that, there was very little I could find. All of her social media profiles were set to private, probably because she was a teacher and didn't want her students to find her photos. Fuck, I wouldn't blame them if they tried. I wanted to see them so bad. I laughed, shaking my thoughts away. I needed to stay married until further notice, but once it was all said and done, I'd definitely sign the divorce papers and forget Isabel existed. It would be better that way. Yes, she was beautiful and had an incredible body, and was obviously fun, but I wasn't going to fuck her. She looked like the kind of woman who would want a relationship and thinking about being attached to another human being like that made my skin crawl. The only reason it worked with Natasha was because we didn't see each other all the time. If she lived here full time, I'd probably broken up with her by now. I turned to look at the New York City skyline from my bed and laughed again. Old Charles Bonetti had a secret daughter he'd married off to me and she was a hot teacher. What were the chances of that?

CHAPTER FIVE

Isabel

THIS EVENT WAS A SNOOZE FEST. I KNEW WILL AGREED WITH ME BY the way he kept squeezing my arm so I could save us from every conversation a new person started. I smiled at him and led him away from each one, claiming that someone else was calling us or that I needed a refill or that I needed aspirin for the headache I was faking.

"I think I should be nominated for some kind of acting award," I whispered when we escaped yet another old man staring at my tits and talking to Will about hunting.

"I think you deserve many awards," Will said, kissing my cheek, and then my lips lightly. I smiled against him and reached up to take my lipstick mark off his own.

"Did you smear me?" I waved a finger over my mouth.

He laughed. "No, but I can."

I rolled my eyes, shaking my head as I laughed. "Maybe our next excuse should be a quickie in the bathroom."

"I've never been a fan of quickies." A man said, and my stomach instantly dropped when I recognized the voice. What the hell was he doing here? Will and I both straightened and turned toward Giovanni, who was staring right into my eyes. I swallowed hard, to regain control of my rapidly beating heart, and the sudden rush of discomfort between my legs. He broke the gaze and looked at Will, giving a sharp nod. "William."

"Giovanni." Will kept his voice even, but from the way the tips of his ears lit up, I could tell he wasn't thrilled to see him.

"Are you going to introduce me to your lovely date?"

Giovanni's gaze swept over my face before slowly raking down my body and back up. It was so obvious that I stiffened. Hell, *Will stiffened* and normally he didn't care.

"This is my girlfriend, Isabel." He grabbed my hand and held it in his, not letting me shake Giovanni's.

"Isabel." His eyes danced with amusement.

"There you are." A tall brunette appeared behind him, wrapping an arm around his shoulder. She was freaking gorgeous. She smiled at me, then at Will, then at me. "Hi. I'm Natasha. Gio's girlfriend."

Will's tension slithered away. I felt it. He let go of my hand to shake Natasha's. I smiled at her as I shook it and introduced myself. I looked at Giovanni with an expression that I hoped he could read as, *"you have a girlfriend, you idiot? Does she know?"* And he arched an eyebrow and looked at me with an expression that said, *"does he know?"* I glared. He smiled, looking over at Will again. It was a fake smile. I could tell. I'd plastered enough of them on my face to recognize it.

"So, William, what's going on with that theater?" Giovanni asked. "You know, the one my permits are held up on for some odd reason even though I pay a shit load of money to avoid these things."

"I don't think this is the place," Will said in a hushed tone.

"Considering I made a hefty donation at the door," he said, then smiled at Natasha. "Two hefty donations. I think this is the perfect place."

"I already told you I have nothing to do with the holdup."

"Really? Because the way I heard it was that your father wants the theater for another cause. Something about another skyscraper?" Gio tilted his head slightly as if this was a totally lax conversation, but his eyes said otherwise.

Gone was the funny, charming man I'd met the other night. He'd been replaced by a menacing, cold, calculated man. And damn him if it didn't make him hotter. Something was definitely wrong with me. Maybe I was finally going through that bad boy phase everyone usually burned through in their teen years. I liked the sweet guys, the sure bets, the ones you could take home to your parents, or in my case, to chaperone the student dance with me once in a while. I'd never understood the bad boy appeal until this exact moment. On that note, I picked up two champagne flutes from the server walking by and handed one to Natasha, taking two steps away from the men we were with. Thankfully, she followed my lead.

"So, what do you do?" I asked, smiling.

"I'm a model." She took a sip of champagne, rolling her eyes. "God, it sounds so fucking pretentious every time I say it."

I laughed. "Hey, it's a cool job. What kind of modeling do you do?"

"Runway."

"Whoa. Really?" My eyes widened. "Any designers I'd know?"

Natasha went on to list the many designers she's worked with and pulled out her phone to show me photos of her latest fashion shows. I just stared and listened in amazement. As she continued scrolling, she reached a photo of her at a beach with the most beautiful clear water I'd ever seen. She was lying on her side, and Giovanni was behind her, wearing swimming trunks, his fit body in full display. Geez. He looked like a damn underwear model. Will had an incredible body, for sure, but he didn't have the body *and* that attitude. Jesus, what was wrong with me? I smiled, taking a sip of champagne, and looked away, my eyes everywhere but her phone screen. I wondered if he had social media. Again, I shook myself away from those thoughts.

"Natasha," Giovanni said suddenly, jaw clenched. "We should go."

"Oh." She pouted her lip at me. "It was so nice to meet you, Isabel! I'm sorry I did all the talking and didn't get the chance to get to know you."

"Oh, it's fine. I'm super boring." I smiled at her, then looked at Giovanni, who looked like he was staring into me with those dark eyes.

For a moment, I thought he was going to say something. Thankfully, Will put his hand around my waist, a movement Giovanni clocked with interest before we walked me away from them without saying goodbye. I glanced over my shoulder one last time and found Giovanni still watching me, fire brewing behind those eyes.

"Everything okay?" I asked, looking at Will.

"Everything is fine." He kissed my temple. "Stay away from that guy."

"I've never seen him before in my life," I said, then asked, "Why should I stay away from him, though?"

"Did you see the way he looked at you?"

I blinked up at him and frowned for real this time. "The way every other man at these events looks at women who are wearing low cut dresses?"

"No." He shook his head once. "Trust me, it was more than that."

It was more than that? I wanted to question him, but also didn't want to make him think I was even remotely interested in Giovanni. I wasn't.

"Hey." Will nudged me playfully. "Let's go find my parents."

"Yeah, let's." I plastered another fake smile on my face and inwardly groaned.

This night could not end soon enough.

CHAPTER SIX

Isabel

So, I LIED TO GIOVANNI THE OTHER NIGHT. SORT OF. I WASN'T *JUST* a middle school teacher. Not anymore, anyway. When my mother left for Spain, she'd handed over the keys to a hole-in-the-wall rum bar. A parting gift, she'd said. It had been a gift from my father to her, and since it was the only thing I had that was both of theirs, I'd been happy to take it over. That, and it made me feel more connected to my dad, who was a rum enthusiast. The Rum Bar had every single type of rum you could imagine. Just rum, though. It didn't make much money, and if I was keeping it one-hundred, the only reason I didn't sell the place immediately, was that my father owned the location and his accountant handled everything from the bookkeeping to the rum deliveries, so the only thing left to do was serve the rum. Luke and Noah did that part, though, so, I had very little to do with is, besides showing up and keeping them company, washing glasses, and pouring rum, something I only did during the summer. Not this summer, apparently. The Rum Bar was only open select days a week and we didn't know what days it would be until that specific week, since it was entirely up to Luke and Noah's schedules. We switched out the sign on the door on a day-to-day basis. If one of us could work the bar, we opened. If we couldn't, it remained closed.

This place used to mean so much to me before I found out Mom was a mistress, and I was their dirty little secret. God. I was so mad I almost picked up the phone and called her, but I restrained myself. Even if she did answer my phone call, she'd probably just brush it off the way she did everything else. I hadn't visited my grandmother this week, but I couldn't exactly depend on her for answers, in the mental state she was in most days.

The door of the bar chimed as it opened, and I smiled when I saw Mike walk through. He was a regular and always sat in the same little table. Everyone who visited were regulars and usually sat in the same spot. Once in a while we got tourists that were staying in nearby Airbnb's, but the bar had a maximum capacity of twenty-five. As I said, hole-in-the-wall. Outside of summer, I only visited on Sunday evenings. Sometimes on Thursdays, which was when Dad's accountant came in and did the books and received the shipments of rum that came in. He'd insisted on doing that job for me, since Dad was paying him. I hadn't thought to question it before, but now, everything was a question.

"You should be at home eating ice cream or something," Luke said, snapping me out of my thoughts. "Isn't that what people do when they're sad?"

"Who do you mean by people?" Noah asked from my other side.

"People who aren't lactose intolerant." Luke shrugged.

"I'll have to keep that in mind." I laughed. Noah shook his head as he poured some Havana Club for someone and walked it over. "Anyway, I'm not sad. I mean, I am, but mostly I'm disappointed. Hurt. Angry. I was sad when he died. I was sad the days that followed. But now? I'm so fucking angry."

"I'm sorry." Luke walked over and wrapped his arms around me tightly. The door opened again behind me, but I kept hugging Luke back because I needed this right now. "Your dad was a good man, Isa. I know he hurt you and what he did sucks, but deep down, he was good."

"Good men don't have secret families in other cities." I pulled away, swallowing my emotions down hard. "Good men don't have two separate families, period."

"Glad you corrected yourself there, 'cause I was about to

say…" Luke smiled. I picked up the towel and smacked him with it. "So now that we've confirmed he was involved in organized crime, are you going to be some kind of mafia princess?"

"We haven't confirmed anything." I laughed, despite myself. "And this isn't the freaking Sopranos."

"I mean, it sounds like it might be."

"Shut up." I laughed, going back to wiping glasses. When I looked up at Mike's table, my laughter died. Giovanni was sitting next to him, his eyes directly on me. My heart hammered. "God, can he not leave me the hell alone for a minute?"

"Who?"

"That's the guy I'm supposedly married to," I said to Luke as Noah was coming back. They both turned to look. Good thing I didn't care if they weren't sneaky, because they would have totally blown my cover.

"Giovanni Masseria?" Noah asked.

"You're fucking joking," Luke said.

My jaw dropped as I turned around fully, letting my back hit the bar as I looked at the two of them. "You know him?"

"We don't know him. We know *of* him," Noah said.

"Everyone knows of him, Isa."

"Not me." My brows rose. "How would I? He's from Chicago."

"Isabel." Luke cocked his head. "Masseria's Italian. You know, where they make the best lasagna."

"Oh." I frowned. I'd never put two-and-two together. It wasn't like I went looking up who owned what restaurant. Besides, I'd never had the lasagna there. "But that's an actual restaurant."

"That his family owns."

"He owns nightclubs," I said.

"You're married to him, of all people?" Noah blinked, shaking his head slowly. "I can't wrap my head around that."

"Me either." Luke's eyes narrowed above my head, and then at me. "Define married."

"I already told you the story. I'm not going to say it again," I whisper-shouted. "I wouldn't have told you if I knew he was going to show up here. How the hell did he know about this place? And why's he sitting with Mike?"

"He's been here a couple of times before." Noah shrugs. "He always comes with Mike. Sometimes he used to come with another guy, but I haven't seen him in a while."

"He was killed," Luke said, "Remember?"

"Oh shit. That's right." Noah nodded. "Nice guy, too."

"Yeah."

I slapped my forehead onto my hand. Apparently, I'd been the only person on the planet who didn't know who these people were. It probably didn't help that I didn't watch the news or read it, for that matter. Or, that I kept my head down and didn't ask many questions. I'd learned that questions often led to disappointment, though, now that it felt like I'd been kept in the dark about so many things, I wished I'd asked a lot more questions. I knew of Silvio Costello, of course. He was huge in organized crime. I'd heard of Anthony Costello as well. So, basically, the Costello's. They practically ran these streets. At least, they used to when we were teenagers. I only knew that because one of our neighbors had gone to jail because of them, or, for them. Noah and Luke both left the bar to take drinks to people. I turned back around, ready to keep wiping glasses, and was met with Giovanni's chest on the other side of the counter. I froze, looking up at his face slowly.

"What are you doing here?"

"This is one of the few places I can always find Havana Club at." He shrugged a shoulder. "I'll have that, on the rocks."

I tapped my finger on the counter and watched him for a beat. He continued to stare at me, into me. It was unnerving, the way he did that. My pulse pounded in my neck. I took that as a sign to pour his drink and move on.

"Here." I set it in front of him, then looked over his shoulder. "How do you know Mike?"

"He's a good friend of mine."

"Really?" I arched an eyebrow. "I don't see it."

"Why?" he looked genuinely confused.

"Because he's nice and you're not."

"Very interesting assumption on your part." He didn't smile, didn't laugh, but I saw the amusement dancing in his eyes.

"About you being mean?"

"About him being nice." He lifted his glass, winked at me, and turned around, walking back to his seat.

He winked at me. And my heart skipped two beats. *What the hell?*

CHAPTER SEVEN

Gio

"**A**NY CHANCE HE WAS HIDING SOME OF THE CARGO IN THE vault?" I asked Mike, who was sitting across from me. I'd known Mike, "The Tailor," as some called him, since I was born and trusted him more than I trusted most. He was a tailor by trade, like his father, who'd taken over the family business from his father before him. They were Jamaican, but owned the best store to get Italian suits, and more importantly, they had vaults behind it, where the five families kept their treasure. The fact that his father was able to gain their trust was mind blowing. To us younger guys, Mike was our brother. To the older guys, though? The Italians of my father's generation? Working this closely with Jamaicans wasn't exactly the norm. My father was the one who changed that, so I had to give him credit there. Maybe he was capable of change. Not that I'd ever say it aloud to him.

"He hasn't been here in months," Mike said, "So it's highly unlikely."

"Any chance he's hiding any in here?"

"Eh." Mike shook his head side-to-side, debating as his eyes jumped on each surface. "We can't rule it out, but I don't think so. He hadn't been here either in a while."

"Really?" I frowned. I'd never paid much attention to Charles Bonetti. He was just another geezer who tried to control what we were doing and put a pause on the changes we wanted to make. He owned this little bar in Queens, though, that only served rum.

The Rum Bar, it was called. Clever, I know. "So, this girl didn't have a good relationship with him?"

"No idea." Mike sat back and focused on his drink.

"You think she'd let us search the place?"

"Isabel?" He let out a laugh. "I can't imagine what excuse you'd give her in order to get her to agree. Whether or not she was close to her father, she's loyal to him."

"She's my wife." I shot him a look and took a sip of my rum, watching the way his face switched from one expression to the next, starting in amusement and landing in horror.

"Tell me you're joking."

"You think I'd joke about that?" I placed a palm to my heart.

"Fuck you, I'm being serious, G. Don't use that shit against her." He sat up and leaned forward. "She didn't ask for that."

"Neither did I, yet here we are." I glanced at the bar briefly. She was talking to one of the old men who'd walked in while I'd been sitting here. Funny how she looked so at ease in here. Then again, she was a middle school teacher and was somehow dating the fucking mayor. She'd have to appear comfortable in any situation. She definitely had the looks for it. When she walked into my office and dropped the bomb of who she was, I could hardly believe it. She looked nothing like her father. It wasn't just in appearances, either. Her father was a cold-blooded killer, with eyes that matched. He hadn't killed in a long time, that I knew of. Once he took over the vacant seat and started buying warehouses to hold cargo in, he focused on that. Still, the fact remained that he looked like a very hard man. Isabel wasn't that at all. She was guarded and open all at once. She was sexy as hell was what she was, but I couldn't let myself think about that too much.

"She's a good girl," Mike said after a moment.

"What do you know about her?" I asked, careful not to sound as desperate as I felt, because I did. I felt desperate to know more about her and I couldn't figure out why, which further pissed me off. I wasn't supposed to *want* to know anything about her.

"She grew up a few houses down from me. A few years younger, but we had mutual friends," he said, nodding at the bar. "Noah and Luke being two."

I looked over again. When I'd walked in, she was hugging one of them. Both big ass dudes that looked like they belonged on a field, not behind a bar, which was an unfair assumption. I knew it from personal experience. When people looked at me they saw only the obvious—rich, flashy, good looking—all good things, sure, but they weren't what made me, me. At least, I fucking hoped not. Before Frankie died, those were things I never thought about. Not once. I'd always used my looks and charm to my advantage in every situation. When those didn't work, I used money. When money didn't work, I used my last name. The guys behind the bar weren't like me, though. I could read that from all the way over here. They weren't who I'd think would run with guys like Mike at all. I turned to him again. "They seem nice?"

"They are." Mike looked at them again. "Their momma sheltered the shit out of those two. Turned out right, though."

"Hm." I took a sip of my rum. When I was a kid, no one tried to shelter me, and even if they had it would have been an impossible task, being the first-born son of Joseph Masseria, and all. And once I found out who the real Evelyn Alvarez was, well, let's just say I always figured I'd end up in jail eventually. Thankfully, I'd been very careful and able to dodge it, had never even gotten arrested. I got one speeding ticket once and my father laid into me so badly that from then out I went one mile an hour below the speeding limit at all times. "What does her boyfriend say about this place?"

"Fuck if I know." Mike laughed. "Who do you think I am? Russo?"

At the sound of Dean's name, I grit my teeth. He still hadn't gotten back to me with the information on Isabel. I'd told him

I'd pay him double, and he was treating it like he had all the time in the world to get it to me. I exhaled.

"I can't imagine he'd be okay with it, as pretentious as he is," I said about William Hamilton.

"You still mad about the permits?"

"Of course, I'm mad about the fucking permits." I looked at Mike again. "I wanted that theater ready by October. It's the middle of June and that asshole is still holding up construction."

"Because his father wants it."

"His father doesn't want it. Silvio and his little team of investors want it. They're just using Judge Hamilton as a front and promising him big bucks. Silvio wants to build a fucking skyscraper."

"I would think you of all people would appreciate a luxury building."

"The theater is historic."

Mike shot me a dubious look. I knew what he was thinking. When did I start caring about historic buildings? The answer was, I didn't. I cared about this one. I wanted to rebuild this one. And I would. If that meant I had to burn Judge Hamilton to the ground, so be it, but it was happening. For obvious reasons, I couldn't exactly burn Silvio Costello to the ground. I couldn't sit in meetings talking about change and do the very thing we were trying to steer away from. I wanted to, though. God, I wanted to.

"Does he come around here?"

"Hamilton?" Mike asked, frowning. "I haven't seen him, but it's not like I hang out here every time they're open."

"How the fuck did they even end up together?"

"They went to school together," Mike said. "High school."

"They've been together since?" My eyes widened.

"No, I guess they re-connected recently." He shrugged.

"Hm." I looked at Isabel again.

She was typing away on her phone. Texting him? Maybe. She was smiling. The moment her eyes met mine, she scowled and turned around. I felt myself smile. At the very least, I knew she was attracted to me, and I knew she wasn't acting this way to play hard to get. I'd met enough women who played that card thinking I liked the chase. I didn't. Isabel wasn't one of those women. She definitely found me attractive, but when I caught her checking me out, I also caught the way she quickly shut down the idea, as if she'd been reminded that I was bad news. I hated that split-second reminder, the moment her light brown eyes told me that she'd told herself *absolutely not.* I didn't know what it was about her that drew me in. I truly didn't, but I knew that for her, I'd chase. In another life, that was.

I was too busy for the remainder of this lifetime to chase someone like her, especially since I knew she wasn't the kind of woman you could just fuck and leave. She was the type who stuck around. The relationship type, and as everyone around me liked to remind me, I was far from the relationship type. She swiped all of her hair to one side of her shoulder, leaving the other bare, her back bare, in that spaghetti strap dress she wore. I swallowed. Took another sip of my drink.

"G, you know I don't meddle in your business," Mike started.

"You always meddle in my business."

"Fair, but not about women. I know you have this thing where you need to fuck every woman you find attractive, but she's not the one. You need to leave this one alone."

"I was just thinking the same thing, actually." I kept looking at her, though, my gaze trailing down the curve of her neck. As if she felt me doing it, she looked over her shoulder, meeting my eyes again. Fuck. *I knew that look.* It was the look you gave someone right before you dragged them to the back room and fucked them. Again, she shuttered it instantly, turning back to her friends, but I saw it. It was still burning into my chest. I looked down at the half-drunk rum in my cup. I shouldn't. I couldn't.

"I'm serious."

"I am, too." I looked at him again. "I'm not going to fuck

her, but I still don't understand how someone like her ends up with someone like Hamilton."

"You mean a rich guy and a poor girl?"

"I mean politician asshole and a wholesome teacher."

Mike laughed.

"What?"

"I forget you're not from around here."

"What does that mean?" I frowned.

"You think she's wholesome."

"You're saying she's not?" I asked, my interest peaking again.

"I'm saying, she's definitely a good girl. She has a good heart. She cares about people," Mike said, staring me down as he spoke. "But she's not one to fuck with either."

"Tell me more."

"Nope. Not my story to tell." He lifted a hand up. "Don't ask me again, either. I would never betray her like that."

A secret then. Damn. I loved secrets. "I'll find out."

"If you do, you do, but there are some secrets that even Dean Russo has no access to." He shot me a look. "Out here, we keep a lot to ourselves."

"Yet, you know hers."

He shrugged. I squinted at him. I knew Mike, though. I wouldn't get any more information out of him. Best friend or not, they didn't only call him *The Vault* because of what was behind his tailor shop. The man did not spill secrets about anyone.

CHAPTER EIGHT

Isabel

I SPENT THE WEEK ATTENDING FUNDRAISERS WITH WILL AND SPEAKING to a realtor in Chicago. I was listing my father's house and selling his truck as soon as possible. I'd told the realtor I'd be there by the end of the week to pack up his belonging while I debated with myself whether I should get a storage unit or keep what I wanted and get rid of the rest now, rather than later. Before then, I needed to visit my grandmother at the home. As it was, I hadn't gone in nearly two weeks and she was used to having me visit once or twice a week. I packed a suitcase and left it by the door, deciding that I'd book my flight to Chicago while I was on my way back from my grandmother's. Will asked me not to go back until Sunday, because that was when he'd be able to accompany me, but I assured him that it wasn't necessary. He kept saying the same thing over and over. *"Be careful, Isa. Please be careful."* Because I was stubborn as a mule, he knew to keep it at that and not try to take over my trip.

On my way to the nursing home, I wished I'd listened and waited for him to get out of work so that he could at least accompany me today. I preferred visiting my grandmother by myself, but right now, doing anything by myself was difficult. Doing anything with someone like Will was also difficult, though. When I got to the home, I made small talk with the women up front, and then the nurses who led me to where my grandmother was, in the television area.

"She's been doing well," the nurse said, "This week, though, she's been waking up in a pool of sweat, saying someone is in her room. It's not uncommon for her to see things that aren't there at this stage, though."

I swallowed and nodded. At this stage of her early dementia. It was one thing I was another thing I was angry at my mother for. She'd moved to another country with a new husband and didn't even think to visit her own mother. She called the nursing home once a week, but that wasn't enough. Since she left, I'd carried the full weight of this responsibility. I didn't like to say it was a burden since my grandmother had given everything up to help raise me, but sometimes, when I'd had a longer day than usual at school and had to come here, it felt like one. It didn't help that I didn't know what version of my grandmother I'd get any given day. Sometimes, she was the sweet woman who made me arroz con pollo and maduros. Other times, the things she'd say to me were evil and made me wonder whether or not she'd always felt this way, or if it really was the disease talking for her.

I stood by the door and watched her, the nurse squeezing my shoulder lightly as she walked away. My grandmother was a striking woman. Not so much these days, since she didn't bother with her appearance like she used to, but she was beautiful, nonetheless. In her day, as she used to say, she was the most sought-after woman in Cuba. She'd married a famous actor, who was equally as handsome as she was striking. Together they had my mother and allegedly lived in bliss for years. That was before the Castro regime got worse, though. Before she fled her country with my mother, just ten years old, in tow, for the promise of a better life.

I never met my grandfather, though I had spoken on the phone with him whenever my grandmother did. When I was eight, he was first arrested by the Cuban government for his vocal activism against what was happening in his country, and then, murdered. With his death, my grandmother's hope died. The hope she'd see him again, that he'd live here with her at some point, that they'd make up for all of the years that had been unfairly stripped of them. She turned into an angry woman then, lashing out at my mother and I, but mostly me, since I was the one who was always there. Up until I was eight, Mima had taken on the role of caregiver, cooking, and cleaning while my mother worked two jobs. She was always telling me stories, brushing my hair, and singing to me. After she lost her husband, everything switched, as if the light inside her went out completely with his death. Growing up, I'd resented her for the way she treated me. Now, I understood that she probably placed the blame on my mother and me. If not for us, she would have gone back and maybe prevented my grandfather's death. It was too late now, though, the damage had been done all around.

I pushed off the threshold and walked over to her.

"Hey, Mima." I kissed her head. She continued to look at the telenovela in front of her for a moment before glancing up at me.

"Anita." She gasped, covering her hand.

I sighed. The last few times I'd visited, she'd called me by my mother's name, and treated me as if I were her. It was never okay. When she wanted to cling on to her resentment for my mother, I had to sit there and take it. When she decided my mother had been the perfect daughter, I had to sit there and take it and pretend she hadn't abandoned us and moved to another country, and I wasn't the one who was visiting every week. I pulled up a chair and sat beside her.

"How are you feeling?" I asked, setting down the bag I brought with me and fixing the blanket on her lap.

"I was fine until that man started visiting." She looked over both her shoulders before leaning in. "He asked where Isabel was. I told him to fuck off."

"Mima." My eyes widened and I bit back a laugh. My grandmother never, ever cursed. She hated it when I did, so I tried not to in front of her. Even though I knew this was yet another consequence of her illness, I played along. "Who is this man?"

"I don't know. I couldn't see his face. I can never see his

face," she whispered, her light brown eyes searching mine. She frowned. "Isabel?"

I nodded, offering a small smile. "What did the man say?"

"He asked for you," she said, now in a rush, "He came last night and the night before. I told him nothing. You need to leave. He'll find you."

"You have nothing to worry about, Mima." I set my hand on hers. "I'm safe."

"Have you spoken to your father?" she asked. "Speak to your father."

My chest squeezed. "Speak to him about what?"

"Tell him to tell you everything."

"Can't you just tell me?" I ran my thumb over her soft hand. She fixated on that. When she looked at me again, her face had changed, and I knew I'd lost her.

"Anita," she said, sighing. "You need to help Isabel."

"I will." I let go of her hand to reached into the bag. "I brought you cheesecake."

"Junior's?" Her eyes widened.

"Of course." I smiled, bringing it out to feed her a slice. "Tell me about this telenovela you're watching."

I spent the rest of the hour watching it with her while she told me about it. Every so often, she'd remind me about the man who visited her. Two weeks ago, the idea of anyone coming in here and asking for me would have seemed far-fetch, but I didn't know what to think anymore. On my way out, I asked the nurse to please keep an eye on her throughout the night and promised I'd be back next week. I'd go to Chicago, clear out my father's house, sell his truck, and hopefully get more information about what it was Giovanni needed from me. If this was at all related to him, I needed to wipe my hands of it as soon as possible.

CHAPTER NINE

Isabel

I HATED THE IDEA OF STAYING AT MY FATHER'S HOUSE, BUT I'D ONLY managed to pack up four donation boxes before I had to stop. By then, it was almost one o'clock in the morning and I was hungry and tired. I ordered pizza. It was the only thing within a five-mile radius that was still open, and even though I'd have to pick it up and hated the idea of going out this late, I had no choice. Thankfully, the pizza parlor had a well-lit parking lot and a space open directly in front of the door. It took me no more than four minutes to pick it up and get back in my dad's truck. The moment the doors were locked, I opened the box and started eating. Every single person I knew would have my head for thinking a pie from a big chain was this good, but I was that hungry. My eyes were closed as I chewed when there was a loud knock on my window. I jumped in my seat and looked over to find a homeless man with pleading hands asking for money. I lowered my window just enough, so I could tell him I had no money. He eyed the pizza. I sighed and looked at the box. I'd eaten two slices. As hungry as I felt, I would've probably had all eight, but if I felt this hungry from not eating for six hours straight, I couldn't even imagine how he must have felt. I closed the pizza box, opened my window a little more, and handed it to him.

"God bless you," he said, taking the box, "You don't know how much this means to me. Please give my regards to the mister."

"The mister?" I'd already started putting my window up again but stopped. "What mister?"

"Mister Bonetti." He nodded at the truck. Shit. It hadn't even occurred to me that my father's truck would be recognized, but now that he'd pointed it out, I wasn't sure if it was a good or bad thing.

"He died."

"What?" His eyes widened. He lowered the pizza box a little, but opened it and took out a slice, taking a big bite of it. Over his full mouth, he asked, "When?"

"Two weeks ago." I searched his eyes, which were clear blue, and the cleanest thing on his face right now. "Did you know him?"

"Of course." He nodded. "Everyone did."

"Did he...how did you know him?" I asked, unsure of what to even ask this man.

"He came by the shelter every month. Brought us blankets and stuff. Sometimes he brought me coffee and donuts." He signaled to the corner of the plaza, where I saw black trash bags and a sleeping bag. "Sometimes the shelter closes before I make it there, and I sleep here. He had me under his care."

"What does that mean?"

"No one could kill me." He shrugged both shoulders, kept eating. "Now, I guess I better get myself a gun."

My eyes widened. Oh, Jesus. I had nothing against protecting yourself, but something told me this man wouldn't really know how to properly use a gun. What did I know, though? He could've been a veteran for all I know.

"Who do you need protection from?" I asked, because I couldn't just leave it.

He laughed. "Everyone. We're getting killed left and right out here."

I frowned. "Who is we? You mean homeless people?"

He nodded gravely, taking another bite, then looked inside

the truck. "You wouldn't happen to have anything to drink in there?"

I frowned. It felt like he was pushing his luck with me, and yet, I reached over and grabbed one of the two bottles of water I'd gotten inside and handed it to him.

"Thank you, thank you." He bowed his head, then asked, "Were you his mistress?"

"His daughter."

His brows hiked up. "Oh, shit. You should use that. His name holds weight around here."

"I'm not planning to stick around."

"I wouldn't either." He pressed his lips together. "I'm Devon, by the way."

"Nice to meet you, Devon. Enjoy the pizza. And the water." I finished putting the window up and reversed the truck.

The polite thing to do would have been to tell him my name and introduce myself formally, but I wasn't about to be polite. Out here, I wasn't William Hamilton's girlfriend or middle school teacher of the year at MS54. Out here, I was my father's daughter. A gangster? I shivered thinking about it. I'd known plenty of gang members growing up, but even though they'd been heavily involved in illegal shit, they looked out for us because we all came from the same neighborhood. Rival gangs from other neighborhoods were bad news, though. I'd had enough traumatic experiences to prove it.

My phone buzzed in the middle of the car as I drove, and I eyed it suspiciously. No one called me in the middle of the night. Unless it was Will, but even he didn't typically do that. We usually had our last call around nine o'clock, and that was usually a FaceTime, where we'd have sex. It was his thing. I just went along for the ride. I picked up the phone and saw Luke's name on the screen. My hands instantly got sweaty. The bar was something I'd been worrying about lately. Keeping it, getting rid of it. Luke and Noah were the only ones holding it together and keeping it now felt pointless. I answered the phone with a shaky hand and set it on speaker.

"Is everything okay?" I asked upon answering.

"Sort of," Luke said slowly. "Someone broke into the bar."

"What?" My heart stopped. "When? What did they take? Was anyone hurt?"

"It must have happened right after we closed for the night. No one was hurt. I have no idea what they could have taken. All of the liquor is intact, even the boxes in the back."

I frowned, grateful to stop at a red light right now. "Did they turn the place over?"

"The office, yes."

"Fuck." I slapped the steering wheel.

"Was there anything in there that they could've been looking for?" That was Noah, which meant I was on speaker phone.

"No. I mean, the physical deed, maybe? But that's in the safe."

They were quiet for a long moment.

"Hello?" I said as I started driving when the light turned green.

"The safe is gone." That was Luke. "What else was in there? Money?"

"Only whatever money you've put in there. I don't go there, Luke." My voice was getting quieter and quieter as the conversation went on. Who would steal the safe? Giovanni? He had been there the other night and he was looking for something, but he'd been so…understanding about it when we spoke at his club. I didn't think he'd do this, but then again, I didn't know anything about him.

"Don't worry about it," Noah said, "We'll get to the bottom of it."

"Absolutely not," I said, my voice no longer quiet. "You two go home to your girlfriends and leave this alone. I don't want

Tina or Piper to kill me over this and I definitely don't want Ms. Smith to think I got you involved in some illegal shit."

"Asking around is not illegal," Luke said. "I'll go to Mike."

"No." Mike was friends with Giovanni. He was also my friend, but I wasn't sure who he was more loyal to. "Let me handle it."

"You? Really, Isa?"

"Yes, really, assholes. Just shut down the bar if you need to. It's not like we're raking in tons of dough." I rolled my eyes.

It was true. Luke and Noah had full-time jobs, they only worked at the bar as a favor to my father, and now, me. Not that they minded. They could drink on the job and chill with the guys from the block, away from their very inquisitive girlfriends. I loved them, but I could see why they needed a break from them for a few hours a night.

"It ain't about the dough and you know it," Noah said. "This is your bar. Our bar. No one should be fucking with it."

I sighed as I reached my father's house and set the truck in park. "Please don't go looking for trouble. We don't know what we'll find."

It was true and it was scary. It didn't matter how many people doing bad things we knew, it didn't matter how many gunshots we heard at night, it didn't matter how many times we received awful news about yet another kid we went to school with. None of it "got old." None of it "became normal." Maybe those who only heard about things on the news were desensitized to it, but we weren't. Whether I lived in a fancy apartment or not, I was still a Queens girl for life. We hung up after they promised they wouldn't go asking, but I had a feeling they'd go to Mike anyway. I knew them. I hoped Mike was on our side. He owed me, but I didn't know how much he owed Giovanni.

CHAPTER TEN

Gio

"**R**EALLY, GIOVANNI?" MY SISTER GLARED AT ME AS SHE STOOD beside the small table where Natasha and I were currently about to enjoy a meal.

My brows rose. She never called me Giovanni unless she was pissed. It was always G. That was what most people called me. G, Gio, most people I surrounded myself with didn't call me my full name, though. It felt too formal. I watched as my sister turned to the table behind her, where there were three seats, but only two people were twirling spaghetti around their forks. Without even asking permission, she pulled the third chair and brought it over to our table, making herself at home in the middle of our date. I couldn't help but smile. She'd always been quiet, only really coming alive on center stage, but ever since she married Lorenzo, she walked around like she was hot shit. Well, at least in front of me. She was still mostly quiet in front of everyone else. This display was a play straight out of my handbook, though. Out of our father's handbook.

"Hello, Catalina," Natasha said across from me, dazzling smile on her face.

"Yeah, hi." My sister looked at her briefly and nodded a few times, before ignoring her. I sighed. She'd never accept this woman and I genuinely couldn't understand why. "You were just going to skip town without telling me?"

"Skip town?" I laughed. *That was what this was about?* "I'm here every other weekend, sometimes every weekend."

"Yeah, well, I'd like to see you from time to time, you know."
Her brows pulled in. "Have you talked to Mom?"

"I should've known this was about Mom." I shook my head.
It was always about Mom, which was borderline comical
since she'd abandoned us and probably never gave any mind to
what we were doing. Catalina had even paused her wedding
plans, just so our mother could be there. She got married in
freaking Italy, where no one was gunning for Evelyn Alvarez,
but she never showed up. She never showed. I was tired of trying to figure her out. At first, I bought the whole story about
her brothers gunning after her for the inheritance her father
left her, but now I knew for a fact it wasn't true. I had pictures
to prove my mother and her so-called-brothers were doing just
fine. So-called, since the three of them were adopted. My sisters
were sent to boarding school abroad, and while I knew they'd
had a very difficult time with all of it, I was the one here, left to
deal with my father's madness. I was the one doing dirty deeds
for him. *Sometimes* when I thought about my mother, I hated her
for leaving. The majority of the time, I was indifferent.

"Shut up," Cat said. "I spoke to Dad, and he said Mom was
coming to New York for something."

"When was this?" I frowned. I'd been avoiding my father's
persistent phone calls for a couple of days.

"Last night."

"And she left when?"

"Last night." She said it like she wanted to hit me. This was
why Lorenzo didn't want that seat. If this was what he was dealing with at home, good fucking luck to him. This was exactly
why I was never getting married. Well, willingly, anyway.

"Don't hold your breath waiting for her call, Catalina." I
took a bite of the lasagna in front of me and nearly groaned with
satisfaction. Natasha was vacillating between her food and typing away, probably telling a friend what a bitch my sister was. If
that was the case, I couldn't blame her.

My sister shrugged a shoulder, "Honestly, I'm done with her."

"Since when?" I stared at her, setting my fork down.

"Since we delayed our wedding three times just for her and then she didn't show up or even bother to call."

I gave an understanding nod and went to pick my fork back up when she spoke again.

"I spoke to Marco," she said suddenly.

"Jesus Christ, Cat." I tilted my head back and exhaled, then I remembered Natasha was still sitting there, so I told my sister, "We'll discuss this later. Stop speaking to Marco."

"Why? He's our cousin."

I drummed my fingers on the table, then looked up at Natasha, smiling. "Will you excuse us for a moment?"

"But I'm eating." She looked at her steak and salad and back at me.

"Cat. Let's go to the back." I folded my napkin and set it next to my lasagna.

I'd been craving it for an entire week, and I knew it was going to get fucking cold while I sorted this out with my sister. I picked up my glass of red wine and started walking to the back office, not even bothering to see whether or not she was following. Once inside, I set my glass on the desk and waited for her to come inside. She was picking up her hair into a bun as she walked in. I took in her attire. Yoga pants, a sports bra, and a see-through crop top.

"What are you doing walking around like that?"

"I was at hot yoga with Emma."

I shook my head. "It's a good thing Dad's not here. He'd never let you walk in with this get up. I'm shocked Loren lets you out like this."

"Please." She rolled her eyes. "Can we talk about Mom coming over here randomly while Dad is over there? Isn't it a little suspicious?"

"I stopped trying to figure her out the night she walked out on us," I said, which was a total lie, but whatever. I lifted the glass of wine to my lips and took a small sip. "I'll get to the bottom of it when I speak to Dad."

"Why are you drinking?" She made a face.

I stared at her. She said it like I had a drinking problem. I didn't, per se. I spent four months getting drunk after Frankie died. One night, my sisters planned a little intervention. After that, I gave up alcohol. I only had it for celebratory occasions, and even then, it was one glass of wine, one glass of whiskey. No more than that.

"It's Natasha and my seven-month anniversary."

"You're joking." She blinked. "You celebrate months? What are you, fifteen?"

"I didn't have a girlfriend at fifteen." I shrugged.

"You didn't have a girlfriend at never," she pointed out. "And this is who you pick? Also, if you're cheating on her, she doesn't count as a girlfriend."

"How do you figure that?"

"What's the point of 'having a girlfriend' if you're going to treat her the way you treat the rest of them?"

"I introduced you to her. That's different."

She rolled her eyes. "You're ridiculous."

"You're the one who doesn't like her, and you've never even told me why," I said and decided to change the subject because this one never ended well. "Also, stop talking to Marco. Why the hell are you even in touch with him?"

"I go to his restaurant sometimes."

"His…" I stopped talking because my jaw dropped mid-way through my thoughts. Our cousin's Colombian restaurant was not in the best part of town. I hadn't even been there out of fear that I'd get kidnapped, not by Marco, but by someone in his crew. It was their MO to hold people at ransom. "Does Lorenzo know about this?"

"Obviously. He comes with me."

I shook my head, processing this. "He's doing business with the Colombians now?"

"We *are* Colombian, G." She crossed her arms. "Do you need a reminder?"

"Of course, I don't need a reminder." I glanced away feeling shitty.

It wasn't that I wasn't proud of my roots. Of course, I was. At least, I had been growing up. After Mom left, though? I kind of turned my back on all of it, including that half of my family. Including Marco, who actually was nice, as Catalina pointed out, and technically wasn't even our cousin by blood, but I didn't bother pointing that out because it really didn't matter. We had aunts and uncles and cousins and people we called brothers and sisters who didn't share our blood, and it didn't make them any less important. The entire Alvarez family had always been nice to us, with the exception of my mother and her brothers. Those three would kill someone on the spot. I'd never actually known my mom to pull a trigger, but I knew she had it in her. Then again, didn't we all, under the right, or wrong circumstances?

"Well, if you think she's going to reach out to me, you're mistaken. Even if she didn't hate me before, she probably does now."

"Why do you say that?"

"The last time I spoke to her, I called her a lying bitch, and you know she doesn't exactly like hearing the truth about herself."

"Jesus, Gio." Cat shook her head.

"If she reaches out to you, call me immediately. Do not meet with her by yourself, Catalina," I said, "Do you understand me?"

"Loren said the same thing. I understand."

I didn't believe her. She held my eyes as she lied, and I had to give her credit because another man may have gone along with it, but I knew liars. I was one. Which meant I needed to call my fucking brother-in-law prematurely, since I still did not have an answer about the locations of the warehouses.

"Is that it?" I picked up my wine and started walking to the door.

"Yeah, I guess," she said, but stayed rooted to her spot blocking the door. I raised an eyebrow. *What now?* "You're not happy, G. I know you think you are, but you're not. This thing with Natasha is a waste of time."

"Maybe I like wasting my time." I walked past her.

She scoffed behind me. "Fucking liar."

I kept walking until I reached the table. Natasha had finished her meal and was now drinking an espresso. I was jealous that she'd gotten to eat alone, in peace, with no interruptions. Cat gave me a kiss on the cheek and waved at Natasha as I took my seat, looking at the lasagna. I pushed the plate away. I could've asked for another one, but I'd lost my appetite after that conversation. Maybe I'd take it home and heat it up, which I never did, but that was how badly I'd been craving this meal.

"So," Natasha said. "Am I going to meet your mother?"

I blinked up from my cold lasagna and found her smiling at me, a hint of excitement in her blue eyes. I almost felt bad. Almost. I waited one second, and another, and finally I sighed, looking away and running a hand through my hair. Fuck, I needed a haircut. I straightened my shoulders and met her gaze straight on, the way I did when I was sitting across from an associate or a capo.

"Absolutely not."

"Wh... well, you don't have to be so mean about it." She frowned. "I thought, I mean, we've been together seven months today, Gio."

"And I have to admit, it was a good run." I looked up at the server and told him to box up my lasagna.

"Wait. You're breaking up with me?" she asked, shocked.

"It appears so."

"On our anniversary?" she squeaked, surely causing every head to turn in our direction, but I wasn't paying attention to them. I kept looking at her.

"I'm sorry," I said. I meant it, too. I hated the idea of break ups. It was why I didn't formally date in the first place.

"For what reason?" her voice rose some more. "I demand to know the reason."

She demanded to know a reason. I tried not to laugh at that as I counted my money for the tip. It wasn't like I paid the bill at my own restaurant, but I always liked to leave the tip in cash. The server came back with my box and a glass bottle of coke, something I always took with me. I thanked him and handed him the cash. His eyes lit up as he thanked me and walked away.

"Giovanni!" Natasha slapped her napkin on the table. "I deserve to know why you're breaking up with me."

"Because, Natasha." I stood up. "My sisters don't like you."

"What?" She let out a laugh. "Your bratty sisters don't like me so you're breaking up with me? You're not fucking them, you're fucking me. Why do you care what they think?"

"You must have not been paying attention." I walked over to her and kissed her lips briefly. "Family means everything to me. Everything they say matters. Especially when it comes to this."

I picked up my doggy bag and walked away after that. She tried to follow me. One of my guys stopped her. I waved at the rest of the staff and the chefs as I made my way through the kitchen and walked out the back door, where Petra was waiting for me outside the SUV. She'd dyed her hair platinum blonde recently. I hadn't gotten used to it yet. It was a striking contrast against her dark skin, but she made it work. Then again, with an attitude like hers, everything worked and if it didn't, it was best not to tell her.

"We have a problem." She set her phone to her side and looked up at me.

"Of course, we do." My whole fucking life was a series of problems.

"That girl, the one who came to the club the other night," Petra said, hesitating.

"Talk," I barked out.

Petra raised an eyebrow. I drew in a slow, steadying breath. This was one of the many reasons why my father didn't employ women. Well, besides the fact that he was a misogynistic asshole. Women had a way of drawing things out and bringing out instead of getting to the point when they thought they were going to piss people off, though.

"She showed up at your house."

"Which house?" I frowned.

"The Lincoln Park house."

"My father's house?" I shut my eyes to try to reel myself in. "What the fuck is she doing there?"

How the hell did she even know where the house was? Maybe the lawyer. That alone was a red flag. How did *he* know where it was? Unless my father had him on retainer, and if that was the case, why was he disclosing private information? I shook my head. Yet, another thing to deal with. If there was ever a time to be grateful that my father was out of the country, it was now. The house always had two guards and two housekeepers, and I had to assume they'd let her in. I wondered how the fuck she'd pulled that off. Over the years, I'd had crazy ex-flings show up and never managed to make it past the gates.

"Yep," she said. "Someone apparently broke into Charles' house."

My eyes popped open. "While she was there?"

"I don't know." She shrugged. "I was literally getting the 411 when you came out here."

"Call Flynn and ask him if he has a plane available here tonight. Tell him it's urgent."

"Got it." She gave a nod and walked away, to the SUV in front of mine.

I got in the back of mine and banged my head on the headrest a few times.

"Airport?" Nico, my driver, asked.

"Yes."

I didn't know who the hell this woman was three weeks ago, and she was already turning out to be a hell of a fucking problem.

CHAPTER ELEVEN

Isabel

I HATED ASKING PEOPLE FOR HELP, BUT WHEN I GOT TO MY DAD'S HOUSE and went inside, I'd been ambushed. They'd tied me up, put a bag over my head, and pointed a gun to the side of my head. My body's first reaction wasn't to scream or run or fight, it was to pee myself. I hated that I did that, but it wasn't really up to me. They'd assured me that they weren't there to hurt me, but I'd heard that line before and it always ended in pain. In the end, they didn't hurt me, not in all the ways they could have. It could've been so much worse, but to me, being tied up and feeling powerless was as bad as anything. Once they left, taking some boxes with them, the boxes I'd packed up to keep for myself, I was able to set myself free. They'd told me, from the door, that the knot had been undone. How I managed to get up to lock the door while still heaving with sobs was inexplicable. How I managed to get to the bathroom and shower and clean up after myself was a mystery to me. I didn't remember doing any of it. I didn't even remember how I stopped shaking hard enough to get back in the car and drive to Giovanni's mansion.

I didn't even want to decipher my thought process in coming here first, but now that I was here, I was glad I'd made that choice. I was sitting in an extra-large white couch, with a cozy blanket over my shoulders and a mug filled with chamomile tea in my still shaky hands. His housekeepers were so nice. His guards, not so much. They'd taken my phone, my purse, my keys, and my jewelry. And that was after I told them what had just happened to me. Assholes. My teeth were still chattering when the chime of the alarm rang alerting of an open door. I was staring at the television, at the words, *"Are you still watching?"* that had been there since the episode of some matchmaking show ended. The housekeepers picked it for me. I had no interest in watching anything.

A man cleared his throat, and I instantly knew it was him. I glanced over my shoulder. He looked like a dark horse, with his hands in his pockets, dressed in all black, eyes so dark they matched his attire.

"I see you've made yourself at home." He walked around the couch until he stopped in front of me, and I had to crane my neck to look up. The mug shook harder. He took it from my hands, setting it down on the table beside me. He dipped the tip of his finger in the tea before handing me the cloth napkin that was next to the saltine crackers the housekeepers left there for me. To soothe my stomach, they'd said. I hadn't touched them. "You don't feel how hot this is?"

"What?" I took the napkin and realized my hands were full of tea. They were red, too. I hadn't felt how hot it was, but now the heat registered. I wiped myself, wincing at the feel of the napkin against my hands, and set the napkin down, my lower lip wobbling. "I can't feel anything."

A frown. "What the fuck happened?"

"I, um…" I paused to lick my lips and take a breath. "I flew in this morning. I'm trying to sell my dad's house quickly. I was packing up and then I got hungry." I stopped again to breathe, hoping to get through this story without crying. "And then I got hungry…"

"You said that part," he snapped. "You got hungry and then what?"

I pulled back, looking away from his face, which meant I was now staring at his crotch. I looked down at my red palms. This man was no Will. Will would have comforted me and kissed my hands and asked if I was okay. But I hadn't called Will. I'd ran here, to him, without second thought.

"I went and got pizza."

"At what time was this?" He looked at his watch and yawned. "Fuck, the sun is about to come up."

"Around one?"

"In the morning," he said, with an edge in his tone. It made me feel like I was an idiot, and that was what made me look up at him. Sure enough, he was looking at me like I was an idiot, and that finally made something inside me snap. Anger I could deal with. Anything was better than numbness. He continued. "You got hungry at one in the morning and decided to drive around Chicago, a city you're not even familiar with, to look for pizza."

"Yes." I bit the inside of my mouth because it was less painful than the bite in his tone.

"I mean…" He shook his head, then waved a hand. "Continue."

"No. Forget it. I don't even know why I came here to begin with." I forced myself off the couch, untangling my legs from the cover and headed toward the front door. I should've left an hour ago. I should've never come here to begin with. I stomped my bare feet against the cold marble floor. "I knew coming here was probably a bad idea, but I didn't have anyone to call or anywhere to go and I thought…I don't know what I thought." Obviously, I hadn't *thought*. That was the problem. I slid my feet into my Adidas slides and set a hand on the doorknob.

That was when I realized I was still shaking, shivering so uncontrollably that my hand couldn't even turn the knob fully. I heard him come up behind me. He didn't say anything. Didn't warn me, either, as he lifted me in his arms. One moment I was opening the door, the next I was cradled in front of his chest as he walked back into the house. It took me a second to react and start wiggling to get out of his grasp. I knew I'd fall on my ass, but I didn't care. I didn't want to be in his arms like this. I didn't want to be touched at all.

"Let me go." I wiggled harder, pushing his chest, slapping his back, his ribs, his face.

He didn't like that. He growled and shifted me so he could look at me, seething, hard, cold, menacing, as his fingers gripped painfully on my skin. I instantly stopped fighting. It wasn't the logical thing to do. When a man carries you and looks at you like he's completely liable to kill you, that's when you should fight. That's when you scream and move. But that look spoke volumes, and this was his house. His territory. His people. His housekeepers were nice, but they were *his* housekeepers, not mine. They wouldn't do anything to help me. I knew that. I crossed my arms, bit my tongue, and let him carry me up the stairs. I was still shaking so hard, that I knew the moment he set me down I'd fall over. He walked into a bedroom, kicked the door shut behind us, and set me down at the edge of the bed.

I tried regulating my breathing, but that was impossible now. I knew it was illogical, too. If this man wanted to rape me, he could've done it by now. Rapists didn't need beds or rooms or privacy, they just took without remorse. Somewhere deep inside me, I knew Giovanni wouldn't do that. How I knew it, I wasn't sure. Maybe it was because I'd known enough men in my lifetime, who took advantage of women. I knew their MO and the way they looked at you. When you really started to break it down, when you really started to notice the way predators around you, it became obvious that the red flags had always been there and had gone ignored for another slew of reasons we used to cover them up. Giovanni didn't have *that* look. He backed away from me, still staring at me with those cold, hard, eyes. Despite all of it, I didn't like being in this space with him. I didn't like that I was in a closed bedroom and that he was looming over me. I summoned all of the courage I could muster, knowing I'd need it to deal with him and whoever else came after.

"I'm not going to tell you what happened," I said quietly, arms still crossed over my chest. I was wearing stripe pajama pants and a navy crop top because that was what I'd brought to sleep in, and what I put on after my shower, but now I was regretting it. At least I was wearing a bra. And still, I felt naked under his scrutiny.

"I guess I'll have to keep you here until someone else tells me what happened then." He started walking toward the door.

"What? No!"

"Don't worry, I'll know soon enough." He kept walking.

"Wait. Wait. Wait." I scrambled to unsteady feet, panic rising into my throat and wrapping around it. "I need my phone. I need my phone and my stuff."

"Your phone?" He stopped at the door, glancing at me over his shoulder, half smiling, but not looking very amused. "What, you want to call your boyfriend to come save you?"

"Maybe." I swallowed, tilting my chin up. "Maybe I already did."

At this, he chuckled darkly and let go of the doorknob as he turned around, leaning against it, crossing his arms and one foot over the other. His eyes were amused as fuck now, and I had the urge to hurl things at him. I would've thrown the bench in front of the bed if I knew I could carry it.

"If you'd called him, someone would have already called me." He cocked his head slightly, pushing off the door.

Instinctively, I backed up, the backs of my knees hitting the bed, making me sit as I looked at him, wide-eyed, while he stalked over. Even the way he walked was nerve racking. This was not the Giovanni who had turned up the charm that night in his club, or at the fundraiser. This wasn't the man who sort of flirted, and then kept his distance in my bar. This man meant business, with the way his eyes stayed zoned in on mine and his defined jaw worked the closer he got. My gaze dropped to his forearms, he'd rolled up his sleeves and gave a glimpse of the roped muscle underneath his clothes that I'd only seen in that one picture in Natasha's cell phone.

I met his gaze again and swallowed hard, moving back slightly, when he ducked down to my level and set his hands on either side of me, gripping the comforter with such force, I felt myself move toward him. I was powerless without my weapon, without steady feet. My lip wobbled on its own accord. I'd been scared shitless once tonight, I'd be damned if I let it happen again, with this man. We were almost nose to nose, his breath on my face smelled of mint, one of those green sticks of gum Luke was always chewing on. I licked my lips. His gaze clocked it momentarily before his cold eyes met mine once more. They were onyx stones shining in the dim light. The way he just looked at me, made it hard to breathe again. I'd almost forgotten what was happening, my head swimming in him, his scent, the hard expression on his face, his gaze pinning mine.

"You didn't call your boyfriend at all," he said, leaning in closer now, brushing the stubble on his cheek against my face. I shivered slightly at that, and the way he dropped his voice low when his mouth neared my ear. "Instead, you ran straight to your husband."

He straightened before I could react, turning and walking toward the door again.

"Stop calling yourself that," I shouted at his back.

"It's what I am." He shrugged those broad shoulders. "You're safe here, but obviously, you know that, otherwise you wouldn't have thought to run here first. Try to get some sleep. It'll help the shock wear off. We'll talk in a few hours."

I nodded, opened my mouth, shut it, felt new tears cascade down my face and wiped them quickly.

CHAPTER TWELVE

Gio

WHAT THE FUCK HAD SHE BEEN THINKING RUNNING STRAIGHT TO the lion's den? Straight to my father's house, of all places. Whoever gave her the address obviously didn't know where I lived. It had to be the lawyer. It didn't matter. If someone had broken into Charles' house, this was the safest place for her to be at the moment. I continued to pace my father's home office, as I waited for a call from Lorenzo and another from Dean. I wasn't sure which I needed first. Lorenzo was going to provide more security detail and mother fucking Dean still hadn't given me the stuff I'd asked him for. It was unlike him. So, unlike him, in fact, that I was starting to worry. I hated that feeling. The reason I had everything from my daily schedule and routine to my meals meticulously laid out was to avoid worrying, so this shit was driving me up the wall. My phone buzzed in my hand. Nadia. I groaned but answered it.

"I'm outside."

"So, come inside." I hung up the phone and tossed it on the desk, confused as to why she'd call me to warn me that she was outside. When the office door opened behind me, I realized why. She walked inside with her husband, Tony in tow, and their five-year-old twins behind them. Jesus Christ. As cute as my goddaughters were, the last thing I needed was to deal with fucking children right now.

"Make yourselves at home," I muttered.

Tony smirked.

Nadia spoke up. "The twins woke up a five-thirty and

wouldn't go back to bed. My mom doesn't get there till eight, so we had to bring them."

I ran my hands down my face. I was hanging on to my sanity by a thread and now had two little girls tugging on my pants. I exhaled heavily and lowered my hands and looked at them. Tried to glare at them, really, but they smiled and tugged again, wide brown eyes. "Uncle Gio. A kiss!"

God damn it. I hated kids. Why'd they have to be so fucking cute? I lowered myself into a crouch and let each of them give me a kiss and hug. "Uncle Gio hasn't gotten any sleep."

"Uh-oh," Lucia said. "You're in a bad mood like Alessa."

"I'm not in a bad mood." Alessa frowned.

"Yes, you are. Because you didn't get any sleep," Lucia pointed out.

I sighed, shaking my head. "It's okay, Alessa. We're allowed to be in a bad mood today."

"Mommy says we're not supposed to take out our bad mood on other people," Lucia said, pointing a finger at me.

I rolled my eyes, grumbling, "Yeah, she's probably right."

"Girls, come over here," Tony said, setting up two separate iPads with the two separate cat headphones I'd gotten them for their birthday a few months ago. He covered them with two separate blankets, and they instantly forgot about us. They were good parents, these two. I had to give them that.

"So, Isabel is here," Nadia said unnecessarily.

"She's in my old room." I pointed at the ceiling.

"The lawyer probably gave her this address," Nadia said, stating the fucking obvious.

"What did she say?" Tony stepped forward. "Do we know who ambushed the house?"

"Dominic is looking into it." Man, I missed Frankie. He would've already found out. He would've already had two of them in a warehouse, tied up and bloodied, but he was no longer here and as angry as I felt, I would never bring up his name right now. I looked at Nadia. "You know I don't want you involved in any of this. That was the deal when I agreed to let you work for me."

She shrugged a shoulder. "I'm only here to tell you William Hamilton's whereabouts for the next few days in case you want to try to have a conversation with him again about the theater."

"Really?" I squinted at her. "At seven o'clock in the morning, you decided to show up with your entire family to tell me something you could've texted me?"

"I want to help," Tony said, taking one step in front of his wife. "You need someone you can trust right now, and I can help. I'll drive you around, ask questions, whatever."

"No. Fuck no." I shook my head. "Out of the question. The last thing I need is for this to go sideways and Nadia to lose another man she needs in her life."

Tony set his lips flat. Nadia grimaced, looking away.

"We all know what we signed up for," Nadia said.

"You signed up to oversee my nightclubs. Nothing else."

"I signed up to do whatever it takes to keep this family safe," Tony said, "That means all of us, including you."

I swallowed, turning around to pace some more because I didn't want them to see the way that got to me. My father had always preached that family was everything, but he'd never been talking about his immediate family. He'd never meant his kids or wife. He meant *The Family*. I learned what loyalty meant from Frankie, Nadia, Mike, Dean, etcetera. Even Lorenzo. Even Vinny before he went and did some crazy ass shit. My sisters were always number one on my list of people I cared about and took care of, but these were the people I dealt with on a day-to-day. These were the people I trusted with my life. Not my father, especially not my father. I ran a hand through my hair as I turned to face them again.

"We don't know what we're dealing with," I said, looking

at Tony. "I know you'll do anything to help, but I don't want you in danger."

Normally, I would have agreed, since as he pointed out, this was what we signed up for. Tony was a soldier, and a damn good one, but it didn't matter. Frankie died the last time shit went sideways. Nadia didn't deserve to lose her brother and her husband. The two little girls on my sofa couldn't afford it.

"He already does dangerous shit, G," Nadia said, keeping her voice low.

"How are you okay with this?" I met her gaze.

"I know what we signed up for." She shrugged a shoulder. "And the seat is important."

Ah, it was about the seat, which I couldn't quite grasp. It wasn't like Tony could take it. The sitting four would never allow that and he'd need someone big to vouch for him, and since my dad wasn't here, that was out of the question. That seat meant automatic control of the import-export and cargo. Lorenzo's operation may have been his, but the way things were set up, to ensure that no one would stab each other in the back, meant he wasn't allowed to act on his own. Charles held control of where everything was stored. And the stabbing in the back? It would happen over this. We all knew it. It wouldn't be me, or Lorenzo, or Dean, but Silvio and my father were wildcards. It was the reason I hadn't formally announced I was going after it.

"Fine. You can interchange with Nico," I said to Tony. "I'm going to have Joey Z stick with Isabel in the meantime, but if shit goes sideways…"

"It won't." He was so sure of himself, and I wanted to believe him, but shit had gone sideways one too many times in the past.

"You have guys who keep their ear to the ground, right?" I said, "Maybe you can ask around. If it was a hired job, it'll be easy to track."

"I'm on it." He took his phone out and started typing as he sat between his daughters on the couch.

"What did she say?" Nadia asked, nodding her head toward the ceiling. "Anything we can use?"

"She didn't talk."

"What do you mean?" She frowned. "She came here though."

I went around the desk and sat in my father's chair. It still smelled like him, this entire office smelled like him, which I tried to ignore since the smell only brought beratement with it.

"You didn't ask questions?" Nadia asked, taking a seat across from me.

"Of course, I asked questions."

"And? What did she say?"

"She went out to get pizza at one in the morning," I said, trying not to grit my teeth as I thought about it. When it came to doing stupid shit, men had women beat by a landslide, but when women went and did stupid shit, they really went all out with their recklessness.

"That was ballsy," Nadia quipped. "And when she got back the house had been broken into?"

I set my elbows on the desk and shut my eyes as I massaged my temples. "I guess."

"You guess?" Nadia's voice rose. "You didn't think to ask?"

"She started fucking crying and tried to leave."

"So, what'd you do?"

"I carried her up to my room and locked her in there." I let my hands fall on the desk and looked up to see Tony trying to bite back a laugh from the couch and Nadia's jaw on the floor.

"You are such a fucking asshole." She shook her head. "You didn't even try to comfort her?"

"Comfort her?" I was sure the look on my face was bewildered. "Have you met me? What the fuck would I even say?"

"I don't know. You seem to know how to charm the shit out

of women when you want to fuck them, I figured you'd know how to handle this situation."

"You want me to fuck it out of her?" I asked, even though I didn't need the answer. Nadia's shrug was answer enough.

I bit my tongue and looked away, my eyes landing on the portrait of my parents. It looked like an eighteenth-century portrait and not one done in the nineties. My father was the reason that everyone expected me to whip out my dick and turn up my charm as a way to *"deal with women"*. It was something I could never complain about without sounded like a pussy, but fuck, in times like these, it bothered me. Nadia wasn't wrong, though. Did I want to fuck her? Absolutely, but the alarm bells my head told me to stay the fuck away. I'd never had alarm bells ring over a woman before, and this time, they were blaring and impossible to ignore. Under any other circumstance, I would have charmed the information out of her. I would've coaxed her until she was sucking my dick and begging to fuck me before I left her there, sleeping in my bed, in sheets that smelled of sex. She'd replay the scene over and over and ask for more. I'd be an idiot to turn it down. From the moment she walked into the office at my night-club with her smart-ass mouth and her perfect body and beautiful face I'd been thinking about bending her over my desk and fucking her. But I wouldn't. This would be the woman I'd leave alone, because Mike was right. She *was* good, and I knew there was something else underneath all of that armor she hid behind. There was a sadness in her eyes, even when she was angry, even when she was smiling. That was the kind of shit that got men like me into more trouble than I was willing to deal with right now.

"You're welcome to try." I pointed at the ceiling. "She's up there."

"Okay." Nadia stood up. "Let's go."

"Let's?" My eyes widened. "Fuck no."

"You're scared of tears now?" She raised an eyebrow.

"Please." I scoffed. "I grew up with two little sisters. You know I'm not scared of tears."

"So? What's the problem?"

I didn't answer. I didn't know what the problem was and that in and of itself was a fucking problem. That was alarm bell number one. I wasn't sure why I didn't like seeing her trying to leave the house, or why I liked the fact that she hadn't called her boyfriend and instead ran straight to me. Two more alarm bells. I mean, I hated the guy, so that was definitely one of the reasons, but it wasn't the only one. It was that look. That sadness. It wasn't I got off on tears. It was more that the sadness and the need to hide it behind a smile, behind harsh words, behind flirting and sex, hit close to home. Fuck it. If she was going to stay here, I was going to have to get used to seeing it. I shrugged and walked out of the office with Nadia.

CHAPTER THIRTEEN

Isabel

THE DOOR OPENED AS I WAS STEPPING OUT OF THE BATHROOM. I'D taken another shower. I couldn't seem to shake the feeling of disgust and even though I knew Dove soap wasn't going to wash it away, I tried anyway. He didn't have many clothes in the closet, which made me wonder if he lived here at all, but I'd managed to borrow a black T-shirt of his and a black pair of boxer shorts. They were both too big, but the boxers stayed put thanks to my hips and ass. I froze when I saw a woman walk inside and Giovanni walk in behind her. He shut the door. I kept my attention on the woman. She was pretty, with short dark hair and light eyes. She was wearing a button down and slacks, which made me wonder if she was on her way to work. It was too early for her to not have slept here, but I'd already met his girlfriend, who was the complete opposite of this woman, so I wasn't sure what to make of this. Giovanni was still wearing the same thing he had been when he got here. He looked tired. Beautiful, but tired. I didn't miss the way his eyes raked over me from head to toe and back, as if he was drinking me in slowly. That look made my heart skip a few beats. I focused on the woman again.

"I'm Nadia," the woman said, stepping farther into the room. She stopped by the bench at the foot of the bed. "Gio's assistant."

"Oh." I blinked. That explained the attire.

"You're Isabel," she said when I didn't introduce myself. I nodded.

"I need you to tell me exactly what happened last night,"

she said, in such a soothing voice as she took a seat at the other end of the bed. She patted it and I didn't think twice as I moved and climbed onto the opposite side, facing her. Giovanni walked to the bench and stopped there, still watching me.

"Tell me what happened."

"I was packing some boxes." I paused, looking at Giovanni. "Does he have to be here?"

"Yes, he has to be here," he said, voice as hard as the expression on his face. "I won't interrupt this time. Just fucking talk."

Nadia shot him some kind of warning look over her shoulder. He didn't even look at her.

"I was packing boxes and when I finished it was one in the morning more or less. I was starving but the delivery apps weren't delivering at that time. I found a pizza place nearby that was still open, so I decided to order and pick it up." I swallowed, waiting for Nadia's reaction to that. She gave none, so I continued. "I ate a couple of slices in the parking lot, but then some homeless guy knocked on my window."

"Jesus Fucking Christ," Giovanni muttered, shutting his eyes briefly. I glanced up at him. He shook his head as if he was exasperated by this already.

"So, I gave the guy the rest of my pizza—"

Giovanni laughed harshly. "Mother fucking Teresa over here."

"Do you want me to tell you what happened or not?" I snapped. "I'm so tired of you and your judgement. I know it was stupid, okay? Fuck."

"I'm sorry." Nadia leaned way in and set her hand on mine. "Please ignore him. He has two younger sisters that he's very protective of, so you can imagine what must be going through his head."

Oh. I looked back up at Giovanni, who was staring into me like he was trying to pull the entire story out of me through my eyes. I was an only child, and even though I considered the neighborhood kids my siblings and would probably take a bullet for some of them—Luke and Noah specifically—I didn't truly know what it was like to have blood siblings. It kind of explained the attitude, though. He was probably picturing one of his sisters doing something this stupid. I looked at Nadia again when she moved her hand from mine.

"The guy asked me about the truck, I told him my dad died, he said something about protection or being protected, I don't know." I shook my head. "Then, I drove back to my dad's house." I looked at the dark gray comforter beneath us. "I parked outside, and I was on the phone because someone broke into my dad's bar back in Queens." I looked up at Giovanni to see if there was any sign that it could have been him, but his face was blank. I kept my eyes on him because it felt like they were anchoring me right now, and I couldn't seem to look away. "I finished my phone call, grabbed the extra water bottle I had, and walked inside. The door was locked, so I unlocked it and went inside. I took off my shoes by the door and before I even turned around they ambushed me." My lip wobbled. I tore my gaze from Giovanni's and looked at the comforter between us. "There were three of them. They wore black ski masks over their faces and like camo clothing otherwise, like military attire but they were definitely not military. One of them had blue eyes. He was the one that stood out the most because his eyes were so blue." I swallowed. "He tied my hands behind my back and told me he wouldn't hurt me." I clenched my jaw, pausing again when I felt a new wave of tears form in my eyes. I tried to bat them away quickly, but they just kept falling. Nadia moved, crawling over to me and pulling me into her arms. I cried openly.

"Did they touch you?" The question came from Giovanni's lips. Venom laced his voice. I glance up and saw the fury behind his eyes now. I knew what he was asking. Did they rape me, but he repeated, "Did they touch you?"

I shook my head, wiping my face as I pulled away from

Nadia. She stayed near, though. "They tied me up and put a gun to my head before they put a bag over my head. They didn't even tape my mouth. They let me scream. No one came." I let out a harsh laugh. "Obviously, no one came. I screamed some more, but then they shoved the gun a little harder against my head and I stopped."

Giovanni's jaw clenched.

"What did they do next?" Nadia whispered.

"They started asking me for a briefcase. I told them I didn't have a briefcase. They yanked me by the rope behind my back as they walked the house, holding a gun against my back the whole time." I paused again.

When I closed my eyes earlier, trying to rest, I could still feel the barrel of the gun against me, I felt their rough hands on me, the way they carelessly dragged me everywhere. I rubbed my wrists together. They were still red, still sore. Giovanni took two steps and was at my side, lifting my arm to inspect. He didn't mean anything by it, I was sure, but his touch did things to me, nonetheless. His jaw working even harder now.

"Go get aloe," he said, looking at Nadia. There was something in his voice that made it impossible to argue with. She climbed off the bed, leaving the room. His hand closed tightly around my arm, just beneath the marks. I looked up at him and my heart hammering at the look on his face. He was pissed off. He was pissed off that they'd hurt me, and that meant something to me. Stupid, maybe, but this was the product of growing up in an uncaring environment. "Whoever did this will pay."

"I don't know what to do now," I whispered, ignoring that. "Do I get to go home?"

"You think I'm letting you go home after what you just told us?" He let go of me.

"If they wanted to kill me, I'd be dead."

"True." He cocked his head like he agreed. "Which means

they want something and if they didn't find it while they went
through the house, they'll come back soon enough."

"What do they want, though?" I whispered. "What
briefcase?"

His face was still so close to mine, I couldn't find it in me
to speak any louder than that. If he wanted to, he could move
forward and kiss me. His eyes searched mine, heated, and I instantly knew he was thinking the same thing. He pulled away
quickly. For some stupid, some crazy reason, my galloping heart
deflated. I screamed at myself for that reaction. I had a boyfriend.
Giovanni had a girlfriend. I'd been attacked not even twelve hours
ago. *What was wrong with me?*

"I don't know," he said, finally, as he stood and began pacing the room. "Maybe the keys and locations to the warehouses
are in the briefcase."

"What warehouses?"

"The ones your father owned. I need those keys from you.
I'm assuming that's why you and I are in the situation we're in
to begin with, to ensure they don't land on anyone else's' lap."

"Oh." I rocked back slightly and decided to get out of bed
because this was suddenly feeling weird now that Nadia wasn't
here. I stood at the edge of it, by the bench, and set a knee there.
Giovanni stopped pacing momentarily, and let his eyes fall over
me again. He looked like he wanted to eat me whole, and I felt
like I might just let him. No. *I have a boyfriend.* I dropped my knee
and straightened. He returned to his pacing, so I spoke again,
"My father didn't leave any keys. Not that I know of, anyway."

"Trust me, he left them. We just need to find them."

"What's in the warehouses?"

He stopped pacing again, looked over one of his broad
shoulders. "It's best you don't know."

"Oh," I whispered, trying to figure out why, then I realized
my father definitely was involved in illegal activity and said, "Oh."

"Exactly," he said, "Which is why it's imperative I find this before whoever came after you does. Did they have accents? Tattoos? Anything you can remember."

I thought about it. "They didn't have accents when they spoke English, but two of them were speaking another language that I didn't know."

"Spanish?"

"I know Spanish," I said. "This was nowhere near Spanish."

At that, he stopped pacing again, just a few feet in front of me. He looked at me again, as if I was some kind of puzzle he couldn't solve. I would have thought a man like him would have all of my information by now, down to my grandmother and mother's names at Ellis Island. Apparently, not, though, because I could see the questions brewing behind those dark eyes. For some strange reason, I wanted to answer each and every one of them. Maybe it was because I'd met a different version of him. A charming, funny one. One that I was sure I wouldn't see again, and somehow, that made me a little sad. I inwardly slapped myself again.

"What were they speaking then?" He took a step forward. It made butterflies come alive in my stomach.

"I don't know. I don't know every language in the world." I looked down momentarily, desperate to get out of the intensity of his stare. "When can I call Will?"

"Not yet."

"But when?"

"Soon, okay?" He shut his eyes and tilted his head back. I kept my eyes on his long neck, the dip of his Adam's Apple. He straightened and looked at me again. I wasn't sure what expression was on my face, but it must have been something he wasn't expecting, something he liked, because he ran his tongue over his bottom lip and looked at mine, eyes darkening again. My chest tightened and it suddenly felt ten degrees hotter in the room. His mouth twisted into a slow, sexy smile that made my pulse race behind my ears. "You sure it's your boyfriend you want?"

Holy shit. My heart went into overtime, as fast as it was beating. The door opened behind him. His smile dropped, expression blank, just like that. In a blink of an eye, he'd composed himself, while I was trying not to clench my thighs together. We both looked at Nadia, who didn't say anything as she walked over to me with a piece of aloe. Not a bottle, but a piece of an aloe tree, broken in half. I raised my arms and turned them over for her to apply it.

"I had to go outside and cut this, so it took a little longer," she said, "And my girls left with their dad, so I had to say goodbye and kiss them twice."

"You have daughters?" For some reason, that soothed me as much as the aloe.

"Five-year-old twins." She looked up at me. "They're the biggest pains in the ass, and the best thing that's ever happened to me."

"I taught first grade for a year," I said, "They're so cute at that age."

"What grade do you teach now?"

"Seventh and eighth mostly."

"God." She laughed, setting my arms down slowly. "That sounds worse than being Gio's assistant."

"Probably equally as taxing." I smiled, looking over her shoulder, where he was standing, still staring at me with that unreadable expression on his face.

"Probably." Nadia laughed lightly. "The housekeeper is making pancakes. You're free to stay here, resting, or go down there and eat. I think it's best if you stay in this house until further notice, though, at least until we know it's safe."

"Okay." I swallowed, nodding. "I need my phone, though."

"No." Gio's voice boomed behind her. "Not yet."

"I won't tell Will what happened," I said. "But I need to tell my friends I'm safe. I was talking to Luke when I got to the house, and they were shaken up about the bar getting ransacked.

And Will is going to call on his way to work, so I need to answer, otherwise, he'll send the cops looking for me."

Gio's jaw worked. "Fine, but I will be present for these conversations."

"That's fine." I shrugged. "You can trust me, though."

At that, both Giovanni and Nadia laughed, as if I'd just told the best joke they'd heard in days. It didn't make me feel uncomfortable, though, because it reminded me that there were people out there who were just as jaded as I was, or worse.

CHAPTER FOURTEEN

Gio

OF COURSE, MY FATHER CHOSE THE MOST INOPPORTUNE TIME TO call me. I'd just taken Isabel's phone out of the drawer to hand it to her. Because I knew he'd continue to call until I answered, I held a finger up for her to wait. My father and I had that in common. It was kind of like a nervous tick. A tell we couldn't hide from those closest to us, since they were the only ones we did this to. My sisters hated that I called too much when I was worried and they didn't answer. My exes hated that I never called at all. I shot Isabel a look to make sure she wouldn't move. She sank down in the chair across from me and nodded.

"Yeah," I said, by way of greeting. Dad hated that more than he hated when I called him by his name, which was why I did both. With men like him, you had to take whatever sliver of annoyances they'd allow.

"What the fuck is going on over there?" he roared into my ear. "You haven't answered my calls in days, and I'm left in the fucking dark."

I set the phone away for a moment and let him continue screaming. He was on the third *"you're a fucking idiot, I knew you would fuck this up, you're going to burn our legacy to the ground"* when I chanced a glance at Isabel, who was now looking at the wall, probably trying to give me some privacy. I didn't really give a shit. My father screaming at me and calling me names in front of people was the norm. He did it to everyone, but he liked to hit me the hardest with it. I'd learned long ago that men who needed to shout and

"Are you going to let me talk or are you going to keep screaming about things you don't know?" I asked, finally.

He huffed, sucked in a breath. "Tell me."

"Charles is dead," I said first, knowing he already knew that, but feeling like I needed to tell him myself.

"Killed?" he asked.

I locked eyes with Isabel, who shook her head, clearly listening. "Natural causes."

"What the fuck," Dad said on an exhale. I knew the loss hurt him, so I gave him a second. They'd known each other since they were born. I knew from experience that losing a friend like that tore you up inside.

"You married me off to his daughter," I said after a long moment.

Isabel's eyes widened slightly, and I knew she finally believed me when I said I had nothing to do with it. Since this was my first time speaking to my father about this, I was going to get a lot more personal in front of her. I should've told her to leave and give me space, but this was necessary if I wanted her to genuinely trust me since I couldn't use sex as a way to get it.

"I did," my father said, no remorse in his voice.

"To secure the seat for me?"

"He owed me."

Charles owed him. I didn't need to know for what, nor did I care, but I needed to know the motive behind this ridiculous marriage plan. My father was a calculated man. Two family members couldn't have seats, so none of this made much sense. Unless he'd found a loophole around it back then. It would have to be a loophole that would secure two positions for him—the one he had now and Charles' seat, where he'd plant me, someone he thought he could use as a puppet. Two years ago, I might've gone for it without second thought, because it would have meant prestige. I wouldn't have cared if I'd gotten it this way, but I was tired of my father doing me half-assed favors that only benefited him.

I was tired of him dictating my life in every single aspect. I was tired of him. I stood up and turned my back to Isabel.

I lowered my voice. "I shouldn't be surprised that you'd do this, after you whored me out all those years, but somehow, you managed to catch me off guard."

"Whored you out. This guy." Dad scoffed. "They weren't paying you for sex."

"Weren't they? They were paying you with secrets that you used against them."

"What's your point?" he asked. *What the hell was my point?* I didn't even know anymore.

"Did it ever occur to you to stop and think about his daughter? Why drag her into all of this?"

"I swear, Lorenzo and his Robin Hood ways is rubbing off on you." He exhaled. "Yes, it occurred to me, Giovanni. I knew the girl when she was a child. I have two daughters her age. Of course, it fucking occurred to me, I'm not that heartless, but in the end, business won, as it usually does. Is she giving you a hard time about the seat?"

"No." I let out a laugh. "She didn't even know what Charles was involved in. She thought...I don't know what the fuck she thought." I frowned, looking at her over my shoulder. She was looking down at her folded hands, her hair curtaining her face. I wanted to yank it into a ponytail so I could see the expression on her face. Instead, I turned around again and looked at the fireplace in front of me. "What is Mom doing here?"

"How'd you hear about that?"

"Cat."

"Right." He exhaled again. "I don't know. She said she had some business."

"Some business? She hasn't been in the country in, what, over ten years? And now she has business?"

"Who said she hadn't been in the country?" my father asked. My stomach dropped at the thought of it, but I knew he wasn't wrong. She'd probably been here countless times and dodged us each and every one of them.

"So, do I call Marco? Is there an alliance there now?"

"Fuck no," he shouted. "With the shit they're involved in, you call him, and we'll all go to jail. Wasn't that your argument when you said you wanted to go legit?"

"Yes," I said, though, it was kind of bullshit, considering I was laundering money and my clubs were filled with drugs. It wasn't that I wanted them there, but they were snuck in anyway, so I figured I might as well make a profit. My father didn't know that, though. Technically, I was legit, as long as you turned a blind eye to those things. "You're a fugitive, Joe. It's only a matter of time before someone goes to jail."

"Not if I stay here."

"Forever?" I asked, and waited, because I knew he knew what I was asking. Was he giving me control for good, or temporarily?

"I still call the shots," he said. "And you know why you can't take Charles' seat, not really, anyway."

I laughed. "Because there can't be two Masseria's, and me taking his place would mean you're out."

"I'm out when I say I'm out."

Right. "I want control of the imports and exports."

Now he stayed quiet for a moment, probably trying to gauge how serious I was about taking him out. Instead of addressing that, he said, "Just get the girl to hand over Charles' briefcase and we'll get whatever is in the vault. Pay her off if you have to. Buy her a fucking diamond necklace. Whatever. We need that and we need the fucking containers."

I bit my tongue. He wanted to rob Isabel blind, on top of everything else. I didn't want to hurt her, since she was innocent in all of this, but I wasn't going to get involved. It wasn't like she'd know what was missing or what wasn't. Up until the other day, she didn't even know her father had the amount of money he had. My mind went back to one thing he'd said. I didn't know anything about any containers. I'd have to bring that to Lorenzo's attention. Or not. I weighed out my next words.

"Who else knows about the containers?" I asked.

"Silvio." Dad made an annoyed growling sound. "Fucking Silvio. If he gets to them before us…it'll mean war. He'll die. There's no way he gets those."

Important shit then. "Right."

"You should've married his fucking daughter, and this wouldn't have been a problem," he spat.

"You married me off when I was twenty-two. Last I checked, you could only legally marry one person at a time."

"We could've voided this one. The Costello's are more important than Charles Bonetti. That line ended with him, unless Vincent is stupid enough to come back, which, for his sake, he better not." He paused, then repeated, "You should've married the Costello girl when I told you to."

"Drop it," I said. "She's too young."

He barked out a laugh. "Never heard a man complain about young pussy."

"Even I have limits on what I'll do for you."

"Find the containers before Silvio does," he barked. "If I was there, I would have already found them."

The line went dead after that. I slid Isabel her phone but didn't look at her. My mind was muddled with containers, a briefcase, the vault, and my mother being here. I didn't have time to decipher whatever look was on her face after that.

CHAPTER FIFTEEN

Isabel

WHILE I WAS ASSURING LUKE THAT I WAS SAFE, MY MIND WAS STILL on Giovanni's conversation with his father. He'd said he'd been whored out for secrets. I wasn't sure what that entailed or when it had happened, but I heard the sadness in his voice when he said that, and it instantly made me sad for him. I fought the urge to get up and hug him, even though I knew he'd probably shrug me off and say something that would annoy me. When I hung up with Luke, I called Will, and assured him I was fine as well. I told him I was staying at an uncle's house. It took me fifteen minutes to convince him my uncle was real, but then he asked me for the address, just in case, and my gaze shot to Giovanni, who was staring at my mouth. It flicked up to my eyes quickly, but my heart was already beating a little faster at that alone.

"The address?" I asked, eyes wide. Giovanni shrugged. "I'll text it to you. I don't know it by heart."

"Okay." Will sighed. "I wish I could be there for you. I'm sure packing up his place is not the easiest thing to do."

"Yeah." I sank into my seat, thinking about the boxes I packed before I'd been attacked. "It sucks. It's like I don't even know who he was, you know?"

"That's not your fault," Will said, "He only let you see what he wanted you to see, and he showed up too late."

"Yeah." I bit my lip and let it go as I agreed.

"Call me at nine, okay?" he said, his voice lowering, and I knew exactly what for. My cheeks heated.

"Yep. I'll talk to you then." I smiled.

I hung up before either of us said goodbye.

"You're not keeping your phone," Giovanni said.

My eyes snapped to him. I gripped it tighter on my lap. "Why the hell not?"

"It's not safe."

"It's perfectly safe. You just saw me speak to two different people and I never wavered. You have to trust that I won't snitch." I shot him a look. "Snitches get stitches. I'm not an idiot."

"Snitches get stiches," he repeated, his lips tugging. "Maybe you should try to keep the seat, after all."

"What is this seat you keep discussing?" I asked. It sounded illegal. "I don't want any seat unless it's one of those cozy massage chairs."

"Cozy massage chair?" he laughed. "The seat is supposed to go to his next of kin. Most people would kill to get this seat. People *will* kill to get this seat."

"Isn't it a man's world?" I couldn't believe I was even pretending to entertain this.

"It is."

"Are there any women in these seats?"

"Nope." He looked pleased with himself when he said that. "But it's yours."

"But it's a man's world, and there are no women currently in whatever this is," I repeated slowly.

"It's the twenty-twenties. The world is your oyster, baby." His eyes twinkled when he said that, and at the sound of the word *baby* coming out of his lips, something inside me trembled.

"I don't want it." I swallowed. "I want a divorce."

"For what? So, you can be free to marry that fucking clown?"

I laughed, despite myself. "He's not a clown. He's a good man."

"He's a politician." He shot me a look.

"But he's one of the good ones. A stand-up guy."

He scowled. "And that's what you like? Stand-up guys?"

I pursed my lips and glanced away to think about it, because I hadn't really given it much thought. Was that what I liked about Will? That he was straight-laced and a stand-up guy? The complete opposite of the guys I'd grown up with. The complete opposite of my father, apparently. Maybe that was why I liked him.

"I guess I like the stability." I looked at Giovanni again.

"You deserve that. Stability," he said, understanding. It shocked me. Then he added, "I'm not sure how much stability there is in politics, though."

"Yeah," I whispered. That was something I was thinking about a lot lately, well, before I found out my father, who I thought was a stand-up, blue collar worker, was involved in this. It bothered me, though. I'd met his employees. I frowned up at Giovanni. "Can I ask you something? Did my father really paint houses or was that all a façade?"

At this, he laughed. It was a loud laugh, with abandon, like the one he'd gifted me with when I met him in his office that night. When I met the charming Giovanni, the playboy who could have anyone's panties on the floor with a wink. He couldn't seem to stop laughing, and I found myself smiling because it was contagious, but then he took a breath and got serious again and my smile slowly vanished.

"You've never heard the term 'paint houses'?"

I shook my head.

"Your father." He smiled, shaking his head, "He was a funny man, I'll give him that. With his legit painting company."

"What does it mean?"

"Yes, he owned a real painting company, but your father was a murderer, Isabel. That's how he made his money," he said, no-nonsense, no sugarcoating. "To paint houses, in this line of work, means to murder people. He was a damn good one, too."

The phone fell from my hands, landing on the hardwood

floors with a loud thump. I didn't care. It felt like the walls were closing in on me slowly, my vision tunneling. *A murderer?* I knew he was into something bad. I thought maybe drug dealing or stealing or I don't know, money laundering? Gambling? But a murderer? My dad? My funny, witty, caring, bear hugging dad? I wiped my tears quickly and looked down, staring at the phone, which was face down. Giovanni moved from his chair and sat in the seat right beside mine, his knees bumping mine. He picked up the phone and set it on the table before lifting my chin with his finger. For a long moment, we just looked at each other. Through my hazy vision, I couldn't see the exact expression on his face, but it looked like concern.

"This is the life," he said. "It sucks that you had to find out this way, but this is the life. That was why he could afford your fancy school and your house and your car and whatever he left you in his will. I don't know if it'll make you feel any better, but he stopped painting houses years ago." He ran his thumb under my left eye, swiping a tear. "Let's go have lunch."

I swallowed, nodding as he swiped another tear and dragged his thumb down to my bottom lip, pressing it there. My pulse zapped, desire washing over every inch of my body as I searched his eyes. He searched mine, his thumb still on my lip. I wasn't sure why I did it, but I snuck my tongue out to touch the pad of his thumb with it. His eyes seemed to darken more as he pressed his thumb farther into my mouth, so far that I had to bite down on it. He hissed, eyes darkening furthermore, and my heart launched against my chest as if looking for a safe place. There would be none. Not with this man. I knew that as well as I knew my name. And yet, something about him was magnetizing. Something about him made it impossible to look away.

He seemed to remember something and instantly shut down the lust that had just filled his eyes, the longing. He took his finger out of my mouth and straightened, going back to business Giovanni as he backed away from me. I was left to lick my lips and taste the remnants of his finger and my tears. He picked up the phone from the floor and walked around the desk, tossing it in the first drawer and meeting my eyes as he shut it.

"The phone stays here."

The moment he put distance between us, I began to feel numb again, so I simply nodded.

CHAPTER SIXTEEN

Gio

I DIDN'T KNOW WHY I WALKED INTO HER BEDROOM UNANNOUNCED that night. Actually, that was a lie. I'd gone up there to demand she give me her phone back, since she'd taken it from the drawer I'd left it in this morning. I was getting ready to scream my head off when I walked in the room, but then, I decided to sneak instead. I knew she had to be talking to William, and I wanted to hear what she was going to tell him, if anything. I needed to make sure she was serious when she said she wouldn't snitch. It had nothing to do with our exchange this morning. It had nothing to do with the way her tongue snuck out and licked my thumb, or the way she bit it when I tried my luck and pushed it into her mouth. It had nothing to do with the way it made me feel like I couldn't breathe for a moment. I told myself that I hadn't walked in here hoping to catch her off guard so I could kiss her, because, fuck, I really wanted to kiss her after that. I wanted to do much more, but I wouldn't. I *really* wouldn't. None of the scenarios I'd pictured in my head could have prepared me for what I walked into.

Isabel was lying naked, in the middle of my bed, legs spread open, angled toward the cell phone she had propped up on a pillow. She was facing the other way and was obviously taking William's instructions on where to touch herself next, so she didn't hear me as I stepped forward to get a better look. A better man would have looked away. A decent man would have left. I was neither. I watched as her hands went up to her breasts, tweaking her small nipples, and my dick instantly hardened in my sweatpants. She was so fucking perfect. Her hair, her eyes, tits, her curves, her ass, her thick thighs. A walking wet dream. The fact that she was William's and was pleasuring herself on *my* bed, made me harder. I heard him say something and she dragged one hand down her stomach slowly until she reached her pussy. My dick was uncomfortably hard now. I should've stayed where I was and enjoyed the peep show, but I wanted more. I needed more. I wanted her to know I was here. I needed to gauge her reaction to my presence, to me seeing her like this, exposed, naked, delectable.

I walked closer to her, but away from the view of the camera. Her eyes were squeezed shut, but when she opened them and saw me, she gasped loudly. William thought it had something to do with him and told her to keep doing that, but her eyes were on me. I braced myself for her to end the call, for her to sit up and tell me to leave. When she didn't, I walked closer to the pillow where the phone was propped up, testing, waiting, but she did nothing, just stared with a look of awe on her face. William barked out an order, for her to move her fingers inside of herself. She complied, looking at him briefly, before meeting my eyes again. I felt my lips move into a smile. This was completely unexpected and sexy as fuck. She was going to get off to me, not him. I knew it from the way her eyes hooded and her fingers moved faster. I brought a hand down and closed it around her ankle, squeezing hard. She gasped loudly, back arching, fingers now moving over her clit. From the strain in William's voice, I figured he was seconds from spilling his load. Fuck him for coming before making sure she did.

He said something else, but her eyes were locked on mine now. Her fingers stopped moving. She was so fucking wet, her pussy glistening. It took every ounce of self-control for me not to launch myself between her legs and devour her right then and there. For a moment, she just stared at me, and I was sure she'd end this, end the call, end my voyeurism. Instead, she brought her foot up and massaged my cock over my pants. I shut my eyes and bit my lip hard to not make a sound. Not because I didn't want the bastard to know I was the one she was with, but because she didn't need more shit on her plate right now. Fuck. This woman. She reached and tapped my belt with her foot before lowering it back onto the pillow. I stared at her. Did she want me to take my pants off? Did she want me to pull my cock out? She wanted this. Maybe she wouldn't let me touch her. Something told me she wouldn't cheat on him, not physically, anyway, but that didn't matter because he'd be out of the picture and I would have her to myself soon enough. I put my hand on her leg again, out of view of the camera.

She looked panicked.

I reached over and ended the call. She could make up some bullshit reason like the signal went out or something. I didn't care.

"If you want me to leave, I'll leave." I kept my eyes locked on hers and waited. "Do you want me to?"

She shook her head but didn't say anything.

"Just say the word and my mouth will be on that beautiful pussy," I said, licking my lips as I imagined what she would taste like, my cock pulsing in my slacks. "Say the word."

"I can't." She inhaled sharply and shook her head. "You can't touch me."

I gave a nod. I figured as much. It was the right call, too, because I knew myself. If I tasted her, I'd want all of her, and she wasn't mine to have. *Yet.*

"You want me to touch myself while you touch yourself?" I raised an eyebrow. She bit her lip and nodded her head eagerly.

"Fuck, Isabel," I groaned.

I was about to say more, when her phone started buzzing again, a FaceTime call from William no doubt. She looked at it and looked back up at me, still wordless, not moving.

I nodded toward the phone. "Answer it, otherwise, it'll look suspicious."

"Are you going to leave if I answer it?" she whispered.

"Do you want me to?"

She shook her head, brought her foot up again to tap my belt. Fuck. My dick grew even harder. I gripped her ankles harder, pulling her legs farther apart. She moaned and threw her head back slightly at that, and I almost came right there.

"Are you sure you want me to do this?" I asked, squeezing her ankles. I'd never asked that question in my life. With her, I felt like I needed to. With her, I was doing a lot of fucking things I didn't normally do.

"Yes." She nodded harder. "Please."

I couldn't remember the last time I'd been this turned on. The phone started to ring for a second time. We both just stared at each other for a moment before she leaned forward and answered the phone.

"I'm sorry, honey. The call dropped," he said. I rolled my eyes. *Honey.* If he only knew his honey was about to come because of me, not him. "Now, where were we?" he asked. "Put two fingers inside."

She complied.

"Keep playing with your tits," he said.

She did.

I unbuckled my belt, dropped my pants, and pulled myself out of my briefs. Isabel gasped, her eyes widening on the length of my cock. I felt myself smile in a way I hadn't since I was a teenager. Back then, when a woman saw how big I was, I'd been proud. Then, it became a job, a chore sometimes, and the attention my cock received no longer held the same meaning, but when Isabel looked at me like that? Jesus. I wrapped my hand around myself and started stroking. She gasped again, looking up at my face. I leaned in slightly, somewhat the same level as her phone. I knew it was the only way she'd keep looking at me, and I needed that. I needed her eyes on me when she came. When I came. I didn't know why, nor did I care to analyze it, but my chest burned for it.

I ran my knuckle along the inside of her calf and mouthed, "Play with your clit."

She nodded quickly, moving her fingers along her folds. William was telling her to return them and keep pumping her fingers inside of her, oblivious to the fact that it wasn't doing anything for her. Fucking clown. She followed my instructions instead, bring her fingers to her clit. I stroked myself to the beat of her hand, going faster when she did, and slowing down when she did. She moaned deeply. I wasn't sure I'd last much longer with her display. William was saying *"that's it"* as if he had a damn thing to do with this, but I didn't even care.

I put my tongue between my teeth and shivered as my balls grew tight. She liked that, her fingers moving faster, her other hand pinching her nipple harder as her back arched. My fingers dug into her calf, making her gasp. We kept our eyes locked. I only lowered mine briefly to look at the movement of her hand, the state of her throbbing, glistening, bare pussy. Fuck, I wanted to eat her more than I wanted anything else right now. I was shaking with the need to do it. Instead, I bit my lip to keep myself from making noise and watched as she started to spasm, legs shaking as she moved her hand over her clit, slowing the movements as her moans grew louder until they were no longer. My release rushed through me, cum spirting jetting on my hand, some on the pillow in front of me. I sighed, throwing my head back, feeling satisfied. Not satisfied enough, but satisfied for now. I moved and reached into the drawer next to me, pulling out the box of tissues and cleaning myself before fixing my pants and buckling my belt. When I looked back at Isabel, her chest was still heaving from that hard orgasm she'd gifted me with.

"Damn," Will said, voice gruff. "I've never seen you come like that. I guess you miss me more than I thought."

I was watching her so closely, that I saw the moment her head began to clear, the moment she realized she'd royally fucked up by letting me be privy to this moment, by including me in it. I couldn't argue there. She'd fucked up in a big way. He wouldn't have her again. I decided that right then and there. She cleared her throat and sat up, smiling at the camera.

"I have to go."

"Okay." He yawned. "Remember I need you at the event on Thursdays. It is for teachers, after all."

"Sure. Yeah." She nodded quickly while I tried to think about what I had on my agenda for Thursday. "Talk to you in the morning."

"Yeah." He yawned again. "You wore me out."

I rolled my eyes. He was worn out already? No wonder he couldn't please her. She ended the call and tossed her phone aside, then grabbed the pillow to cover herself. A little late for that, especially since some of my cum was on the pillowcase, but I didn't bother saying it aloud. I waited. She waited. I'd wait longer, though, she had to know that.

Finally, she cleared her throat. "You shouldn't be in here."

"It's my room."

"That I'm staying in unwillingly," she said. "You saw what I was doing, and you walked in anyway."

"Yep."

"This is so fucked up," she whispered, looking at me like I was crazy. She had no idea.

"Maybe, but it turned you on. You wouldn't have gotten off if I hadn't been here. We both know it."

"It still doesn't give you the right to do that!"

"You wanted me to stay. I asked you. I asked you before you answered his call and you told me to jerk off in front of you. Admit it, Isabel. You wanted me here. You had your pussy spread out, wet as fuck, because I was here, not because of him."

"Oh, my God. This is wrong. This is so wrong." She swallowed and looked away. "This can't happen again."

"I agree. You need to break it off with him." I started walking away. I needed a cold shower and to jerk off, and another cold shower after that.

"What?" She laughed behind me. "You're crazy if you think I'm going to break up with my boyfriend over this."

"You said it, this was wrong." I raised an eyebrow, turning around again. "You don't think this is cheating?"

She opened her mouth. Closed it. Opened it again. This time, her eyes filled with tears and her lip wobbled as she said, "I'm not a cheater."

I believed her. I was a cheater, though, and I knew how these things worked. Give a finger, they'll take a hand, and once you do, you might as well admit that you're a fucking cheater. I also knew I'd driven her to this. I took advantage of the situation, but I didn't care and wouldn't take it back. I knew if I was William and she did this to me behind my back I'd burn this place to the fucking ground. Then again, if I was William, I wouldn't have let her out of my sight for this long. The women I dated and I were never exclusive. Seeing other people was never discussed. We were just on the same page about it. My reputation preceded me in that sense. None of them ever gave me an inkling that they thought they'd be the one to tame me, sort of speak. None of them wanted to even try. Natasha had been the first, and even that went sideways in the end, as Nadia pointed out.

"It won't happen again," she said, voice low. "And I'm not breaking up with him."

"Suit yourself." I shrugged a shoulder and walked out, shutting the door behind me.

She would break up with him. It was only a matter of time. She didn't belong with him. She sure as hell didn't belong with me, either, but fuck if that didn't make me want her even more. She was pure, despite the fire that lurked inside. She was good. She was a helper. And that was the problem. I was a sucker for helpers because they rarely had people who helped them in return.

CHAPTER SEVENTEEN

Isabel

I T HAD BEEN TWO DAYS SINCE THAT INCIDENT, AND I HADN'T SEEN Giovanni at all. I should have been pissed off at him for walking in on me like that, but instead, I'd welcomed it. And he wasn't wrong. I would have never gotten myself off if I'd continued with Will's suggestions. I would've never gotten off without seeing him touch himself. God. He'd been so hard, so big, so incredible. I should've been burning with shame from merely remembering it, but I wasn't. I felt alive. I felt unstoppable. Sextiming was something we did often when Will traveled, and every time I'd have to wait until we ended the call to get myself off. Even if Giovanni had just stood there, not touching me at all, just watching me through those dark hooded eyes, I would have come, but he'd touched my legs, and then he'd touched himself. And it was so good. Too good. It could never happen again, though. I wasn't sure if the space he was giving me had anything to do with that, but I was grateful for it.

In his absence, Nadia was visiting me. She brought her daughters yesterday and we spent most of the day together, though she seemed preoccupied. Today it was the same. She was sitting there, staring at her phone, while the girls played with their dolls.

"I need to go home," I said. "I know I'm not supposed to leave, but I have to go back. I can't just stay here forever."

"What do you need? We'll fetch it for you." Nadia looked up from her phone.

Fetch it for me, like it was no big deal. I shook my head.

"I need to see my grandmother. And I'm supposed to go to an event for teachers. With Will."

"With Will." Her brows rose for a second, then she started typing away on her phone. "When is the event?"

"It's a luncheon. Thursday."

"In two days."

"Yep."

"And you need to also visit with your grandmother."

"Yep."

"Ok." She set her phone down on her lap.

"Okay, what?"

"Now we wait."

"For what exactly?"

"Permission." Her eyes gleamed with amusement.

"Are you all like this? Excited about having people's lives in your hands?"

She laughed. "Not particularly."

"How does a person like you even get involved in this stuff?" I asked, then whispered, "You're a mom."

"I know," she whispered back, smiling as she looked at the girls. She leaned forward to fix one of their hair bows. "I'm not involved in 'this stuff.' My brother was. He died a couple of years ago."

"I'm so sorry."

"Me too. I miss him every single day." She smiled sadly. I swallowed back tears. I missed my father, too, but I couldn't imagine losing a sibling. She cleared her throat and said, "Anyway, I'm only in charge of things that pertain to the clubs, the restaurants. That stuff."

"The legal stuff."

"What else is there?" She asked, still looking too amused for my comfort.

"I don't know. Painting houses," I mumbled. Thinking

about it made my heart hurt. "It was what my father apparently did."

"Gio doesn't paint houses."

"Does he have people to do that stuff for him?"

"This is where this discussion ends." She smiled. "Try not to worry yourself with what he does and doesn't do. Unless you're asking because you're interested."

"In him?" My eyes widened. A blush creeped up on my neck. I hoped it wouldn't reach my cheeks. "No way."

"Good."

"Why good?" I frowned. "Just out of curiosity."

"Well, for starters, you're with William Hamilton. Gio loathes him and vice versa," she said. "Secondly, you like men like Will, and Gio is not that."

"I'm not sure how much longer I'll stay with Will," I said. "Completely unrelated to Giovanni."

"Why? You don't think you're cut out to be a politician's wife or girlfriend."

"I know I'm not cut out for it. I don't know if I can do the whole keeping up the perfect image thing forever."

"You'd probably have to give up teaching," she added.

"I don't think so, but it would be a possibility, I guess, depending on how far he takes his political career."

Those were things I'd discussed with Will, but not extensively. Only in passing on our way to events together. Never sitting down, having a heart-to-heart. By the time each of us got home from our jobs, we wanted to eat and go to bed. I thought about what it would be like to be with someone like Giovanni and that somehow seemed worse. Sure, there was undeniable chemistry there, but what would I do? Sit at home all day to wait for him?

"How do you do it?" I asked Nadia. "How do you let your husband walk out of the house knowing he may not come back?"

"It's part of the job. How do police officers' wives do it? Or firefighters? Or military wives? They know what they sign up for when they get married. Is it easy? Hell no. Is it worth it? God, I hope so. For me, it is," she said, smiling sadly, "If there's ever a day he doesn't make it home, it'll be devastating for me and the girls. But losing is the price you pay for falling in love with anyone, regardless of what they do for a living."

CHAPTER EIGHTEEN

Gio

I WATCHED WILLIAM HAMILTON WALK INTO THE MOVIE THEATER WITH his security detail in tow. I wanted to pounce right now, but I needed to wait until Dean Russo finished his cigarette—which he was taking his sweet ass time with—so he could finally give me the information I'd asked for. I'd learned to keep my cool and practice patience from him. It was an art to him. He once told me he'd gotten three men to crack without physical torture, just by sitting across from them smoking his cigarettes. I didn't have half the patience he had, but I tried. In front of him, especially. Still, I was fighting the urge to pace the sidewalk.

"Will you chill out?" he said beside me.

He couldn't be serious. "I'm just standing here."

"You're fidgeting." I wasn't fidgeting. I looked at him. He wasn't even looking at me. I sighed. "What did you find out? I asked for this over a week ago."

"Your girl," he said as he tossed his cigarette, and damn I liked hearing him refer to her as mine for some weird fucking reason. "Is Charles' daughter, as you know. He met her mother, Carolina Marrero, in Miami where she was a waitress at a club he frequented. She was with him for about eight years on and off, while he was married to Vinny's mom. Isabel was born there after they'd been together six years, raised by her mother and grandmother. They moved to Queens when she was fourteen, probably to be closer to Charles."

"Where's the mother now?" I asked, since I already knew

where the grandmother was. Isabel was visiting with her at the nursing home, as I stood there.

"Spain. She remarried just after Isabel finished high school." Dean took a breath, exhaled. "There's really not much on her. It's probably one of the reasons Will picked her. No dirt to bring up during elections, teacher, middle class, half-Latina, half-Italian. It makes him look good."

"Does she live with him all the time?"

"The house in Queens is vacant but looked after. They either have a cleaning lady come once a week, or she stays there sometimes. She hasn't been here long enough for me to have her followed."

"Mike knew her from the neighborhood. He mentioned something about her being fierce. The way he said it...I didn't like it. Any idea what it could mean?"

"Honestly, dude, no clue. The girl's past is squeaky clean. Eerily so."

"What does that mean, eerily so?" I met his eyes.

"When you've been doing this as long as I have, you always find something. Something usually stands out. If this girl wanted to disappear, she easily could, and even I probably wouldn't be able to find her."

Fuck. That rattled me more than anything else. "What about the containers?"

"I got the locations. No keys, but unless you have beef with your Colombian cousins, you can get to them."

"Colombians?" I frowned, clicking the file he'd airdropped me. "You sure they're the right containers?"

My father was adamant about not doing anything with the Colombians, whether I was related to them or not. For him to keep his precious cargo anywhere near theirs was odd. I looked at the drone images of the containers, and sure enough, they were in Colombian territory. Why would he lie about this? I knew there had to be a good reason for it, and maybe whatever it was, wasn't important enough to dwell on. Not right now, anyway. I looked back up at Dean, who had moved on to something else.

"Where are the locations and keys?"

"They have to be in Isabel's possession…or the vault? Maybe a safety deposit box under Charles' name?"

I thought about the break-in. She hadn't gone back to her father's house after it happened, not because I didn't want her to. I had enough men who would surround and protect her. She said she couldn't face it. That was the only thing she'd told Nadia. *"I can't face this yet. I need to process it and lock it away in my memory before I go back."* Those were her exact words, according to Nadia, who'd text messaged me as soon as they left Isabel's mouth. I wondered how many other things she'd had to process and lock away. I looked at the movie theater again. Her stupid boyfriend watched a movie with his mother every Thursday morning without fail, before the theater opened to the public. It was just another thing I hated about him. I shouldn't have. It wasn't his fault that my mother was a piece of shit.

"Any news on my mother?" I asked, hating that I had to since it meant admitting that my family wasn't unified, the way we tried to make it seem to the public.

"She's moving around."

"You gonna tell me where?" Jesus, this fucking guy.

"Do you really want to know what your mother is up to?" He lowered his phone and angled his body to me, paying full attention. My stomach dropped at that alone. It had to be bad. *Did I want to know?* No I didn't, but I probably should know anyway. He seemed to read the answer on my face, because he shrugged slightly as if to say "your funeral." My stomach clenched again. "She wants the seat."

It took me a second to process that. "Charles'?"

Dean shot me a look. Obviously Charles' seat.

"That would be impossible." I shook my head.

Women didn't take seats. It was why I was supposed to

stay married to Isabel in the first place. Every time I told her to claim it, I'd done it to find out what she wanted and whether or not she was power hungry. She wasn't. My mother on the other hand…fuck. That wasn't the kind of news I expected. I wondered if my father knew about this. He couldn't have, otherwise, he'd have called me a thousand times by now, demanding I stop her from doing whatever stupidity she was thinking about doing. What *could* she do, really? What *would* she do to control the import-export system we had going? My stomach churned. If I knew anything, it was that my mother was more money hungry than anything else, and the containers and warehouses and the contacts that came with it, was worth a lot.

"Is she behind the robberies?" I asked.

Dean looked away, eyes on the movie theater. "I'm sure you can figure it out."

"Fuck. Me." I ran a hand over my face. "She's not even Italian."

"Obviously," Dean said, "Especially since Silvio is all but declaring war on her if she tries."

This would turn into a bloodbath. We both knew it would. I doubted my mother wanted the seat. What she wanted was control, and I knew she'd stop at nothing to get it, even if it meant taking us all down. I shut my eyes momentarily before looking back at the theater.

"What are you going to do about him?" He nodded at the building.

I didn't know. Any other guy I would've at the very least, had roughed up by now, but doing that would mean driving Isabel back into his arms and that would only happen over my dead body. I'd agreed to let her go to her little teacher luncheon, because she seemed genuinely excited about it. That was what Nadia told me. I'd been avoiding Isabel since the night in her bedroom. She made me feel things I shouldn't, made me want things I shouldn't, like dig into her past, even more so now that I knew not even Dean could get any details on her life. I shouldn't want to know.

I should just do what I was supposed to do—stay married on paper until the fateful meeting where I'd take the Bonetti seat, gain control of the import-exports, and then cut her loose. It was the right thing to do. Maybe that was why I wasn't interested in it. Maybe that was why when I was alone in bed at night and I closed my eyes, it was her brown eyes that popped in my head, her thick dark hair and her plump lips, and her perfect fucking body. It was worse now. Before, it was just a fantasy. Now that I'd seen her naked, that she'd played with her pussy and rubbed her tits in front of me...fuck. Now, it was something else.

"I'm going in there to have a little chat with him."

"Is this about the theater permits?"

"The asshole still has everything on pause."

"For the life of me I can't figure out why you want to renovate that place." He eyed me. "Is it for your sister?"

I grunted my response. No use in lying to him anyway. "It's my wedding gift to her."

"A year later?"

"It's a big fucking gift."

"Right." He started walking away. "I'm out. Good luck with the mayor. And with Isabel." He shot me a pointed look. "She seems like a nice woman. My advice? Don't get involved."

Right. I nodded slowly as he got in his car and drove off. I'd lost count of how many people had now said that to me. Nadia told me the same thing last night. I wasn't sure why they did it, knowing damn well that telling me not to do something would drive me to do it even more. I turned around and told Tony to keep the engine running as I headed inside the theater and made my way to theater four. They usually watched old movies, the black and white kind that I'd never been a fan of. I stood by the door and watched them. There was a time that I was intimately acquainted with Emily Hamilton. I wasn't even twenty-one then.

She'd been one of the nice ones, though, one of the heartbroken ones who wanted a shoulder to cry on about her own husband's extramarital affairs. The irony of it all was disgusting.

I gave a nod to his security detail. It was laughable, really. The same people he paid to keep him safe, I paid to keep tabs on him. It wasn't only about the money, though. It was my name. My reputation. My father's, and his fathers before him. We'd made it so that people owed us favors, sometimes that meant losing a job, or their lives, but they offered it up anyway if it meant their family would always have our protection. That was always what it came down to. Family. As I sank into the seat directly behind Will and his mother, I thought hard about that. She was kind and I really didn't want to do this in front of her, but he'd left me no choice. I leaned forward on the side opposite of her.

"Here's what's going to happen."

He jolted at the sound of my voice, jumped out of his seat, and pressed a hand to his chest. His mother turned quickly to see what was happening, eyes wide when she saw me, recognition sparking instantly. He still had his hand on his chest when he said, "Mom, wait for me outside."

"What's this about?" she asked.

"Emily, so nice to see you. It's been a while," I said, flashing a smile at her. She blushed fiercely. William looked at her, then back at me, as if he was trying to figure out how we knew each other.

"Wait for me outside," he said, voice stern this time. He turned to look at her, but she was still looking at me, still blushing, and he'd have to be a complete fucking moron to not know. *He had to know.*

Emily walked out of the row.

"How the fuck did you get in here?" he asked as soon as she was no longer in sight.

"Here's what's going to happen," I started again, ignoring his idiotic question, because he had to know the answer to that one as well. "You're going to have the city approve my permits and allow construction to continue."

"That's what this is about?" He lowered his hand. "You couldn't have waited until the luncheon? I saw your name on the list."

"No, I couldn't have waited until the luncheon," I said, mimicking his stupid voice. "Every time I talk to you at those events, things go in one ear and out the other. I figured maybe crashing your weekly outing may get me somewhere."

He shut his eyes. "My father has a deal with Silvio Costello."

"Your father is a fucking judge. The fact that he's making sweetheart deals with a criminal is juicy," I said, "Don't you think? The media would have a fucking field day with it."

"And with you," he said, eyes narrowing. "If you try that shit, I'll go to the media with shit I know about you."

"What exactly do you know about me? That I used to fuck your mom on Thursdays while you and your father were out playing golf with your buddies?" I raised an eyebrow. His entire face drained of color. I thought he was definitely going to throw up. Or hit me. I would've hit me. Hell, I wanted him to hit me. "We own the fucking construction companies. You can't lift a finger without my say so. This entire thing is a fucking waste of time and I've wasted enough time." I started walking out of the row. He still hadn't recovered from the comment about his mom, I could tell. I stopped at the edge of the row and turned one last time. "One more thing, Mr. Mayor. Lose the girl."

"What girl?" he asked, sounding genuinely confused.

"You know exactly who I'm talking about."

"I'm not, I can't just, you can't tell me what to do in my personal life," he said.

"I just did." I walked away again.

"I'm not afraid of you," he called out when I reached the door.

I smiled as I turned around. I looked at his security detail, standing there, watching me, waiting for one simple word. That was all it would take to blow his fucking head off. I wouldn't give that order, though. It would be way too messy.

"I'm not," he shouted again, "I'm not afraid of you or your goons."

"Well, William, the only thing I can tell you is that you really fucking should be."

CHAPTER NINETEEN

Isabel

THERE WAS SOMETHING TO BE SAID ABOUT REPRESSED MEMORIES. I hadn't thought about the night that I'd been pinned down by two guys just feet away from a party I'd attended with Eloise. It happened so quickly; one minute I was waving goodbye to her and another friend, and the next I was on the ground, my back sliding against the wet grass beneath me as they held me down. There were countless memories I'd tried to bury, but that one was the worst. After being ambushed at my father's house, I'd had nightmares, not of the ambush, but of that night in college. It wasn't the last time I'd been cornered by men trying to take advantage of me, but it was the only time it had worked. After that night, I became obsessed with self-defense. I couldn't afford the classes, but I mentioned to my father that it was something that interested me, and he paid for a few sessions. Just enough that I'd be able to stop someone in the moment. Taking classes beyond that meant I would've had to explain myself, so I YouTubed and practiced on my own. It hadn't helped me the other night. I'd been completely caught off guard and off my game.

It wouldn't help me today, either, considering that I was standing in the corner of the luncheon that Will was hosting for select teachers. I'd been speaking to some of them when I caught a whiff of a familiar cologne, and those memories came flooding back. I excused myself and stood in the corner near the door, watching and praying Will wouldn't spot me and call me over. I watched as he shook hands with the man, smiled and laughed with him, all while my stomach roiled. I couldn't do this. I thought I could, but I knew it was just a matter of time. My conversation with Nadia replayed in my head. It was the first time I'd said, aloud, that I wasn't cut out to be a politician's partner. Even if it hadn't been for the cologne, I'd know it was him. I'd know him anywhere. After all, it was because of me that he had a scar on his cheek.

"Trouble in paradise?" Giovanni's voice made me jump.

"Nope."

"Liar." His voice was low. Under any other circumstance, it would have turned me on. He seemed to notice that was the case because his demeanor shifted. I hadn't even looked at him, I was still staring at Will, at the man he was speaking to, but I felt the instant Giovanni's demeanor shifted from flirty to on edge. "Who's he talking to?"

"I don't know." I swallowed.

"You're shaking." He touched my shoulder, and I nearly jumped out of my skin.

"Don't touch me," I snapped, finally looking up at him. He dropped his hand, dark eyes unwavering on mine. I knew he was trying to read me, and I knew he wouldn't. Couldn't.

"Who is he?" There was an edge to his voice now, a gruffness that pulled at me because it told me he was in my corner.

"I don't know," I said again. I really didn't. I'd never found out his name. I couldn't even point him out in a lineup if it ever came to that, because I couldn't remember his face. At least, I thought I couldn't, until this moment.

"Does William know how you feel about this guy?"

"I don't feel anything about this guy." I gritted my teeth and made myself look at him. "Stop. Asking. Questions."

He stared at me for a long moment, those dark brown eyes far more in touch with the storm brewing inside me than I wanted to give him credit for. He'd kept his distance up until this moment. Given the circumstances, I shouldn't have felt this tug that magnetized me to him, that made me yearn to reach out and touch him, that made me want to tell him everything about my past because I knew he wouldn't judge me and he'd protect me. I wasn't sure how, but I knew that deep in my marrow. I wondered if this was what all of the women felt when they let their guard down for him, when they let him waltz into their lives with the force of a tornado and leave them just as quickly.

"You're going to tell me," he said. "Maybe not right now, but you're going to tell me."

At that, I laughed, and I was so grateful for it. "You seem sure about that."

"I am sure about it."

"Good luck trying to get anything out of me," I said. His eyes danced; it was the only indication that he was enjoying this. Otherwise, his jaw was set and his expression was lethal, and fuck if it didn't turn me on more than the damn charm he threw around.

"I always get what I want."

"That doesn't surprise me." I smiled and decided I needed to change the subject. "Where's Natasha?"

"No idea."

"Wow. I thought you'd keep tabs on your girlfriends the way you seem to keep tabs on me."

"I don't keep tabs on my girlfriends." His eyes were dancing again, his mouth pulling into a slow, sensual smile. "I only keep tabs on my wife."

I groaned, rolling my eyes, and looking away, hoping to hide my blush and how much those words affected the area between my legs. Why they did, I didn't know, but every time he said it, I reacted. My eyes landed on William again, who was slapping the man in the back as he said goodbye and moved on to someone else. My eyes stayed on the man as he walked in our direction. He was leaving, which was great, but we were standing next to the only exit, which meant he'd see me. I held my breath, but refused to look away, refused to cower more than I'd already cowered. Even if I felt like throwing up, I'd keep my eyes on him and let him know I was doing just fine, that he hadn't broken me. It was a lie, but it was a lie he didn't need to know. He glanced up from his watch and looked straight at me. I saw the moment realization kicked in. His entire neck and face burned. He looked at Giovanni beside me, and suddenly it was him who looked like he might puke. If I needed a sign about Giovanni's reputation, that reaction said everything I needed loud and clear. His feet shuffled faster as he made his exit. I exhaled shakily and felt my eyes burn with angry tears. I counted to ten, breathed through it, blinked, and composed myself. Giovanni didn't say another word and I was immensely grateful because if he had, I might have lost my shit. Will caught my eye then, waving me over with a huge smile, until he saw who was beside me, and then his face paled a little.

"You're better off without him," Giovanni said quietly.

"Of course, you'd say that." I swallowed. "Let me guess, you'd step right into the doting boyfriend role."

"Maybe." There was a challenge in his eyes that made my pulse quicken.

"Isabel," Will called, smiling again, "Join us. I've been raving about my incredible girlfriend for an hour now and telling them that I got all your favorite flowers for the center pieces and your favorite food catered, but without you here, they're going to start thinking I'm lying about you." The people around him laughed. "Really, she's absolutely amazing," he continued, raving on about me as I started walking away.

"Still think you can be a better boyfriend?" I paused, smiling over my shoulder. I hadn't even finished turning back around when he grabbed my arm and pulled me flush against his chest.

"I don't have to be a better boyfriend," he growled against my ear, sending a shiver down my spine. "I'm your fucking husband."

He let me go, then. It took me three full seconds to compose myself and keep walking without my knees buckling and giving out beneath me. I joined Will and played the part of good girlfriend, but in my heart, I knew I'd end this before the day was over. It would hurt. I'd probably cry. He'd probably demand answers. But it wasn't fair to continue on the way we were, knowing that, even without Giovanni in the picture, our relationship had an expiration date.

CHAPTER TWENTY

Gio

SHE WAS SLOWLY CONSUMING ME, AND I HATED EVERY BIT OF IT. It was the way she baited me. The way she looked at me square in the eyes and treated me like I was just some random guy off the street. She was getting to me, and to top it all off, for some idiotic reason, I kept reminding her that I was her husband. I didn't know why it felt so satisfying to say those words aloud, to see the reaction she gave me. I didn't expect her to admit that she liked it, but the fire in her eyes seemed to crackle when I mentioned it. Maybe I liked it, too, the idea of belonging to someone like her. A helper, a teacher. I shook the thought away. I didn't belong to anyone. Mike would joke that I belonged to the streets, and he'd be right. Mike, who I was currently waiting for in her rum bar while she was sitting in my condo. I'd let her see her grandmother and go to the luncheon, but that was where I drew the line. There would be no secret meetings between her and that clown. There definitely wouldn't be room for them to have sex. She was mine now. For the time being, anyway. Mike walked in the door, finally, and waved at the guys behind the bar before sitting across from me.

"For someone who doesn't drink rum, you sure love coming here all of a sudden," he started, "Why are we meeting here and not my place?"

"I wanted to assess the damage." I nodded toward the bar. "I thought maybe I'd be able to figure out who was here."

"And?"

I shook my head. No dice. They didn't break anything. Didn't take any rum. Didn't even check for money.
Dean said it was probably my mother, but if it had been, she
would have made it a point for them to steal things so that it
looked like a robbery. Whoever it was went straight to the office in the back, straight to the safe. By now, everyone knew
about Charles' death, which meant everyone knew he'd
handed everything down to her. It could virtually be anyone
who was after those warehouses and containers. The containers, we'd secured, but the warehouses were still MIA. I'd
have to sit down with Isabel and tell her the truth about all
of this. Maybe if I did that she'd understand the gravity of it
all. I should've already done that, but I thought we'd be able
to do this without getting her too involved. I was sure she'd
hate knowing the extent of her father's deceit. Then again, it
couldn't possibly be worse than the things she already knew.

"I was at a luncheon today," I said, "Isabel wanted to go
with William, and it would've looked weird if she didn't show
up, especially after he bought her a first-class ticket to fly over
here."

"And you were there doing what? Securing the perimeter
that your security detail had already secured ten times?" Mike
raised an eyebrow, shaking his head. "I'm telling you, man.
She's not the one. I know you have a teacher fetish, but go find
another one to bother."

"I can't." I set my glass of carbonated water and lime
down.

"Jesus." Mike chuckled. "You're unbelievable, you know
that? You've slept half the female population, not all by choice,
I'll give you that, but you still have so many others you can get
with. Why can't you leave her the hell alone?"

"If I knew the answer to that question I'd leave her
alone." My eyes snapped to his. "At this luncheon, there was a
guy, probably around her age, he had blond hair, slicked back,

light blue eyes, almost see-through, and a scar that went from his hairline down to his ear. Ring any bells?"

"No." Mike frowned, thinking about it, then shook his head. "Could be one of the Russians?" He said, then added, "Or the Mexicans?"

"Nah. This guy was American through and through."

"You think he's involved in this?"

"No."

He sat back and watched me for a moment. "This is about Isabel."

"She was spooked by him," I said. "I saw her right after she'd been tied up and had a gun pointed to her head. I know when she's terrified. That's what she looked like at this luncheon when she saw him."

"Maybe his eyes were familiar? Maybe he was part of the robbery."

"No. This guy, whatever he does, it's legit. Why was she spooked?"

"How the fuck am I supposed to know?" He nodded at the bar. "Ask her."

"I did. She wouldn't tell me."

"Go ask them." He nodded at the guys behind the bar.

"I already asked them, genius. They don't know any men with blue eyes."

Mike rubbed his jaw. "Fuck, man, I don't know."

"You said she's fierce. Not one to fuck with, to be exact. Why?"

"No. Fuck no. I'm not going there." He started to get up. My fucking best friend. That alone made my stomach drop.

"Please."

His eyes widened slightly. He sat down again. Mike was watching me warily, but I wasn't going to say it again. He got one plea from me. That was it.

"You're never going to fucking tell her I told you this," he said. "You never mention it—period—because if you do, she'll know where the information came from and that's not gonna go over well with me the next time you see me."

"I'm not going to tell her anything. I just need to know."

Mike let out a laugh, shaking his head. "Never thought I'd see the day."

"Shut the fuck up. Just tell me."

"This isn't going to get you any information about whoever you saw today. I really don't know who that could've been."

"Out with it, Mike." I was getting impatient and no amount of channeling my inner Russo was going to help matters.

"There were a few incidents. This was back when she was in college, since I hadn't seen her around in a while. I was closing up the shop when I heard a woman scream," he said. My fists clenched on my lap. "I ran toward the scream because, well, it could've been anyone, a friend, a cousin, my own mother. By the time I got there, she'd managed to kick the man on top of her in the nuts. He ran away when he saw me, probably knowing I'd take him down easily." Mike paused, rolling his eyes when I shot him a look. "Okay, when he saw the barrel of my gun pointed directly at his chest."

"Did he do anything to her?"

"He didn't get to, he said. "That was how it was, though. I couldn't tell you how many stories just like that one we heard weekly, daily sometimes."

"Fuck." I exhaled, but it did nothing for my anger. I pictured her in that situation. I pictured my sisters. I wanted to kill every fucking asshole who would ever do that to a woman. "What's the other incident?"

"Ah." Mike laughed, scratching the back of his neck. "Some guy pulled a knife on me when I was closing the shop.

This was maybe six months later? There were a lot of new faces here, some who moved from rival areas."

"So, someone pulled a knife on you," I said, so he could get back to the point.

"So, he pulled a knife on me, and this fucking girl, Isabel, comes out of fucking nowhere and disarms him right in front of me. I didn't even have time to react. It was like, movie shit, vigilante shit. I told her to never do that shit again, but she saved my fucking life that night."

"Who was the guy?"

"Some gang banger." He shrugged. "He was shot a few days later."

"What a coincidence," I said. I couldn't even imagine a scenario in which Isabel would overpower anyone, but it felt good to know she did. "That's it?"

"She had one more incident after that, with two female gang members. Isabel ended up with a black eye and something else, a broken rib maybe? I don't know. I heard it from Luke. One of the girls who attacked her ended up with a cut from here." He pointed at his shoulder blade and ran his hand down to his elbow. "To here." He shrugged a shoulder. "No one around here fucked with her after that."

"What about Charles? He never found out?"

"I doubt it."

"Her mother? Grandmother?"

He let out a single laugh. "I'm sure this is going to shock you, but some people don't have anyone looking after them, even your asshole of a father was there for you from time to time. You looked up to him once. She didn't have that at home."

"I thought you didn't know her well enough?"

"I didn't. I didn't have to."

I swallowed that bitter truth. I didn't like the idea of Isabel being alone in the world.

"So, she's a knife girl," I said after a moment, trying to imagine that. She really surprised me at every turn. *Impressed me.* Was that where the man's scar came from? I wasn't sure what happened between them, but I intended to find out. If I thought I wanted her before, it was nothing in comparison to now.

"I know that look, man," Mike said, shaking his head in disapproval. "She doesn't deserve to have you shower her with attention and lavish dinners and shit just to be discarded when you find someone new that interests you."

"I know." I did. That was the reason I'd tried to deny myself this.

My phone rang in the pocket of my suit jacket. I pulled it out and saw Petra's name as I answered it.

"G, you need to come get your girl because I don't want to hit her, but I might have to."

"What are you talking about?"

"She demanded to go to William Hamilton's apartment. She was going to call the police if I didn't bring her, so we did—"

I stopped breathing. "Who's we?"

"Me and Joey Z."

"Where are you now?"

"I'm standing outside the apartment. Joey's downstairs by the front door."

Jesus Christ. Joey Z was a monster of a guy. If Isabel was able to boss him around, she must really have wanted to go there, which further pissed me off, because what the fuck? Was she in the apartment alone with William? Was she fucking him? Kissing him? I felt an uncomfortable burn in the back of my neck. A loud sound came out of my mouth that sounded both annoyed and pissed off. The few people at the bar turned to look at me and went right back to their rum.

"Stay put. I'm going over there." I hung up the phone and stood up. "Talk to you later."

"This is about Isabel?" Mike asked, standing. "She okay?"

"She's fine. For now." I stalked out of the bar and went straight to the back of the SUV.

For now, because I wanted to fucking strangle her for this. Tony must have sensed how mad I was because he didn't even try to make small talk as he drove me to the apartment. All the way in fucking Chelsea. Fuck me. He slowed down as we neared the sidewalk, and I saw Isabel walking out of the building. Tony hadn't even set the car in park before I was out of there, making my way toward her.

CHAPTER TWENTY-ONE

Isabel

I 'D JUST LEFT THE APARTMENT I SHARED WITH WILL, WITH WHATEVER I could pack. I promised him I'd come back for the rest when he was at work and leave the key with the doorman. Break ups were the worst, even when they were inevitable. I hadn't even wiped the last of my tears or taken three steps out of the building when I saw Giovanni. He was a force, walking with purpose and a pissed off look on his face. *No.* I'd seen him pissed off before. This went beyond that. He was looking at me like he wanted to rip me in half. I wasn't one to back down, but I also wasn't crazy enough to mess with this man right now. Then again, I already had, hadn't I? I'd visited Will without his permission. *His permission.* I knew why I needed it. I knew it was for my safety, but that was the word that finally made me snap and do it anyway. I'd never even needed my own mother's permission for anything, so this was not something I was familiar with, and I wasn't sure what to make of it. As he got closer, my heart galloped, and I decided that I liked it. Maybe I was an idiot, but the fact that he cared enough about me to be pissed off like this, warmed my body. Instinctively, I took a step back and clutched the handle of my bag a little tighter. He stopped just steps away from me, fuming, as he looked first at Petra, then at Joey Z, then at the SUV parked beside us along the curb.

"Ride with Tony." The order was barked at them.

Neither of them argued. They walked toward the other SUV, and Joey Z threw the keys for Giovanni to catch. I waited. I was shaking a little now, but it could have a lot to do with the emotional outburst upstairs. I'd just broken up with the nicest man—hands down—I'd ever dated. And yet, he'd never made my entire body sing the way the man standing in front of me had every single time we locked eyes. Tonight, those eyes were different, though. They held warning and darkness and promise. Even knowing how mad he was, and how he could easily over-power me with his size and strength, I felt safe. His presence au-tomatically made me feel safe, even though it shouldn't, and I didn't know what to do with that. He took one more step for-ward. I planted my feet so that I wouldn't retreat again and tilted my head to look at him.

"Get in the car." It was an order.

It wasn't loud like the one he'd given his crew, but it was still an order and for some reason, I felt a thrill deep in my core. I thought about defying him, but there was really no point in doing that, so I swallowed and got in the car, tossing the bag to the backseat. Giovanni climbed into the driver's seat but didn't turn on the car. He just sat there, both hands gripping the steer-ing wheel. He looked like he wanted to scream. Or reach over and kill me. He looked like he was going to fucking lose it, so I just sat in silence and looked out the window, focusing on the old wooden door that I'd never walk through again. He turned the car on and drove off, slamming a fist on the dial to turn off the music that came out blaring through the speakers. He didn't speak the whole three blocks it took to get back to his apartment. I didn't either because I didn't want to add fuel to the fire, and I didn't know what to say.

When we got to his apartment, he parked his car in the ga-rage and shot Petra and Joey Z a look I didn't understand, but they stayed put and didn't move to follow us. In the elevator, he punched the code for his penthouse and looked back at me. I set my bag down by my feet and wrung my hands together. If this was what my students felt like when they explained a bad grade to their parents, I didn't think I'd be handing out any more of them for the time being.

"I told you to stay put," he said through his teeth, taking a step toward me and bringing both hands to either side of my head, caging me in with the warmth and anger that rolled off him. "I told you to stay in my apartment. I..." He stopped talking and inhaled then exhaled deeply. I still didn't meet his eyes. I couldn't.

The elevator reached his floor and opened up to his grand foyer. The moment it closed, I set my bag down again and he walked me back against the door, the cool steel against my bare shoulders making me shiver as he caged me in again like he was scared I might run. As if reading my thoughts, he pushed a button next to us and I heard some kind of closure behind the elevator doors behind me. A locked door.

"What the fuck were you thinking, Isabel?" he asked, breathing heavily against me.

"I needed to do something," I said quietly, still unable to meet his gaze.

"What, exactly, did you need to do?" He spat out each word harshly, shifting in his fancy dress shoes as he kept his arms on either side of me.

"I needed to pick up some things."

"We could have done that for you." He took a breath. "Was he up there? William?"

I nodded, swallowing as I looked at the way his throat worked. I still couldn't chance a glance at him out of fear that I'd either scream at him and slap him or be turned on and kiss him. So far, the latter was winning and that seemed much worse than the aforementioned.

He slapped his right hand against the wall nine times, in sequence with his words" "What–the–fuck–were–you–doing–up–there–alone?"

Oh, my God. Something pooled between my legs. This time,

I did look up. His face was so close to mine. Too close to mine. His eyes narrowed and fuming and sexy as hell. I considered it. I knew he'd be mad if I went since he told me to stay put and wanted to keep me safe, but I hadn't considered another reason, and that made my heart skip a beat.

"Are you jealous?"

"Answer the fucking question." His jaw clenched as hard as his fists did in my peripheral. "What were you doing?"

"I wanted to ask him a question and get some things." I licked my lips. His gaze fell to them. His nostrils flared as he met my eyes again.

"Tell me."

I shook my head. "It's not important."

"It's important to me."

"Why?"

"Fuck. I don't know." He pushed off the wall, his voice bouncing in the space. When he looked at me again, he looked menacing. "Because you're my fucking wife and I have a right to know."

Again, with the wife thing. I had to laugh. It was the only emotion I had left today. That made him even more angry, the lines of his face hardening as he took a step forward again.

"You think this is funny?"

"Kind of. I don't know." I shook my head. "I don't know what to think of it. I don't understand why you want to know so badly."

"I *need* to know." He breathed out, I breathed it in. His eyes flared again. "What were you doing? Were you fucking him? Just tell me."

"For what? So that you can judge me or tell me he's a clown or not good for me or whatever else?" I swallowed, lifting my chin. "No, we weren't fucking. I was breaking up with him."

"Jesus fucking Christ. This woman." He breathed out, as if

a heavy weight had been lifted off his shoulders and pushed off the wall again and turned around to pace the other way.

He looked like an animal that had been caged too long. Like one of those panthers in a zoo exhibit that pace while you watch them, daring you to try something stupid so they could ravish you. When he turned around and looked at me again, he didn't look any less pissed off, but there was a new heat in his eyes, and I braced myself for it because I knew I'd certainly be his next meal. He didn't even give me time to process what was happening. He put his hand around my throat and squeezed as he pulled me into him, his mouth crashing into mine hard, punishing, ruthless. I moaned deeply as his hands moving up to my jaw and squeezing my cheeks tight so that I have no choice but to open my mouth and let his tongue inside. There was nothing soft about this man. Not his body, not the way he looked at me, not the way he kissed me, and though we hadn't yet, I was certain, not the way he fucked. I realized I liked it that way. I *needed* it that way. Maybe it was what I'd been missing all those months I'd spent with William.

Giovanni used his tongue thoroughly, as if he's erasing any other kiss from any other person who's ever touched my lips. That's what makes me moan against him. That's what sets me into a frenzy, taking off his jacket and unbuttoning his shirt. It was tucked in, and I couldn't seem to get it out of his pants fast enough, so I sank my hands in it instead and planted my palms on every single muscle on his torso. He growled against my mouth, letting go of my face, my throat, as his lips pulled away from mine and he dragged them down my chin, down my throat. He ripped my shirt open easily, the buttons flying all over the marble floor, then he worked on my bra, and lowered his face to my breasts, breathing, not licking, not touching, just breathing against the middle of my chest.

"Fuck," he groaned, as if he was trying not to do more, as if he was trying to hold himself back. I ripped the buttons of his shirt and he pulled away, searching my eyes. "If we do this, there's no going back."

He waited a beat after he said those words, letting them sink in. My brain was mush, my body burning with how turned on I was. I would have agreed to anything in that moment, and he seemed to know this. He waited and waited as he watched me. I moved against him, but he held me in place.

I let out a harsh breath. "Okay. Whatever you say."

"No." His eyes were hard on mine. "Not 'whatever I say.' If we do this, there's not going back. There's no volleying between me and that fuck face. If we do this, you're agreeing to being mine."

My heart thundered in my ears, eyes nearly falling shut at the thought of that. Being his. Why'd that sound so good? So dirty? So dangerous. I'd been with petty criminals when I was a teenager, kids I used to kiss in alleyways on our way to and from corner store. Nothing more, though. Not actual relationships. This felt bigger than that, and Giovanni wasn't just a petty criminal. He wasn't slinging drugs on the streets. I wasn't even sure exactly what it was he was involved with, outside of the clubs, but I knew it was something I wouldn't like. He leaned in, taking my bottom lip in his mouth and sucking hard, letting it go slowly, with a bite. I groaned loudly, heart pounding so hard it hurt.

"Yes. Just do something. Please," I panted, finally, pushing myself against him, lowering my hand to touch him over his pants. I groaned at the feel of him and tilted my head back. "God. Please, please do something."

He made a sound like he had no choice but to do something just before his mouth closed around my left nipple. I gasped, my head rolling from side to side as he gave the same attention to the other. He nipped my breasts and licked his way down my stomach as he knelt in front of me, unzipping my pencil skirt and bringing it down. When he saw my black lace panties, he inhaled sharply and looked at me again.

"You wore these for him?"

I shook my head.

"For me?"

"I wore them for me." I bit my lip, took a breath. "But I'm glad you're the one seeing them."

"Fuck." He grabbed my ass and pulled me against his face, nipping me through the lace.

My knees began to shake, and he hadn't even done anything. He brought a hand up and ripped the panties off so hard, it left a sting between my ass cheeks. I didn't have time to dwell on it or joke before he lifted me beneath by thighs and started eating me out. He used his tongue like a sword, striking down on my folds. He feasted on me with abandon, as if it was a treat he'd been waiting for, lapping and sucking and gripping my thighs, pulling me closer to his mouth while he did it. It didn't take long for him to pull the first orgasm out of me as he sucked on my clit. The next one came when he started pumping his fingers inside of me.

"Oh, fuck." Was all I could chant over, and over, as the orgasm washed over me.

He nipped the insides of my thighs then kissed his way back up my body as he set me down on wobbly feet.

"I don't think I can stand," I whispered, meeting his gaze.

He smirked, clearly proud of himself.

"Just for a second." He reached into his back pocket, took out a condom, tore it with his teeth as I began unbuckling his belt, undoing his button, his zipper, pulling everything down quickly and shakily, needing more of this. Of him. I watched, barely able to breathe, as he rolled the condom over himself. I'd seen him that night, through a haze of lust, but seeing him about to fuck me was different. I was sure I wouldn't be able to take him inside of me, but then he wrapped my legs around his waist and thrust himself inside me until he was seated with one swift motion that made me scream and clutch onto his shoulders.

He groaned, meeting my eyes then. I wasn't sure what I saw in his. Something wild. Untamed. Powerful. He squeezed my ass as he began to move in hard, deep strokes, I gripped his shoulders tighter, burying my fingers into him, clawing him when he moved faster, harder, deeper. I gasped as another orgasm built inside of me. Surely, I couldn't. I'd never come like this. He looked at me once last time before taking my lips in his, slower this time, less brutal, but not any less passionate.

"You feel so fucking good," he growled against me, his grip tightening even more on my ass. "So, fucking good. Come on my cock, baby. I know you're close."

On the next thrust, I saw stars. My legs began to shake as the orgasm hit me hard. He buckled against me a few more times, deep, slower thrusts as he found his own release. We panted against each other, foreheads pressed together as we tried to regain consciousness. He kissed my lips hard one last time before pulling out of me and making sure I could stand on my own. It hit me, as I picked up my scattered, ripped up clothes, and the bag I'd picked up from Will's place, that I'd just broken up with someone. *Just.* I should've felt guilty, but I didn't. I felt something. I felt *alive*.

CHAPTER TWENTY-TWO

Isabel

"You're staying in my bed," Giovanni said from the other side of the kitchen counter as I walked out of the guest bedroom.

I'd showered and changed into loose gray shorts and a matching T-shirt. I wasn't sure how I managed to even shower, since every single muscle and bone in my body felt languished. I sat down in the center barstool, across from where he was. He'd also showered and changed into sweats and a T-shirt, all black.

"Keep looking at me like that and I'm going to fuck you on the counter in the next ten seconds." He raised an eyebrow as he set a plate of mac-n-cheese on the counter.

"I'm not sure my vagina can take you again right now." Even as I said it, I felt my face flame.

He got himself a plate and set it in front of him, but instead of grabbing a chair, he just started eating as he stood across from me. "We still need to talk about what went down at Will's apartment."

"Oh, God." I rolled my eyes. "The sex wasn't enough to convince you it's over between me and him?"

"You would've let me fuck you back in Chicago that night," he said pointedly before putting a spoonful of mac-n-cheese in his mouth.

"I'm not sure I would have," I whispered, looking down at my plate. "This is so freaking good. Did you make it?"

"Of course, I made it."

"From scratch?" My brows rose.

"From a box." He laughed like I was being ridiculous. "I added milk and butter and stirred it up in the stove though, so I'm taking credit for it."

"Well, it's amazing."

"Do you know how to cook?"

"Are you kidding?" I laughed. "I started cooking when I was twelve. Otherwise, I would've..." My words trailed off as the smile fell from my face. I didn't want to get into that right now and mar the temporary bliss we had going.

"Finish that sentence." He set his bowl down in front of him.

"I don't want to talk about it right now," I whispered.

"But you will. Another time, you will." He pinned me with those serious eyes of his, and I merely nodded, not because I would, but because I wanted to move past this topic.

"What did Will say about you breaking things off?" he asked.

"He..." I frowned. "It was almost like he knew it was coming."

"Hm." He kept watching me as he ate.

"Like, he was ready to accept it." I took a sip of the water he'd set in front of me. "I mean, he did try to convince me to stay with him."

"He did, huh?" His jaw worked, eyes suddenly gaining that darkness he normally didn't keep in check. "How'd he try to get you to stay?"

"Not by fucking me against the wall." I raised an eyebrow back at him. He laughed, eyes twinkling. Yeah, he was hottest when he laughed like that.

"Good. Otherwise, I would've had to kill him."

I grew serious instantly. If anyone else said that, I'd take it as a joke, but not someone who had any relation to what my father did. "I thought you didn't 'paint houses.'"

"I don't, but I make some exceptions for people who touch what belongs to me."

"I'm not your property, you know." I shot him a look. "I'm

not even your wife, legally, so as much as you like to throw that in my face, we both know it's bullshit. That document was forged."

"The law thinks it's legal."

"And you care so much about the law, right?"

His lip twitched. "In this case, absolutely."

Why that made me get butterflies in my stomach, I didn't know. I looked back down at my plate and continued eating.

"My father's lawyer called," I said, licking my lips as I pushed the plate away. He picked it up and started doing the dishes.

"What did he say?"

"There's a safety deposit box," I said. Gio's eyes snapped to mine. "I can't imagine they'd be there though. The keys you need. I mean, why would he keep keys that he needs somewhere he can't readily access?"

"That would be logical, but Charles was…" He shook his head. "They might be there."

"If you really think about it, those guys who broke into my dad's house would've just kidnapped me if they thought that would be in a safety deposit."

He lifted an eyebrow. "Is that what you would do?"

"Obviously."

He laughed, shaking his head as he set the plates down in the drying rack. "You continue to surprise me, Isabel."

"Just because I can try to think like a criminal, doesn't mean I am one."

"Not yet." He was joking, I knew it, but it still made me shake a little inside.

"I'm a teacher," I said unnecessarily. His eyes darkened. I frowned, smiling. "What? That's a turn on to you?"

"You have no fucking idea."

"Really?" My nose scrunched. "That doesn't seem like you."

"What seems like me?"

"I don't know." I shrugged a shoulder. "Natasha." I gasped

the moment the name left my mouth, clasping a hand over it. "Oh my God. Did you just cheat on her with me?"

"Would that be the worst thing in the world?" He looked entirely too amused with this conversation. I scowled.

"Yeah."

"Says the girl who touched herself in front of a man while she was supposed to be having a sex call with her actual boyfriend."

I clamped my mouth together. He wasn't completely wrong. I thought of something and felt a slow smile bloom on my face. "Except, it wasn't just a man I did that in front of. It was my husband."

"Oh, fuck this." He walked around the counter quickly and hauled me out of the barstool.

"You may have a marriage kink, not a teacher one. I'm not sure which one is more surprising." I laughed as he threw me onto his bed and came down over me, enveloping me with his body.

"I don't have a marriage kink." He nipped my jaw, my neck. I sank my fingers into his hair. He glanced up at me. "I have an Isabel kink."

My laughter died in my throat. My heart fluttering uncontrollably. Hell no. I could not, would not actually fall for this guy, right? It would be the gravest mistake I could make, for a plethora of reasons. I didn't even have enough space on a sheet of paper to name them all line by line. Having sex, sure, yes, I'd take that, but falling for him? The thought made a surge of panic run through me.

"What?" He paused and lay beside me, propping himself up on his elbow. He brought a hand to my face and pushed my hair away from my cheek as I turned to face him, my heart pounding in my ears.

"This can't happen."

"What, you and me?"

I nodded.

"You agreed to this." He raised an eyebrow. Him and his agreements.

"I know, but still." I swallowed. "It's a terrible idea."

"That's all I've been hearing from everyone from the moment I laid eyes on you." He leaned in, kissed my mouth, sucked my bottom lip into his. "You really think that'll stop me from having you?"

"Well, yeah, if I'm the one telling you it can't happen." I was smiling when I pushed his shoulder hard. He fell on his back with a low chuckle and pulled me on top of him. I straddled his hips, throbbing between my legs when I felt his rock-hard erection there.

"Is this you telling me it can't happen? Because I really fucking like it." He rocked his hips up. I bit my lip to stifle a moan.

"What happened to Natasha?" I asked breathily.

"You're really going to bring up another woman while you're in my bed, looking like you're ready to fuck my brains out?" His hands skirted down to my thighs, his fingers gripping as they moved up, under my shorts, easily pushing the thong I had aside.

"Gio." I groaned, throwing my head back. "Please. I need to know."

"Hm. How badly do you want to know?" He kept a hand under my thong, his thumb circling my clit as his other hand came up under my shirt, squeezing my breasts, tweaking my nipple. "Does it make you wet? Me having a girlfriend?"

"No." I gasped, rocking against his thumb.

"No?" he asked, smile in his voice, though my eyes were still screwed shut as the orgasm rocked through me. I shuddered, he took his hand back, and as I opened my eyes and looked down at him through a haze, I saw him stick his thumb into his mouth and suck it with a pop. I shuddered again.

"I need to know," I said again, looking at him seriously.

He sighed heavily. "I broke up with her."

"For sure?"

"Yes, for sure." He frowned. "I wouldn't lie to you."

"When did you break up with her?"

He turned his face and looked away, but he was still hard beneath me. I rocked my hips. He hissed, grabbing my thighs again, right on top of the small bruises from earlier. I bit my lip at the pain, the pleasure. I liked to feel what I did to him. I liked what he did to me. I knew if I kept rocking against him like this, I'd come again, without the help of his hand.

"Can we talk about this after?" He brought a hand up under my shirt again.

"Nope." I ground my hips again.

"Fuck." His eyes popped open, sharp gaze on mine. "The night you showed up at my house."

"What?" I stopped moving and planted my hands on his hard chest. "Before or after you found out I was there?"

"Jesus, Isabel." He pulled in a breath and let it out, tweaking my nipple. I bit my lip, but the moan left my mouth, nonetheless. "Before."

"So, not because of me?"

He chuckled, grabbing my hips and turning us so that I was beneath him on the bed. I kept my legs wrapped around him. "Is it going to make you even more wet if I say yes?" He pushed a hand into my shorts, into my thong, and groaned. "Damn. You're so fucking wet now. So ready for my cock."

I shuddered as he ran his fingers over my sensitive clit. I was too sensitive. Too raw. He kept rubbing, though, and I kept riding his hand.

"It wasn't because of you," he said, bringing his lips down to mine, his fingers slowly moving up and down my wet folds, teasing. "But I would've broken it off the moment I saw you if it meant I could have you. Is that a good enough answer?"

"Y-yes. I think so," I gasped, arching my back.

"Good, because if I don't fuck you in the next five minutes I might die."

And he did. He fucked me slower that time, biting my shoulder, my arm, my lip when I kissed him. Slower, but he still made me orgasm twice, and I couldn't even protest when he pulled the covers over us and turned off the lamp once he was finished. I didn't think of Will or my father or what would happen next. I didn't think of the break in or the man I'd seen earlier in the day. Gio consumed my every though, my very existence, and left no room for anything else. I should've been terrified, but it was thrilling.

CHAPTER TWENTY-THREE

Gio

I DIDN'T MIND WOMEN SLEEPING IN MY BED. SOME MEN SNUCK OUT IN the middle of the night or didn't like the idea of sharing a bed because it made them feel like they were sending the wrong message. I never gave a shit about the message. If I wanted something in black and white, I stated it that way. If they didn't like it, I got rid of them. With Isabel, things already felt more complicated than that. I wanted her body, and I got it. I'd wanted her thoughts, and she gave them, most of the time. Information was tricky, but only when it came to personal information about her about her past, which was what I wanted. I wanted a list of every single fucking person who had wronged her. The why didn't matter. It just was. She opened her eyes slowly, adjusting to the light coming into the room.

"Are you watching me sleep like a creep?"

"Yep."

She smiled. "What a strange man you are, Giovanni."

No one called me by my full name unless they were angry at me. When she said it, it sounded sexy as fuck. When she said it as she was coming, it was a slice of heaven.

"What did you speak to Will about?" I asked, watching her closely.

"Oh, my God." She groaned turning and pushing her face into the pillow. "You're going to start the day with that?"

"I need to know."

"I need to go to the bathroom and brush my teeth." She fought with the covers as she got out of bed and I watched her ass sway in underwear that looked like boxers, but were too small for any man to fit in. Maybe they were William's. I pushed the thought away instantly. I didn't want to think about him or anyone else she'd been with. I got out of bed and followed her, crossing my arms and leaning against the door frame as she wiped herself and flushed the toilet.

"Hello? A little privacy."

I let out a laugh. "Your pussy was riding my mouth a few hours ago. I think we're past privacy."

"In that case, can I borrow your toothbrush?" She looked at me in the mirror as she washed her hands.

I pushed off the door frame and popped open the cabinet below the other sink, then opened a new pack of toothbrushes and handed her one.

"Thanks." She smiled as she spread toothpaste on it. "For some reason, I can't imagine you buying that."

"Well, Petra bought them, so you'd be right about that."

She rolled her eyes and spit. "Of course."

I shrugged and joined her, reaching for my toothbrush then brushing my teeth beside her. It felt weird. This was a simple thing, brushing my teeth next to someone, but I'd never done it. I'd also never walked into the bathroom while a woman was peeing. I usually did allow them privacy. Natasha would've screamed her head off if I'd ever walked in on her doing something like that. She had this thing about keeping pretenses. So much so, that she always made sure to get up before me to apply her makeup. With Isabel, it felt...normal. We rinsed and set our toothbrushes down, wiping our faces as we continued to look at each other in the mirror.

"Please tell me what you spoke about," I asked.

"Please? Wow." She raised both eyebrows and turned to face me. "I didn't know that was part of your vocabulary."

"Apparently, it is now," I mumbled, looking at our feet momentarily. Apparently, it really fucking was, though, since I'd used it more times this week than I had in all the years of my life. I could play nice when I wanted to, but damn she was making this difficult for no reason and I didn't like it. My eyes snapped back to hers. "Are you going to tell me or what?"

"Why do you want to know?" She crossed her arms over her chest. She was wearing her gray T-shirt, but something told me she felt too exposed to have this conversation. Good. I wanted her to feel exposed to me.

"I don't like being kept in the dark about things."

"Even when those things have zero to do with you."

"Especially when those things have zero to do with me." I felt my lips pulled when she laughed and shook her head.

"You're ridiculous."

"I know." I pulled her to me, telling myself I was just doing it to make her comfortable enough to open up and tell me what went down in that clown's apartment, but she felt undeniably good in my arms, and I wondered why the fuck I didn't hug women more often. Or ever. I set my chin on her head. "Tell me."

She sighed heavily. I braced myself because instinctively, I knew that whatever it was would piss me off. "I told him to re-consider being friends with that man we saw him talking to. You are the company you keep and all that."

I ignored that since, well, I was the company she was keep-ing at the moment. "The one with the scar by his ear."

She nodded under my chin, making my head bob along. "Who was he?"

"No." She pulled away and put a good five steps between us, as if that would deter me from touching her if I wanted to.

"Isabel, I need to know."

"Why?" her whisper was soft, almost broken. "Why do you *need* to know?"

"Because I do."

She watched me for a long moment and must have real-ized I wasn't going to drop it until she told me, because the next words out of her mouth were, "If I tell you, you have to promise to never bring it up and forget about it."

"Fat chance."

"This is why I don't want to tell you." Her shoulders dropped. She took another step back. Six steps between us now. She could make it eight, ten, twenty-thousand, and it still wouldn't be enough to keep me from pulling her into my arms again if I wanted to. She squared her shoulders and tilted a chin up, defiant. "I've moved on from it. I don't need you coming around and drudging all of this up and making me experience things all over again for the sake of your curiosity."

"You didn't move on from it, though. You were scared when you saw him. Terrified. Do you think he was one of the men who robbed your dad's house?" I asked, even though I knew the answer to that.

"No." She bit her lip, crossing her arms again. "He's a lawyer. The guy."

"What's his name?"

"I'm not going to tell you his name." Her eyes widened; her arms dropped at her sides.

I reminded myself to breathe. Rein it in. I wanted answers and I knew I wouldn't get them if I lost my cool. Still, I was two seconds from losing my cool and taking the six steps to crowd her so she'd tell me. I ground my teeth together and stayed put.

"Who was he?" My eyes narrowed slightly. "I'm not going to ask again."

"Oh." She raised an eyebrow, laughing as she walked out of the bathroom and into the room. "That's a funny demand, since it's *my* problem and I don't remember saying I *wanted* to tell you."

I stayed by the door, watching as she pulled on her sweatpants and started walking out of the bedroom. Panic rose inside me, reaching my throat and clasping. I knew she wouldn't, couldn't leave, and yet, I felt my skin crawling at the thought of her walking out on me. Chalk it up to mommy issues. Hell, to mommy and daddy issues. I didn't appreciate people walking out on me unless I was finished with them, and I wasn't finished with her. Not by a long shot. I followed her through the kitchen, through the living room, and into the guest room. She started picking up the few things she'd taken out of her bag when she showered in here last night.

"You can't leave," I said, a reminder, a threat.

"I'm well aware." She met my gaze, expression hard. "But I'm assuming we're going back to Chicago. To Dave's office for whatever it is he needs to give me."

"I just want to know what he did to you, Isabel. Put me out of my misery and tell me and I'll leave you alone. I swear."

"Jesus Christ." She let her head fall back with a groan. "You're really not going to let this go, are you?"

"Nope." It was the truth. I wouldn't.

"I've never even told anyone." She swallowed again, bringing a hand up and chewing on the tip of her finger like she'd done to mine as I was pounding into her from behind last night. Fuck. Not the time to think about that right now.

"Tell me," I said, voice quiet, hoping I sounded calmer than my insides felt.

"Fine." Her eyes flared on mine. "I'll tell you, but you do not get to touch me again until I say so."

"What?" The panic rose again. "Why?"

"Do you want me to tell you or not?"

"Yes." I groaned. "How long is this for, the no touching thing? Like right now in the next five minutes?"

"Until I say it's okay," she said, and the fire was back in her eyes, so I knew she meant business. "Definitely not in the next five minutes, maybe not in the next five days. Maybe not ever."

"Fuck." I ran a hand through my hair, heart pounding. "I don't like this agreement."

"If you want me to tell you, that's the agreement." She continued to stare at me. I stared back. I didn't say anything. I weighed it out. How long would she not let me touch her for? *An hour? A day? A week? A month?* Panic rose each time a new thought formed. I couldn't promise her that. "And you can't talk to me the entire ride to Chicago. From the moment I tell you until the moment we get to the house."

"Fine." I took a deep breath and let it out. I could do this. I hadn't touched her until last night even though I'd been dying to, what was one more day, or week, or month? The thought clawed at me, though. I gave a nod. "I always keep my promises." It wasn't a lie. If I gave you my word, I gave you my fucking word.

"He raped me," she said simply, as if reading the fucking weather. I felt the air swoosh out of my lungs as I stared at her. Not what I'd been expecting. I was expecting...fuck, I don't know? A bully? Someone who'd threatened her? An asshole ex-boyfriend? But rape? I clenched my fists when I felt myself begin to shake and let her continue speaking without interruption. I owed her that much. "We were in college. I'd just left a party and him and a friend of his...they just...yeah. They raped me." She blinked rapidly, trying to obviously hold back tears. She wiped them before they could fall. "I hadn't seen him again until yesterday. I didn't even know I knew what he looked like."

"I'm the only one who knows?" I asked, voice hoarse. I swallowed to clear it.

She nodded.

"You didn't go to the police? You didn't report it?"

She scoffed, wiping her face again. "Please."

"Isabel." I took a step forward.

"Don't you fucking dare." She shot me a murderous look, holding a finger up. "We had an agreement. You said you keep your promises."

"I do. I just...I need..." I took another step forward.

"I don't care what *you* need, Giovanni," she shouted, backing away. "This isn't about you."

I stopped walking, then took half a step to see if she'd change her mind.

"I swear to God, if you touch me, I will shank you." She reached into her bag, grabbed a black switchblade, and held it up. Under any other circumstance, this would have turned me on. Fuck, it nearly did right now, but I was still stuck on the rape thing.

"Isabel."

"I will cut up that perfect face of yours," she said, and I knew, I *knew* she'd put that scar on his face. "And I'll never tell you anything personal again. Ever."

That was where she got me. Not the cutting up my face bit, but the not telling me anything personal thing, because I wanted more. I needed more. I nodded and retreated a step back, then another. She lowered the knife but kept her eyes on mine. I wanted to fuck the fire out of them. I wanted to hold her and tell her it would be okay because anyone who'd ever hurt her would pay, but I didn't. Words without actions were just letters strung together. Meaningless. I'd make them mean something, though.

"Who was the other guy?" I asked when I managed to get my throat to work again. "The friend."

"I don't know." She shrugged a shoulder. "I'm not kidding, I really didn't remember what he looked like until I saw him. Until I..." she shivered hard, wrapping her arms around herself. "Just, please stop it with the questions. You can't imagine how hard it is for me to say this out loud."

"Thanks for telling me." I swallowed again and gave a nod as I turned around and walked out of the room. "We're leaving in thirty minutes. There's coffee in the kitchen and Eggos in the freezer."

He'd raped her. That no-good-fucking-asshole. I was an asshole, I knew that. I wasn't boyfriend material and I'd treated some women in the past like they were just objects to discard. But rape? Fucking rape? By the time I reached my bedroom, I was shaking. My entire body buzzing with a rage I hadn't felt in years. Even when I'd found out my sister was dating Lorenzo, who I'd seen as a potential enemy at the time, I hadn't felt like this. I'd been mad, yes, but not like this. Even when Frankie was killed. Even when Vinny kidnapped my sister. Even when my father didn't kill Vinny, like he should have. Even when my mother walked out on us like we were meaningless. Even when my father knocked me around or called me names.

Even when I was a teenager and heard all of the things the older women said about me behind my back, the way they spoke about my body like it was just a plaything. Even then, I hadn't felt this kind of rage. This blind, white heat that shielded my eyes from reason. I slammed my door with the back of my foot and paced the room, taking deep breaths. Focusing on that. Focusing on getting my heart rate back to a normal speed. If I made a call right now, I'd sound like a deranged man. I took one last breath as I took my phone out and pushed Dean's name on my caller ID.

"I need a name," I said when he answered. "Lawyer, blue eyes, went to Rutgers's, graduated the same year as Isabel, maybe a little before or after. Has a scar coming down his hairline to the side of his ear."

"He practices in New York?"

"Yes." I let out another breath. "He was at William Hamilton's luncheon yesterday."

"Give me an hour." He hung up the phone.

I threw mine on the bed and growled in frustration. I hadn't been lying when I told her I didn't kill people. I didn't. I had, but I *didn't*. It wasn't something I enjoyed. Some people liked it; men and women I employed genuinely liked it. They got a sick power buzz from it, from the torture, from the killing, from having someone's life literally in their hands and then taking it. I'd never found it appealing. To me, it had always been a means to an end, or when I was a soldier, an order I couldn't ignore if I wanted to move up in rank. This guy, I'd kill though. This guy, I'd torture.

My pulse was racing at the mere thought of seeing the helpless look on his face. And still, it would never be worse than what he did to her, and who knows how many others. My phone buzzed with a text message. I lunged for it and sat at the edge of my bed. It hadn't even been four minutes and he'd found the man.

Dean: Carson Riley, esq.

He sent another text with the address.

And another with background information about the man. I clicked on it and read a few points, but it wasn't like it would make a difference. It could have been said he was a loving husband and doting father and it still wouldn't change his fate. Maybe people changed. Maybe we shouldn't cast judgement on others, especially when we had dirt on our own hands. *Maybe, maybe, maybe.* I didn't give a fuck. He was dying today. I got my shit together fast, the adrenaline still buzzing through me as I opened my door and walked out. Isabel's was still closed as I headed toward the elevator. When I reached it, I unlocked it, pushed the button, and called Petra as soon as I stepped inside.

"Yep," she said as a greeting.

"Take her back to Chicago. To my place, not the house. Don't let her out of your fucking sight this time."

"I didn't let her out of my sight last time, boss," she said, and I could hear the cockiness in her voice. I clenched my other fist tight as she added. "We were right outside."

"Don't leave her in a room with a fucking man, Petra," I growled. "Or a woman. Or a fucking dog for that matter. You go to the fucking bathroom and stand there as she takes a shit if that's what it'll take to keep her safe."

"Got it." She had the nerve to laugh. "You're real testy about this one. I like it."

"Shut up." I hung up the phone.

When the elevator reached the first floor, I found Tony sitting in a chair, on a FaceTime call with Nadia. When I approached, Nadia's eyes widened on the screen.

"Someone's pissed off," she said. Tony turned around quickly.

"We need to go," I said to him, then looked at Nadia. She must have read the expression on my face correctly because her eyes widened.

"Be careful," she said quickly, looking at me, then at her husband. "Please be careful."

I gave a nod. Someone would die today, but it wasn't going to be us.

CHAPTER TWENTY-FOUR

Isabel

BOARDED THE PRIVATE JET WITH PETRA AND JOEY Z IN TOW. IT WAS a different one than the one we'd taken the other day. It was always a different one, but it was always the same two pilots and the same woman handing us drinks and snacks. Neither of them spoke much. They just smiled when they were supposed to and gave as much (or little) information as they could. I appreciated that in a way, especially today. I kept looking between the window beside me and the door, which was still open, waiting for him to waltz in at any moment. He hadn't ridden with us. He hadn't even been there when I got out of my bedroom. I didn't know why, but I needed to look in his, just to make sure he was gone, and he was. The bed was unmade, the sheets all wrinkled from our night together. My heart felt heavy as I left the apartment and followed Petra to the car. Something changed after I told him what that man did to me. I knew it would. Maybe that was why I'd never spoken about it. There was an underlying shame to it all. Like maybe I'd been at fault for it. In my nightmares, I'd replayed it over, and over, trying to figure out what I'd done or said or worn or what kind of smile I must have had on my face for them to target me. I knew it wasn't any of those things. I knew I wasn't the problem. I knew that if the world were a good place, I'd be able to walk outside completely naked and not worry about a man thinking my nudity had anything to do with him. But that wasn't the world we lived in.

Giovanni had been the first person I told. Maybe because I knew he wouldn't judge me, not really. And he didn't, but he did get pissed, and that made me get even more mad because what the fuck? I'd been the one who endured that night and every single night after that. I'd been the one to pick myself up and take myself to a therapist when I realized the nightmares weren't going away and that I couldn't just go back to class and finish my semester. I'd been the one to fight for online schooling for the remainder of my college years and miss out on the full experience, because if the full experience meant dealing with entitled assholes who thought everything, including other people's bodies, belonged to them, I wanted no part in it. I'd been the one to get up every morning, look in the mirror, and make the choice that I wouldn't let it define who I was. So, for him to be upset? It annoyed me. Maybe I should have felt proud or happy or turned on? But I didn't. I felt annoyed and through the annoyance I tried to tell myself it was irrational, but I knew it wasn't. No feeling was irrational. Feelings were feelings, and we were free to experience them and make of them whatever we wanted. So, annoyed it was. I was grateful I'd made him promise not to touch me, too. I was grateful when he agreed and grateful when he stopped himself. It took pulling a knife on him, but he didn't come any closer. Whether or not the knife was the deterrent, I wasn't sure.

To men like Giovanni, sometimes a knife was just a knife. A tool they could easily conquer and dispose of. It hadn't been that way with that guy that night, though. It wasn't a knife I'd used. It was a shard from a broken Corona bottle lying nearby. I'd already resound myself to my fate by that point, my mind checking out as he took advantage of me, but when I saw that glimmering piece of glass, I grabbed it and aimed for his face, his arm, anything I could sink it into. I became interested in knives after that. My father couldn't understand it, but he bought me this one anyway. My gaze fell to the pocket I'd stored it in. It was engraved with my initials: IEB. *Isabel Emilia Bonetti.* I'd learned how to somewhat do things with it from YouTube (thank you, internet), but I'd never used it on a person. The first time I'd even threatened someone with it was last night. God. I shivered. I would've used it, too. I knew that as well as I knew this entire thing between Gio and me would blow up in my face. I glanced at the door as the woman closed and locked it.

"No one else is coming?" I looked at Petra. She looked up from her phone and shook her head, then went right back to it.

The remainder of the flight was silent for the most part, except when Joey Z took the seat across from me and opened up a foldable chess set.

"You play?" he asked. "I can teach you."

"I think I remember." I picked up the black pieces and set up my side of the small board. "My dad taught me when I was around seven."

"Was he any good?"

I let out a laugh, looking at Joey. "I don't know. He was the only person I've ever played with."

"I learned in prison," he said, like it was no big deal, like it was a normal place to visit.

"Interesting." I moved a pawn.

"I learned how to read there, too."

"And people are always talking about how bad our prisons are," I said, mostly joking, because I couldn't even begin to imagine how terrible it must have been in there.

"I don't like it." He moved a piece. "Some guys do though. They get used to it, feeling caged. Don't know what to do when they're out here, you know."

"I don't know, but I can imagine." I moved a piece. "What were you in for?"

"Robbery." He shot me a look. "I was the getaway, not even the fucking robber, but whatever, I'm not a snitch."

"You were still involved." I bit back a laugh because this conversation was fucking insane, and I was having it anyway. "The getaway is still involved in the robbery."

"That's what Judge Rosalyn said."

We continued to play in silence. He beat me twice before we landed and I decided that tonight, I'd watch YouTube videos on how to play chess, because no way would he beat me a third time. Not that I was planning on sticking around much longer. I did need to get back to work in August. It wasn't like I had all the time in the world to sort this stuff out with the marriage and the warehouses and whatever else they needed from what my father left. I knew it would be much easier if I just gave them access to all of it, but I didn't want to. As it was, they had more than enough information. I needed to focus on packing up his things, selling the house, and getting the hell out of here. It didn't matter how much Giovanni affected me whenever he was near me. It didn't matter what spark we had or how good he was in bed. None of it mattered. I didn't belong in this life any more than I belonged in the life of a politician.

We pulled up to a luxury building, where Joey parked in the garage and the three of us got down. I looked around, unsure of what we were doing here. It didn't matter. It wasn't like I was going to stomp my feet and get out of here. I knew I was safe with these people, so I let them lead me inside, to the elevator, and up the building to the penthouse. I instantly knew this was Giovanni's. All this luxury had his name written all over it. When the doors opened, I paused in the elevator. Damn. At least the man had class. He must have paid an interior designer a lot of money, because it looked straight out of a Restoration Hardware catalog. Everything was sleek and dark. The floors were black stone, the walls were black stone, the mirrors were huge, but the furniture itself was just clean and minimal. And then, the hall opened up to the living room and kitchen and my jaw dropped. He had the most perfect view of the city I'd ever seen. I walked over and stood by it, not setting a hand on it out of fear that I'd dirty the glass.

"Wow," I breathed.

"It gets me every time," Petra said behind me. I turned around to face her. "Make yourself at home. I'll give you a tour so you can see where everything is in case you get bored."

I nodded and followed her as Joey took my bags up the winding stairs. There was a glass wall there, but I couldn't see anything else. I wondered if it was some kind of loft. Petra took me into the kitchen and showed me how to work the filtered water and fridge. She showed me the hidden pantry that was organized to perfection, and where the pots and pans and mugs and coffee were. Then, she showed me one guest room, then another. The third room was massive. It was a game room slash movie theater. The movie theater portion had three rows of chairs in front of a big screen. The game room portion had a pool table, foosball table and Pac-Man arcade game.

"His personal favorite," Petra said, tapping the Pac-Man game. It was my favorite, too. I killed that game every time. She added, "He holds the highest score and talks about it non-stop when we hang out here."

"Do you hang out here often?" I asked. Not because I was jealous. I wasn't. I just wanted to know. It was something I needed to ask him, though. It was a conversation I'd need to have if I chose to continue sleeping with him. If. Big if. I looked at Petra. "I'm sorry. You don't need to answer that."

"Nah, I get it." She smiled. It was the first genuine smile she'd given me. "We have never, are not, and will never be together."

"Thanks." I felt myself smile back. I didn't ask why, or whether or not either of them had tried. That wasn't for me to ask her or for her to disclose.

"Would you be jealous if we had been?" she asked as we left the room and headed toward the stairs.

"Honestly?" I sighed heavily.

Yes, I would have been jealous, and that scared the hell out of me. I wasn't jealous or possessive. Hell, William had been flirted with heavily, by women right in front of me, and I'd stood there, smiling and trying to bite back laughter sometimes. Thinking about Giovanni with another woman, though? That set ice in my veins. I bit my lip. When we reached the second floor, she turned to me, brow raised, waiting.

"I'm taking that as a yes."

"Yes, but I shouldn't be."

"Because of his reputation or because you're not cut out for this life?" She turned back around and continued walking. Joey walked out of the room we were standing near.

"Have you been talking to Nadia?"

"Maybe." She smiled again. "Not many people are cut out for it, but if it makes you feel any better, he's removed himself as much as possible from anything that may land him in jail."

"Really?"

"Eh." She moved her head side to side. "I mean, most things."

I laughed, shaking my head as I followed her into the room we were standing in front of. The faint smell of wood hit me first, but that was just before my mouth dropped. It wasn't a massive room, like I'd expected, but the view was incredible.

I looked up and realized there was a second floor. "What's up there? Bathroom?"

"Nope, bathroom's down here." She walked toward a door and opened it. Okay, the bathroom was big.

"How does all of this fit in one space?"

"Well, when you know people and convince the architect to design something a certain way..."

"Wow," I breathed, taking it all in. "He must have really good connections."

"You can say that." She laughed as we walked up stairs. "You really hadn't heard of him or his family?"

"I mean, I've heard the last name because of that Italian restaurant that claims they have the best lasagna in the U.S., but not really, no."

"That's wild." She shook her head as we reached the second floor.

My eyes widened. He had a bookcase, a small bar, and a cozy looking couch that faced the floor to ceiling windows across the room. I turned around and stared at it for a moment.

"How the hell do those get cleaned?" I asked.

She laughed. "Some guys do it. It's cool to watch. I mean, unless you happen to be getting dressed and forget to push the privacy button. That might be awkward and I'm pretty sure Gio would gauge their eyes out when it comes to you."

My heart thundered. "Why do you say that?"

"He's very protective of you."

"I'm sure he's protective of all of the women he's currently fucking."

Petra set a hand on her narrow hip and shot me a look. "Gio doesn't give a fuck about the women he's fucking."

"That's…kind of sad." I thought about Natasha. "He seemed to care about Natasha."

Petra rolled her eyes. "Well, he may have been the only one, because we certainly didn't."

She went over to the door and opened it. I felt the cool air and smelled the outdoors and nearly fell to my knees. He had a rooftop? All the way up here? I mean, in the elevator, there were only seventeen floors, which put us on the eighteenth, technically, so it wasn't the tallest building ever, but still, it was way up. The outdoor area was smaller than I anticipated, but it felt perfect. It was just big enough for a barbecue, a small pergola, a couch that fit about four people, and two lounge chairs. There was a table between the seating area that had to be custom, the way it was. The parameter was surrounded by tall, see-through planes that reminded me of the that time we took a field trip to the Empire State's observation deck. Definitely not tall enough that anyone could climb or go over.

"It feels safe." I said. Petra nodded beside me. "Does he barbecue?"

"If he does, I've never seen it." She shrugged. "Joey or Nadia could tell you. I hang out, but I like to hang out with my brother and his family on my day off."

"I get that." I smiled. "Are you from here?"

"Southside, baby." She smiled proudly.

"How'd you end up working for him?"

"You mean, how did a skinny black girl from southside end up working for a Masseria?" she asked, raising a brow. I nodded, because yeah, that was exactly what I meant. "He picked me off the street."

"What?" I blinked.

"My brother and I were pick pocketing near one of his clubs. We were tired as hell and hungrier than hell, and Gio saw us steal some guy's wallet and gave us jobs." She shot me a look. "Not important jobs. John washed his cars. I filed papers at the club. Shit like that."

"Does your brother still work for him?"

"Oh, yeah. He's in New York. He oversees some of his businesses over there." She gave a small smile. "I know all of this is a lot, but Gio really takes a chance on people and when he says he's in, he's all in. No one, especially his father, wanted us here. Most of the old guys, they only want full Italian lineage, which is understandable, but Gio's not that, and he doesn't try to be."

"Maybe that's why he hires people from so many different backgrounds," I said. "I mean, forget background, you're a woman. And Nadia? That's pretty different, from what I've seen in the movies, anyway."

"Yeah, this is nothing like the movies." She laughed. "Well, maybe a little."

She didn't explain what that meant, and I didn't ask. I was grateful she'd shared that with me, even if it did leave me feeling more conflicted than I already felt.

CHAPTER TWENTY-FIVE

Isabel

GIOVANNI NEVER CAME HOME LAST NIGHT. I DIDN'T KNOW WHY I was expecting him to. I knew even less why I'd been so disappointed that he didn't. I meant it when I told him I wouldn't let him touch me. I'd already given him enough. He couldn't have every single part of me just because he damn well pleased. Besides, him touching me again, fucking me again, it would only complicate things more when it ended. My feelings were already more involved than I wanted them to be. I got out of bed and went through the motions before I headed to the kitchen. Joey and Petra were there, finishing up whatever they were eating.

"Joey made pancakes," Petra said. "Eat at your own risk."

"You said they were good." He frowned at her as he set his fork down.

"They are good." She smiled at him, and the moment he lowered his head, she widened her eyes at me like they weren't.

I bit back a laugh and went into the kitchen, brewing myself a coffee pod. As I waited, I turned to face them. "I have to go to my father's house. To finish packing up. When do you think that can happen?"

"Tomorrow," Petra said. "We're going to do one more sweep to make sure no one has gone back or is staking out there."

"Okay." I could wait until tomorrow. I looked around. There was enough for me to do here to entertain myself. "Can I have my coffee up on the rooftop?"

"Of course," she said. "We're only here to protect, not hold you hostage."

I stared at her.

"Okay, fine, we're also kind of holding you hostage." She started washing the dishes. "But it's for your own good."

"Yep. I got that part."

I took my coffee, toasted a bagel, spread cream cheese on it, and headed up stairs. Out there, I felt free. Maybe it was the wind or the smell of the city or the fact that I felt weightless. It was probably the combination, but I felt free. I knew I wasn't, of course, but I'd learned long ago that you could trick your mind into believing anything, so I was sticking to this.

I spent the rest of my day watching a movie on the big screen and playing Pac-Man. I was determined to beat the highest score. I didn't care how tired my eyes and hands got. That was what I was doing when the door opened and two women walked inside. They were probably about my height, with thinner body frames, and dark hair, red, or brown, I couldn't tell, both had fair skin. One had lighter eyes than the other. The one with the darker eyes seemed to stand taller, hold her chin up a little more. They had to be sisters, though. I just wasn't sure what the hell they were doing here.

"Hm," the one with the darker eyes said, eyeing me up and down with such scrutiny, I almost crossed my arms. I didn't, though.

"Interesting," the other one added, also eyeing me up and down, but she was nicer about it. When she was done, she nodded at the game beside me, where one of my hands was still holding the red control. "So, what's your highest score?"

I looked at the screen. "So far, eighty-five thousand."

"Oof." The other one shook her head. "Gio's is two-hundred-and-thirty thousand."

"I can beat that." I felt myself frown. I could. I could definitely beat that. I just needed more time and less interruptions from women who were clearly very familiar and comfortable in this space and Giovanni.

"Fine." The one with the lighter eyes said, sighing as she stepped forward, extending a hand. "I'm Emma."

I shook it, still frowning. "Isabel."

"Catalina," the other one said, stepping forward and shaking my hand as well. So formal, these two.

I took a step back and looked between the two of them. "So, who are you and why are you here?"

The one with darker eyes smiled slowly. "We're either your worst nightmare or your best friends. That's yet to be determined."

"Oh." Relief rushed through me. "You're not his girlfriends or anything, then?"

"God, his reputation sucks," Emma said, laughing.

"We're his sisters," Catalina said.

"Oh." I blinked. "Oh."

"I know. We don't look alike," Emma said. "Some people say our mother had an affair with an Irish man."

"Emma." Her sister nudged her, then looked at me. "Ignore her. She just got back to the U.S. and doesn't remember her manners."

"Oh. Where were you?"

"Medellin." She smiled proudly.

"Colombia?" I raised an eyebrow. "I hear it's beautiful there."

"It is. The place, the people, the culture, the food," she said with a groan. "Oh my God, the food is to die for."

"Considering you could've died, that's not a funny joke," Catalina said, glaring at her.

"Oh, please." She rolled her eyes. "I was trying to visit our father, but that didn't work out, so I had to come back."

"Oh." I stepped away from the machine beside me and licked my lips. They started walking toward the couches, and I followed, taking a seat near them. "Your brother's not home. I'm not sure when he will be. I'm sure you know this since Petra's out there."

"Yeah, that's why we're here."

"Because he's not?" I frowned.

"We wanted to meet you. He never introduces us to his girlfriends," Catalina said. I opened my mouth to tell her I wasn't his girlfriend, but she just continued on, "Well, that's not true. Most of the time we run into him with them and that's how we're introduced."

"Except for Natasha," Emma said, then looked at me. "She was the worst."

"The worst," Catalina agreed.

"She seemed nice."

Both their jaws dropped before they recovered and asked at the same time. "You met her?"

"Yeah. Twice, actually."

"How the hell did that happen?" Emma asked.

"I was with my boyfriend, and they happened to be at the same events."

They shared a look, a long one that was obviously some kind of unspoken conversation between siblings. I'd always wanted that growing up, that connection people seemed to have with their kin. Found families were definitely heaven sent, but there was something special about this kind of bond.

"Tell us everything," Emma said.

I laughed nervously and gave them a short, very minimal, version of the story. As it was, I wasn't sure where these two stood on the whole "illegal" side of things, but something told me they were sheltered from it. Maybe it was the way their eyes lit up when they spoke. Petra's didn't, not really, anyway. Nadia's didn't. I wasn't even sure that mine did. We ordered take out from an Italian place nearby. We were sitting around the kitchen counter, eating our food and sharing a bottle of wine as I told them the funniest and absolute worst things my middle schoolers had said to me. Apparently, what I'd found offensive, they all found hilarious. Even Joey's laughter boomed through the penthouse, and I couldn't help but to laugh along.

"But why were you wearing Birks?" Emma asked, wiping her tears, still laughing. "Who wears those?"

"Listen." I shot her a look. "Don't knock 'em, till you try 'em. I thought they were ugly until I tried them on and now I have three pairs."

"Nope." That was Petra, also laughing. "No, ma'am. I'm good."

"Whatever." I shook my head. I was still smiling when I heard the sound of footsteps in the hall.

We all sobered up fast and turned to look. My heart raced, knowing it was him, finally, and that felt like a knife to the heart because I knew that even though I'd merely dipped my toes in what was this thing with Giovanni, I was already I was in too deep. His dark eyes met mine first. He was wearing a white button down, no tie, and charcoal dress pants. He looked tired, like he hadn't slept at all, his face covered in a shadow that surpassed five o'clock, for sure. He looked sexy as hell. I swallowed down that thought as I took in the rest of him. That was when I noticed his bloodied bandaged hands and gasped unwillingly. I met his eyes again, questioning, but he gave nothing. He finally tore his gaze from mine and looked at his sisters. That was when he smiled. For them, he smiled, a real, comforting smile that made me want to cry because I wished it had been directed at me first or second or at all.

"Why are you here?" the demand in his voice was a contrast to the expression on his face.

They both stood up and gave him a hug. I didn't miss the way his eyes flinched at that. They pulled away and took a seat back where they were, pouring more wine in each of their glasses. I continued to look at him, to examine his hands, what I could see of his body, which was nothing really. When I looked at his face again, I found him staring at me, that unreadable look on his face, his jaw set as if was trying to hold something in. Words? Questions? I wanted so badly to find out. I wanted so badly to stand up and launch myself at him, to show him the relief I felt at the fact that he was here, but I wouldn't. I wasn't his girlfriend. *But you're his wife,* a little voice reminded me. I took comfort in that, even if it was hidden comfort and I'd never say it aloud.

"I'm going to shower and change," he said, finally, tearing his gaze away from me as he walked past us and headed to his room.

I made myself stay in my chair. I made myself pick up my glass of wine as if nothing out of the ordinary was happening, because what else could I do?

I looked at Petra and whispered, "I think I should move rooms. Since he's back and all."

"Good luck," she said, "You're free to go tell him that if you want. I'm not getting yelled at tonight."

"Why would he yell?" I shot her a look, then looked at his sisters who were both wearing the same expression on their faces— lips pressed together as they shot me a sympathetic look.

Catalina broke the silence, smiling softly. "Give him some time."

I nodded, but even as I nodded I knew I was going over there, not because I needed to hug him or touch him, because that would be extremely hypocritical of me, but because I wanted to make sure he was okay. He didn't look okay. The only second, he seemed okay was when he smiled at his sisters, and even that was short-lived. I waited as long as I could, which turned out to be two minutes, according to the clock on the microwave. His sisters laughed lightly. Petra pressed her lips together, shaking her head, seemingly telling me not to go. Even Joey flinched. I made my way to him anyway.

CHAPTER TWENTY-SIX

Isabel

I FOUND HIM IN THE BATHROOM. HE WAS WEARING GRAY SWEATPANTS, but remained shirtless, as he re-tried to bandage his left hand. His right hand looked bad. Really bad. As if he'd punched glass repeatedly. His eyes snapped to mine in the mirror. He didn't even hide his annoyance or his glare or the fact that he looked like he was ready to kill me.

"You should go back to the kitchen."

"I should." I took a step forward, then another, until I finally reached him. I kept my eyes on his hand. He kept his on me. I knew this not only because my skin was prickling with the awareness of it, but also because his hand was still frozen in mid-air, the way it had been when I walked in. I swallowed. "Let me do this."

"So, you can touch me, but I can't touch you?"

I met his eyes, narrowing my own. "This isn't touching you. This is helping you since you seem to be struggling with it."

"I'm not struggling with it. I'm fine." He dropped his hands, glared right back. "Just leave."

"No."

"No?" he raised an eyebrow. "Get the fuck out, Isabel."

"No." I held my ground, even though hearing those words coming from his mouth hurt a little.

"You gonna let me touch you, then?" His eyes narrowed.

"With what hands, Giovanni?"

"I don't need my hands." His gaze smoldered. It was so sudden, that change from cold to hot, that I physically shivered.

"No," I said again.

"So, no." He shrugged, those wide shoulders of his.

"For the love of God, please let me help you do this." I looked at him for a long moment.

I hadn't reached for his hands yet, but I wanted to so badly. Instead, I set a hand on the edge of his shoulder. It wasn't meant to be interpreted as anything more than that. Joey could've touched him there and he wouldn't have batted an eye, but the moment my skin touched his, he shut his eyes and inhaled sharply. He opened them and pinned me with his gaze. There was a storm brewing in there. I felt it inside me as well.

"Isabel," his voice was a whisper.

"Let me help you." I took my hand from his arm and turned it over, holding it out for him to place his hand in it.

He didn't. He was trying to rattle me. He was trying to get me to cave, to kiss him, to touch him, to fuck him, I knew it. I could feel it because those were the things I wanted to do. But I wouldn't. I'd said no and I meant it. I truly wasn't ready to do that again, not after what he knew, not after how he'd handled it, by disappearing and not coming home and making me feel dirtier than I already felt. Finally, he set his hand on mine and I couldn't stop the relieved exhale that left my lips. I unwrapped what he'd already wrapped and hissed when I saw his hands.

"Jesus, Gio," I whispered, looking up at him. He gave nothing. "Did you disinfect this?"

He nodded at the counter. I grabbed a cotton ball and pressed over his wounds, applying balm after and a gauze on top before I began to wrap it. "You could've been a nurse."

My lip twitched. "I thought about it."

"Why didn't you go for it?"

"It's a long story."

"I have time." He angled his body toward me. My glanced up and stared at his abs, wishing I could lick him there, then looked back down and continued to wrap.

"I've already told you enough about myself," I whispered.

"I want to know more."

My eyes snapped to his. "Why?"

"Because I'm nosey."

I snorted a laugh, went back to the task. "I had a neighbor. Luke and Noah's mom, actually. She was a nurse. *Is* a nurse. Sometimes she'd take me to work with her for daughter-mother-work-day."

"Where was your mother?"

I shrugged. "Who cares?"

"I'm pretty sure you care. I care," he said, voice so low I almost missed the words. I looked up at him again.

"I don't."

"My mother left us," he said suddenly. "Just picked up and went. Didn't tell us about it, didn't call, write, nothing."

"That sucks." I finished wrapping that hand and moved on to the next.

"Yeah." He chuckled. I felt it in my core. "It did suck, actually. It still sucks."

"And your dad is a complete asshole," I said, "so that didn't help."

"How do you..." he started, but stopped, probably remembering that I'd been present when he'd spoken to him on the phone. "Yeah, he is an asshole, but so am I. It was fine."

"You're not." I looked at him again. "I mean, you are, but you're not."

"That makes a lot of sense."

"It does in my mind." I felt myself smile as I tossed the cotton on the counter and started wrapping the hand.

"I want to know what's in there," he said, jutting his chin up, "In your head."

I shook my head, unable to look at him. "Nope. I told you enough."

"Not nearly enough," he growled softly. My insides shook.

"More than enough." I looked at him then. Fuck, I wanted to kiss him. I looked away.

"Let me touch you."

"Nope."

"What if I beg?"

"Will you beg?" I raised my eyes and eyebrows as I looked at him.

"No." He scowled.

I had to laugh. Of course, Giovanni drew the line at begging. It was good to know. We slept with a pillow between us on the bed. It was massive. Custom. Bigger than a king size. A replica of a mattress made for Shaquille O'Neal, he'd said. When I asked why he wanted a bed so big, and followed up with, "For orgies?"

He'd only laughed. I got the feeling it wasn't for that, but still, it left a bad, jealous, taste in my mouth and despite how comfortable it was, I kind of felt like burning the damn bed.

CHAPTER TWENTY-SEVEN

Gio

THIS WOMAN WAS GOING TO KILL ME OR GET ME KILLED, AND IF I had to pick between the two, I'd take the latter because death by Isabel would somehow be more excruciating than anything else I could experience. I'd known her less time than I was with my ex, and somehow, she'd managed to reach something inside of me that no one else before her had. She treated me like I was just a random guy off the street, and for some strange reason, I loved it. I'd grown so used to women already having a certain image of me, and delivering accordingly, that I'd forgotten how to be. With Isabel, I just *was*. I was myself, not a pretense of myself that I thought she wanted me to be. It was dangerous. I knew deep down that I should give her up and just walk away from this now. It would be the smart thing to do, to let her keep her secrets and her body, but the more I thought about it, the more I wanted all of her. I hadn't gotten my hands dirty in years—years—before I paid a visit to Carson Riley the other night.

In the past, I'd dealt with a couple of people because my father expected it from me, but with this scumbag, it was personal. I didn't know what it felt like to want to rip apart a human being until I looked into his eyes after I knew what he'd done. Tony had called Lorenzo and Dominic for backup because he couldn't drag me out of the warehouse I'd tied Carson Riley in. Even the memory of his name brought the taste of blood to my mouth. I sat up in bed with a sigh, propping my right arm on one of the pillows Isabel set between us. She wasn't in bed. I groaned, letting myself fall back onto my pillow. She wasn't letting me touch her, could barely look into my eyes, and was making me sleep on the other side of my own bed. Not even the side I normally slept on. Nope. She'd pointed at the right side of the bed and told me that was where I would be sleeping, and normally I would have said something, shouted a reminder that this was my house and we played by my rules, but I was so tired. So fucking tired. I would've slept on the couch. My phone buzzed on the nightstand beside me, and I blindly reached for it, groaning when I saw my brother-in-law's name on the screen.

"What?"

"You good?" he asked.

"Splendid." I yawned. "What the fuck time is it?"

"Twelve."

"In the afternoon?" I bolted up. What the fuck? I'd never slept this late.

"You practically just got home," Loren said on the other end. "Take a fucking day."

"I can't. You know I can't." That was all I said. All I had to say. "I have to go. We'll be in touch. By the way, your wife is in Chicago. She was here last night hanging out with Emma and Isabel, and I'm almost afraid to know what they said and how they treated her because I don't want to lose my shit two days in a row."

Loren laughed. "My wife is currently on an airplane coming back home, and she told me Isabel was her new best friend, so I don't think you have to worry about this one."

I frowned and ended the call.

New best friend? That was new and unexpected. What the fuck had they talked about? How long had they even been here? I hadn't even gone back to the kitchen after Isabel wrapped my hands and told me where I would sleep in my own bed and what I would and wouldn't be doing with her in my own house. As much as I loved my sisters and wanted to spend time with them,

I couldn't go back out there. They understood. I knew that much. They were used to me, used to my moods and my need for solitude. I looked at my phone. Twelve-oh-five now. Fuck. I got out of bed and made myself get ready for the day as if it was just any other day, because it was. Every day was the same shit around here. The only thing that would be different about today was that I'd have a little chat with Dave, the lawyer, about the manila envelope he was supposed to hand over to Isabel. Another day visiting another lawyer. Hopefully, his fate wasn't anything like the last guy's.

I was shrugging on my jacket when I walked out of my room and stopped short. There was music playing. Fucking music. In my house. At least it was wordless music, just rhythm. Brazilian, maybe? And it wasn't loud, just background noise. Whatever. If she wanted to listen to music, she was allowed. I kept walking. In the kitchen, I found Isabel and stopped short again, something in my chest squeezing a little for God knew what reason. I swallowed. It was the exhaustion. She was wearing a dress that was covered in little flowers. I took her in as she spoke on the phone, a smile on her face. Her long brown hair was down and moved whenever she animatedly moved her hand as she spoke. The dress had sleeves that covered half her arms and wasn't skin-tight. In fact, you couldn't see much of her curves at all, but I knew they were under there.

Fuck, did I know they were under there. My dick twitched just thinking about it. She moved toward the refrigerator, and I saw the rest of her. Hell no. Absolutely fucking no. Now I understood why the dress was so modest up top. It was way too short. Way too short. One gust of Chicago wind and we'd have a second Marilyn Monroe type of picture, except it would be on a cell phone and posted on social media and I'd have to track down the asshole who took it and threaten him until he deleted all signs that he'd ever taken one. Her legs were so beautiful that a part of me didn't want her to cover up at all. Either way, I'd have to pretend it didn't bother me. That was the thing about women like her, if you told them what you wanted them to do, they'd go and do the opposite. I'd had two of those pains in the asses growing up, though Catalina was definitely a little more of a people pleaser and rule follower. Emmaline was the opposite. I cleared my throat, as if I needed to alert her of my presence—IN MY OWN HOUSE—and stepped forward. She turned quickly, those big brown eyes widening a touch when she saw me. I watched as her eyes made their way down my body all the way to my shoes and back up. I saw the way she visibly swallowed. Knowing she wanted me just as much as I wanted her, made me breathe a little easier. What that asshole had done to her justified what I did to him, but knowing she wanted me, knowing she'd be mine again when she was ready, made it that much sweeter.

"I gotta go," she said, hanging up the phone once she finally composed herself and stopped gawking at me.

I stepped into the kitchen. "Are we going to hug or kiss or what?"

"What?" Her eyes widened. She took a step back. "No. Why would we hug or kiss?"

"How do you greet people in the morning?" I turned my back to her to hide my amusement as I set a pod in the coffee maker. I was crowding her space. Maybe I was a bastard for it, but it was the closest I could get to her without touching her and she set these stupid rules, not me. I turned and faced her, pressing myself onto the counter and setting my hands on either side of myself as I waited for the coffee.

"The only people I greet are classrooms full of tweens and teens." She scrunched her nose as if thinking of something gross, then added, "And a lot of them come in right after physical ed."

"Sounds lovely." I felt my own face scrunch, because that was fucking gross. I stood straight when my coffee started to pour into the mug I'd set there.

"I was thinking," she said, and I already didn't like where

this was going, "After we go to the lawyer's and figure out that mess, I want to go back to my dad's house to finish packing."

"That's fine. I have to go to the office anyway to sign some contracts. Petra and Joey can take you while I'm there." I grabbed the mug and took a sip. Her nose scrunched again. I sighed. "What now, Isabel?"

"I should've known you take it black."

"How do you take it?" I asked, biting my tongue to not add what I *really* wanted to add. She knew it too, the way she blushed a little and looked away quickly. I couldn't help my smile.

"Two creams, one drop of sweetener."

"Drop of sweetener?"

"Yeah, the ones that have no real sugar." She mimicked squeezing a dropper. "You just boop it into the mug."

Boop it into the mug. This girl. I shook my head and laughed. "You belong in a fucking Disney show."

"Oh, my God. That was my dream growing up." Her eyes grew wide. "Are you kidding? I watched all those shows at night and wished so badly that I could jump into the screen and just magically be a part of those families or friends with those kids."

"What was wrong with your family?" I asked, taking a sip of my coffee.

"Well." She leaned against the island counter behind her and crossed her arms over her chest. I'd never been more grateful to be holding a hot cup of coffee in my life because this would have been the first time I'd broken a promise. I was dying to lift her up and have her legs around my waist as I felt her up underneath that short ass dress. She snapped her fingers. My attention snapped back to her face. She continued, "Apparently my father had a whole other family I didn't know about in Chicago, so if that's anything to go by, you already know some of what was wrong with my family."

I sighed heavily. That was uneventful. Here I thought she

was going to open up and the only thing she was doing was shutting down. I couldn't understand it. Fuck it.

"I'm doing everything you asked me to do," I said. "Doesn't that mean you'll at least let me in that beautiful head of yours?"

"It's been two days, Giovanni." She bit her lip and looked away, the blush on her face again.

I'd never been a fan of women blushing. I liked women who owned their shit. I couldn't think of a woman who owned her shit and blushed. For some reason, the combination was apparently, yet another thing to add to my list of kinks. Right under teacher. Middle school teacher, to be exact.

"Are you going to eat?" she asked, uncrossing her arms and moving out of the kitchen, putting way too much distance between us.

"Did you eat?"

"Yep. Had a bagel with cream cheese and lox."

"Good." I set my empty mug in the sink. "I don't eat in the mornings."

"Oh." Her brows pulled.

"I usually wake up at five, work out, shower, have a smoothie while I get ready, and have lunch at the office," I said.

I was telling her my God damn daily schedule and she couldn't tell me about her fucking family. Ridiculous. This entire thing. When we reached the elevator, I texted Petra to let her know we were on our way down. She was waiting with Joey and Tony. Probably talking shit about me as I stood here. Probably taking bets on when Isabel would tell me to go to hell and leave me for good. My chest squeezed again. I rubbed it. I shouldn't have skipped my workout. Now I was liable to have a fucking heart attack. We stepped inside. I pushed the button to the garage, looked straight ahead, trying not to look at her, but she was all I could see in our reflection anyway.

"Don't you think you'll be cold in that dress?" I asked finally because I fucking couldn't not. At least I'd worded it carefully.

Something else I'd learned from having two sisters who were constantly PMSing.

"I think I'll be fine." I saw the smirk from the corner of my eye.

"Are you doing this on purpose?"

"Doing what on purpose?" She glanced up at me, genuinely confused. "Wearing my favorite dress?"

Ugh. "It's a beautiful dress."

"Thanks." She smiled wide, a beautiful smile that reached her eyes and hit me right in the groin. God damn. She was going to fucking kill me.

CHAPTER TWENTY-EIGHT

Isabel

MY DRESS MADE ME FEEL CONFIDENT, BUT WHAT I WORE underneath, even more so. Too bad no one would be seeing it except for me. Somewhere between the kitchen and the car ride over here, I'd decided that I was going to open up to Giovanni. He'd said he was trying, and I believed him. Last night, he'd just nodded his head and gone to bed where I told him to, even though I damn well knew that wasn't the side of the bed he slept on (my pillow smelled like him). I could tell it was taking everything in him not to touch me and I'd expected to have a full argument about the length of my dress. It was short, but not that short. It was short and flowy enough that I could sit down carefully, without putting on a show, but I definitely couldn't bend over in it. He made a comment, of course, but I'd expected worse. Then again, Natasha had been naked in some of her modeling shoots.

Maybe he really didn't care about wardrobe at all. He was also asking personal questions, which, I'd told myself I wouldn't answer, but I figured I might as well get to know the man I was married to on paper, right? Yes, it was a sham of a marriage, but I wasn't sure how much longer we'd be stuck together, so I might as well ride it out. I hadn't decided on the sex thing. Of course, I wanted him, but I was nervous. I'd never told anyone I had sex with what happened to me. I'd seen the way he looked at me when I told him. A part of me was afraid that he'd start having sex with me and then halfway through decide he couldn't do it. Maybe it was irrational, but I never claimed to be a logical thinker. I tried, but in this case, I couldn't. There was no logic to trauma. I felt what I felt.

I got out of the car, careful not to flash anyone who may be outside. Giovanni was standing near the door, blocking my view anyway, so it didn't matter. He hadn't wanted to ride over here with me. I should've been hurt by it, but I was grateful for the distance, grateful for the silence and the time to sort out my feelings. We rode the elevator with Joey, Petra, and Tony. The three of them were strapped and pretty obvious about it, with the way they walked. Petra was the least obvious, but her face told its own story, and it wasn't one with a happy ending for whoever dared to cross her. Giovanni walked next to me. My heart galloped every time his arm brushed against mine. Tony opened the door to the conference room for us and the three of them stood outside. It seemed like overkill, but whatever. Walking in there again felt different, as if a different person had taken over my body. Maybe it was having Giovanni at my side. Maybe it was my damn dress. Whatever the case, I walked in with my head held high.

"Isabel, pleasure seeing you again," Dave said as he shook my hand.

"I can't return the sentiment," I said with a smile, "Nothing personal against you."

Giovanni laughed behind me. He shook Dave's hand as well and introduced himself, as if Dave didn't already know who he was. "I'm only here as an advisor," he added.

An advisor. I rolled my eyes. I turned toward the table just as Giovanni pulled out the corner chair for me, which was unexpected. He knew he'd shocked me, too, judging by the way his eyes twinkled when I thanked him. He sat next to me.

"I'm sorry it's taken me so long to give these to you," Dave started, taking a seat at the head of the table, next to me.

His eyes assessed me, then Giovanni, and I knew he was trying to figure out how the heck this happened, or what the heck was happening. I wanted to say, *hell if I know*, but I wasn't about to answer anything that wasn't verbalized. He cleared his throat after a moment and kept his eyes on mine the entire time he spoke.

"We only open each safe twice a month," he explained, "There were a couple of things in the first safe."

Giovanni pulled out his phone quickly beside me and started to text someone. I ignored him. He was only here for the keys anyway. The damn warehouse keys. Dave reached for a suitcase beneath the desk. I didn't miss the way Giovanni stiffened next to me, like he's bracing himself for something to go sideways. At a lawyer's office. He lowered his phone slightly. I glanced at him. He didn't even look at me. Didn't even blink. He kept his eyes on the briefcase. The only thing that ran through my mind was, *what kind of life has this man led that would make him this paranoid?* Followed by, *is this the kind of person I'll become if we gave this a real shot? Someone who can't sit still at a private office out of fear she'll get killed?* I definitely didn't want that. Again, my mind, overthinking and messing with my previous plans. I turned my attention back to Dave, who twisted the briefcase in our direction to show us stacks and stacks of yellow manila envelopes. Money? I pulled the briefcase closer to me, but look up at Dave again, who was also looking inside, waiting.

"Do you know what's in here?" I asked.

"Yes," he said, "It's confidential, of course. I would never disclose it. There's a checklist. It has your father's initials. He counted the items every month."

"Counted it," I repeated, pulling out the first envelope.

I opened it just a tad, so only I could peek in. I saw a diamond glittering. At least, I thought it was a diamond. Giovanni didn't get closer, or speak. He just sat there. He might as well have been a statue. My advisor, he'd said, but even an advisor would speak, right? Maybe he was really just being supportive. The next three envelopes were more of the same. Tiny diamonds.

The only thing I could think about were the amount of people who died for these damn diamonds. Digging for them and moving them around here before my father got ahold of them. Who knew how many? The fourth was a gold band. His wedding ring, maybe? I closed that one quickly and set it down as if it burned me. I opened the next. This one held a driver's license. I pulled it out. It was my father's face, but it was a Colorado license. I didn't know him to have ever even visited Colorado. The next one was the same, Florida driver's license. Same photograph, different name. *What the fuck?* I opened a larger envelope and peeked inside. There were rings. More wedding bands? The licenses I understood. I didn't want to, but I did, but I couldn't imagine why he'd need so many different wedding bands, unless he married these many women? The idea made my stomach churn. They were different colors, too, different styles. One in particular caught my eye, because it seemed like it was dirty. I picked it up and examined it. It looked like blood. I turned to Giovanni. His eyes were on mine in an instant.

"Does this look like blood?" I whispered, hoping Dave couldn't hear me.

Giovanni looked at the ring in my hand and gave one sharp nod. That was it. His mouth set hard, expression blank, and a sharp nod. I dropped it back inside the envelope and shut the briefcase with a loud thump. I'd seen Dexter. Both the regular and the sequel. I knew what trophies were. The thought of these being trophies made me want to vomit. Really vomit. I set the envelope back in the briefcase. There were two other big ones, but I didn't want to look. I couldn't right now. Instead, I buried my face in my hands, trying to breathe through the nausea. I'd never known him, not really. All of these years, twenty-eight-fucking-years, and I'd never known him at all. I was trying to keep myself from crying, but I knew the chances were low. A phone buzzed loudly on the table.

"Shit." Giovanni stood up. "I'll be right back. Emergency."

I nodded, face still in my hands. I waited until I heard the door close behind me before lowering them and looking at Dave. "What is this?"

"I never asked for details. I just know the envelopes are numbers, for the checklist."

"The checklist. Right." I opened the briefcase back up to look for it.

There were a series of numbers and two letters on them that matched the numbers on the envelopes. State acronyms? I set it back in there and shut it again. *Painting houses*, my ass, though, based on Giovanni's explanation, I had to assume my father painted houses up and down the United States. I shivered at the thought. There were more contents in the briefcase that I knew I wouldn't bother to look at today. This was enough.

"I just want to go home," I whispered, finally.

The more I thought about it, though, the more I wondered what the hell I was even going back to. I wouldn't be living with William anymore. I could move back to the Queens house, but I hated the Queens house. The Queens house was picture-perfect, but the memories were dark. I wouldn't go back there. I'd inherited enough money to move, that was for damn sure, if I decided I'd use it. Blood money. That was what it was. Blood money, blood diamonds, and bloody wedding bands. I hadn't noticed I'd started crying until Dave shoved a box of tissues at me. I thanked him and patted my face.

"I'm sorry." I let out a laugh, wiping my tears. "It seems like I only cry in your office."

"Maybe you're comfortable here." He offered a small smile, setting his hand over mine. "If you need someone, if you're in trouble or you know, want to get away from people, or someone, you can call me. I don't expect you to trust me, a complete stranger, but I hope you trust me enough to do that."

"Thank you for saying that." I swallowed, nodding. He seemed genuinely kind, but unless I needed to get out of jail, I had no use for a lawyer. He kept his hand on mine as I finished wiping my face.

"Are we done here?" Giovanni's voice boomed so loudly behind me, that I nearly jumped out of my seat.

Dave took his hand back. I did as well, setting the box of tissues down.

"I think we are. Right?" I looked at Dave, who smiled. I stood up and grabbed the briefcase. Extending my hand for him to shake again. His was almost touching mine when he dropped it and turned around.

"Shit. Sorry. I almost forgot this." He pulled up yet another manila envelope, this one was much bigger, though, and much fatter than the rest. He handed it to me and set a paper on the table. "I also need your signature." He chuckled lightly, scratching the back of his neck. "I'm glad I caught it, otherwise, you'd be making another trip here tomorrow."

Giovanni grunted something behind me. I signed both papers and set the pen down.

"Now, we're officially done." Dave smiled wide.

We shook hands. "Thank you for everything."

"You're welcome." He lowered his hand and looked at me. "I mean it, Isabel. Please use my number. Call me."

I nodded a couple of times, turned around with the suitcase and envelope and nearly ran into Giovanni. He didn't shake Dave's hand this time. Didn't even say goodbye as we walked out of the conference room and into the hall. A little rude, but I wasn't going to point that out. I had things in my hand that I didn't know what to make of. The irony was that none of it was heavy. It was easy enough for me to carry both things in my right hand. I hadn't even opened the envelope, and I didn't know if I wanted to do it today. This was a lot as it was. When the elevator arrived, Giovanni shot Joey and Petra a look. It looked like a warning. Whatever it was, made them take a step back. I frowned as the elevator doors closed between us and them. I turned to

Giovanni just as he started pushing every single button on the elevator from this floor to the parking garage.

"What are you—"

"'Please use my number? Call me?'" he asked, mimicking Dave's voice. "What was that about?"

My heart skipped a beat as I turned to face him, a shiver rolling through me when I saw the look on his face. Dangerous, pissed off, and definitely jealous. I swallowed. The elevator stopped on the next floor, opened, he pushed the button, it shut, kept moving. He was still waiting, so I reminded myself to breathe and answer.

"He was just saying that if I was ever in trouble to call him," I said, looking at the next floor the elevator doors opened at, shut, kept going. "You know how lawyers are."

"I know exactly how lawyers are," he mumbled, looking at his wrapped fists. "He was touching you," he said. "He was fucking touching you."

"He was touching my hand," I said.

"Still counts as touching." He shut his eyes and backed into the furthest wall from me, breathing hard. It seemed to me like he was really, really, trying not to lose his shit. Why that turned me on was a mystery to me, but it did.

"It does," I said quietly. His eyes opened and he pinned me with a look that I could only describe as feral. My heart skipped ten beats as I held his gaze, fully expecting him to pounce at any minute, to break the damn promise I'd make him make me. He didn't, though. He just stared. The elevator stopped again, opened. This time, there were two men in suits there, about to walk in.

"Take the next one," Giovanni said, no room for argument in his voice. Their eyes widened as they backed away, letting the doors close.

"Why would you do this?" I asked, pointing at the panel. It still had about ten more numbers lit up.

"It gives us time."

"For what? To talk about a man that I'm never going to see again in my life touching my hand?" I asked. "Is this your way of telling me you're jealous? Of staking a claim on me or something? Is that what's happening?"

He took a step forward, then another. I didn't know why I'd chosen today to wear flats. Maybe because I knew I was already wearing a short dress and I didn't want to risk tripping over my feet. Regardless, I had to really crane my neck to keep eye contact. He stopped as close as he could get without touching me. My heart pounding frantically.

"I don't have to stake my claim on you," he said, his voice low, gruff. "You're my fucking wife."

I knew he was going to say that, and I still gaped at him. The words and the way he said them sent a shock between my legs. My nipples pinning against the thin bra I wore. Suddenly, I couldn't remember why the no touching rule was even a rule and why I'd thought he'd be the one to cave first. I felt my breath coming in a little faster as he looked at me, his dark eyes bouncing between mine, a contained fire in them that I felt blaze through my entire body.

"I would bet my life," he said, inching forward, still not touching me. "That if I put my hand up your dress and dip it into whatever sexy as hell underwear I know you're wearing under it, you'd wet as fuck." He didn't touch me, though. I swallowed, pressing my thighs together. "I can tell you want me. I *know* you do. Say the word, babe. Say it and I'll make you come on my fingers before we reach the next floor."

My mouth popped open. God, I wanted that, but I shook my head, it wasn't a firm shake, but it was a shake.

He groaned, throwing his head back slightly. "God damn it, Isabel. Let me fucking touch you."

"I can't give you everything," I whispered. His eyes snapped back to mine. "You either get my body or you get my secrets. Which one do you want? You can't have both."

"Why the fuck not?"

"Because if I give you both, you'll leave me with nothing." I tried to swallow back tears, but I was still freaking out about the stuff in my hand, the briefcase biting into my fingers as I gripped it, a reminder. A tear fell, then another. He breathed even heavier, his chest expanding fully with it, nearly brushing against my breasts. "Don't you understand that? I'll have nothing. I already have nothing. I can't risk losing myself, too."

The elevator opened on the garage floor. Finally. Giovanni took one huge step back, eyes narrowed on mine. Tony was waiting for us right outside. He walked out first and looked around, then made way for me to walk out. It reminded me of the movie The Bodyguard, except I was no Whitney and Giovanni Masseria was certainly not my knight. The way he walked out and looked to make sure I was safe, though, I liked that. He was quiet as we walked to the SUV that Petra and Joey were standing by.

Petra raised both eyebrows but didn't say anything as she opened the door for me. I set the briefcase and envelope down, curling and uncurling my hand to fight the cramp it'd gotten from gripping it so tightly. I turned to face him, to say something or wait for him to say something, I didn't even know what I was expecting. Maybe for him to answer and tell me what he wanted from me. Maybe for him to say fuck it, and just take it without asking. I wasn't expecting just silence or the way he was looking at me with that blank expression, as if he was done with the conversation all together.

"Are you riding with me?" I asked, finally.

"I need to see what's in the big envelope." He gestured toward the back seat with his chin.

"Oh. Right." I turned around and grabbed it, opening it as my back was facing him. I took out a folder and opened it.

There was a handwritten letter addressed to me. Damn. My hands shook as I read it.

Isabel,

If you're reading this, please know that I'm sorry. You were the best thing that ever happened to me. The only good thing that ever happened to me. You have to know that. I'm so sorry. I hope one day you'll forgive me for all of this. Those days at the ballpark, the park, the mall, the museums, those were the days I was allowed to let my guard down and be myself. I was always myself with you. Go to those places while you're here and remember the good times. Go and think of me. Please don't look at the rest of this. Find Joe Masseria and give it to him. He'll take care of you.

Love always,
Your pop-pop

My pop-pop. He had some nerve signing off like that. I swallowed as I folded the letter. I probably would cry about it later. No, I knew for sure I would later, but right now, I was too busy running through the motions. I shut the envelope and followed his instructions. God only knew that the last thing I wanted was to get involved in whatever this was. I wondered if I was really supposed to give it to Joe Masseria or if any Masseria would do. Either way, I knew which one I'd be handing this over to. I turned around and faced Giovanni. He had his bandaged hands in his pockets and was looking at the floor. His hair was messy, as if he'd run his hands through it a million times from the time he'd left his house to now. He sensed my eyes on him and looked up. My heart pumped harder, the way it did every time he looked at me. God, why was this happening? With *him* of all people?

"He wanted me to give this to your dad." I held the envelope up.

Giovanni closed the distance between us, my heart gripping

tighter with the way he was looking at me. I would've killed
to reach into his mind and sort through all of his thoughts. I
handed him the envelope. Our eyes widened on each other's as
the tips of our fingers brushed in the exchange. He gave a nod
and walked to the other car. A nod. Like we were fucking associates. Maybe I had my answer after all. Maybe he didn't want
my secrets or my body. I laughed at myself as I shut the door of
the car. I wasn't even mad at it. Then again, I couldn't be mad at
it right now. I couldn't feel anything at all.

CHAPTER TWENTY-NINE

Gio

WE HAD SOME SCATTERED LOCATIONS AND SOME KEYS. Unfortunately, scattered meant really fucking scattered. He had a warehouse here, one in New York, and two in Florida. I couldn't even be mad at him, though. Two years ago, some of our locations had been robbed and torched, or maybe only torched, it wasn't like we could recover enough to figure it out. Collector's items, family heirlooms, you name it, we lost it. We still hadn't found out who was behind it. At first, we thought it was the Colombians, but they gained nothing by doing that. Their business was entirely separate from everything we did. The Mexican cartels were always a possibility, but why? We sold weapons, not drugs. There was no reason behind it. We had no issues with them either. It couldn't have been an inside job since we'd all been targeted. Or it could just be a really fucking smart way to throw off the scent so the dogs couldn't find out. Either way, we were remaining vigilant and trusted no one. Well, no one outside of the ones in this car at this moment.

"You think he was doing business with other people?" Dominic asked.

"He must have been," I said. "You don't keep containers in Florida, near a dock, and not get involved with drugs."

Even though I had no interest in moving drugs, I couldn't keep them out of my nightclubs. They nodded and continued to sit in silence, probably trying to figure out who he could have been doing business with and why. It wasn't like he wasn't making enough money off us. Lorenzo, Dominic, Dean, Tony, and I were on our way to the first warehouse. Dominic and Tony as were talking about wrestlers for the third time during the ride, as Tony drove. Lorenzo and Dean were texting on their phones.

I was looking out the window, my eyes and thoughts on everything and nothing at all. Somehow, my thoughts always ended with Isabel. I exhaled heavily. Fucking Isabel. I didn't even know of her existence until a few weeks ago and somehow crawled under my skin and decided to get cozy in there. I hated it. I wanted nothing more than to cut myself open and get rid of her. If it were that easy, I would've done it already. I'd already had her body and I wanted more. I wanted it again, and I wanted more. I wanted everything. I couldn't figure out why now or why her? If she asked me that question, I wouldn't even have an answer for her. What was I supposed to say, "It's a feeling I have for you"? That sounded like bullshit. It might also be the only answer to that question. Natasha asked me that once, the second time I took her out. She'd turned to me, smiling, and asked, *"Why me?"* I'd shrugged and said, *"Why not?"* She'd accepted that and sucked my dick in the car on our way to my apartment as a way to prove how much she liked the answer. It was so simple with her. So, fucking simple.

And then I met fucking Isabel Bonetti. Scratch that. I didn't meet Isabel Bonetti. Meeting her would mean I'd sought her out somehow or had been formally introduced to her. No, I didn't *meet* her. She'd barged into my life like a fucking tornado, ripping the very ground I stood on and tossing it God knows where, because I still couldn't tell you where the fuck I was standing. What was worse was that I couldn't seem to quit reminding her that I was her husband. It wasn't like I was actively trying to do it, either, but whenever I felt her pulling away or even looking at another man, the urge to remind her of that ripped through me. I never even wanted to get married, for fuck's sake. It had never once crossed my mind. Not marriage, not kids, not a perfect house with a fucking dog. I liked my life just fine. I had everything a man could possibly ask for—money, power, pussy. What the fuck was there to life? So, yeah, Fuck Isabel Bonetti for stirring shit up and making me question everything.

"Where's your wife?" Dominic asked from the front seat, not bothering to hide his amusement.

"Mind your fucking manners." I glared at him. He didn't know when to shut the fuck up. He was young and thought the entire world was wet for his cock. He reminded me of me at times, and that wasn't necessarily a good thing.

"I'm just saying, I haven't seen her."

"Fuck off, Dom." I sighed, closing my eyes.

"Who died?" Dean asked from behind me. He was sitting in the third row of the SUV. I was sitting in one of the captain chairs, and Lorenzo was at my side in the other. Dean was lounging in the middle of the bench, legs splayed out. Fucking relaxing and shit as my head split open with this god damn headache and these god damn questions. I opened my eyes and turned slightly, frowning at his question. He nodded toward my bandaged hands. "If it's that bad, I'm assuming someone died."

"No one important."

"I thought you went legit," he said.

At that, Lorenzo laughed. "Money laundering in his clubs is going legit?"

"Fuck you," I muttered, but felt my mouth tug at one side, because that shit was funny.

"You know what I meant," Dean said. "I thought you didn't get your hands dirty anymore."

Dominic's shoulders shook lightly as he turned around to look at Dean. "He shoved a gun up a guy's asshole the other day. I can't imagine his hands not being dirty after that."

I sighed heavily. "Yeah, let's discuss my private business, Dominic."

"Fuck," Dean said, laughing. I knew he was shaking his head in the back seat.

I also knew he didn't care one way or another. Yet, he had this concept in mind that involved all of us taking over the five seats. After all, our lineage followed all of the fucked-up bastards that came before us. The concept was that we'd fill the seats and work together. *Together,* together. As in, everyone's business was supposed to be discussed at the dinner table like we were on a fucked-up version of Family Matters or something. We all laughed about it and made fun since it didn't feel like that would be a possibility any time soon, unless we took the seats from our fathers, but it really wasn't a terrible concept. We had all been fucked over in the past by our own flesh and blood and deep down we wanted *something* unconditional.

Unconditional loyalty, support, whatever. So, Dean didn't really give a shit whether or not I'd killed a guy, but he wanted to know details so that he'd know what we were up against if it blew up in my face. It wouldn't. I'd made sure of that. I may not have gotten my hands dirty in a long time, but I wasn't a fucking amateur. I also didn't want to discuss it. Everyone in this car knew what happened, whether they were there for the aftermath or not. I turned around and shut my eyes again.

"He did it for his wife," Dom said, all prideful and shit.

"Fuck off."

"No, I'm serious, it's honorable. I dig it."

"Thank you for that, De Luca. I was really hoping to earn your respect." I massaged the area between my eyes, hoping he caught the sarcasm. Knowing him, he'd take it as a compliment.

"I just think it's crazy that you did it and she's not even going to stay your wife for long," he said.

"Stop fucking talking about it," I snapped, opening

my eyes and staring at him. I swear to God if the man kept talking, I'd choke him with his fucking seatbelt. He must have either heard the threat or seen it on my face, because he shut his mouth and turned around, looking at Tony and starting back up again with the wrestlers.

"I haven't seen you around with any other women," Loren said.

"You haven't seen me around at all, dickhead."

He chuckled. "I'm just saying, it seems like you haven't gotten bored of her."

"Jesus fucking Christ." My jaw twitched. They were goading and I knew it and still I couldn't stop them from getting to me. "Can we *please* stop talking about Isabel?"

"Whoa." Tony, the fucking quiet one, looked at me through the rearview. "The motherfucker said please. Hell is freezing the fuck over."

I raised a middle finger at all of them.

"He's not wrong," Dean said.

My head whipped around. "I thought you were above this petty shit."

"I never said I was above anything." He looked amused. "This chick has gotten to you."

This chick. "Fuck you, Russo." I turned back around, closing my eyes as he chuckled behind me. "For the record, I never said I wasn't fucking anyone else."

Thankfully, that response seemed to work. Dean changed the subject and went back to the matter at hand. We needed to find the warehouse with the weapons since those needed to be shipped out ASAP. I needed to find the one with alcohol, since I needed to stock up my clubs. Dean needed whatever the fuck Dean needed for his gambling facilities. Loren needed whatever he was selling on the black market. Dominic, well, Dominic was basically coming along for the ride since he was Loren's right hand and lowkey enforcer, though Loren would never refer to Dom as an enforcer. No one really would unless you saw him in action. The kid looked like a fucking runway model. A runway model full of tats, but a model, nevertheless. He was a stealthy motherfucker, too. By the time you saw him, you were practically dead. If I hadn't seen it with my own eyes, I wouldn't believe anyone who told me.

Originally, I'd suggested we split up to search the warehouses, but Dean shot that down quickly. He'd said if the Russians, or the Irish, were sniffing around and only saw one of us, we'd go down, but they didn't have the balls to kill all of us at the same time. Unless Silvio hired the hit. Then, they'd gladly do it. Snake ass Silvio. He probably wouldn't have a problem taking us all down at the same time. It hadn't yet been confirmed, but I was almost positive he was the one sniffing around for the keys, sending men to tie up Isabel. Sending men to her bar. Maybe my father was right, after all. Maybe I should've fucked his daughter so I could slap that in his face. I could've lied, of course, but the poor girl didn't deserve that. Nor did her mother. Silvio should be thanking whatever higher power he chose to believe in for the women in his life every night before he went to bed, because it was out of respect for them that he was still breathing.

"You going to the club tonight?" Dom asked.

"I should. I have a shit ton of work to catch up on."

"You're not going to stay open long if the liquor isn't in one of these warehouses," Loren said.

Fuck. He wasn't wrong. Charles had been importing liquor from the Caribbean and Russia for me. It was another thing to worry about. The operation was a big one. Whoever took over that seat would have it made, though. None of us had discussed it. We should've, but we were kind of walking on eggshells about it. No one wanted to be the asshole to say "vote for me. I'd be better than the rest of you."

"Fuck," I said, eyes still closed. "The liquor isn't here."

"How do you know?" Dom asked.

"He has a warehouse in Brooklyn. He has a rum bar in Queens." It really didn't take a rocket scientist to put two and two together.

"Is it near the docks?" Loren asked.

"Looks that way." I opened my eyes and clicked my phone, turning it for him to see.

"God damn it. I guess we're going to Brooklyn tonight. If the alcohol is there, the weapons will most likely be there. We still have to check out this warehouse though." He lifted his phone to his ear, probably to call Flynn and check if he had a plane here. "Fuck Charles for this. Cat's going to fucking murder me for having to cancel our anniversary dinner."

I scoffed, closing my eyes again. I guess I wouldn't be seeing Isabel tonight, after all. It was probably for the best anyway. It would give us both time to process whatever the fuck this was. She'd said she didn't want to give me everything because she was afraid I'd leave her with nothing. She'd said she was alone as it was, which meant that unless *I* was willing to give her everything, I had to try to respect that. Still, I couldn't *not* have her. My entire life I'd gotten easy pussy, which wasn't to say anything bad about the women who gave it to me, but I'd never really had to chase anyone down. I'd grown up my father's son, my last name alone, preceded me. That wasn't a good thing in a police precinct or a court, but from a woman's standpoint, it meant money, trips, and good dick. Of course, the only one I was trying to chase was making it harder than it needed to be, but that was okay. I'd have her secrets and I'd have her body. My phone buzzed on my lap, and I looked down to see Mike's name on the screen. Mike usually sent texts. He hated phones. I answered quickly.

"Yo."

"The vault was broken into."

"What?" My stomach dropped. Every head in the car

turned in my direction. I looked at Tony and pointed at the nearest empty spot along the road. "Stop the car. Park right there."

Once he did, I got out of the car in a hurry, trying to breathe. "When? What did they take? Who did they steal from?"

"They didn't take much. They had no time. I had it set up so that it would ring the cops immediately. They must've seen the address and been around since they got here at record speed."

"Who did they steal from?" I asked again.

The vault was where all five families kept their shit. The important shit, anyway. Art, mink coats, jewelry, personal items no one wanted to lose. I'd heard Charles even had slabs of actual gold and endless diamonds in his, amongst other things. I had cash in mine. A lot of it. I'd put it in there for safekeeping while I opened a new bank account and had yet to go back and get it. My father had nearly everything he owned of value in there. The vault was basically a robber's wet dream, but only the five could get in there. We were the only ones who knew the location and had access to it.

"They went into your stash and Silvio's," Mike said after a moment. "I looked at the cameras. It happened half an hour before I got here. It was a rushed job, but whoever it was knew and knew the place well."

"How did they fucking get in there?" A different kind of panic rose inside me. A series of things flashed in my head all at once. Whoever did it was also most likely counting on the fact that we'd be on this fucking scavenger hunt. Whoever did it, knew our movements. My heart beat even faster. I asked again, "How did they get in there, Mike?"

"It was open. The vault was left open."

I let those words sink in as I tried to think about what I had in there. What we all had in there. My father was going to fucking…I didn't even know what he'd do. I didn't want to think about it. Few people had the code to our safe. We shared ours with Costello. I said this to Mike.

"Some of the Costello stuff is also missing, but not much. Not enough time."

"Fuck, Mike." I ended the call and gripped my temple with my thumb and pointer as my headache grew.

I wouldn't be surprised if my head exploded like a grenade, that was the size of the headache I had. It also might very well be the best outcome, because a lot of people were going to start pointing fingers quick.

CHAPTER THIRTY

Isabel

I T HAD BEEN THREE DAYS AND GIOVANNI HADN'T COME HOME. HE hadn't called or sent a text or any kind of sign that he was alive, but Petra told me. Not outright, but she'd mention him in passing when I was in the room, so I knew he was okay, at least. I'd spent two days packing up Dad's house and figuring out where to donate all his furniture and clothes. I hadn't even looked through the rest of the contents in the briefcase since I'd spent the two days reading his letter over and over and crying until I was too exhausted to do anything else. Yet, I'd woken up every single night, looking at the empty space on the other side of the fortress of pillows I'd set up between us. Each time, wondering where he could be. *Was he with another woman?* It was plausible and I really shouldn't care, but the mere thought of that made my stomach twist painfully.

Tonight, I'd decided to take melatonin and go to bed early. I couldn't keep re-reading the letter or looking for Giovanni and hoping he'd be beside me when I opened my eyes. I didn't even know why I wanted him to be beside me, considering I'd told him I didn't want him to touch me, and I meant it. I still meant it. Once this was over with Dad's house and whatever else was done with Dad's involvement in their organization, I would go back home. I'd get a new place and live on my own. I'd go back to school in August and continue living as if nothing had happened and he'd continue on with his nightclubs and his model girl-friends. That was how it all played out in my head. It sucked, but it was for the best. We weren't meant to be together. Technically, we weren't even meant to meet.

I wasn't sure what time it was, since I'd been sound asleep, but suddenly, I felt the bed shift beneath me. For a full second, I panicked, but then I remembered where I was and who they'd have to go through to get to me. I sat up slowly, rubbing my eyes to adjust to the darkness, and saw the outline of his lean frame as he sat on the other side of the bed, his back turned toward me.

"Where have you been?"

"Working." He reached over and switched on the light beside his side of the bed. Now, I could see more, but not enough since he had it at the lowest setting.

"For three days straight?"

"You worried about me, Isabel?" His voice was rigid as he threw a smirk over his shoulder.

"Yes," I whispered.

"Yes?" He turned a little more, surprise written on his face.

"I was worried."

He looked at me for a long time, so long that I couldn't help but wonder what was running through his mind. Maybe I should have moved to the guest room, after all. Maybe he needed his space and I was all up in it, demanding things he didn't, couldn't, give me. Maybe he would rip the Band-Aid and tell me he'd moved on. It was best if he did. It would break my heart, but that was what should happen.

When he finally spoke, his voice was low, a near whisper, "Are you going to let me touch you?"

I'd not been expecting that. The question nearly took the air out of me. I looked down, focusing on my fingernails, and shook my head slowly. It wasn't that I didn't want it. I seemed to want it more and more as the seconds ticked by, and even more in this moment, but he had to understand that it was the only way to shield myself from him encompassing me entirely.

"Was that what you were doing?" I asked quietly, lifting my gaze to his. "Touching someone else?"

"No." His eyes narrowed. "The only person I'm interested in touching is sitting in my bed, denying me." He turned back around and switched the light off, lying down. "Good night, Isabel."

I turned my back and did the same. I wasn't sure why his answer brought such relief, but it did, and I finally got a good night's rest.

The next morning, he was gone. I showered and looked in the mirror. I looked awful. With a heavy sigh, I set down my makeup bag. I needed something to help the swelling from all the crying and lack of sleep. I went to the kitchen, made myself coffee, and grabbed an ice pack from the freezer. The house was quiet, so I went back to the room, pressing it to my cheeks. When I heard the elevator door opened, I quickened my steps and shut the bedroom door quietly behind me. It could've been Petra or Joey or whoever else, but I didn't want to see them yet. Not yet. I headed upstairs, grabbing a blanket to throw over myself as I went outside. I sat down on the couch, setting my mug down to wrap myself better before picking it up and lifting it to my lips. I shut my eyes and breathed the natural Chicago air. It always seemed to be chilly in the mornings, the gusts of wind seemingly picking up every so often and crashing against my skin.

I set the mug down again and leaned back on the couch, closing my eyes as the sun hit my face. It felt like heaven. At the feel of the couch dipping beside me, I startled, eyes popping open as I looked to find Giovanni. He wasn't looking at me, his eyes were set on something in the distance. The extensive body of water of Lake Michigan, I assumed. He was wearing black shorts and a gray T-shirt that was wet, his hair messy in a way that made me want to tame it. I realized he must have been working out. After three days of non-stop work, he'd gotten up early to work out. I shook my head. His jaw was working with much more than just a five o'clock shadow now, and I had to fight the urge to run my fingertips over it, just to feel the prickle of hair against them. He did look exhausted, but still unfairly gorgeous. Meanwhile, I was holding an icepack to the bags under my eyes.

"When I was fourteen, my father decided I needed to get laid," he said, voice gruff as he spoke. My attention snapped back to his face. He was still staring at the lake, or the sky, or whatever, just not at me. "It wasn't like I had lack of options. A lot of kids my age were already getting action. I just..." He shrugged. "I wasn't in a rush to do that, if you can believe it." He let out a harsh laugh, shaking his head. "But one of my best friends at the time, Vinny, your half-brother." He paused to glance in my direction for a beat, then looked away and continued. "He had gotten laid and was boasting about it to anyone who would listen, so my father decided that no way in hell was one of his associates' sons going to one-up his son." He leaned back on the couch, crossing his feet at the ankles. "So, he drove me to someone's house, dropped me off for a few hours, and I got laid."

There was a pregnant pause there, and I licked my lips, unsure of what to say. He went on before I could even form a thought.

"It turned out to be the wife of some guy." He waved a hand. "The mom of one of my friends, actually." He shook his head as if the whole thing annoyed him. "I fucked her, or she fucked me, rather, and I left. The next week, my father dropped me off there again. It became this weekly affair, where we'd fuck, and then she'd tell me things, and my father would pick me up, and demand to hear those things." He glanced at me again, "I was a honey pot, essentially. A spy for my father, who used sex as a means to extract information from the wives of the men he wanted control over. The list was endless."

I nodded my understanding but still didn't speak. What could I possibly say to this? That I was sorry? That seemed like a slap in the face. I knew that was how I'd take it if someone apologized for some guy raping me. Thankfully, Giovanni continued to speak.

"I never had a girlfriend. I mean, I did, but that didn't last very long." He laughed again, unamused. "How could I keep a girlfriend if I was constantly fucking other women?"

I flinched, looking away this time. "Why are you telling me this?"

"I figured it was only fair to tell you my secrets in exchange for yours." He shrugged a shoulder.

"Like a honey pot?" I felt my brows crease.

"I mean, if you want to give me your body and secrets, I'm not going to turn down the offer." His lips lifted, but the amusement didn't last long.

"I don't." I tore my gaze from his, shutting it down before I looked at him again. "I already told you. You have to pick, and based on this conversation, I'm assuming you picked secrets."

"Hm." He shut his eyes shifting his body lower so that his head was resting against the back of the couch. My eyes fell on the gray shirt, which was plastered against his muscled chest and arms. I wasn't sure if to take this as a confirmation or what.

"What do you want to know?"

"Everything." He opened his eyes and pinned me with his gaze. My heart dipped. "I want to know everything about you."

"Everything." I let out a laugh, as unamused as his had been. "I don't know where to start."

"Where were you born?"

"Miami."

"And then you moved back to Queens when you were in high school."

"Someone's been asking questions." I shot him a pointed

look. "If you have all the answers, why the hell are we having this conversation?"

"Would you rather we not talk?" His gaze traveled slowly down my face, down my chest. I began breathing a little heavier under his scrutiny. He met my gaze again. "Would you rather do something else with that mouth of yours?"

"You said you wanted secrets," I whispered. He got up so quickly, I didn't get a chance to move.

He set his hands on either side of me on the couch, his nose just inches from mine. "I said I wanted everything."

"*Everything* is not on the table." I licked my lips.

His eyes darkened as he watched me do it. Instead of asking something else, or saying something else, or even *doing* something else, he sighed heavily and straightened, turning to walk away. He looked at the lake one last time, pointing at the mug on the table with a finger without even looking in my direction.

"Use a fucking coaster." With that, he left me there, heart in my throat, wondering what the fuck had just happened.

CHAPTER THIRTY-ONE

Isabel

I PACKED UP YET ANOTHER BOX ON AUTOPILOT. THESE WERE PILLOWS and throws that I'd be donating. Petra and Joey were sitting outside on the porch, rocking in chairs and smoking a joint, listening to Bob Marley on a small boombox my father kept in his kitchen, as if this was just a casual afternoon. They'd taken care of calling a moving truck to handle the big items while the realtor showed the house virtually. She'd already gotten offers, and no one had even stepped foot inside of it. So, technically Petra and Joey had helped, some, but every time I put tape on one of the boxes, I glared in their direction. Neither of them noticed, or cared, or even offered to help. The least they could've done was offer me some of what they were smoking, but no, they didn't share that either.

I went down to the small basement and looked around. There wasn't much, just a television, a couch, and a small desk with minimal things on it, an old laptop and some small black notebooks. I'd been here countless times and never stepped foot near this desk. There was nothing interesting about it. Now, I sat on the chair and looked at it, really looked at it. He had a calendar that took up nearly the entire surface. On it, he had pictures of us together on the right-hand corner. One of me and him at a Cubs game, smiling at the camera in one of them as he took a selfie, and just him smiling as I kissed his cheek in the other. My dad, the man who was always smiling, always joking, always doing kind things for strangers, was a killer. I couldn't seem to process how those two truths could make up the same man.

I leaned back in the chair and looked around. The house had always felt cozy and unassuming. Everything about him was low key. He didn't buy new clothes or shoes unless he needed them. Didn't wear watches or flashy jewelry, with the exception of the pinky ring finger he never took off. My thoughts narrowed on that. I looked at the pictures, and sure enough, there was the ring. I'd had him buried with it since it was the only thing I knew he loved to wear all the time. Even as I sat there, in a room I'd been in countless times growing up. One we'd watched movies in whenever I was in town. One that still smelled like my father, the immense feeling that I just wanted to go home hit me. It wasn't like I had people waiting for me, besides Luke and Noah and my grandmother whenever she remembered my existence, which wasn't often at all, but it was still home. I was still comforted there, in my city, walking my streets, smelling the disgusting sewers, taking the pain in the ass trains that only worked when they wanted to, listening to people bicker and laugh and joke and try to con everyone out of a dollar. I missed everything about home. My phone buzzed on the table, and I reached for it quickly, frowning when I saw Will's name on the screen.

"Hey." I answered.

"Hey." He paused. "I'm just calling to check up on you."

"Oh. I'm at my dad's house, packing up boxes," I said, "Well, taking a break and resting my arms from packing up boxes."

"I figured you'd be in Chicago," he said. "You're by yourself?"

"Yeah," I said, because I didn't want to explain the guards outside the house.

"So, I owe you an apology."

"What for?" I frowned again.

"I said some pretty mean things to you that night in my— *our* apartment."

"It was warranted." I sat back in the seat.

"That doesn't mean it wasn't mean. I've been feeling like shit over it ever since."

"Well, I forgive you." I sighed, still staring at the picture of me and my father. "I figured since you didn't try to come after me, it was for the best."

"Try to..." He laughed. "How could I go after you? Giovanni Masseria made it clear that wasn't an option."

"What?" I sat straight up in the chair, heart thundering in my ears. "What are you talking about?"

"Wow. I should've figured he'd keep you in the dark."

"About what?" I snapped. "Tell me."

"He told me to stay away from you. He also threatened me and made me back away from that fucking theater he's determined to renovate for who knows what reason, probably to have another place to launder money through," he mumbled, practically whispering the last part to himself.

"I didn't know." I licked my lips. "Not that it's worth anything, since the outcome would've been the same."

"I supposed." He cleared his throat after a beat. "Anyway, I'm in Chicago for a couple of days for a conference. If you're free..."

"Where are you staying?"

"The Four Seasons."

"Are you free at night?" I asked, eyes on the photograph again.

"I can make myself free."

I smiled at that. "Maybe we can catch a Cubs game?"

"Shoot me a text. I'll be around."

"Okay." I hung up, still smiling.

I realized it was the first time I'd genuinely smiled in days. I knew Giovanni wouldn't be happy about me going anywhere with Will, especially after what he'd just told me, but I was definitely going to keep the plan in my back pocket. If Giovanni didn't come home again tonight, I was going to that damn game.

CHAPTER THIRTY-TWO

Gio

SHE WAS FUCKING RECKLESS. RECKLESS AND SELFISH. SHE'D FOLLOWED my rules of taking Petra and Joey everywhere, all right. She'd taken them straight to Wrigley to watch a game with William fucking Hamilton. I was in the middle of a fucking disaster, on the burner phone with my father. I'd considered calling Silvio to straight up ask him if he was behind all of this, but I knew better than that. He didn't settle things verbally, on the phone, or ever. With Silvio, if you crossed him, you were done. In this instance, I was positive my father was regretting the day they'd kissed each other's pinky ring and called each other brothers.

"He needs to be taken care of," my father kept saying. "Take care of this, Giovanni."

I nodded, even though he couldn't see me, and drew in a breath. When I looked down at my desk, a text from Petra was coming in telling me that Isabel was going to a game with William Hamilton. I could barely push through the rest of the conversation with my father, as enraged as I was. That was how I found myself on a treadmill, running as I listened to the sound of my feet on the belt beneath me and my breath as I tried to maintain it level. This usually worked. This and fucking, but I wasn't doing the latter, and I was regretting that this moment. I picked up the phone and called Dean first. He always had answers, and I was hoping by now he had a hint of who went into the vault, but he didn't answer his phone, so I assumed he was still working on getting them. I hit dial on Lorenzo next. He answered and I told him more or less what my father told me, leaving out the obvious words since you never really knew who could be listening to these conversations.

"You know I can't say anything about that," Lorenzo said.

I knew he couldn't since Silvio was his fucking uncle, but I hoped he would since he was my brother-in-law and friend. I exhaled heavily as I got to my third mile.

"Did you look at the camera feed?"

"Yeah. Black ski masks. There was one short guy and two average build, they were covered in camo head to toe, as if they were expecting war."

"But they weren't. Someone let them in."

"Do you think…"

He didn't even bother finishing the sentence. It was what we'd all been wondering. Was Mike screwing us over? Did he set this up? He easily could, but why would he? I couldn't fathom it. He had to know he'd be killed for it. Fuck. I hated that thought. People often thought that it was easy to kill someone who betrayed you, but you only felt betrayal from those closest to you and getting rid of them was gut wrenching. It wasn't something I'd ever had to do. I knew my father had to once. Dean had to once. I'd never wanted to be put in this position, so I'd chosen to surround myself with people who wouldn't turn into Judas.

"I don't know what to think." I shut off the treadmill.

"I don't want to think what I'm thinking," he said. "We can't do anything about it right now. Let's take the night. I have some guys working on it and they'll keep working on it until they find something. Get some rest, G. You look like shit."

"You can't even see me." I scowled as I headed to the showers.

"I've been seeing you these last few days and you've looked like shit the entire time. Get some sleep. We'll continue this tomorrow."

"Call me as soon as—"

"I know." He hung up on me.

I showered, taking extra-long under the spray of hot water.

The robbery was stressing me out, and somehow, instead of obsessing over my missing Rolexes and Phillip watches, I was obsessing over Isabel being at that stupid game. Lorenzo told me to take the night and I was going to. I was tired as fuck. It wasn't like I didn't need one, but with every second that ticked by my fury rose little by little until I felt like I was going to explode with it. I finished my showered, changed, and went back to my office. Nadia was still there, going through numbers, rubbing her eyes as she looked at the screen.

"You need to go home."

"I thought you were going home early?" She looked up at where I was standing by the door.

"I went downstairs."

"To work out?"

"What else is downstairs?"

"Why don't you just go home? You need rest, G."

"I've heard." I dragged a hand through my hair.

"You're a little more on edge than usual," she said. I shot her a look. She ignored it. "The liquor is getting to the club tonight. Are you going to be there?"

"I'll have John handle it."

"Are you on edge like this because Isabel is at a game with William?"

That was definitely the current reason. I stopped pacing, turned to her. "Petra told you."

"Isabel told me." She pressed her lips together. "She was trying to gauge how upset you'd be."

"And?" I asked, trying and failing not to shout.

"I told her you wouldn't like it."

"And?" I said again, louder.

Nadia flinched. "Jesus, lower your fucking voice."

I growled and started pacing again, shutting my eyes as I tried to breathe through the anger. Breath in, breath out. Repeat.

I'd just taken off the damn bandages today and I already felt like I needed to punch something else.

"She said you were never home anyway," Nadia continued, "Which, I told her was exactly what she should get used to if she chose to stay with you. A lot of lonely, sleepless nights."

"You told her that?" I stopped walking in front of the desk and stared at her. "Why would you say that?"

"Because it's the damn truth, Gio." She shook her head. "Anyone who tries to tame you deserves to know the ugly truth about that up front."

Tame me. I scoffed. Like I was some wild animal. What a load of shit. People didn't get tamed, they chose to be tame. I took a seat in a chair across from her and picked up a stress ball she had sitting on the desk, squeezing it. "I take it she didn't like that answer."

"It seemed like she already knew that. She said if you didn't call or come home after work, she was going to the game, so she did."

"She could have called me and told me she wanted to go to the fucking game." I threw the stress ball against the wall. "I would've taken her."

"Really? You would have left your meeting, left whatever else it is you're trying to handle right now, and gone to the game with her?"

"Yes."

She raised an eyebrow. "Really, G?"

"I said yes, god damn it. Why is this happening?" I buried my face in my hands and tugged on my hair. "This woman is going to give me a god damn heart attack."

"Seems like it," Nadia quipped. "Still no news on Evelyn?"

I groaned at the sound of my mother's name, pressed the heels of my palms harder against my eyes. "Nope."

"She hasn't called Cat or Emma?"

"Nope."

"Geez."

"Mother of the century, am I right?" I dropping my hands.

"Right." She eyed me peculiarly. "I heard the meeting got pushed forward."

"Yep. Fucking Silvio." I stared at a dark spot of wood on her desk. That was another curious thing, Silvio wanting the meeting moved forward to fill that seat ASAP.

"It'll mean Isabel can finally go home and leave this all behind," she said. I didn't like the sound of that at all, and Nadia seemed to notice, because she added, "I guess you could try courting her the way a normal person would if you truly wanted to date her."

"Maybe I will."

"Do you even know what that entails?" She raised an eyebrow, looking entirely too amused for my liking.

"I've courted people, Nadia." I shot her a look.

"Name one and if you say Natasha, I'm going to throw this stapler at your face."

I sighed and looked away. That was exactly who I was going to say.

"Natasha was all over you the moment you met. It was just, we're together now, and that was that." Nadia laughed. "Kind of funny, really, since she was the one who asked you out on your first actual date, so I guess in a sense, she courted you."

"I like women who take initiative." I shrugged. I did.

"And Isabel doesn't."

"Isabel won't even let me fucking touch her."

Nadia's brows hiked up. "So, I'm assuming you're seeing someone else at the moment."

"Wrong."

"You're, what, practicing celibacy?" Nadia laughed loudly, throwing her head back.

"It's not fucking funny."

"It kind of is, G. When was the last time you tried to do this?"

"Never." I scowled. "Why would anyone do this willingly?"

"*You're* doing it willingly, moron."

"No, I'm doing it because Isabel won't let me touch her. I thought we covered this already." I kicked the desk by mistake as I tried to get comfortable in the seat. The fucking stapler shook and fell over. "I'm over here, running six miles, waiting around, not even paying any mind to any woman who even looks in my direction, and she's at a fucking baseball game with her ex-boyfriend."

"So, go to the game." Nadia shrugged.

Fuck. "If I go, I'll kill him."

"Why?" She laughed again.

"Because I feel like it."

Her laughter died instantly, her eyes bouncing between mine as if she was trying to figure something out. "You're serious."

"Glad we're finally on the same page."

"Holy shit." Nadia sat back in her seat. "You're in love with her."

"She won't open up and tell me anything about her past. How the fuck could I be in love with her? What even is that?"

She pressed her lips together and shook her head slowly. "I don't know, G. It seems like you are."

"I'm not."

"Okay." She shrugged, reaching for her phone and typing something. She stared at it while she waited for a response to whatever she'd sent someone, then tilted her phone so I could see the screen. It was a picture of Isabel sitting next to William. She was wearing a too-big-for-her Sammy Sosa jersey and a backwards Cubs cap, her head thrown back in laughter as William smiled at her. The look he was giving her. I knew that fucking look. I stood up, the chair I'd been sitting on tipping over with the force of my movement.

"Yeah, he's dead."

I walked out of the office, calling Tony on my way down.

CHAPTER THIRTY-THREE

Isabel

WILL AND I WERE WALKING SIDE BY SIDE AS WE EXITED THE stadium. We left at the bottom of the sixth inning, since the Cubs were winning by a landslide, and Will had to be up at six in the morning for his first meeting. It was me, Will, Petra, Joey, and one of Will's security guys. Five of us, yet the moment I looked forward and saw Giovanni leaning against his black SUV, I knew we'd be no match for him. He was looking at me like he wanted to douse me in gasoline and set me on fire on the spot, his jaw tense, his expression blank, but those eyes, fuck, those eyes said everything. I swallowed. My heart raced as I continued walking, keeping my eyes on his, silently praying that he wouldn't do anything stupid.

"I guess someone is trying to stake his claim," Will said beside me. He stopped walking. I stopped walking. The other three people also stopped walking, creating somewhat of a barrier between us and Giovanni, but I knew that was as much of a façade as the nonchalant expression on his face. Will and I faced each other.

"Thanks for coming," I said.

"You know I'm always here for you." He smiled. "Always."

"You've always proved that to be true."

"Well, I guess this is goodbye, for now." He opened his arms and enveloped me in a hug.

I returned it kind of half-assed because I swore I could feel Giovanni's rage kick up ten notches from all the way over here. When we separated, he walked away with his security guy, shooting a quick look over his shoulder in Giovanni's direction. I let out a breath as I turned to where he stood. He looked so casual against the SUV, that if not for the hard expression on his face and the darkness brewing in his eyes, I would've thought he was picking me up for a date or something. I closed the distance between us, stopping two steps away from him and crossing my arms.

"I'm surprised to see you here," I said. "I didn't know you ever got off work before dawn."

"Right." That was all he said, eyes unblinking, hard on mine.

"I guess you're here to berate me for going to a game with Will, but before you even start, I want to make it clear that it wasn't a date. He was just accompanying me to a ball game. As a friend. That's all." I searched his eyes. Nothing. His jaw, though. He might need to visit the dentist office tomorrow as hard as his teeth were grinding.

"Who's is that?" His eyes dropped to the jersey I wore.

"My dad's."

A nod before he looked away. My heart sank into my stomach. I was completely out of my element here. Will was nice, readable, easy. Giovanni was the complete opposite. He was difficult and seemed impenetrable, though he had his moments. At least, with me, he had his moments. The things he'd confessed to me were real, and personal, and had clearly hurt him. *Still* hurt him.

"Gio," I whispered, finally, unable to take it. He looked at me. "Can you say something? Anything?"

"What would you like me to say?"

"Well, you can start by telling me what you're doing here."

"I was going to go inside to watch the rest of the game with you, but obviously I got here too late for that."

"Oh." I felt myself frown. "Why?"

"Why what?" he asked, voice clipped.

"Why would you want to watch the game with me?"

He shot me a look.

"If you say because I'm your wife, I'm going to claw your eyes out," I warned.

At that, he smiled. This guy. "I'd take it because that would mean you have to touch me. That's where I'm at right now, Isabel. I would rather you claw my eyes out than continue to put this distance between us, or whatever the fuck it is you're doing."

I swallowed, pressing my lips together and looking away briefly, eyes on the buildings across from us, filled with people cheering and watching the game from rooftop bars. I was envious of them in that moment, even though I knew seeming carefree for a few hours didn't mean you didn't have worries. I thought about what I was about to tell him. It may seem like nothing at all to him. My story seemed like nothing in comparison to some of the students I had over the years. I'd learned, though, that it didn't matter who had it better or worse. Everyone went through their own kind of hell. Just because I hadn't been physically beat at home, didn't mean the things I'd endured were any less traumatic. I took a deep breath and looked at Giovanni again.

"When I was eight, my grandfather died. I never met him. He was back in Cuba. My grandmother was holding on to the hope that he'd move over here at some point, but instead, he was murdered. Brutally murdered. Because he'd spoken up against the government." I licked my lips to pause. "My grandmother was the closest thing I had to a parent. She was kind and fun and made me forget that I lived in a broken home, but when he died everything changed. Overnight, she became callous and began acting like she couldn't even stand the sight of me. My mother was already barely there, and when she was, she was just as bad, so I had two mean people in the house, constantly telling me I'd never be enough. Never be pretty enough or smart enough. Every day, I heard that reminder from sunup to sundown. They never hit me. Maybe once or twice, but their weapon of choice was words. They didn't hug me, kiss me, nothing. They fed me and kept a roof over my head and that was enough to be grateful for, I guess." I took a breath. "The only time I felt happy was when my father picked me up. Genuine happiness. I'd beg to go live with him. I'd beg him not to drop me off. I never told him why, of course, but he must have known. How could he not?"

I looked down at the dirty white converse on my feet. "I obviously started looking for attention elsewhere. Luke and Noah's mom helped as much as she could. When boys started paying attention to me, I felt special, until I didn't." I scrunched my nose as I thought about it. "I liked the emotional attention, but they were handsy and I wasn't interested in that. Every single man I've ever come into contact with wanted my body, wanted to use me, you know." I shrugged a shoulder. "I was able to fend most of them off, until that night in college. Then, suddenly, I felt truly powerless. Then, suddenly I did feel unworthy and like a failure." I took another breath to continue. Gio remained quiet and unmoved. I didn't know if he was even listening, but now I needed to purge myself of all of it.

"So, anyway, you know what happened that night. I went home, got Dad to buy me a knife." I smiled sadly. "Learned how to use it from YouTube videos. Took some self-defense, blah blah blah, stabbed some people, blah blah blah. Went back to college even though I had daily panic attacks and vivid nightmares. I roomed with a friend, Eloise, because I was so scared to be alone. I graduated, got my masters online because at that point I was holding on to my sanity by a thread and couldn't be on campus anymore. I got a job, kept my head down, hung out with Dad when I could. Mom had already left for Spain with this new guy that I don't even know. Mima's in a nursing home. Mima's my grandma." I paused to make sure he was

still following. "She has onset dementia. Sometimes she re-
members me. Most of the time she thinks I'm my mom and
sits there insulting the fuck out of me." I laughed, shaking my
head. "It's actually pretty funny when I think about it. I'm the
only one who cares enough to visit her, despite everything, and
she still treats me like shit."

Another deep breath. People cheered in the distance,
drunk people walked out of the stadium. I looked up at him
again, noticing that his expression had finally softened slightly.
"So, yeah, I re-connected with Will at an event for school, we
started dating, and the moment he mentioned moving in, I said
hell yeah."

"Because you hate to be alone," he said, startling me when
he finally spoke.

"Pretty much." I nodded. "He's a good guy. A great guy,"
I said. Giovanni's jaw clenched again. "I just wish I'd felt differ-
ently about him."

"How do you feel about me?"

I let out a surprised laugh. "You make me feel crazy."

"Then, we're on the same page."

"That's not a good thing."

"Because you'd rather go home to your boring, vanilla
boyfriend and fake smile for cameras for the rest of your life?"

I glanced up at him, narrowing my eyes. "Who said the
smiles were fake?"

"Were they real?" He straightened. I bit my lip and looked
away. "Isabel." I looked at him again, wondering if this was
when he'd finally touch me. I'd let him. I wouldn't even hold it
against him if he did. Instead, he said, "What happened to you
wasn't your fault, and no matter what anyone told you, you are
enough."

"Thank you for saying that," I whispered, swallowing and
blinking away the tears I felt pricking my eyes.

"So, can we go now?"

"Where?"

"Home." He looked at me as if to say, *where else?*

"Okay."

We rode in the backseat of the SUV together, in silence. We were sitting on complete opposite ends of it. He was so close to his door, I thought he might open it and jump out at any moment. I kept replaying his words over and over. *What happened to you wasn't your fault. You are enough.* I hadn't realized how badly I needed someone to say those things to me until that moment.

"So," I started, since I never finished my story. "All of my best memories were with a man who was lying to me the entire time."

"And you think I'd be that man." He glanced over. "You think I'll let you down eventually?"

"I don't want to think that."

"But you do." He shook his head, looked away again. "Just like you thought I was fucking another woman just because you weren't touching me."

"I didn't know what to think."

"Not that." He met my gaze again. "I know my reputation sucks, but I don't want you to ever worry about that. I wouldn't do that to you."

"Okay." I swallowed. "Still, you have to understand why I'm not cut out for this...life."

"I understand why you think that. It doesn't mean I agree."

Nothing else was said. We arrived at his place, took the elevator up. Everyone else kind of idled downstairs. I walked straight to his room, taking my shoes and socks off the minute I walked in the door and doing the same with the jersey I wore, but one of the buttons was stuck. Underneath, I was wearing a white sleeveless camisole and a white lace bra that matched my underwear. I wasn't going to completely undress in his bedroom, though. It would give him the wrong idea. Or maybe the right idea. I didn't even know anymore. Giovanni walked in the room. I turned and watched him shut the door with the back of his foot. He looked at the bed for a moment, which I'd made before I left, and then looked at me, pinning me with an intense stare. My heart began to gallop. I forced myself to look away, focusing on the stupid button again.

"Isabel."

"What?" I stopped fidgeting with my clothes.

"Let me touch you."

My eyes widened, snapping to his. "What?"

"Let me touch you." He closed the distance between us and held his hand out, turning it over again, waiting for mine, the way I had when I'd wrapped his hands that night.

I stared at it for a moment. Alarm bells went off in my head, telling me to back away, to not give in, but my need for him screamed louder, tearing all of those warnings apart. As terrified as I was, something inside of him called to me. I knew giving myself completely to him meant he'd keep large pieces of me forever. I'd end up broken and alone once he was done with me. I knew I would.

"I told you my secrets," I whispered, still staring at his hand. "Isn't that what you wanted?"

"I told you I want everything."

"You can't." I met his eyes again. His hand was still there. "*I* can't."

"Give me a reason." He dropped his hand.

"One?" I scoffed. "I have a lot."

"Start with one."

"You're not a boyfriend kind of guy."

"You can't know that. We haven't tried. And for you? I'd fucking try every day, I promise."

I inhaled sharply at that, my eyes growing wide again. I knew he meant that. I felt it deep in my core. "Do you think you can be a *one-woman* kind of guy, though?" I swallowed, looking down. I hated asking that question. Hated the silence that followed it.

"Look at me."

I did.

"In the past, I haven't been, but now I know that I'm a one-woman kind of guy." He searched my face. "I need you to trust me. Do you think you can do that?"

"I don't know," I whispered, searching his eyes. "Will you trust me?"

His eyes widened slightly. He wasn't expecting that. After a beat, he said, "I trust you completely."

"Even when other men say or do things that you don't like, you'll trust that I'm yours?"

His eyes darkened. "You're mine?"

"Isn't that what we're discussing? Me being yours and you being mine?"

"Fuck." He let out a harsh laugh with an exhaled breath as he looked up at the ceiling for a moment. "Now I really need to touch you. Is there anything else on this ridiculous list of yours?"

My heart skipped. "Yes. You don't know me, not really. And vice versa."

"I know everything I need to know." His eyes dropped to my mouth and moved back to my eyes. "Whatever we don't know, we learn together."

"Oh my God." I laughed, looking up at the ceiling for a moment. "This is insane."

"That you're considering it?"

I met his gaze again and nodded. I wasn't even *considering* it anymore, and he seemed to know that. He lifted his hand again, turning it over. This time, I put mine in his and he pulled me into him with such a force, my cheek hurt as it crashed into his hard chest. His arms engulfed me as he squeezed and breathed me, inhaling me deeply.

"Thank fuck," he said against my hair. "God, I needed this."

"A hug? All this time and what you wanted was a hug?" I smiled against his chest.

"I want everything." He exhaled against the top of my head, letting out a chuckle that permeated through me. "I guess William Hamilton will live to see another day, after all."

"He didn't do anything, Gio." I laughed against his chest.

"He had his arms around you." He pulled away slightly, setting a finger under my chin to tilt my face up. "If Natasha walked over here and gave me a hug like that after I told you that you couldn't touch me, how would you feel?"

"I'd want to stab her between the ribs."

"Fuck, Isabel." He shook his head as he looked at me for a moment before stepping forward. He brought his mouth to mine and kissed me then, a slow, thorough kiss, his tongue exploring my mouth and teasing my tongue. I moaned against him, pressing into him even more. He pulled away, keeping his lips against mine. "You'll be the death of me, I swear."

My exhale came out shuddered as he pressed his lips back to mine, his fingers skating down the sides of my body. I lifted my arms for him to pull the camisole over my head. He took a step back, closing his eyes and groaning momentarily before opening them again, a new fire blazing in them.

"It should be illegal for you to walk around wearing this underneath your clothes." He shook his head slowly as he tugged the thin straps of my bra, letting them fall over my shoulders. He reached behind me and took it off. He pinned me with his gaze. "Any other night, I'd make you keep this on and fuck you in it." He started working on my shorts, letting them pool over my feet, biting his bottom lip when he saw the white lace matching thong. He brought his eyes back to mine. "Any other night, but I'm starving for you, desperate to have you again." His hand dipped into my panties, his head lowering to catch a nipple in his mouth.

"Fuck." I set my hands on his shoulders, gripping the suit jacket he still had on. "Take this off."

He stepped back and obliged, kicking his shoes out of the way and shrugging out of the blazer. I worked on the buttons of his shirt while he took his pants off. We were in a lust-filled craze as we ripped at each other's clothes, kissing in between each item we tossed aside. He grabs my breasts, massaging them in his hands as he leans forward to lick a trail up my neck. A shiver rolls through my entire body.

"I'm going out of my mind for you," he said below my ear before taking my earlobe into his mouth and sucking. He moved back to my breasts again, taking each nipple into his mouth and sucking, biting. I gripped his shoulders, sinking my nails into his shoulder blades. He sucked harder. I threw my head back with a moan and he let go of my nipples and started sucking on my exposed neck, one hand moving to cup me between my legs, sliding his fingers up and down my folds. "Now that I have you, I don't even know where to start."

"Anywhere," I breathed, grinding against his fingers. "God, that feels good."

He took my mouth into his again, still moving his fingers as he turned us and guided me down to the bed, an edge to his expression as he watched me and continued to move his fingers, dipping one, then two, inside of me, before bringing them out and running them through my folds, to my clit. I began to move against his hand again, chasing the pleasure that was building.

"I want you to fuck my mouth like this," he said, voice low and gruff, adding another finger, pushing against my clit, sucking on my chest. It was all too much at once. The orgasm crashed into me like an unexpected wave. Gio didn't relent. He moved down my body and gripped my ass as he lifted me off the bed, putting his mouth where his hands had just been.

My hands found his hair and tugged as I shook. "I can't."

Lick.

"Gio. I can't," I said, legs shaking, core clenching.

He sucked my clit, groaning against me as the second orgasm hit me. He licked around his mouth as he set me down, a wild look in his eyes as he watched me come down from the orgasm. He left me briefly to take off his boxer briefs, and I sat up on me elbows to look at him. He was truly a marvel of a man, chiseled and hard and huge. He reached into his nightstand and pulled out a condom, ripping it with his teeth as he moved back between my legs, but I sat up quickly, grasping his shaft with my hand and stroking it. His fingers sank into my hair, gripping and pulling me up so we're both on our knees, my hand still moving between us. He stared into me as his breathing deepened, his hand gripping tighter with each stroke. He leaned in, crashing his mouth to mine in a punishing kiss that feels like it'll instantly leave a bruise. I kissed him back with the same intensity, tasting myself on his mouth as I stroked him, his grip in my hair making my eyes prick with hot tears. It hurt, but it also felt so good. After another stroke, I leaned in and licked the tip.

"No. Fuck no." He growled, yanking my hair back so that I couldn't put my mouth on him. If you do that, I'll come right now."

My breathing quickened at his words, at the realization that this man wanted me that badly. I licked my lips as I watched him roll the condom over himself. He leaned back into me, kissing me again, lying me down on my back as he pulled my legs up to settle between them. He gave no warning before thrusting in, deep and hard. I heard a scream rip out of me as I arched my back at the feel of him as he stretched me.

"That's right. Scream for me, baby. Let everyone know

you're mine." He fucked me harder then, his cock so deep inside me, that I could barely breathe, let alone utter coherent words, but scream, I did. Another orgasm tore through me, this one shaking my entire body against him. When I opened my eyes, I shuddered again because he was looking at me with an expression I'd never seen on his face. Open, vulnerable, so fucking scary, because it felt different. It made me feel different. He moved in slow thrusts, sucking the tips of my fingers as I lowered them from his hair, kissing the backs of my thighs as he rearranged my legs, setting them down on the bed, keeping his movements slow and gentle. "You feel this, Isabel," he whispered, "I know you fucking feel it."

My pulse throbbed behind my ears. Something passed between us in that moment. I didn't know what, but it was definitely something I'd never experienced before. Something that both terrified me and excited me. He brought his forehead down against mine before taking my lips in his again, a slow, sensual sweep of my mouth with his tongue. My heart pounded harder and harder with each thing he did. Another orgasm shot through me when he said my name again, and again, and again, tensing above me, grunting with one final thrust before coming down over me with an exhale. I let out an oof sound as his body crashed into mine. He was too heavy for me to move. I froze beneath him. It was something I wouldn't have normally allowed. I was always on top and when I wasn't, I didn't necessarily like to be hovered over too much. Our breaths fell into the same rhythm after a moment, and instead of pushing him away and demanding he get off me, I wrapped my arms and legs around him.

"Hey, Isabel," he murmured against my neck.

"Yeah?"

"Can we get rid of the fucking moat between us on the bed?"

I laughed loudly, and he squeezed me as he turned us over so we were facing each other. "Yes, Gio."

His eyes searched mine. "I like it when you call me that."

"Yeah?" I felt my brows pull in slightly. "I thought you liked it when I said your name."

"I do, but this makes me feel like you're finally comfortable with me." He kissed me again, softly, before getting up and walking over to the bathroom.

I stayed in that position, staring at the pillows. I *did* feel comfortable with him. It was an odd thing, considering his reputation and the way he discarded women. When he walked back to the bed, he threw the pillows to the other side of the room as he climbed back in and pulled me to his chest, wrapping his arms around me tightly.

"I would never hurt you," he said against my hair. "You have to know that."

I nodded against him. I believed him. He made me feel safe, though. Comfortable. He made me feel—period. I should've probably been terrified, but I was tired of playing it safe.

CHAPTER THIRTY-FOUR

I WOKE UP WITH GIO'S HEAD BETWEEN MY LEGS, HIS TONGUE LAPPING my folds and his mouth closing over my clit, sucking. I gasped, sitting up on my elbows as I looked at him, my hand reaching, fingers threading into his hair.

"God, that feels good." I rocked against his mouth.

He groaned deeply, the sound radiating through me with such force, I had to bite my lip to keep from crying out. He swiped the back of his tongue over my clit, his dark eyes meeting mine as I continued to move, unable to stop my hips from rocking. The hand he had gripping my inner thigh moved and he slipped one finger inside of me, pressing his mouth against my clit again. Two fingers, then. My back arched, hips bucking. Three fingers.

"Yes," he growled against me. "Keep riding me, baby. My hand, my mouth. Keep riding me."

"Fuck. I'm going to—" I inhaled sharply.

"I know. I got you." He really started to feast on me then, fingers and mouth finding the exact spots I needed him to press in order to push me over the edge.

The orgasm rolled through me, blinding me for a moment with its power. I was still panting when he moved between my legs, pressing both hands on either side of my head. His forehead tipped mine, and I raised my eyes to his. The way he looked at me was indescribable. I'd tried to put it in words when I sorted out my thoughts and how I felt about him, but it was impossible. It had never been this way for me with anyone, and I knew that to be true for him as well. We were both out of our element here. Somehow, that made me feel better about the situation. We were both figuring it out together, as he'd said we would. He pressed his mouth to my forehead. I reached and grabbed his ass in my hands, squeezing him closer to me, hoping he'd apply pressure where I needed him, but he remained unmoved, a statue above me.

"Gio," I whispered.

"Give me a moment." He swallowed, mouth still pressed against my forehead.

I couldn't imagine what he needed a moment for. He was hard and thick, and the tip of his cock was glistening with pre-cum. The urge to reach out and wrap my hand around him was immense, but I did as he said. He lowered his face, pressing his mouth to the side of my neck, sucking there, licking, biting, still unmoved above me. I started to writhe beneath him. I needed him inside me, needed it like I needed air.

"Patience." He pulled back slightly, shooting an amused look at me.

"Please," I breathed, biting my lip. I was whining, but I didn't even care.

"You want my cock inside you?" he moved me so that I was higher in the bed and wrapped a hand around himself as he began moving the tip of his cock over my clit, up and down my folds.

"Fuck." My hips circled. "Please. Please."

"Tell me you want me." He locked eyes with me, then, the darkness in his eyes brewing. "Tell me."

"I want you." I grinded against his cock, taking whatever, he could give me, needing him to make me come again. "Please. I want you. I want you so bad."

"How bad?" He cocked an eyebrow, sliding his cock down my wet folds again, applying pressure right at my entrance, but not thrusting inside.

Oh, my God. My head slammed back onto the bed. "You're going to kill me."

"There are worse ways to go."

"I can't imagine." I wrapped my legs around his waist, pulling him closer, but he didn't budge. He was staring at me, that stupid smirk on his face that normally I liked but right now I wanted to kill him for. I let myself drop onto the bed, my back flat, and brought my hands to my breasts, tweaking my nipples as he looked down at me.

"Fuck." He bit his lip, thrusting against me, still not inside. "You're so wet."

"I know."

"Soaking, baby."

"I know." My hips moved again, my fingers twisting my nipples. I felt the orgasm building again, my legs shaking slightly with it. I was close. He grabbed my wrists with one of his hands and held my arms over my head, stilling against me. I gasped. I was right there, right there, and he'd stopped. I shook my head side to side, eyes wide on his. "No, no, no. Please keep going."

"This okay?" he asked, squeezing my wrists over my head. I swallowed and nodded. I knew what he was asking, but I trusted him. He leaned down, pressing a kiss to my lips, then my jawline, my neck. He brought his mouth to my ear. "You sure?"

"I'm positive, Giovanni, but for the love of God, please fuck me."

He chuckled, pulling away again. "I fully intend to."

"Right now." I moved my entire body as much as I could, which admittedly wasn't much with the way he was on top of me. "Please."

"Hm." He groaned against my chest, lowering slightly to pull a nipple into his mouth. "I love it when you beg for my cock."

My eyes squeezed shut. "Please, please."

"You want your husband to fuck you?"

My eyes popped opened. I nodded fiercely.

"Say it. Tell me."

"I want my husband to fuck me." I arched my back slightly.

He let go of himself with the hand that wasn't holding my wrists and started playing with my clit again. "Oh my God."

"Is your pussy mine, Isabel?" He bit my earlobe.

"Yes." I moved my hips. "Fuck. Yes. It's yours. I'm yours."

"You gonna let me fuck you like this?" he asked. No condom, that was what he meant. We'd already had a conversation about this. An unsexy one, as we brushed our teeth yesterday. I'd confided that I'd never done it that way. He'd said he only had once, when he was fifteen, and then he panicked, so he'd never done it again.

"Tell me." He gripped his cock harder, breathing heavier as he slid up and down the folds of my pussy. I was so wet. So wet.

"Yes," I gasped. "Please."

"Please what, baby?"

"Please fuck me like that. Now."

"Why?" He searched my eyes, fire blazing in his.

"Because I need it. Because I need you. Because I'm yours." I shuddered. "Please, Gio."

He made a sound in the back of his throat that made a shiver roll down the length of my spine as he took his hand off my clit and impaled me. That was the only word for it, as I screamed, my entire body bowing off the bed, my arms coming up with the force of it, but he held them down as he fucked me in hard, deep thrusts, that I felt everywhere inside me. My legs started to shake uncontrollably, now, another orgasm crashing through me with force. He slowed his movements then.

"Look at me," he said, his voice low above me. I did, my heart skipping a beat the moment our eyes met. "You feel this, Isabel."

I bit my lip as I nodded my response, my eyes falling closed again.

Holy shit, I was going to come again. I felt it building, but just as I was about to fall apart, he'd stop and slow his movements even more. Tears sprung in my eyes. It was too much, too much pressure and too much pleasure. I forced myself to open my eyes again and look at him. What we shared was insane, and yet, I couldn't imagine my life without him anymore. When I thought about that possibility, I wanted to curl up into a ball and die. It was powerful. He let go of my wrists. I brought my hands to him, to his chest, clawing his pecs, and to his jaw, scraping my short fingernails down his jaw, his hair pricking the tips of my fingers. I watched as he thrust into me slowly, his head falling back with a deep groan.

"I love you," I said on a breath.

He stopped moving, eyes popping open as he looked down at me. He stayed inside me, though, his cock pulsating, bringing me a ting of pleasure even without the movement. His gaze was unreadable, making me squirm slightly, but I wouldn't take the words back. I meant what I'd said, and even if this wasn't who I was supposed to be with, this was what I felt for him.

"I love you," I said again. "You don't have to—"

"I love you, Isabel." He brought his face down and closed his mouth on mine with a punishing kiss. He started moving again, thrusting deeper, harder. "Fuck. I love you."

I came again. There was no stopping it this time. He emptied himself inside me, my name on his lips in a chant I'd grown to love. Afterwards, he wrapped his arms around me and turned us sideways on the bed, kissing my shoulder, my neck, squeezing me in his arms.

"I'm never letting you go."

I smiled at his words and closed my eyes, falling asleep again.

CHAPTER THIRTY-FIVE

IOVANNI'S PANCAKES WERE TEN TIMES BETTER THAN JOEY'S, BUT I didn't say that aloud since I didn't want to hurt Joey's feelings. It was comical since the complete pancake mix had come from the same box. All you needed to do was add water. Petra and Joey both got up and cleared their plates, washing them quickly before announcing they were going downstairs. I was still working on mine, lathering it with syrup. When I looked up, I found Gio watching me with a funny look on his face. Disgust? Maybe. Either way, it made me laugh.

He pointed at my plate with his fork. "You use a little boop of fake sugar in your coffee, yet you drown your pancakes in syrup?"

"It's my cheat meal." I shrugged, smiling as I popped a piece of the pancake in my mouth and closed my eyes with a groan. So, so good. When I opened them Gio was now watching me with a completely different expression, one that went straight between my legs.

"Why do you visit your grandmother?" he asked suddenly.

"What do you mean?"

"If she was so shitty to you, and still is, why put yourself through that each week?"

I drank some chocolate milk—something Gio said he had every time he made pancakes—and shrugged as I set the glass down. "Maybe I'm a masochist."

"No, you're not," he said, amusement lighting up in his eyes.

I looked up at him as I cut another piece of my pancake. He was watching me, waiting for me to give him an honest answer, but I wasn't sure I had one. No one had ever asked me that question before. Once I was done chewing, I set down my silverware and gave him, and that question, my undivided attention.

"I know what it's like to feel like you're alone in the world, and if I can show up for her right now, I figure I should." I shrugged.

He watched me closely while he chewed, as if looking for an underlying answer or something, but there was none. That was the truth. That was the real reason I went there, time and time again, even when she treated me like shit. Once upon a time, she'd been kind, she'd been loving and caring, and I liked the times when I caught a glimpse of that version of my grandmother. Maybe it was more selfish than it was selfless.

"Does your mom ever visit?" he asked after a moment.

"No. She calls her, though."

"Yet, you make the journey there each week."

"Yep."

"It still doesn't make sense to me." He stabbed another pancake on the plate between us with his fork and set it on his plate.

"You wouldn't visit your mother if she was in a nursing home?" I raised an eyebrow.

"My mother?" He chuckled darkly, shaking his head. "Fuck no."

That made me sad, but I understood that side of things as well. I looked down at the pool of syrup on my plate. I'd never realized how difficult talking about this with someone would be until this moment. It was difficult to explain to anyone, but it felt even more difficult to say it aloud in front of him, since I knew he'd experienced similar circumstances, and he'd been genuinely able to write off his mother in a way that I hadn't. It wasn't like I ever spoke to my mother, but that was a mutual choice at this point. I'd lost count as to how many times my calls went unanswered, so I just stopped trying, and she never did.

"Sometimes she's nice," I said quietly, eyes still on the syrup.

"And that's enough of a reason for you to go? Because sometimes she's nice?" He shook his head, chewing another piece of his pancake and waiting until he swallowed.

"Like I said, I know what it's like to feel alone, but imagine being old and alone. It's sad. So many of the people in there have no one who visits them. Maybe they were all sucky parents, what do I know? But it has to be heartbreaking to selflessly give your all to your children and then not have them return the favor when you're unable to do things on your own."

He looked at me for a long moment, his eyes bouncing between mine, searching my face, skimming down my body, even though I was wearing one of his T-shirts and a pair of shorts, so it wasn't like he could see anything, and yet, goosebumps scattered over me as he did his slow assessment. When his gaze met mine, he shook his head again.

"What?"

"I don't deserve you." He shrugged a shoulder and before I could say anything he added, "I don't think anyone on earth is worthy of you, but if you want to give it to me, I'm going to take all of it. I shouldn't, because I'm a bastard, but I'm too selfish to let you go."

"You're not a bastard." I smiled at him.

"If you knew everything I've done in my life, you'd say I was."

"Well, you don't paint houses," I said with a shrug. "That counts for something."

"Of all the things you now know about your father, is that what bothers you the most?"

"Yes."

"What if all of the people he killed were horrible humans?"

"It would still bother me."

"Why?" he looked completely dumbfounded by this.

"Because, Gio, we're not the ones who should be judging

who's good or bad or getting rid of people," I said. "Besides, people change."

"You really believe that?"

"I'm telling you I do."

He shook his head. "Most people don't change, they just adapt."

"Same difference."

"Not really. Change is change. Adapt comes from the Latin word *aptus*, which means 'fit,' so you're not really changing, you're merely lessening whatever it is you were already doing so the people around you can feel comfortable. Change is a concept and concepts are just perceptions."

"So, what you're saying is that you can't change your philandering ways?" I pointed my fork at him, raising an eyebrow.

"I said *most* people, smartass." He walked around the counter, stopping in front of me and wedging himself between my legs. He ducked down to kiss me, suck my bottom lip into his mouth. "Most people don't have you."

"Only one person has me," I said against his mouth.

"You're goddamn right." He lifted me off the seat and carried me back to his room.

CHAPTER THIRTY-SIX

"SO, ALL I HAVE TO DO IS ACCEPT THE OFFER AND SIGN THE PAPERS and then we're done?" I asked Josh, the realtor, who nodded.

"Basically. It's a good offer," he said, "A cash offer."

"Which will make it painless," I said, since that was what I'd gathered from the first ten times he'd said that it was a good offer. It was, apparently. The value of the home was almost triple what Dad paid for it when he bought it. That in itself was beyond my comprehension. It wasn't that it wasn't a cute home, but it didn't really have much of a yard or even that much space, despite having a basement. I didn't tell the realtor, but I was planning on accepting any offer. I just wanted this done already.

"It'll be the most painless transaction I've made this year, I'll tell you that."

"I believe you." I looked at the papers in front of me and signed on every X necessary. When we finished, I shook his hand and walked out of the real estate office, with Petra and Joey in tow.

"I worked at a realtor office once," Joey said. Petra and I shared a confused look. Joey shrugged. "I did. I cleaned the office every night after they closed."

"Oh. That's more up your alley," Petra said.

"I'm not going to let that offend me."

I laughed. "I actually think you'd make a good realtor."

"Really?" They asked in unison.

I nodded. "This Josh guy virtually did nothing. He put up some pictures and the offers just rolled in."

"You calling me lazy?" Joey frowned, but I could see the smile in his eyes.

"Not lazy." I smiled. "It's just similar to what you do now. You sit, and sit, and sit, and then boom something pops off and you spring into action."

"Shit, how much do realtors get paid?" Petra took out of her phone.

Joey and I laughed as we reached the SUV and headed back to Gio's place. It had been an amazing week. Blissful, even. So much so, that I was afraid to let myself get too excited out of fear that it'll blow up in my face, but deep down, I knew there was really no reason for me to feel that way. Luke and Noah told me the same thing. *"Stop being negative. Just stick to the happy stuff,"* Noah said. Meanwhile, Luke couldn't believe I was actually dating Gio. He couldn't wrap his head around any of it, but the more we spoke, the more he agreed that I sounded genuinely happy and Gio sounded like a decent guy, despite everything he'd heard. It was another thing I was grateful for. Because I hadn't really heard of Gio before all of this, I couldn't impose judgement on him. I could only do that with what I had now, and somehow, I'd truly fallen in love with him and decided that it didn't matter who he was before or who he'd be tomorrow, because I still loved him.

His car was in his parking spot when we got back to the condo. Butterflies instantly swarmed my stomach. At the sight of his car. I inwardly laughed at myself. I'd seen so many women go through this and never thought I'd be one of them, yet here I was. I moved quickly, aching to get upstairs and see him again, even though I'd seen him this morning and he'd left late to the office. Joey and Petra stayed downstairs while I took the elevator up to the penthouse, which I didn't question, since they often stayed behind unless Gio called them and told them to come up.

When the elevators opened, it was completely silent. Not unlikely, since Gio apparently didn't listen to music while he was home. He wasn't in the kitchen or living room or his bed-room. I found him in his closet, shirtless, wearing only jeans as he looked through T-shirts. I'd never seen him wearing jeans be-fore, and I took a moment to admire the view. His eyes snapped up when he heard me.

"You're home early." I crossed my arms and leaned against the doorframe of the closet.

"I figured I'd take you on a date." He set the stack of folded T-shirts down on the island in the closet and walked to-ward me, his eyes taking me in entirely as my heart beat wildly against my chest.

"For real this time?" I asked, unable to speak louder than a whisper, with the way he was looking at me.

He closed the distance between us, brought a hand up to my chin and tilted it slightly to kiss me, just a peck, then another, be-fore pulling away. I kept my arms crossed because I knew if I un-crossed them and touched him, the way my fingers were burning to, we would never leave. It was what happened every other night when he promised he'd take me on a date. We'd start touching, kissing, fucking, and always ended up staying in. I wasn't com-plaining, but I did want to go somewhere.

"For real this time." Another peck before pulling away again and walking back to the T-shirts.

"Where are we going?" I asked, trying and failing not to ogle him again. It was impossible, though. My eyes trailed down his body and caught the love marks on his torso, the scratches on his shoulder. My stomach dipped as I thought about all the things we'd done the last few days.

"Isabel," he said, the seriousness in his voice beckoning my eyes on his. "If you keep looking at me like that, we're never going to leave the house."

"I know. I'm sorry." I bit my lip and turned around. He chuckled. I heard him walking over and felt his warmth on my back as he wrapped his arms around my middle. I closed my eyes as he kissed my neck.

"I'm not complaining," he murmured against my ear. "I just really want to take my wife out."

"Gio," I whispered, a slight shiver running through me.

"Tell me where you want to go. What's another thing you used to do with your dad?"

I opened my eyes and turned in his arms, looking up at him. "Navy Pier."

"Really?" The look on his face said he really didn't want to go.

"What? It was fun."

"How old were you exactly?"

"Young." I laughed. "Why? Is it bad?"

"I wouldn't say bad, but it's not where I'd go."

"So, just take me somewhere you'd go."

He searched my eyes for a second. "No, let's go to the pier."

"Why are you so paranoid?" I asked, looking up at Gio, who was looking around as if there may or may not have been a sniper aiming a gun at his head from above.

"There are a lot of people here." He let go of my hand and hugged me to the side of his body. "And we're not in the clear, you know."

"Isn't this the safest place to be, then?" I looked around. There were a lot of people here.

"Hardly."

"Really?" I shot him a look. "I'd think it would be impossible to get away with something when there are these many witnesses."

"That's because you've never had to get away with

something." He winked at me. Despite his words, butterflies swarmed my stomach.

"What could they possibly do?"

"Create a diversion. Maybe shoot something, someone, get people running in all different directions, and then come for us."

"You've done that?" I whispered, barely able to breathe at the thought.

"Do you really want to know?"

"Yes." I swallowed. "We said no secrets."

"No." He shot me a half-smile. "I've never done that."

I released a relieved breath, then frowned as I thought of something else. "I thought you said things had settled. And no one has even tried to come after me again. Maybe they figured whatever they stole from you was valuable enough."

"Maybe." He didn't sound convinced.

"What did they steal from you?"

"Stupid shit." He shrugged the shoulder behind my head. "Replaceable shit."

"Hm." I didn't push because I'd learned when he didn't want to outright tell you something, he wouldn't. "You know what I would kill for right now?"

He chuckled. "Let's hear it."

"Chicago pizza."

He dropped his arm and stopped walking, turning to face me. His face was serious, but his eyes were glimmering in amusement. "Did you say Chicago pizza?"

"Yeah, like the deep-dish stuff." I bit my lip. "Why? You don't like it?"

"Oh, I love it. I'm just surprised you do. Do the people in Queens approve of this?" He raised an eyebrow.

"We're not going to find out, because we're not going to tell them." I shot him a look.

"I don't know, I kind of want to see Luke's reaction to this."

"Don't you dare, Giovanni." I laughed when he lunged for me and picked me up.

"Don't worry, I won't tell, but it'll cost you."

I kept laughing. "What will it cost me? A blowjob?"

His chest rumbled in approval. "You said it, not me."

We drove to a pizza place and were instantly ushered to a table in the back. When we reached the booth and slid in, side by side, I glanced over at him.

"Let me guess, your family owns this place."

"Nope." He grinned.

"Someone you know owns it."

"Yep."

I shook my head and picked up the menu, looking through it, then set it down. "Maybe you should just order."

As soon as the waiter stood in front of us, Gio ordered some things. It sounded like enough food for an entire village, though, and when the waiter walked away, I said as much.

Gio shrugged a shoulder. "We have enough mouths to feed."

"Do you always order extra when you go places?"

"It depends where I go. Joey and Tony love this place, so I usually get extras here."

"You really treat them like family."

"They are family." He paused to thank the waiter for our water.

"Did you know my half-brother?" I asked. Gio, who was drinking water when I asked, shot me a wary look. He set the cup down and cleared his throat.

"Yeah."

"Well?"

"Yes."

"What happened to him? How did he die?"

"That is a very difficult question to answer." He chuckled darkly.

"That bad?" I felt my brows raise. I didn't know anything

about Vincent besides the fact that we shared a father and that he was dead. Maybe I shouldn't have wanted to know more, but I'd always wanted a sibling, and now I knew I'd had one at one point in time, so I was a little curious.

"Not bad enough, if you ask me."

I sat back a little, pulling away from him. He'd said the words so nonchalantly, that it felt like the complete opposite of the Gio I'd come to know in private. I reminded myself of that, though. If my father's death taught me one thing it was that everyone had different sides to them, and who they showed depended on who they were with. In my case, Gio showed me a multitude of sides, but he definitely kept the darker one hidden for the most part. I decided I didn't like it. I wanted to know everything about him, even the ugly.

"Tell me." I angled my body toward him as much as the booth allowed.

"We thought he was dead," he said, "And two years ago, out of the blue, he came back, kidnapped Catalina and killed my best friend, Nadia's brother, Frankie."

My mouth dropped. It was a lot to take in, but I kept going back to two years, and they thought he was dead. Did that mean he was a live, or had they been responsible for his death, ultimately?

"Did you kill him?" I whispered.

"No. We should've, though." He held my eyes as he said the words, there was no remorse in his face at all and I knew he meant it. My stomach clenched.

"Is he dead?"

"Who knows?" He shrugged a shoulder. "Who cares?"

"Do you think he'd..." I licked my lips. "Do you think he's responsible for all of this?"

"I seem to be the only one who thinks it's a possibility. He makes the most sense."

"Why do they think he wouldn't be responsible?"

"He has a family now. A wife, kids. They don't think he'd risk his life, or theirs, by coming back a second time."

I sank farther into the booth, letting that settle. My half-brother had a family. He had kids. I would never be a part of their lives for obvious reasons, and even though I didn't know him and hadn't known he existed before all of this, it stung a little. Maybe it was because in a sense, he was the only person who could truly understand what I was going through. Unless he'd known about me, then he couldn't possibly fathom what all of this had been like for me.

"He's not worth your thoughts or concern." Gio set a hand over mine. I met his gaze.

"But what if it is him?" I asked. "What if he is the one coming after me? Will you...you know."

"Kill him?"

"Yeah."

He took his hand from mine and shrugged both shoulders. The pizza got there just in time for the conversation to be cut short, but it stayed on the back of my mind. I couldn't imagine Gio killing someone he was close to, let alone someone he knew was a father, but again, maybe that was the side he hid from me, the way my father had all those years. I wasn't sure how to feel about it. A big part of me hated the idea of him being callous, of course, but another part of me understood that this was the way they were raised. Still, it didn't mean I approved.

CHAPTER THIRTY-SEVEN

Devil's Lair was opening a new area, and Gio said I needed to go with him.

"My wife should be there," he'd said, biting into a piece of toast with butter, as I rolled my eyes. He'd pointed the bread at me, raised eyebrow. "She should."

"Yeah, yeah." I smiled. "I need to visit my grandmother, though."

"That's fine." He shrugged. "We'll have lunch, and you can go visit her while I do a walk-through at the club. Petra and Joey can take you there afterwards." He shot me a pointed look. "Is that plan to your satisfaction? I don't want you switching shit up on me."

"I won't." I rolled my eyes, still laughing. "But your sisters want me to get drinks with them before I go to the club, so maybe there's a tiny switch of plans?"

"You're joking." He cocked his head.

"Nope. The bar is right by Devil's Lair, though."

"We have five bars at the club. You can't just drink there?"

"With all that loud music?" I pulled a face. "No way."

"Fine, but no switching up this plan."

I blew him a kiss. "I already told you I wasn't doing that again."

"Good." He walked around the counter and pressed a kiss to my lips. "Let's go, wife."

"Oh my God, Giovanni." I shook my head, hopping off the barstool.

"Yup. I seem to recall you screaming that a lot last night."

He looked down at me. "And the night before that. And in the shower and—"

"Okay, okay. I get it." I laughed. "I was there, too."

"Oh, trust me, I know. I have the bite marks to prove it."

I shook my head as we walked to the door. "You're unbelievable."

"Another word you used."

"Jesus Christ." I laughed as we walked into the elevator.

I got to the nursing home much, much, later than I anticipated, which meant I'd be pressed for time in getting ready. Just in case, I was wearing one of the dresses that was an option for tonight. It went down past my knees, hugging every curve on my body, with a nude bodysuit lining that was covered by a black mesh material that was see-through. It was one of those that made you do a double-take and wonder if I was naked underneath it, which was what I loved about it. I could already picture Gio's face when he saw me. My stomach fluttered at the thought. Because there were men in the nursing home, I wore a trench coat closed over it to cover me up. I'd also left my heels in the car, opting to wear my black converse. It was definitely a vibe, as Petra pointed out. *"Not the right one,"* she'd said, laughing, *"but still a vibe."*

In the elevator, I'd asked Petra to hold the bag of food I was carrying—two slices of cheese pizza and a slice of cheesecake, courtesy of Gio, who was adamant about grabbing lunch at my grandmother's favorite places so we could spend a little more time together—and opened my trench coat, taking a selfie of myself in the mirrored elevator.

I texted it to Gio.

Petra shook her head, laughing. "I know he says it jokingly all the time, but I really do think you might just kill that man."

I laughed, grabbing the bag of food from her as the doors

opened in front of us on the second floor, where they'd moved my grandmother a few days ago. According to the nurse, she wouldn't quit complaining about being on the first floor, so they finally moved her when a room on the second became vacant. Petra fell into step beside me. Joey was downstairs, "manning the door," because that was totally necessary in a nursing home, but I didn't argue. I was learning to pick my battles with these people. My phone buzzed in my hand.

Giovanni: fuuuuuck. When did you get that?

*Me: *wink face**

Giovanni: What are you wearing under it?

Me: lol I'm not going to spoil the fun

Giovanni: I'm going to drag you into my office the moment you get here.

Me: I can't wait

God, I couldn't stop smiling. I set my phone on airplane mode as we reached the door, knowing full-well that once Gio got going with texts or phone calls, he wouldn't stop. It was odd, feeling this way about him, "of all people," as Luke pointed out. It wasn't like I hadn't thought about it more than a few times. I was still so angry about my father, yet I'd fully fallen for someone who was technically in the same "line of business," if you will. The difference was, Giovanni didn't kill people. I didn't know much about what went on behind closed doors outside of the night-club business, and I didn't want to, but as long as he didn't kill people for a living, or for any reason, I could deal with the rest. Taking a life was just something I couldn't justify doing outside of self-defense. I didn't actively practice religion, but I certainly didn't think any of us should be playing God and taking lives.

The more I thought about it, the angrier I felt at my father.

I didn't know the reason he'd done it, but I wasn't an idiot. I knew it couldn't have been self-defense. Maybe once, twice, but over three-hundred times? I shivered uncomfortably, my stomach clenching at the thought of it. When we reached the door, I knocked twice and eyed Petra. When I opened the door, she stepped inside, did a quick sweep of the room, and headed back to the door, where I was still standing.

"I'll be out here. I'll check in with you in about twenty-minutes." She set the timer on her watch, then looked down the hall. There was a nurses' station and a vending machine on the other wing that we could see from here. "I'm going to grab a coke and be right back."

I let her step outside before walking into the room and shutting the door behind me. This room was colder than her last one, she probably loved that, my grandmother used to set the air at sixty-eight every night. She would've set it lower if my mom hadn't screamed at her so many times to stop messing with the thermostat. I looked at my grandmother. Her eyes were closed, but the television was on, so I knew she must have either just dozed off or was pretending to be asleep. She'd done both on multiple occasions. I sighed heavily and leaned in to kiss her cheek, pulling up the chair to sit beside her.

"Mima," I said.

No response. Before sitting down, I set the bag of food I brought on the movable take next to me, taking out the box with the two slices of pizza and the smaller box with the cheesecake. Sometimes, she'd open her eyes when she smelled the food. Sometimes, she waited as long as she could. It didn't matter. I sat back in the chair and looked at the television, set on Univision, for a few minutes, before pulling out my phone and taking it off airplane mode, after all. The texts were instant.

Giovanni: I can't stop staring at this picture

Giovanni: Does it come in other colors? I'm buying you another one

Giovanni: fuck, Isabel. What the fuck are you doing to me?

I laughed to myself but didn't respond. I wanted to wait until I saw him in person. Instead, I opened up the news app on my phone and started scrolling. It was always the same heartache, wars, a mass shooting, murder, and some crooked politicians. Then, I caught sight of a face, one that sent a cold shiver down my spine. Beside the face, the headline read: *Carson Riley, MISSING.* Next to that, the last date he'd been seen. I opened my calendar app and scrolled back, my stomach plummeting. Images played out in my head, the bloody knuckles, the anger, staying back here while I went to Chicago ahead of him. Fear gripped my heart. Had he killed him? Did I care? I truly wasn't sure, and that scared me more than the possibility of him having done it.

Through the haze of emotions, I decided that I did care, but mostly because he'd lied to me. He did kill people. I knew in my bones he'd killed this man, a poor excuse for one, sure, but it wasn't like people didn't change. I couldn't believe my own thoughts, but it didn't make them wrong. Some of my middle schoolers had convict parents, who had turned their lives around for the sake of their children. Some of them were already headed toward a dark future, initiating in street gangs, and trying to prove themselves with their fists. I tried extra hard with those. Extra attention in class, extra care in the way I spoke to them, and extra help afterschool when they needed it, and even then, I knew it wouldn't change the trajectory of their lives. I thought of Gio, who technically, had everything he could possibly ask for growing up, and yet, he was unhappy, angry, would have changed so much about his life if given the chance. Really, that "life" they called organized crime that he was involved with was no different from those street gangs. They liked to think so, of course. When I brought that argument up to him, he'd said that they were absolutely different, since they were organized. He'd emphasized that word, too. I'd argued that it didn't change the things they did, and once again, he'd reminded me that he didn't kill people.

Despite my rapidly beating heart, and the sudden urge to vomit, I clicked on the article. He was married, the rapist. Married and his wife was pregnant. My chest squeezed when I read that line, when I saw the look of devastation on her face at a recent vigil, where she'd pleaded for information on his whereabouts. I didn't feel bad for the rapist, I felt bad for his family. I felt bad for his wife and unborn child. Granted, I didn't know what kind of person he was at home, I didn't know if he'd changed at all or turned his life around, or if he'd raped others, and yet, I felt bad for his wife and the kid who would never meet their father. I swallowed thickly as I text messaged Gio the article. Beneath the link, I wrote, "I thought you didn't paint houses."

He called me before I could even set the phone down on my lap. I answered, but didn't say a word, just breathed into the line, waiting.

"I don't," was the first word he said.

"You lied to me."

"I didn't. I've never lied to you." His voice sounded composed and left no room to argue with that. He sighed into the line and lowered it, "What are you thinking?"

"I'm thinking that you asked me to trust you, and I did, and now I'm second guessing that," I said, keeping my voice low.

"No." I heard something slam on a hard surface. His fist, probably. "Don't say that, Isabel."

"I don't know if I can do this," I whispered, my eyes instantly watering. My own words were ripping me apart. "I don't know if I can just…" I exhaled, wiping a tear with my other hand. "How would this work anyway? I'm a teacher. You own nightclubs and do whatever else it is you do when you're gone, lying to me about—"

"When have I ever lied to you? Name one time." His voice was hard.

I swallowed.

"Don't do this."

"You lied about this," I said. "Did you not?"

He was quiet on the other end of the line for a moment. "We should have this conversation in person."

"Did you do it?"

"Yes." He sighed.

My heart stopped beating for what felt like an eternity. I knew he was involved in some things that I probably wouldn't condone, but killing someone? There was no way I could justify anyone doing that, even if it was a man who took something from me, because that was what he did that night. He'd taken my dignity, my confidence, my safety. He'd reached into me and taken the light from inside me. Before then, I'd been in awful situations, sure. I'd been in a not-so-good situation at home. None of the horrendous things that happened before then could ever reach that level, because that night, I felt stripped of everything that made me, me. It took a while for me to find it in myself to even smile, let alone sleep with another man, and that didn't happen until I rekindled my friendship with Will. I'd tried, of course. I'd tried to sleep with other people as a way to regain my strength, thinking that it would give me what I needed to move on, but each and every time they tried to climb on top of me, I stiffened and pushed them away. Until Gio. He was the second man I'd trusted with my life and the second man I'd found out was capable of taking a life.

"And you know what?" he continued, snapping me away from my thoughts. "I'd do it again. You weren't the only victim, you know? He had a long trail of women accusing him of this shit."

I swallowed hard as guilt gnawed at me. That had been my only fear when I didn't go to the police when it happened. Days later, weeks later, I thought that maybe me going would make a difference to someone else, but I didn't. I stayed quiet. I didn't know how to process what had happened to me, let alone verbalize it. I didn't know if I wanted to.

"I'm going to come get you," he said, a hint of impatience in his voice. "I don't like talking about this without being able to see you."

"Don't."

"Isa—"

"I'll see you later, okay?"

A pause. "Are you still going to come over here?"

"Yes." I took one last shuddering breath. "I'm still going."

"I love you, Isabel." He breathed into the phone. "Please don't leave me over this."

I shut my eyes, my heart stumbling in my chest before dropping and cracking a little at the plea. I knew it would hurt him if I left him. I knew I didn't want to leave him. I didn't want to be with a man like my father, though, who held secrets, who killed people, who kept wedding bands as reminders of it all. I felt sick when I thought about it all. Yet, I knew that Gio only wanted to be loved like the rest of us. He wanted a sure thing, someone who wouldn't walk out of him when things got rough. I just needed to figure out whether or not I could be that person, knowing what I knew, and not asking questions about what I didn't.

"Just, at least wait until we see each other and discuss this in person," he added quickly. I could tell he was on edge, probably pacing his office as he spoke to me.

"I'm not going to leave you, Giovanni." I sighed. "I just need a moment to process all of this."

"Okay."

"Okay."

"I don't do that, Isabel. I swear I don't. This was different."

"Okay," I whispered again, because I didn't want to even think about it anymore.

Besides, what else could I say, really? He'd done it. He'd admitted to it. I hung up the phone and clicked out of the article. I didn't condone murder, but I never wanted to see that man's face ever again. When I set the phone aside, my grandmother was opening her eyes. She looked at me, at the food, and back at me.

"Isa." She smiled wide. "My favorite *nieta*."

I shut my eyes for one second, smiling at that. I wasn't sure how long the good mood would last, where she acted like I was still seven years old and the light was still in her eyes, and her husband was still alive, but I was certainly going to enjoy it.

"Your only *nieta*," I said, standing and rolling the table over her bed and opening the box of pizza.

"You're still my favorite." She smiled, looking at the pizza. "Cheese?"

"Yep."

"From Joe's?"

"You know it." I smiled as she sat up and took a slice in her hand.

"Best pizza in town." She took a bite and looked at me as she chewed.

"Do you like this room more? Are you sleeping better?"

She stopped chewing, her eyes clouding, and I inwardly kicked myself for ruining the moment, silently praying that she wouldn't remember how much she hated and blamed me for taking time she would've rather have been with her husband than with me. She started chewing again before she asked for water. I poured her some in a plastic cup and gave it to her.

"I like this room better," she said after a moment. "It's colder and there's no balcony that leads to the parking lot."

I smiled softly. "So, no more visits from the boogey man."

"That's right." She finished the slice of pizza. "I think I'll have my dessert now and save the other slice for when Dolores comes in trying to feed me the disgusting mashed potatoes and pork chops they made today."

"That doesn't sound that bad." I laughed, closing the pizza box and opening the cheesecake.

My grandmother was chewing her first bite of the

cheesecake when I heard a sound behind me. My skin prickled, an uneasy feeling settling in my gut, but when I glanced over my shoulder, I saw nothing, merely shadows moving beneath the gap on the bottom of the door. Nurses, probably. Petra, most likely, if she'd come back from the vending machine. I turned back to my grandmother, who was smiling at me, that light in her eyes again that I hadn't seen in so long, so, so long. I heard a noise again, this time, the door handle, and my heart launched to my throat.

When I turned around again I saw a man standing there, covered in camo from head-to-toe, like he was about to go into a forest for a hunt or somewhere for war. A ski mask covered his face, and if that wasn't enough to knock me off kilter, the huge gun he was pointing at me was. I stumbled back, my ass landing on the edge of my grandmother's bed, as I stared up at him, my heart pounding in my ears.

"Leave her alone," she said behind me, grabbing my right arm.

I only took my eyes off him for a moment to look over his shoulder. Where the hell was Petra? She should've been standing outside. My eyes bounced back to the gun, and I really looked at it now, noticing the silencer on the thin barrel. I only knew what it was from movies I'd watched, where they used those to not alert anyone else of shootings. I stopped breathing. He was really going to kill me. I couldn't, for the life of me, figure out why. He must've been mistaken, that was my only thought.

"What do you want?" I asked shakily.

"You." That was all he said as he brought the gun closer to me, setting the silencer between my eyes.

I squeezed them shut. If I had to die, at least let it be quick. Please, God, let it be quick. As I sat there, with my eyes closed, everything flashed before my eyes, but the most prominent one was Gio. This was going to tear him apart. I knew that. He'd told me about his best friend who died a couple of years ago, and how that had nearly broken him. I knew this would be ten times worse, not because I thought I was more important than his friend, but because it would be two people he loved and lost back-to-back.

"Get up," the man said. My eyes popped open. I stood.

My grandmother yanked my arm, pulling me back toward her bed. "Let her go. She's a ch—"

Before she could finish her sentence, he shifted the gun from my forehead to her and heard the sound of air whooshing past my ear. Her hand instantly dropped from my arm, going limp beside me. I opened my mouth and screamed. It was the only thing I could do. That was when the real panic kicked in. He grabbed me by the arm and dragged me toward the door as I looked over my shoulder. The only thing I could see was blood. I screamed again, and again. I wasn't sure if anyone could hear me, or if they were just hiding out because they were scared, but I screamed regardless. I looked around for Petra. God, where was Petra? She could help me. We were almost at the elevator when I saw her, lying in a pool of blood. A shuddering sob raked through me as I screamed again. Please no. Please, please, no. I felt something jab me and suddenly, everything went black.

CHAPTER THIRTY-EIGHT

Gio

LOOKED AT MY WATCH AGAIN. I KNEW ISABEL WOULD BE LATE, BUT she should've been here by now. The nightclub was in full swing, women dancing on stages on the first floor, the dance floor overflowing, and the VIP area on the second floor completely full. All of it was technically perfect, but she wasn't here. Normally, I'd have drinks with the VIPs or stand around watching everyone dancing beneath me. Normally, I'd be thrilled over this turn-out. Tonight, it all felt stupid, empty, boring. I looked at the time again. She couldn't possibly still be at the nursing home. I knew I should've gone earlier. The moment she called me, the moment I heard her broken words as she asked me all of those questions, I should've left this place, but she'd asked for space, and I was trying to give it to her. Now, I was beginning to worry she'd changed her mind about me, and I was starting to panic a little. I started making my way back to the office, where I'd left my phone charging. Tony turned around with me.

"Have you heard from Petra or Joey?" I asked him.

"Was I supposed to?" He took his phone out of his pocket.

"Call them. I want to know where they are," I said, forcing a smile for the tables I walked by on my way out.

"They're calling you back over," Tony said. I stopped walking. He nodded back. "The women at that table."

I looked over my shoulder to see if I recognized anyone. I didn't. I kept walking forward. I'd play nice and stop for regulars, friends, family, and VIP, but I wasn't going to waste my time on thirsty women. I only had eyes for one, and seeing as she wasn't here, I knew there was a high chance she was in my apartment sulking and overthinking this entire thing. Fuck. I was going to have to leave my own grand opening, and I didn't even fucking care. At all. As far as I was concerned, this was just another club. Isabel, though? Was irreplaceable. If I had to beg her to stay with me, I would.

"They're not answering," Tony said.

I stopped walking again, looking over at him. "Neither of them?"

"I tried both twice."

The fear that trickled into my veins was slow, but once it was settled, it overrode every other emotion I might have been feeling. I ran to my office, barging in both doors. John stood quickly, and looked up, falling in step behind us when I ran past him. I practically threw myself onto my desk, where my phone was, and picked it up. No calls. No texts. Nothing. Oh, fuck. I picked it up and dialed Isabel. No answer. I dialed again. No answer. I dialed Petra, no answer. Joey, no answer. I gripped it in my hand and tried to calm down, but I was shaking, my sight blinding as I staggered into my chair. Something was horribly wrong.

"Boss?" John said, snapping my attention to his face, waiting for me to give an order.

"Go down to the nursing home. Tony will give you the address. Your sister, Joey, and Isabel were there, they were supposed to have left, but..." I didn't want to finish that thought or sentence. I shook my head. I looked at Tony. "Go to my house."

"What if you need to go somewhere?"

I shot him a look. "Just go and call me when you're there."

They both got the hell out of my office, Tony with his phone to his ear, assumingly talking to Nadia.

I picked up my phone and called Catalina. She answered quickly.

"I'm almost there. Geez."

"Did you see Isabel today?"

A pause. "No. She never showed up at the bar. I assumed she ran out of time and went straight to the club."

My heart stopped.

"G? Is something wrong?"

"Where's Loren?"

"Driving us over to—"

"I need to speak to him."

"Yeah," Lorenzo said.

"Something's wrong. Isabel went to visit her grandmother with Joey and Petra, and none of them are answering the phone."

"Maybe they're on their way back. Don't they have to cross the bridge to get here?"

"It can't be cell phone reception. It doesn't take that fucking long to cross the bridge."

"In traffic?"

I tried to reason that, breathe through it, but I couldn't help the sinking feeling in the pit of my stomach. "Something's wrong. I can feel it."

"Fuck." He exhaled into the line. "I'll call you back."

I walked back around my desk and slammed my fists on it. I didn't even know what the fuck to do. I had John going to the nursing home. Maybe that would bring answers. After a moment, I made a call to Dominic, Dean, and Rocco. Rocco hadn't been here long, he'd just moved from Rhode Island, but he'd been in the life since he was a kid and was well acquainted with Silvio and Charles before he passed. None of them had answers for me, but they promised they'd look, they promised they'd call, they promised they'd fight, if it came down to it. I hoped it wouldn't. I started running through worst case scenarios and couldn't land on any specific ones that were a possibility. She had two of my best soldiers with her. There was a slim chance shit could go sideways while visiting a nursing home. Unless something was wrong with her grandmother? Maybe she'd died while she was there, and her phone ran out of battery? That was a possibility.

I knew Isabel would hate me for thinking it, since she was all about saving lives and shit, but I hoped that was the reason behind this. Her grandmother was old, and not Isabel. Maybe that made me a bastard, but I didn't care. I wanted her safe and with me. My knee started bouncing under the desk. I couldn't remember the last time I felt this out of sorts. Maybe the night I killed that disgrace of a human being. Maybe afterwards, when I was still running on adrenaline and anger. It was nothing to what I felt now, though. My phone buzzed on the desk. John. I answered.

"This place is crawling with police officers and ambulances."

"What?" My stomach dropped. "Can you get in there? Do you see the SUV anywhere?"

"I'm going to check for it now. I don't know if they'll let me in. I have to look for a side door."

"Do it."

"I'll call you back." He hung up and I wanted to scream at him to stay on the phone with me, but I knew that would only make him move slower. I stood up and started pacing the room.

Finally, I called Nico. "Have the car ready. We need to go."

By the time I went downstairs, Nico was waiting with the car running. We headed straight to the nursing home. On our way, Tony called and said the apartment was empty. The knot in my stomach grew tighter. I couldn't remember the last time I felt this kind of fear. When my sister was kidnapped by Vinny. That had been the last time. And even then, I knew Vinny and what he was capable of. I knew that underneath his anger, he wouldn't hurt Catalina. He may not have ever been in love with her the way he was in love with his wife, but he loved her nonetheless. He'd been our brother once. I'd never spoken to him after the fact since I had nothing to say to him and I was liable to shoot him on sight for what he'd done. Now that I was convinced he wasn't the one behind any of this, I wish I'd had him in my corner. He was just like Frankie. The same bullseye, fearless, mentality. I'd run into a burning building if it meant rescuing someone I loved, but I didn't do shit like that for the fun of it, the way Frankie had and Vinny had. The only other person I knew who was crazy enough to run into burning buildings for kicks was Dominic. Jesus. What was the world coming to, that I had to turn to Dominic De Luca, of all people?

CHAPTER THIRTY-NINE

Gio

"ANY INFO?" I ASKED AS I ANSWERED DEAN'S CALL.

"You still on your way to the nursing home?"

"Yes. We were stuck on the bridge for forty-fucking-minutes." I clenched my jaw, trying not to kick and punch the doors of the SUV like a child, even though that was what I felt like doing. "Any news?"

"Based on logic, Silvio is the only one who could be behind this," he said. I shut my eyes. I was really, really, hoping it wasn't him, but fuck it.

"He wants the briefcase?"

"What else could he want?" Dean asked. "Like I said, it's the only logical explanation. No one has talked or slipped up, which means he's not using hired guns."

"Does Midas know?"

Dean scoffed. "Loren would've shut this down before it got this far, and he would've told us about it."

"Do you really believe that?" I closed my eyes. I didn't know what to think anymore. I didn't want to doubt my brother-in-law, but right now, I felt like I had a bandage over my eyes and everyone was a prime suspect.

"Boss, we're here," Nico said.

"I'll call you back." I hung up on Dean and looked at the scene in front of me.

There were news helicopters flying above, police tape everywhere. My heart stopped beating for what felt like an eternity. I jumped out of the SUV before it even came to a complete stop, running toward the building. Two officers stopped me immediately, pushing me back, telling me I couldn't go in there. I pushed them both away, yanking myself from their grasp. I couldn't even see their faces to know if they were one of mine. I couldn't see anything.

"Masseria," someone called out.

My head whipped in the direction of Detective Marchetti, who told the officers to let me go. They did immediately. Marchetti was one of ours. Well, technically not one of ours. He was one of them, the boys in blue, the ones who laid their lives out on the line for the people of this city, but he also happened to be Rocco Marchetti's older brother, which meant, he was one of ours, whether he liked it or not. We'd all grown up in the same circles, called each other cousins, went to birthdays and saw each other during holidays sometimes. Detective Marchetti didn't really like mixing business with pleasure, especially when business meant more than half of the people in his family were involved in organized crime. He could've easily turned us all in, but he wasn't a rat, and he especially would never sell out his little brother.

"What the fuck is happening?" I asked, walking over to him.

"There was a shooting," he said. That much was obvious, based on all the police tape and people everywhere, but it still made my stomach sink. "A couple of your people were in there, right?"

"Where the fuck are they?"

"Petra Spellman was taken to the hospital. Joey Zaffino…" Marchetti shook his head softly, sadness in his eyes, and I just knew. Fuck. I looked down momentarily.

"They were here with my girl…my wife," I said. There was no way for him to hide his shock and I had no time to be offended or explain. "She was visiting her grandmother on the second floor." I swallowed thickly. "I need to get in there."

He looked around for a minute, before lifting the police

tape for me to walk through with him. By the main door, I saw dried up blood. We were walking inside while John was walking out. We stopped in front of each other. He shook his head. I could see the desperation in his eyes, it was the same thing that was clawing at me inside.

"She's in the hospital," he said. "Isabel isn't here and Joey Z—"

"I know." I set a hand on his arm and squeezed. "Go be with your sister."

"I can—"

"She needs you, John. You've done enough. Thank you." I squeezed his arm one more time before letting go and walking toward the elevator.

The entire place looked like a scene out of a horror movie. There were things thrown everywhere and blood all over the floors and walls. John said Isabel wasn't here, but I needed to see for myself. I needed to see so that I could convince myself that she was okay. Maybe she was hiding. She was smart. She could've been hiding. I was sure that, as a middle school teacher in today's world, she'd had enough training on active shooters. The thought gave me a sick feeling in the pit of my stomach, but nothing in comparison to what I saw when the elevators opened on the second floor. There were crime investigators everywhere, taking pictures, laying down tape where they didn't want us to step over. There was blood everywhere. I couldn't imagine how many people lost their lives today. Normally, I was able to compartmentalize that, reminding myself that even when you aimed for a target, those around them could become collateral. But this was an old people home and they were innocent in all of this. I continued walking. I knew what room her grandmother had been in because Petra gave me all of the information, so I headed in that direction, stopping short next to a vending machine that also had a puddle of dried blood beside it. Whoever did this, showed no mercy. I turned to Marchetti.

"How many people died?"

"Three."

"Three?" That was a lot less than what it looked like.

"A lot injured," he said, as if reading my mind. He shook his head. "I don't know what this is about or what your involvement is, but even you have to see how fucked up it is."

"I do see it." I slowed down as we got to her grandmother's door. "Were all of these rooms searched?"

"Every single one."

I pushed the door open, eyes instantly taking in the food on the floor, the bag Isabel had brought it in. The rolling table was knocked over as well as two chairs. The bed was empty, but there was blood everywhere.

"Who was taken from here?" I asked, hating the way my voice came out so quiet, so shaky.

"An old lady."

"And no one else?"

"No one else."

I put my head in my hands for a moment, just breathing. Whoever did this was targeting Isabel. If they were trying to get to me, why hadn't they called for ransom or sent a picture letting me know they had her?

"We need to get out of here," Marchetti said. "It's only a matter of time before someone starts breathing down my neck about you being in here."

I gave a sharp nod and straightened, heading toward the door.

"Any idea who did this?" He huffed. "Not that I'd expect you to tell me."

"If I knew, I'd tell you." I looked him dead in the eye. "I need to find my wife."

"Why do you keep saying that? When the fuck did you get married?"

"It's a long story." I jabbed the button for the elevator. "Her name is Isabel Bonetti. She's about five-five, long brown hair, caramel skin, light brown eyes. I don't know who took her or what they want, but whatever it is, I'll give it to them."

He looked at me for a long moment before nodding in understanding. Normally, I wouldn't really consult with him. His brother, sure, but not him. This wasn't the time to play cops and robbers, though. Half the force was on our side, anyway, and the longer Isabel was gone, the worse the outcome would be.

CHAPTER FORTY

Gio

WHEN I FOUND HER AND ENSURED SHE WAS SAFE, I WOULD LET her go. I'd decided that on the ride from the nursing home. It wasn't because it was the honorable thing to do, because fuck that, but I couldn't go through this again. If it weren't for me, she'd still be in New York, pouring drinks to old men in her little rum bar while she waited for the school year to start. If it weren't for me, she'd be with William Hamilton, and even though I fucking hated the man, I couldn't deny that he'd give her a good life. A safe life. How many people had warned me against going for her? How many had reminded me that this wasn't where she belonged? Too many, and I'd ignored each and every one of them, because I was selfish and I wanted her anyway. Nico pulled up to the warehouse and parked across the street. I didn't even bother looking over my shoulder as I stomped to the door, punching in the code before stepping in and kicking the door shut. I felt like I hadn't been able to take a breath since I spoke to Isabel this afternoon. I kept replaying that conversation over and over and wishing like hell I'd gone over there when my gut told me to go. After a moment, I walked in.

The warehouse had been converted into a hang out. It had a full bar, furniture, a pool table, and a round table that Dean had brought in for us to sit in and discuss shit like he was King fucking Arthur. He was already sitting there with Loren, Dominic, and Rocco. I frowned at the sight of him here.

"The fuck are you doing here?" I asked, nodding at him.

"I invited him," Dean said.

I took my usual seat. I didn't care one way or another if Rocco was here. In fact, he belonged here just as much as the rest of us. I just wasn't used to him being around. Ever since he moved here, he'd been working with Dean in the gambling rings, making sure people were paying what they were supposed to and stiff-arming them when they weren't. He was Dominic's age, just a baby when the old *Patriarca* had come for his family back in Rhode Island and stole his mother's last breath. It was the reason his brother, Michael, became a detective. It was the reason Rocco became a gangster. We all had our own ways to deal with pain. Some of us went straight and arrow, while others took a darker path. We do what we have to in order to survive.

"Every second that goes by is another second that Isabel's life is in danger," I said. "There hasn't been a ransom call, a picture, nothing. Who the fuck has her?"

"Silvio's men were seen sniffing around the nursing home." Dean popped the laptop in front of him open and clicked something before turning it to us. Sure enough, Albert, Silvio's trusted enforcer, was walking out of the nursing home. I looked at the date.

"This was weeks ago."

"He went every day for two weeks. He missed Isabel by seconds the last time she'd gone."

My stomach coiled. "He's been watching her."

"He's been watching her grandmother," Dean said, shutting the laptop. "Her grandmother had just gotten moved to the second floor after complaining about a man who kept visiting her."

"Why is this the first we're hearing about this?" I looked at Dean, at Loren, at Dom. Not at Rocco since he'd just gotten involved, but the rest of the guys knew enough to have their ear to the fucking ground.

"Her grandmother had dementia. She said a lot of things, saw a lot of things," Loren said. "She would've most like have told Isabel about the man and she probably shrugged it off like anyone else would've."

My eyes lowered to the wooden table. It had marks on it from all the times these assholes hadn't used a coaster. Mostly Dominic and Frankie. I rubbed the back of my neck to relieve the tension that came at the thought of my best friend. Worse, at the thought of my best friend linked to Isabel. I hadn't lashed out, hadn't called Mike or her friends yet, hadn't really done anything besides go to the nursing home. I was helpless. Helpless and hopeless as I waited for a fucking call from someone who could tell me why they had her, where they had her, and what the fuck they wanted in exchange for her. If they'd gone to these measures, they had to know I'd give it to them, whatever it was.

"G." At the sound of Dominic saying my voice, I snapped out of my trance and looked up. "Do you want us to send Silvio a message?"

I looked around the table, all eyes on me, all ready to follow whatever call I made. It was just the way it was with us. My eyes landed on Dean again, the oldest one, though not by much, but certainly the most respected.

"I want Silvio's operations burned to the ground." My voice was eerily calm, but that's how I felt all of a sudden. Maybe I was tired, maybe I was just going through the motions until something happened. "And I want his location. I'll handle him."

"Gio." Dean's eyes widened slightly as he shook his head. "We'll have someone do that."

"I want to do it myself. Whoever took my wife is going to die by my hands." My voice left no room for argument. Everyone's eyebrows shot up, but that was the only confirmation I got that they were fine with me handling it. I looked at Dom. "I'm going to need you to come with me."

"I'll go with you," Rocco said, his eyes shooting to his boss briefly. Dean gave a nod, permission. "He usually comes by the laundromat on Washington. The one near Holland Tunnel."

I sat back. Dean had too many locations for me to keep track of, but if there was one near the tunnel you had to cross to get to or from the nursing home was, it could mean Silvio had taken her there. I said this aloud to them. They agreed that it made sense.

"He has a Bingo Hall on sixty-ninth, by Joey's."

"I know the one." I pushed off the desk and stood quickly, walking to the armory closet.

We normally didn't bring weapons to the table. The big five, the geezers, they didn't allow weapons in the building at all when they met up. They didn't trust each other, though. The only supposed alliance they had was to their own blood, and we'd all seen how little that meant to them when push comes to shove. We all knew that the only reason they were in the positions they were in was because they'd killed someone in their own family. Or had them killed. It was the same shit. I picked up an M17 and the Walther. I loaded both before moving on to the knives. I didn't know what the fuck to do with a knife, if I was being honest, but I picked one up anyway because if it came to close contact, I'd use the fuck out of one.

Rocco reached down for his backpack and took out the weapons he had, making sure they were loaded before setting the safety back on. It didn't surprise me that he had this many, but I hadn't expected him to be carrying them with him. I didn't ask. We waited for Dominic. Loren and Dean stood up. Loren walked over to me, handing me a bulletproof vest, which I took and put on, even though we all knew we'd most likely get shot in the head and there was nothing that could save us from that.

"What can I do?" Loren asked.

"Go get the briefcase."

"Chicago?"

"Under the bed, I think. Call Nadia. She'll get it for you and meet you at the airport."

"I'll call Flynn." Loren sighed. As he walked away.

Fuck, I should've looked inside that fucking briefcase. I didn't think to, since I'd seen the envelopes she opened. Rings, diamonds, more rings, more diamonds. Those were valuable, sure, but something else must have been in there for this to happen and I should've checked for it.

"Loren," I shouted. He stopped walking and turned around. "Call John to check on Petra. And don't tell me sister about this."

He didn't comment as he turned around and kept walking. I didn't know what that meant, but I knew he wouldn't

Dean patted my shoulder and told me he'd look at the camera footage on that intersection in case he saw something, before turning to speak to Rocco quietly as Dominic and I left the room and headed outside. Nico, who was smoking a cigarette, threw it down, eyes wide when he saw us. We either looked completely deranged or like something out of the movie. By the time we reached him, Nico was in the driver's seat starting the car. Dominic walked out of the warehouse, looking around for a second first. He'd been the only one out of the three of us to take care to do that. I couldn't even berate myself for not doing it. I just wanted to go. He jogged to the SUV and shut the door after getting in. Nico started driving, looking at me.

"Where to, boss?"

"Sixty-Ninth and…" I looked over my shoulder at Rocco.

"Grand," he said.

Nico gave a nod. Shit, he was in Joey's enough to know exactly where we needed to go. My heart pounded faster as we drove closer, the adrenaline finally kicking in again. My phone buzzed in the center of the car, and everyone froze. I picked it up quickly, looking at the screen. Blocked Caller. My heart pounded harder as I answered it and held it to my ear.

"What do you want?"

"You know what we want." It was a man, but I didn't recognize the voice.

"I don't make assumptions." I bit my tongue hard to keep my voice steady and not add more to that statement.

"Maybe you should," he said, and suddenly I heard Isabel's scream. My hand gripped the phone tighter. "The briefcase. Where is it?"

"I'll get you the fucking briefcase, but if you hurt her, you're dead," I growled.

"Well then." The man tsked. "I guess I better start looking for a plot."

Anger punched me in the chest, but I tried not to react, tried not to give anything else away. They already knew how much she meant to me. Whoever this was knew me and had still done this, which meant they probably wouldn't mind hurting her or killing her if it came to that.

"Where do I meet you?" I asked.

"I'll be in touch. Your little girlfriend told us the briefcase was back in Chicago, so I'll be patient and give you a few hours."

I ended the call, then screamed and punched and kicked the shit out of my car. I knew it wouldn't help, but it was the only thing I could do with the pent-up rage I felt right now.

"He wants the briefcase." That was Rocco. I turned around quickly and stared at him.

"How the fuck do you know that?"

"Word on the street is people have been asking around for it, from Queens to Jersey, trying to figure out who would have it."

I turned as much as I could in my seat. "Who wants it?"

"Silvio for sure. Some other guy, tall, blue eyes, black hair. He never says his name, but he's been sniffing around."

Blue eyes. Fuck. I turned around and kicked the dashboard again, then faced him. "Any idea who it might be?"

"If I knew, we wouldn't be here right now."

I turned and faced forward again, picking up the phone again.

"Anything on the bingo hall?" I asked.

"I'm looking at surveillance footage as we speak," Dean said, distracted. "One of Silvio's cars parked in the back alley last night around the time we're looking for and it hasn't moved since, so either someone sleeps there on the regular or your chick is there."

I shut my eyes, wishing I could feel some kind of relief, but I didn't. The only thing I felt was determination. It was better than anger. Anger made people do stupid shit. Anger could get her killed and I couldn't live in a world that Isabel wasn't a part of. My best friend had already been ripped from my life, and most days I was okay, but somedays I was barely holding on. Isabel gave me hope, though. Isabel the helper, the teacher, one of the strongest people I knew. She'd survive this. She had to, or else I wouldn't.

CHAPTER FORTY-ONE

Isabel

MY HEAD FELT LIKE IT WAS ABOUT TO EXPLODE. MY JAW HURT. MY cheeks hurt. My teeth even hurt. *What the hell?* The overpowering smell of fabric softener was making it worse and giving me nausea. I tried to open my eyes, and even that hurt, but I managed. When I did, I was met with pitch black. Something was in my mouth. I reached up to remove whatever was covering my face, and realized my hands were tied together. My feet too. Fear rolled through me in an instant. Oh my God. I'd been kidnapped. I instantly thought of my grandmother and remembered the man shooting her. I thought of Petra and Joey and wondered where they were. They'd be here, right? They'd come for me. And Gio? Ugh. He was going to think I purposely didn't show up to his club. I tried again, to fight against my restraints, but I could barely move. *Was this payback for what Gio had done to that guy? Was it the same people that raided my dad's house?* It had to be them. It had to be. What the hell did they want with me, though? A sob raked through me. The darkness, the ties around me, the thing in my mouth that was making it difficult to breathe, the feeling of helplessness that I tried to avoid at every turn of my life, it was all too much.

I was still crying when I heard footsteps approaching. My stomach coiled. They were getting closer, closer, closer. It sounded like boots. Something, or someone heavy. The fabric covering my head was snatched off suddenly, with such a force, that I nearly tipped over. I was on the floor. I blinked until my eyes adjusted to my surroundings. All I saw was concrete on every side. A boot stepped on my arm and turned me roughly, and I saw the man above me. Blue eyes. I knew it was him, the man from my father's house. He didn't wear a mask this time, which made my stomach turn even more. As I'd said, I'd watched Dexter. I knew what happened to loose ends and whether or not I gave them what they wanted, I'd be a loose end. He said nothing, this man. Behind him, another man came into view. A much shorter, much wider man. He looked harmless, wearing a short sleeve button down, slacks, and big eyeglasses. He looked like a math teacher. He walked until he got to me, and then he crouched down beside me, turning his face so I could see him upright, since I was on my side.

"I'm sorry about all of this." He waved a hand at me. "I was told they'd be gentle, but I can see they haven't been and that pains me." He reached out and took the gag out of my mouth. I took a harsh deep breath, and another, and another, my head woozy. "Calm down," he said in a calm voice that matched his demeanor. "Calm down. Breathe."

I breathed. Finally, I took one last breath and licked my lips. "You killed my grandmother."

"Also, not on the list of things they were supposed to do." He craned his neck and narrowed his eyes on the blue-eyed guy, shaking his head. "A disgrace, I tell you." He looked at me again, green eyes soft. "Do you know who I am?"

I shook my head, tears filling my eyes. "What do you want from me?"

He barked out a laugh, taking off his glasses as he stood, and cleaning them with the bottom of his shirt. "I'll take that as a no."

"Why am I here?" I asked, my voice hoarse.

"You have something I want."

"I don't have anything." I began to sob again, unable to hold it back. "I don't have anything."

"On the contrary, you have something everyone wants," he said, walking back a few steps. "The briefcase."

I blinked. The briefcase. This was all over my father's fucking briefcase? My grandmother dead, Petra and Joey... Oh, God. I swallowed. "Where is Petra?"

"She's insignificant." He put his glasses back on. "Where is the briefcase?"

"Is she dead?" I whispered, a wave of new tears filling my eyes.

"I don't have the answer to that question," he said, "As I stated, she's insignificant. Where's the briefcase?"

"I don't have it."

He took a step back. Blue eyes took a step forward, planting his boot on my side. The math teacher looking guy narrowed his eyes on mine. "I don't want to hurt you. I was great friends with your father, and I told him I'd look after his daughter if he died before me, since he'd promised to do the same for mine. So, I don't want to hurt you, but that doesn't mean he won't."

"He works for you. It's the same thing," I tried to shout, but my voice wouldn't project, and it was just another broken whisper.

"Nope." The man started to turn around and walk in the direction he came from. My heart began to pound harder, louder. I looked up at blue-eyes above me, who looked like he'd enjoy doing a lot of things to me if he had the chance. I was already tied up. We were about to be left alone. It wasn't like he needed permission from anyone to rip my dress apart and have his way with me if he wanted.

"Wait," I said through a sob. The man stopped walking and turned around, small smile on his lips. "The briefcase is in Chicago."

"*Where* in Chicago?"

I bit my lip hard.

"Does your boyfriend have it?" he raised an eyebrow.

"I don't have a boyfriend." I swallowed.

He chuckled, shaking his head. "Is it in Giovanni's apartment?"

I nodded softly. He gave a nod and turned around again.

"Wait," I said again. "Wait wait wait."

The man stopped walking and turned to me, eyebrow raised, waiting.

"Please don't leave me alone with him." Tears welled my eyes as I pleaded. "Please."

"He won't touch you. Isn't that right, Ricardo?"

Ricardo sighed above me and nodded. The man turned around and left, not turning around again, leaving me with Ricardo. I shut my eyes and cried quietly.

"I wasn't planning to rape you," he said. My eyes popped open and met his. "I take no pleasure in that."

I swallowed. "Only in killing old ladies?"

"Ah, I didn't take pleasure in that. It was a means to an end." He pushed his back against the wall behind him and sank down right by my head, bringing a rough hand to my face and wiping my tears. "I've never been a fan of criers. It's a weakness. At least, that was what my father used to tell us." He let out a laugh. "Crying is for pussies," he'd say. "What do you think about that?"

I swallowed hard, my throat hurting each time I did so. He grabbed a fistful of my hair and brought my entire body up with it, tears springing my eyes from the pain.

"I asked you a question." He stared right into my eyes.

"I think…" My lip wobbled as I answered, my words coming out jaggedly. "Pussies are made of steal."

He opened his hand, letting go of my hair and my face went down hard. I caught myself just as it hit the concrete, but not well enough. My cheek stung with pain, blood pooling in my mouth quickly. I took a breath, then another. This man would probably be the one to kill me. He'd probably do it as I was tied up, too. Like a dick.

"My sister, she takes pleasure in ending a life," he said after a moment. "Well, she would probably say she doesn't, but I've seen the gleam in her eye."

I started to shiver, the palms of my hands vibrating with it.

"She wants to meet you," he said. "She's curious who managed to steal her son's heart."

My eyes went wide. Holy shit. Holy shit. Holy shit. Gio's *mother* was behind this? A small part of me hoped he wouldn't find out, for his sake, but mostly, I wanted to get out of here and I knew the only way to do it would be for him to bring the briefcase to his mother.

"Of course, it doesn't matter," he added. "Whether my nephew likes you or not doesn't really matter. Soon enough he'll find someone to replace you with. He'll be sad, I'm sure, based on how we've seen him looking at you, but he'll survive."

I squeezed my eyes shut. More tears trickled down my face.

"What are these? Scars from small cuts?" He lifted my hands. I yanked them out of his grasp, bringing them back against my chest. He stood up, setting both feet on either side of my torso. My pulse sped up, eyes wide on him. He said he wouldn't. He said he wouldn't. How many times did people make promises to do one thing and did the complete opposite? Too many. In my experience, way too many. He lifted me by the front of my trench coat, until our noses were nearly touching. He smiled then, in his eyes and his mouth, a smile like if he was about to tell me the fucking weather. He started setting me back down, and just as I thought I was in the clear, he punched me and I lost all consciousness.

CHAPTER FORTY-TWO

Gio

WE'D BEEN PARKED ACROSS THE STREET FROM THE BINGO HALL for thirty-minutes. I wanted to barge in there and demand to see Isabel, but I knew that wasn't the right move. Silvio would have her killed before I reached her. I had no doubt about it. Loren wasn't back with the briefcase yet. I didn't expect he would be, but I wished he'd hurry the fuck up. I picked up my phone and called my father. He wasn't the person I wanted to speak to at the moment, but I knew he'd tell me what was going on. Whether he liked me or not, he was depending on me to hold shit down here. No answer. I tried again. No answer. I tried again. No answer. I banged the back of my head against the headrest, growing angrier by the second.

"I can't do this anymore," I said, "I can't just sit here knowing she's in there."

"We don't know for sure yet," Rocco said. "Let's give it five more minutes. Dean will get back to us by then, and if he doesn't, fuck it."

"If he doesn't, we'll ride like the wind, Bullseye," Dom said, smiling, until he saw my glare and then he dropped the smile and said, "We'll go fuck shit up."

"Try not to sound excited about that." I shook my head and turned forward in my seat, eyes on the building again.

My phone buzzed with an unknown number. It wasn't blocked, but I answered it anyway. I couldn't take any chances.

"*Qué hubo, pues?*"

I frowned. "Marco?"

"Who else?" He let out a laugh; it sounded strained.

"Why are you calling?" I asked tentatively because I was one second from losing my shit and if he was calling to tell me he had something to do with this I'd have to light his restaurant on fire and my sister loved that place.

"I have some information I thought you'd like."

"Okay," I said slowly.

"Do you remember Luis?"

"No."

"Well, he's our cousin. He lives in Barranquilla."

"Good for fucking Luis. What the fuck do you have to tell me?"

"Your father's dead."

My mouth dropped, a wave of panic, grief, anger, dizziness, hitting me all at once. It sucked the air out of my lungs. My father was dead. I'd always known I'd hear those words at some point in my life and I always tried to picture what my reaction would be. I did that a lot, set up scenarios and played them out to see how I'd react. Complete paralysis was not what I'd envisioned in any of those scenarios. Finally, I gathered my thoughts and found my voice.

"Who killed him?"

"Who else?"

"My mom's brothers."

"Yep."

"Fuuuuuck."

"Yep." He sighed into the line. "I'm sorry."

I let out a laugh. "Yeah, right."

"I'm not sorry he's dead. I'm sorry you lost your father though. I know how hard that is to bear."

I swallowed thickly, emotions threatening to rise. Marco's dad passed away a few years ago. Cancer. I'd met him a handful of times, if that. I never went to the funeral. Never called Marco or his sister to give them condolences. And now I felt like shit about those things, because here he was, calling me to say this.

"Your girlfriend is in the Bingo Hall on—"

"Sixty-Ninth, yeah I know. How do you know?"

"Word on the street."

I shook my head. "Apparently your streets talk more than my men listen."

"You should call me more often," he said, then added, "So, you know?"

I felt my brows pull in again. "I know that she's at Silvio's bingo hall, yeah."

"Oh." He paused, as if he was considering potentially not giving me more information. His tone sounded the same to when he said my father died, and my heart squeezed so hard in my chest I was sure it would detonate.

"Did something happen to Isabel?" I asked, gripping my phone tighter. "Are you calling because you heard something happened to her?"

"I'm calling because I heard Tia Evelyn is involved in this."

The phone fell out of my hand, landing on the floor, between my legs. I was staring outside but looking at nothing. My mother. First, my father dead, now my mother involved in my wife's kidnapping? What the fuck was happening? I breathed in and picked up the phone again.

"Why are you giving me all of this information?" I asked, my voice low.

"Because you're my cousin."

"And? We haven't seen each other in years. We're practically strangers."

"Cat and I aren't strangers," he said, "Besides, Evelyn already killed one brother and I'm sure I don't have to tell you who put the hit out on your dad. This information is just me trying to make sure she gets what she deserves."

"What have you heard?" I demanded and had him detail every fucking thing he'd heard.

He didn't hold back, so either he was fucking with me, or he was trustworthy, like he claimed to be. Right now, everything was a shot in the dark though. I grabbed my gun and got out of the car. Nico stared at me. Dominic and Rocco climbed out, no hesitation, ready for war. As we jogged to the other side of the street, I took one last look at the block that I knew so well. My dad used to bring me here all the time when I was a kid. There had been an arcade right next to this bingo hall that he'd let me play at before getting me Joey's across the street. I took one last sweep of it, because it would never look like this again once I was finished.

CHAPTER FORTY-THREE

Isabel

WHEN I OPENED MY EYES AGAIN, I WAS SITTING UPRIGHT, MY ankles no longer tied together. My wrists still were, though. Across from me, there was a woman sitting in a chair in the center of the room, staring at me. I inhaled sharply when our eyes met. It was like looking at Gio's sisters. He looked nothing like her, but his sisters might as well have been her clone. She was wearing a purple pantsuit and black heels, looking like she was going to an office meeting or something.

"I take it you know who I am," she said, her accent much thicker than her brother's. It reminded me of my grandmother's.

"The woman who abandoned her kids," I said, voice hoarse. If I thought my head was throbbing before, it was nothing in comparison to this. My cheek felt like it was broken.

"Ah. Is that how they tell it?" she asked, smiling.

"How should they tell it?"

"Do you want me to give you the rundown?" She crossed her legs. "We have some time."

I shrugged. If her speaking would buy me time, I'd listen to her recite the fucking dictionary.

"Have you met Giovanni's father?" she asked, then added, "No, of course not. He hasn't been here since you came into his life." She smiled again. "We met in Barranquilla. He was vacationing with his first wife when he met me in a club. I was waitressing then. Well, I was dealing drugs under the table, but I was also waitressing." She shook her head, still smiling as if she was remembering it. "I wasn't really interested in dealing drugs. It was something one of my brothers talked me into doing since it would be easier for me to get away with it than him, but I became addicted to it. The rush, the money, not the drugs." She shot me a pointed look. "Joe went in that night and bought everyone drinks. Bought some people bottles. His wife was sitting there looking horrified, as if she didn't know who he was anymore." She rolled her eyes. "Needless to say, we clicked, and he brought me back to New York, and then Chicago."

"And then you had three kids and abandoned them?" I asked.

"That came later." She waved a hand. "In the beginning, it was blissful. Not for my brothers, though. They were out for blood. They felt Joe had stolen their prized possession, which, technically, he had." Her eyes sparkled. "We were so in love. We owned this fucking city. Chicago, too. The moment we stepped foot somewhere, everyone wanted to help us. That's the thing about this last name, it brings money and status and power." She grinned. "So much power. Giovanni loves that. He loves the power. He loves the money. Do you?"

"Not really."

"No, of course not, you're a teacher," she spat.

I bit the inside of my cheek. I was used to being treated like my job wasn't important, as if teaching and nurturing other people's kids was no big deal. We spent more time with those kids than their own parents, and somehow, we still were underappreciated. Underappreciated and underpaid. It was astounding, considering all the new shit we had to do in order to keep their kids safe in an environment that should already be safe for them. Teachers were no longer "just teachers," were also babysitters, counselors, guardians, teachers, and bodyguards. And still, we were belittled, underpaid, and underappreciated.

"Giovanni likes the flashy life," his mother continued. "He likes the cars and the clubs and the revolving door of women. I'm sure you understand why this could never work between the two of you."

"I'm not discussing my love life with you, and I'm definitely not discussing Giovanni with you. As far as I'm concerned, he has no mother."

She looked at me for a beat, then laughed. "You're brave, I'll give you that. All tied up, at my mercy, and you're talking back."

"I'm not, but okay." I looked at the ground, then at her heels, then at her face again. "You were getting to the part where you abandoned your children."

"Right. I had the money, the power, the respect. I had everything, but I was still just Joseph Masseria's wife. That alone should have been enough, of course, but I knew that had I stayed back in Colombia, I would have been the boss. There's no doubt in my mind about that."

"So why not stay?"

"Because I fell in love." She shot me a look. "Keep up."

I nodded, licking my lips. I still tasted blood in my mouth.

"Joe wanted children, so I gave him children. I demanded nannies, of course. It wasn't that I didn't love my children, I did, I do, but I didn't feel that momma bear thing that other mothers seemed to feel. Maybe I was broken. I had no mother, after all. I was orphaned at a young age, went from home to home, then to the streets. I just needed to survive. My father, the man who took me in, he didn't show me love, not in the way the movies show it, so let's just say that was why I didn't feel that maternal instinct. Do you think that's fair?"

"I don't know." I shrugged my left shoulder, hissing as a sharp pain hit me. It hurt like a bitch, and I didn't know why since I'd been lying on my other side most of the time. "I think it could be that, or you could just be a psychopath."

"Both are very possible," she agreed. "Nevertheless, I did not want to be a mother. I stuck around for a long time. You have to give me credit there. I stuck around and pretended every single day that I was happy just being a housewife. Every day until they hit their teen years, and then I couldn't take it anymore. Joe begged me not to go. He kept asking what he should tell the kids." She let out a laugh. "That was what he was worried about."

"One of you had to be," I said, even though I knew what a monster Gio's dad had turned out to be in her absence.

"Personally, I think they were better off without me."

"Can't argue there."

She laughed again. "You really are something. I can see why my son likes you."

I didn't bother saying what I wanted to, which was that she knew nothing about her son. I needed her to keep talking.

"So, yeah, I'm not sure what bullshit story Joe made up for me, but he did, and I fled."

"Fled?"

Her eyes widened slightly, as if I was missing something. "Do you really think Joe was just going to let me go? After everything I knew?

"So, you fled from him."

"I did. I went down to Miami, stayed there for a while, then went back home."

"And now you're the Queen B of Barranquilla," I said.

"No." She smiled. "I do like the way that sounds, though. It's not very often that I'm seen out. I do everything behind closed doors, quietly, to not get caught. Joe wanted me to come back. He called every day at first, then every week, asking me to come back, but I was done with this life. I was done being in his shadow."

"And now?" *keep talking, keep talking, keep talking.*

"And now, I'm back to claim my throne." She smiled wide.

"You mean the seat my father left vacant?" I asked. Her eyes flashed suddenly. Surprise, excitement, I couldn't be sure. I continued, "I heard you have to be Italian to be in that little club. And not a woman."

"I've heard a lot of things in my lifetime. It hasn't stopped me from getting what I want," she said. "They can keep their stupid little seats and their stupid little all-boys-club. I'll still control what I need to control. They already lost."

I had nothing to say to that. I didn't know as much about any of this as she did, and I didn't want to. I wanted to get out of here. I wanted to see Gio again. I wanted to go home.

"So," she said, getting out of her chair. "How 'bout we play a game?"

"What kind of game?" My eyes widened as I looked up at her as she walked closer to me.

"The kind where I silence you and put an end to all of this."

My heart bounced in my chest. "You don't have to kill me."

"I don't." She walked even closer, and I caught a whiff of her perfume. It was flowery and gentle, the complete opposite of her. "But I might. I haven't decided. We'll see how this plays out." She crouched in front of me and gripped my cheeks so tight I had no choice but to open my mouth. "Do you know where I make the most of my money?" she asked. I tried to shake my head, but her grip was too tight on my cheeks. "Selling women. Usually they're much younger than you, inexperienced, stupid. Probably a lot like your little middle schoolers, but I'm willing to make an exception." She smiled then brought her other hand up to put a pill in my mouth. I gagged and moved my tongue, trying not to swallow it, to spit it back out. She looked at me hard. "The only thing you gain by doing this is that you'll taste it more. Either way, you're taking it. Would you rather me inject you? Because that can be arranged."

Tears filled my eyes. I should have just taken it. I should have been okay passing out for the millionth time, but my hatred for this woman grew by the second. I hated her as much or more than I hated my own mother. I hated everything she'd done to me, to Gio, to his sisters. I hated that she was involved in sex trafficking and showed no regrets about it. So, instead of taking the fucking pill. Instead of swallowing it like I probably should have, to avoid being shot, I head butted her as hard as I could. She stumbled backwards, landing on her ass. I knew she wouldn't be disoriented long, so I pushed against the wall and got myself up, running toward the door they kept using. My hands were still tied. I wasn't sure how far I'd get or what would happen, but I needed to try. I needed to at least fucking try.

CHAPTER FORTY-FOUR

Gio

I DIDN'T LIKE CASUALTIES. DOM KNEW THAT, SO HE POINTED HIS GUN at the five old people sitting in a table playing bingo and told them to get the fuck out. They did it, but that meant it was only a matter of time before the police showed up, so we had to be faster. Dominic went first. He rounded the corners and pointed his weapon. We reached the door that separated the bingo hall from the shit that really went down here. From the few times I'd been here, I knew the bouncer would be sitting in a stool just to the right, so the moment Dom was about to cross the threshold, I pulled him back by his bullet proof jacket and stopped him. He glanced at me over his shoulder, question in his eyes. I nodded in the direction the bouncer normally sat in, and he pointed his gun there. I stepped forward. It was empty. We looked at the door in front of us, the three of us taking a collective breath and letting it out as Dominic kicked it down and we rushed. A dozen men stood up, guns aimed at us, but we were ready. We started shooting man after man after man. Once I knew they'd be fine on their own, I went straight to Silvio's office in the back, kicking his door open. He was on the phone, behind his desk, when he looked up at me, wide-eyed, scared.

"Honey, I love you. I'll talk to you later," he said, setting the phone back in its cradle. He put his hands up. "Your mother is behind all of this. She was the one who—"

BAM.

I didn't let him finish his sentence before I shot him between the eyes.

BAM.

BAM.

Two more for good measure. I walked out and opened the door next to his, which led to a stairwell. A basement? I started walking down the stairs. I heard her before I saw her. I heard her crying and struggling against something, someone. I walked as fast as I could without making noise. When I looked over the ledge, I saw two things: Isabel with her hands tied, struggling to get away, and a man's arms wrapping around her. Then, I only saw red.

CHAPTER FORTY-FIVE

Isabel

RICARDO WAS SHOT IN THE HEAD, JUST INCHES AWAY FROM MY FACE. His blood splattered everywhere, and all I could do was scream as I fell down with him and scream again when I saw the state of his head. I was shaking as I kicked away from him, trying to get to the wall, to anything, even though I knew this was it. I knew it was over. This was where I'd die, down here, in a stairwell God knows where, alone. The alone part never used to bother me. I used to think I'd die alone. I was neither happy nor sad at the prospect. I figured when it was my time, I'd have to go. Never did I think it would be like this. Even as a teenager, when once in a while we'd here of a kid on the block who had gotten shot down, or someone being hit by a stray bullet, I didn't think it would ever be me. Even during those drills, we practiced constantly in case of a school shooting, even then, I didn't think I'd die by a gun. Maybe it was better that way. Maybe it would be painless. A sob raked through me. I couldn't see through the haze of my tears, through the blood coating my hair which was covering half of my face. I couldn't hear, my ears ringing loudly, so loudly, that even swallowing wouldn't help them pop. Someone grabbed me, crouched down in front of me, shook me hard, so hard my head went forward and back with it. I cried harder. I swallowed again and my ears adjusted slightly.

"Isabel." He shook me harder. "Isabel."

I blinked. "Gio?"

"It's going to be okay. Oh, my God, thank God you're alive. It's going to be okay, baby," he said again, and I couldn't tell whether he was saying it for my benefit or his. Over his shoulder, I saw the outline of a person. The outline of a gun. It was a one second decision. I gasped, pushing him off me as hard as I could. I heard the BAM. I felt it as it hit me, pushing me back against the wall, my head slamming with the impact. I heard two more.

BAM.

BAM.

Everything went black.

CHAPTER FORTY-SIX

Gio

WHEN WE WERE TEENAGERS, FRANKIE AND I USED TO PLAY A GAME. We'd rattle off ways you could die and rate them from one to five, five being the absolute worst. Frankie always picked old age. Every single time. I'd laugh, and he'd say, "I'm serious, bro. Imagine being so old that someone has to wipe your ass for you. Imagine not being able to get it up." He'd shiver at that.

Shiver, the way we shivered when we were outside in Chicago in the dead of winter, as if it was the most horrible thing in the world. I knew he meant it because he never rated the rest of them a five. Death by drowning? Four. Death by gunshot? Three, depending on where you got shot. Death by knife to the femoral artery? Eh, maybe four and a half, but death by old age? Easy five. He got his wish, I guess. That's the thing about death, though. The person who dies actually rests in peace. It's the rest of us who stay restless. Some things keep us up. The day-to-day monotony, the day-to-day excitement when you're working on something new, but at night, at the end of each day, you're still left alone with that restlessness and that pain. Fuck. That pain alone I'd rate a five and a half. That pain doesn't go away. People say grief gets easier with time. It doesn't. We just learn to ignore it better. We push it to the back of our minds and occupy ourselves with whatever the fuck we can in order to not think about it, to not feel it.

I never rated any death a five. I usually rated all of them four-and-a-half, though, and Frankie would call me a little bitch for it, since he'd rate the rest of them a three and sometimes four. I was never going to stop missing my best friend, never, but I knew I had to push past the pain and keep on going. At least, I hoped I could. The only thing I knew for certain was that I was completely in love with Isabel Bonetti. I would die for her, no questions asked. I would kill for her, no hesitation. And now, I had to let her go. Just like that. I had to get out of this uncomfortable chair in her hospital room and walk out the door and not look back. For her sake. For my sanity. Fuck. For everyone's sake. I got up and walked over to her bedside, taking her in one last time. Even with the bruises, the black eye, and the broken nose, she was fucking breathtaking. I leaned down and kissed her forehead, then her lips as softly as I could, and I walked out of that room with no heart in my chest. She'd taken it, like the little thief she was, coming into my life and stealing my air, my time, my sanity, my thoughts, everything. If I could turn back time, I wasn't sure that I'd do it all over again. Someone once said it was better to have loved and lost than never to have loved at all, but that was complete bullshit. I didn't want to love Isabel. I didn't want to love anyone. It just happened and I was going to do everything in my power to make sure it could never happen again, because this emptiness? This bottomless feeling? I'd rate that a five too.

Yeah, I'm a little bitch. I know. Fuck off.

CHAPTER FORTY-SEVEN

Isabel

WHEN I OPENED MY EYES IN THE HOSPITAL, I PANICKED, GASPING
for air, until the nurses settled me down. I couldn't settle
down, though, everything hurt, and I saw no sign of Gio.
When I asked if I had any visitors, the nurse who was with me
that day said yes and my chest expanded with hope, only to see
Nadia and Petra walk in. I swallowed, chest aching so much I
was sure they'd need to replace it with another. Petra's right arm
was in a cast, her face looking like she'd seen better days. Both of
their expressions were grim and did nothing for the panic I felt.
When I closed my eyes, the only thing I saw was Gio's face in
front of mine, eyes wild and scared as he took me in, and then I
heard the gunshots. The gunshots were so loud in my memory.
My ears still felt like they were ringing from it. What I couldn't
remember was what happened. Someone tried to shoot him.
There were so many gunshots fired. So many. Whoever it was
probably hadn't missed. Seeing the way Petra and Nadia were
looking at me, I knew it was bad news.

"Did he…" My lip wobbled so hard I could barely talk.
Before the question was even out of my mouth, I began to sob.
"Please tell me he's okay."

"He's okay." They both rushed to my side.

"Hey." Petra smoothed my hair out of my forehead, tears
in her own eyes. "He's okay."

"Did he get shot?" I looked between the two of them. They
both shook their heads. I let out a sigh of relief, but it didn't
last long. "You're okay." I grabbed the arm that wasn't in a cast.

"God. I was so scared. I saw you lying on the ground, and I thought—" I shook my head, swallowing, then flinching at how much it hurt. Nadia stood on the other side of the bed, patting my cheeks with a tissue.

"I'm okay." Petra smiled, tears filling her eyes. "It got scary."

I nodded, not saying anything else to that because I couldn't. I couldn't.

"What happened?" I whispered, looking at Nadia. "Gio was there and then I was shot and then I heard more gunshots, but I was gone."

Nadia's lips pressed together as she swallowed, and I braced myself for the worst. "Evelyn died."

My heart stopped. She'd been the one holding the gun, I realized. I hadn't seen her face, but it had to be her. She'd pointed the gun at her own son, shot me, and she was dead. It didn't take much to put the pieces together. My lip wobbled again. Poor Gio. I couldn't even imagine what he was going through.

"How's Gio?"

"Fine. Well, physically." Nadia paused. "He killed his mother."

"So, he's not okay," I whispered.

"He's as okay as someone who had to kill their own mom can be."

"What do you remember?" Petra asked.

"I don't know," I whispered. "I remember screaming. I remember blood, so much blood. I remember Evelyn having a gun aimed at him. I moved him and then I remember nothing."

"That's Gio's account too," Nadia said. "You saved his life."

"He saved mine."

He had. In so many ways, but if he hadn't gotten there when he did who knows what his mother would have done to me. I hated her. I'd never wanted to actually kill anyone, but she may have just been my first victim. I shivered at the memory of her.

A terrible mother, a sex trafficker. Ugh. It was mind-blowing that her children had turned out as well as they had.

"She was a horrible human being," I whispered. "How long have I been in here?"

"A week." Petra held my hand. "You've been in and out. Mostly out."

I looked down to examine myself. Holy shit. "What *isn't* broken?"

Nadia laughed lightly. "You have some cracked ribs; your shoulder got some real damage from the gunshot. Your face looks like complete shit, but I'm sure you feel it, so I don't think I need to tell you."

"And you're supposed to be the nice one," I mumbled. Nadia smiled a little. "Where's Gio now?"

"Taking care of some things. His father died the same day his mother did, so, he lost both parents."

"Do Cat and Emma know?"

"Yeah," Nadia said. "Gio told them everything that happened. They're sad, and relieved, but mostly sad. They're a mess about their dad, though."

I could imagine. I didn't say anything, though. I looked at Petra. "How's Joey?"

She shook her head, the sadness returning, tears welling in her eyes instantly.

"No." I gasped.

"He was a good soldier," Nadia said. "He saved a lot of lives that day. Who knows how much worse it could've been if he hadn't stopped the second shooter from going in there?"

I swallowed, bringing a hand up to flick more tears off my face. "I'm so sorry."

"It's not your fault." Petra wiped her own face. "It's none of our fault."

I looked down again. "Is Gio not going to visit me here?"

"He was here in the beginning," Nadia said. "But he thinks

you're better off without him. I'm sure he's torn up about his parents, but I think he's mostly grieving the loss of you."

"The loss of me?" That hurt, too. "I'm right here, though. I'm fine."

Petra's brow shot up. "You're not even close to being fine."

"But I'm alive. I'll be fine."

"He feels guilty. If he hadn't pulled you into this mess, you'd be living your life with your friends, and work and William Hamilton." Nadia gave a shrug.

"So, what, he's walking away?" I blinked.

"He's made a promise to stay away."

"That's bullshit," I whispered, blinking as fresh tears fell. "He can't just break up with me without actually breaking up with me."

"Trust us, it's killing him, but he truly feels this is the right thing to do."

"Since when does he care about doing the right thing?" I asked, my voice rising.

"Since you."

"That's total bullshit."

They laughed.

"How 'bout you focus on getting better and then figure this out?" Nadia said in her mom voice. "If you still feel the same a month from now, then, I don't know, call him or something."

"You really think he won't call me first?"

"He won't." Petra let go of my hand with a sigh. "He's a stubborn motherfucker."

He was a stubborn motherfucker, but so was I.

CHAPTER FORTY-EIGHT

Gio

TWENTY-EIGHT DAYS. THAT WAS HOW LONG IT HAD BEEN SINCE I last saw her. Between my sisters and her friends Luke and Noah, I knew she was doing okay. Physically, at least. She'd moved into a new apartment. It was so close to mine that it hurt to breathe whenever I passed by it. And yet, I continued to drive by it, hoping to catch a glimpse of her. As if in a city of over a million people, I'd see her randomly walking to the subway or a store. According to Luke, she'd transferred to a new school, one that was around here. Classes hadn't started, but she'd met the teachers and apparently, she loved it there. I was happy for her. I was.

Meanwhile, I was in the process of selling my place in Chicago so that I could move to New York for good. We'd already sold our family home, so this was the next step. It wasn't that I didn't love Chicago. Hell, I definitely preferred it to New York, but Isabel was in New York. Yes, I let her go. Yes, I was keeping my distance, and I would continue to do so. I wouldn't even intervene if she met a good guy she liked. I wouldn't even intervene if she wanted to marry him. The thought of that made my stomach hurt. I fucking hoped she didn't get any ideas. I let her go, but that didn't mean I liked the thought of either of us moving on. She hadn't called, though. I didn't know why I'd expected her to, or why I'd expected it not to hurt as much as it did. She knew I wouldn't call her, but she hadn't called either, and that was what told me she must have been trying to move on.

I was still staring at the sidewalk when I caught William

Hamilton walking into her building and felt my heart clench. My hand closed over the door handle. I gripped it hard, ready to jump out of the car, but I made myself close my eyes and breathed through it though. *Change is hard. Change is necessary. Change is good. Change hurts like a motherfucker.* I sighed and signaled at Nico to drive past her building and head to the warehouse. The five of us—Dean, myself, Lorenzo, Dominic, and Rocco—were it now. Not exactly the way we'd planned to form this group, but it happened, nonetheless. Lorenzo, of course, still had his dad in his ear, but now that he'd officially taken over the import-export thing, things would definitely run much smoother. I'd take over construction, instead. I liked it. It was something else that would keep me busy. After we talked about what was on our agenda for the week, we moved on to the case of the vault. We still couldn't figure out what happened or who took the stuff or what was done with it. Mike was on it, though, and he was serious about it since he wanted to make sure no one dragged his name. We wouldn't. Well, I wouldn't. I knew Mike better than to think he would rob us. And even if someone argued that I didn't know him as well as I thought I did, I knew for a fact he didn't want to die.

The briefcase was another situation all together. The fucking briefcase. We discussed it every single time we got together. So many people died because of it and as far as we could tell, it was full of trinkets and diamonds. Maybe it had been the diamonds they were after. We just couldn't figure out why. There was a code to Charles' vault in it, too, but there was nothing that particularly stood out. The slabs of gold and the diamonds, sure, but we all had valuable things in ours. It didn't make any sense. According to what Isabel told Nadia and Petra, my mother had been involved in human trafficking. That was the only thing I could think of. Maybe Charles somehow had access to something, a container or something, that would fuck up their operation. Fuck if we knew, though. At least, not yet. Thinking about the human trafficking alone made me feel sick. It also made me understand why my mother was okay with my father handing me around all those years ago. To her, a body was just another weapon to wield and control. Sometimes, when I shut my eyes, I could still see the look on her face when she realized I'd been the one to shoot her. It haunted me. Her eyes wide in surprise, as if she didn't think I had it in me. That was the thing about actions, though. You never think you have it in you until you're put in a situation that pushes you to find out. It didn't mean I was proud of it. It didn't mean it didn't feel like a fucking knife was wedged between my ribs when I relived it. I pushed all thoughts of my mother away when I heard Loren call out my name from across the table.

"Shit. I spaced out." I did that a lot these days.

"The sanitation workers are talking about going on strike," Loren said.

"No wonder it reeks every time I step out of my building." I scrunched my nose at the thought. "What do they want?"

"Better pension. More money."

"Shit, good for them." I shrugged a shoulder. "What's that got to do with us?"

"The city's looking to hire someone to do the job in the meantime."

"Isn't that up your alley, Marchetti?" I looked at Rocco. Even though he was deep in the gambling ring, he also practically owned the private sanitation company that picked up the garbage in places the city didn't, not because the city couldn't, but because the Marchetti family struck a deal with them early on and stiff-armed them into it and even though his father was still somewhat involved, Rocco had practically taken over.

"A lot of those guys are paid by us on the side. I don't think going against them is in our best interest."

"So, what, you're going to turn down the contract?" I asked.

"It might start another war if they don't," Dean said.

"So, to be clear, you think he should turn it down?" Dominic asked, seemingly as confused as I was.

"I think he should take it and take the guys we're already paying with him. Offer them the incentives they're asking the city for," Dean said.

"Smart."

"So, I guess that's settled," Dom said, looking at Rocco, who looked like he was still thinking about it.

When we finished discussing, we walked over to the bar and sat in the couches, everyone grabbing a drink to sip on. It was like this every week. We'd meet, talk business, then drink and talk shit. It was still better than the therapist my sisters dragged me to. Well, Catalina dragged me, Emma, and Loren to see the therapist, and had given Dean, Dominic, and Rocco his card as well. She said we all needed serious help. She included herself in that category, so we couldn't even be offended by it. What I liked was that we didn't talk about our feelings. Not really, anyway. We just talked. And talked. And talked. And Jeremy (our therapist) listened, took notes, listened some more. We didn't get into details, of course. We mostly talked about our fucked-up parents.

"I'm out." I stood up after finishing my ginger beer.

"Such a lightweight these days," Dom said, shaking his head. This kid, I swear.

I threw up a peace sign and headed to the door, where Nico was waiting for me, and asked him to drive me to Cat and Loren's place. After all the shit I went through with her wedding present, I was going to give her the deed and the keys. It wasn't finished. It was nowhere near finished. We'd stalled construction more times than I could count, but if I've learned anything these last few years, it's that you just have to do the thing, whatever that thing is. The doorman opened the door for me, and I waved at the guy sitting behind the counter as I let myself up. I rang the doorbell, and she opened the door with her phone pressed to her ear, her eyes going wide when she saw it was me. My heart did that thing it did when anything that involved Isabel was happening because I knew, I knew, she was talking to her.

"'Kay, I gotta go. See you tomorrow," she said with a smile, hitting the end button and taking a step back to let me in. "I thought you were with Loren?"

"I was."

"So, where is he?"

"Still at the place."

That's what we called it—The Place—because we had no other name for it and that one somehow made sense. It was just another reason I employed women. I was sure my sister could come up with a better name, but it didn't matter. It was just a place.

"Interesting." She eyed me suspiciously. "What's in your hand?"

"Ah." I smiled, handing it over. "Your wedding gift."

"Didn't you get me money?" she frowned, opening the envelope, eyes still on me. "I could swear you gave us money."

"I did. Open the fucking thing."

"Why are you giving me a second wedding gift? Is Loren going to propose again or something?"

"Why the fuck would he do that?" I shot her a look.

"Some people do that. They propose to their partner every year, or every few years or they do this thing where they have a little ceremony and say their vows again."

"Who are these people?" I blinked. "They sound like idiots."

She rolled her eyes and took the paper out of the envelope. "You're giving me an old theater?" She paused and kept reading, then glanced up at me. "I'm very confused right now."

"It was an old theater. It now has new flooring, new roofing, new plumbing. It still needs a lot of work. There needs to be a stage, and better box seats that the ones currently there, because, who wants to go to a ballet and not sit up there?"

As it slowly dawned on her, Catalina started blinking back

tears. She swallowed and whispered, "You got me my own ballet theater?"

"I figured you deserved it."

"Gio." She shook her head, openly crying now, then laughed and punched me in the arm before pulling me into a hug. "I hate you for this."

The door opened behind us and shut right away. I looked up as my sister kept squeezing me and crying into my shirt. Loren looked like he was either about to walk right back out or kill me. Either was a real option. I could see it in his face.

"What is happening?" he asked slowly.

"Gio got me my own ballet theater." Cat pushed away from me and wiped her face, holding up the deed. "My very own theater. It's our wedding present."

"You already gave us money."

"I wouldn't be surprised if you remember the exact amount."

"I actually do." His lip twitched. He looked back to my sister as he walked over to her. "Your own theater. Holy shit, Cat." Then he looked at me, glaring. "I'm never going to top this gift, you fucking asshole."

At that, I laughed. "Well, that's my cue. I have to be at the club tonight."

"Again?" Catalina asked, sighing heavily. "Can't you just take a break?"

"Nope."

"You know, I was talking to Isabel when you got here." My sister glanced up at me, shifting in her feet, as if I was going to attack her for saying Isabel's name aloud or something. It hurt to hear it, but it was something I needed to learn to cope with, especially being that my sisters had formed a friendship with her, and it wasn't something I'd take away from any of them. It hurt, though. It fucking hurt.

"I figured," I said, finally.

"She asked about you."

I swallowed, looking away. "Don't tell me. That was the deal. You stay friends, but you don't give me details. I don't want to hear it."

"Hm." Cat shook her head.

"You really look like you could sleep for two months, G," Loren said, changing the subject.

"I feel like it, too." I gave my sister a kiss on the head and patted his shoulder. "No rest for the wicked and all that."

"Even the wicked die, G." He raised an eyebrow. "You should rest."

"I will." I walked out. "Someday."

CHAPTER FORTY-NINE

Isabel

H E'D SENT ME A MASSAGE CHAIR.

I'd once told him the only chair I wanted was a cozy massage chair, and the bastard actually sent me one. That was as much of a sign I got from him that he was still alive and thinking about me. Of course, I'd spoken to Cat and Emma. We'd even grabbed drinks a few times, like we did a couple of hours ago, and now I was back in my apartment, sitting in the massage chair. I'd given Gio enough time. I'd given myself enough time. Every day, I woke up and asked myself if I was where I needed to be, and I answered yes. Then, I asked myself if I was happy, and the answer was also yes. Then, I asked myself what would make me happiest, and the answer was always Giovanni. There was no way around it anymore. I couldn't continue to pretend that this wasn't what I knew it was. I was in love with him, and I wasn't going to fall out of love with him any time soon, if ever. So, tonight, I'd grabbed Luke and Noah, and their girlfriends, and we headed to The Devil's Lair.

Was it a good idea? Probably not.

Was I going to do it anyway? Hell yeah.

At the very least, I knew we'd get inside, which was all I needed. Luke and Noah went off to the bar, making me promise I'd text to let them know how it went. They already knew the drill, though. If they didn't see me back here within the hour, it had gone well enough. They were fine with it, since they knew Petra was involved and I wouldn't get physically hurt in here. I shot Petra a text to let her know I was here. She'd already warned me that Gio was in one of his bad moods, but she said that every night when I checked in, so that wasn't a surprise. When I reached the second floor, I bypassed the VIP, waving at the new bouncer working there, and headed to the door. Petra walked out as I was getting there, shaking her head. She was wearing dress pants and a nice blouse, no longer in a cast.

"I need a drink," she said, dropping a kiss on my cheek. "Good fucking luck in there."

I walked in and shut the first set of doors behind me, then practiced breathing as I reached the doors to his office. I opened them slowly and let myself in. He had both arms on the desk, his head resting between them, the way my students do when they fall asleep in class.

"Really, P? If it's not an emergency, don't fucking bother me. I don't have time for this."

"You can't even make time for your wife?"

His head snapped up. Those dark eyes met mine and I immediately felt faint. He stared at me, just stared. Not seeing him as long as I'd gone without him, and seeing him now, felt like a blow to the chest. Adrenalin propelled me to move forward. I walked over to the desk, standing on the other side as he shifted in his seat and looked up at my face, still staring as if he wasn't entirely sure he was seeing things or if this was real. I'd been the one to finally show up here and I felt the same. It all felt like a dream I'd played out in my head a million times and now that I was here, I needed to do something, say something.

"I know you don't go back on your promises, but I was thinking that maybe we could come to some sort of agreement, since I came to you and not the other way around." I tapped the tips of my fingers on the desk.

He continued to stare, and I wasn't sure how to decipher the expression on his face. At first, it was surprise, but now, it was just intense, like he wanted me to hurry up and tell him what I wanted. I just wasn't sure if he wanted me to get it over with so he could kick me out and tell me this was a bad idea or what. It didn't matter. Good idea or bad, he'd have to hear me out.

"What kind of agreement?" he asked, voice hoarse.

"For starters, I want the right side of the bed. I know you think that's your side, but it's mine," I said. He pushed a little deeper into his seat, as if he was having a difficult time processing the words coming out of my mouth. I walked around the desk. He turned his chair in my direction and waited. I walked closer, stepping between his legs, noticing the way his chest expanded with a breath. He was nervous. Giovanni Masseria was nervous. I bit my lip to hide my smile, but it was no use. I set both hands on the arms of his chair and leaned in, getting close to his face, but not close enough. "You're only allowed to make mac-n-cheese *once* a week. If we make it a nightly thing, well, you may not suffer, as much as you work out, but my thighs can't afford that."

I could tell he was having a difficult time keeping his hands to himself, but he did. He licked his lips. "I can make other things."

"Like what?"

"Like grilled cheese," he breathed against my face. "I can make a mean peanut butter and jelly."

At that, I laughed, pulling back slightly. "Peanut butter and jelly? Really, Gio?"

"Isabel," he said, his voice barely audible, eyes searching mine as if in agony. "You're not supposed to be here."

"I thought a wife was supposed to always stand beside her husband."

"Please, Isabel." He shut his eyes and swallowed hard.

"I love you, Giovanni. I'm not going to stop loving you. God knows I've tried." I blinked away tears as he opened his eyes and stared at me again. "I know you're scared. I know you hate yourself for what happened, but I'm fine. I'm not made of glass."

"You said you weren't cut out for this life."

"Are any of us really cut out for life at all?" I asked. "We're all just treading in the deep end, hoping for a life jacket to drop out of the sky. That's life, period."

"You said—"

"I know what I said, and I'm telling you now that none of that matters. I love you. I want to be with you. If that's still something you're interested in, let me know. Otherwise, I'll leave, and you'll never see me again, but I had to try." I pushed away from his chair and started to take a step back when he moved forward and wrapped his arms around me, the side of his face on my hip. He shuddered against me once, twice, squeezed me tighter before letting go and pushing his chair back as he stood. I looked up at him.

"*If* that's something I'm still interested in?" he asked. "I've been interested since you barged into this office the first time."

"Liar."

"I'm not lying. I don't lie to you. You know that." He brought both hands up to the sides of my face. "I'm so in love with you that it hurts. It physically hurts to think about you. So in love with you that being without you feels worse than death. On a scale of one to five, it's a ten." He swallowed. "I'm so in love with you that I was going to wait one more week before I went for you, because you're the only person who can push me to break my promises, because I fucking need you more than I need air, more than I need anything. I'll give all of this up, every single thing, if you tell me to, and I'd be happy to do it."

"I wouldn't ask that of you," I whispered, swallowing as fresh tears formed. "I wouldn't want to change you. I want *you.*"

"Fuck, baby," he growled before setting his mouth on mine. It wasn't a hard kiss, like I'd expected. It was slow, and gentle, his thumbs grazing against my cheeks, picking up any tear that fell. He pulled away slightly and looked at me. "Tomorrow, we're going to buy wedding rings."

"Really?" My brows rose, a laugh escaping my lips.

"We're already married." He shrugged. "If you want a

wedding, I'll give you the wedding of the century, but in the meantime, we need rings."

"And you're going to wear yours?"

"I'm never going to take it off." He kissed me again, and again, and again, soft pecks against my lips. "And we're moving all of your shit to my place ASAP."

"I like my place." I frowned.

"You did the living alone thing, and it seems like you enjoy it, but I need you with me. All the time."

"All the time?" I laughed. "Are you going to come to school with me?"

"You want me to?" His brows rose. "I'll sit in the back and fantasize about all the ways I'd fuck you in the classroom."

"Gio." I slapped his hands away playfully, feeling his words between my legs.

"Let's go home." He grabbed my hand and pulled me away from the desk, then stopped when we got to the door to give me a full once-over. "I swear you're going to fucking kill me."

I laughed as I followed him. Petra threw her hands up with a laugh when we walked by her. Nico hugged me when he saw me. I called Luke and Noah and told them what happened, and promised I'd be at the rum bar tomorrow night.

"I'll be there too," Gio added beside me. "Make sure you stock up on Havana Club."

I hung up the phone and smiled at him. "You don't even drink."

"Oh, I'm drinking. I'm celebrating the fuck out of this." He wrapped an arm around me and pulled me into him, almost on top of his lap. "My wife deserves to be celebrated every day. And she will be."

He kissed me again, and I felt all of my worries drift away. He felt like the home I'd always wanted. And now, I was his.

EPILOGUE

Gio

I T WAS ALWAYS SOMETHING.

We were sitting in my rooftop, grilling, and Rocco, the absolute fucking moron, set one of the umbrellas on fire, so now we had the entire fucking fire department on the rooftop, hosing everything down, while I bounced between wanting to strangle him to death or throw him off the roof. He was lucky I couldn't do either. Mostly, he was lucky Russo decided to attend this little party, and my wife was standing next to me, so I couldn't do either *right now*.

"I mean, at least none of the furniture burned," Isabel said beside me.

"That's one way to look at it."

"Are you upset that it was your steak that burned?" I could hear the smile in her voice without looking at her, and my own lips itched to smile back, but I didn't.

"I'm upset it wasn't his face that burned."

"Giovanni." Isabel slapped my arm with a laugh. "He didn't mean it."

"He didn't, but him and Dom are always goofing off. He shouldn't have been grilling to begin with."

"Well, if it makes you feel any better, I prefer it when you grill anyway."

At this, I faced her fully. She was smiling as she stepped into me and wrapped her arms around my waist. She set her chin on my chest and looked up at me. She was wearing flats today. Flats and a yellow summer dress that made her look like she was glowing. Everything from the smile on her face to the twinkle in her eyes radiated happiness, and knowing I played a role in bringing that to her made me feel invincible some days. I wrapped my arms around her and kissed her forehead.

"You smell like a forest fire now."

"Ew." She started to pull away, but I held her tighter.

"Just stay," I whispered. "Stay right here."

She melted into me, and I shut my eyes. I heard the firefighters talking to someone, Loren, I thought, maybe Dominic. If they had any sense, they wouldn't direct any questions in my direction, especially when having Isabel in my arms was the only thing keeping me from losing my shit. The wind picked up slightly, blowing her hair into my face, but I kept my eyes closed as I held her.

"I love it here," Isabel said against my chest. "I really, really, love it here."

"Yeah? You have a thing for rooftop fires?"

She laughed, pulling away from me. I let her this time, mostly because I wanted to see her face. I took my eyes off hers briefly, looking over at the chaos I'd been trying to avoid. The firefighters were gone, and everything seemed to be back to normal. Even the burned umbrella was gone. Maybe Rocco had some sense after all. When I looked back down at Isabel, she was still smiling at me. Every time she smiled at me like that, it knocked me off my feet all over again.

"I have a thing for *you*," she said, then waved a hand in the direction of the chaos. "And this? This is family. This feels like the home I never had."

"It does, doesn't it?" I glanced back at them.

Everyone was bickering, even Cat was jabbing a finger in Loren's chest as he looked down at her, unmoved, letting her complain about whatever it was my sister was complaining about, probably smelling like fire, if I had to guess.

I looked at Isabel again. "You feel like home."

"Yeah?" her eyes lit up.

"Yeah." I leaned down and kissed her softly, deepening it when her fingers threaded into my hair and pulled.

"Oh, please, get a fucking room," Rocco called out.

"What, so you can set it on fire too?" Isabel called out as soon as she pulled away.

I couldn't help my laugh.

This woman.

My wife.

She'd have my heart forever.

ACKNOWLEDGEMENTS

Jan Cassi, Rea Loftis, Rachel Van Dyken (who seriously saved me with all of her help!), Stacey Blake, Liz Trice, Kay Springsteen, Everyone at Valentine PR (especially Kim Cermak, Nina Grinstead, Kelly Beckham)

My kids, who are the best hype-people anyone could ever wish for

My husband, who lets me take parts of his personality in order to create all of my heroes. It's a good thing you're a Gemini and have a couple of those lol. Happy Birthday, best friend.

ALSO BY CLAIRE

ClaireContrerasbooks.com

Twitter:
@ClariCon

Insta:
ClaireContreras

Facebook:
www.facebook.com/groups/ClaireContrerasBooks